J. M. COETZEE AND THE NOVEL

OXFORD ENGLISH MONOGRAPHS

J. M. Coetzee and the Novel

Writing and Politics After Beckett

by

PATRICK HAYES

OXFORD
UNIVERSITY PRESS

OXFORD

UNIVERSITY PRESS

Great Clarendon Street, Oxford OX2 6DP

Oxford University Press is a department of the University of Oxford.
It furthers the University's objective of excellence in research, scholarship,
and education by publishing worldwide in

Oxford New York

Auckland Cape Town Dar es Salaam Hong Kong Karachi
Kuala Lumpur Madrid Melbourne Mexico City Nairobi
New Delhi Shanghai Taipei Toronto

With offices in

Argentina Austria Brazil Chile Czech Republic France Greece
Guatemala Hungary Italy Japan Poland Portugal Singapore
South Korea Switzerland Thailand Turkey Ukraine Vietnam

Oxford is a registered trade mark of Oxford University Press
in the UK and in certain other countries

Published in the United States
by Oxford University Press Inc., New York

© Patrick Hayes 2010

The moral rights of the author have been asserted
Database right Oxford University Press (maker)

First published 2010

British Library Cataloguing in Publication Data

Data available

Library of Congress Cataloging in Publication Data
Library of Congress Control Number: 2010925675

Typeset by SPI Publisher Services, Pondicherry, India
Printed in Great Britain
on acid-free paper by
The MPG Books Group, Bodmin and King's Lynn

ISBN 978–0–19–958795–7

1 3 5 7 9 10 8 6 4 2

For my mother and father

Acknowledgements

Above all I would like to thank Peter D. McDonald, who supervised my doctoral thesis on Coetzee: his example will remain for me the model of what, at its best, doctoral supervision can be. I am also extremely grateful to Derek Attridge, David Attwell, Ron Bush, Sam Durrant, and Hermione Lee, who advised on my work in detail.

My special thanks go to St John's College, Oxford, who offered me a 'Lamb and Flag' studentship during my doctoral studies when other funding avenues were closed. This support provided me with a year of full-time research that was crucial to the development of my work. I also thank the AHRC for funding the final stage of my doctoral study.

It has been my pleasure and privilege over the past few years as a tutor and lecturer in Oxford to spend time with an outstanding and diverse group of students. Their insights, questions, and enthusiasms have been a constant source of inspiration during this project.

My other debts are too extensive to be listed in full. I am immensely grateful to Sarah for her patience and encouragement. This book is dedicated to my mother and father, whose love and support over the years have made everything possible.

Contents

Introduction

'For a novelist [*pause*]; for a writer working in the medium of the novel . . .'

(J. M. Coetzee, describing himself, in interview with Paul Bailey)[1]

Debate on Coetzee has focused on the vexed and complex question of political responsibility, and the two most important studies of his work have each tackled this question in different ways. In *J. M. Coetzee: South Africa and the Politics of Writing* (1993), David Attwell established Coetzee's political seriousness by revealing the extent of his engagement with the specificities of South African political culture; in describing his work as 'situational metafiction', Attwell emphasized the self-consciously critical energies of Coetzee's writing.[2] In *J. M. Coetzee and the Ethics of Reading* (2004), Derek Attridge drew attention to the way in which Coetzee's fiction explores the complex relationship between politics and ethics, taking his lead from the thought of Derrida and Levinas. Thanks to this work, Coetzee's reputation as a serious and responsible writer is now largely uncontested, and there is room to evaluate his significance— including his significance as a political writer—in different ways.

This book is an attempt to do just that. Following Coetzee's own abiding concern with the origins, history, and ongoing cultural

[1] 'Interview with Paul Bailey', *Third Ear*, BBC Radio 3, 18 Dec. 1990.
[2] David Attwell, *J. M. Coetzee: South Africa and the Politics of Writing* (Berkeley, 1993) 18.

legacy of the form of the novel—an interest most explicit in *Foe* (1986), but equally evident elsewhere in his work—my main concern will be to define and evaluate his own innovativeness as a writer within that tradition. Coetzee has often suggested that his work may be understood in this way, not least when he responded to a question on Samuel Beckett's 'anti-illusionism' in the following terms: 'Anti-illusionism is, I suspect, only a marking of time, a phase of recuperation, in the history of the novel. The question is, what next?' (27). For Coetzee, this question about the future of the novel is deeply related to what it means to be a novelist 'after Beckett': when he started attempting to write in the early 1960s Beckett's fiction stood out as the most engaging and disturbing avant-garde handling of the novel to date, and Beckett remained his most important literary influence. Coetzee has chosen to draw attention to his debt to Beckett on a number of occasions, describing him as a 'clear influence on my prose', and emphasizing that his engagement with Beckett's fiction was a matter of serious study: it was a 'conscious process of absorption' in which his concern was above all to discover what he called the 'secret' of his prose style—'a secret of Beckett's that I wanted to make my own' (*Doubling the Point* 25). An abiding concern of this book will therefore be with the style of Coetzee's fiction, in particular with the highly wrought tension it creates between the serious and the comic—a prose style which, writing of Beckett, Coetzee has described variously as a 'fierce comic anguish', as a 'comic energy, with [the] power to surprise', and even as an 'anguished, teeth-gnashing...intellectual comedy'.[3] Indeed, one of my central claims will be that this aspect of Beckett's legacy (and not only Beckett—other modernist writers such as Kafka are also important to Coetzee for reasons of literary style) has been neglected

---

[3] See J. M. Coetzee, Preface to *Samuel Beckett: the Grove Centenary Edition*, iv (New York, 2006) p. xi; 'Eight Ways of Looking at Samuel Beckett', in Minako Okamuro, Naoya Mori, Bruno Clément, Sjef Houppermans, Angela Moorjani, and Anthony Uhlmann (eds.), *Borderless Beckett/Beckett sans frontières* (Amsterdam, New York, 2008) 23.

at substantive cost to our understanding of Coetzee's distinctive approach to the politics of writing.

It might already seem to some readers that my concern with the intricacies of Coetzee's style and his dialogue with the tradition of the novel, and perhaps above all my special emphasis on the dynamics of the reading experience, together constitute a rather regressively 'literary' approach to a 'postcolonial' writer. But what I hope to show is that there is nothing regressive or depoliticizing about either Coetzee's abiding concern with genre and prose style, nor with the concept of literariness that governs my decision to give attention to those concerns. My central argument is that Coetzee's writing should be understood in the broadest terms as an attempt to move beyond a long discursive tradition—one that includes certain powerful and enduring constructions of the form of the novel—which attempts to position literary value, or literary truth, or most generally 'culture', as superior to, or even transcendent of, politics. It has recently been argued that this tradition, for all its many differences of emphasis, should be described collectively as 'metacultural discourse', as its shared characteristic is the deployment of a 'cultural principle' that 'dissolves the political and takes up the general labour proper to it, assuming the role of a valid social authority'.[4] In short, 'metacultural discourse' is an attempt to arbitrate properly political questions from a position, often named 'culture', that is assumed to be somehow systematically beyond, or at least superior to, the terms of political debate. I will argue that Coetzee's complex engagement with the form of the novel should be understood as an attempt to find a way out of the assumptions made by this tradition, yet a way out that

---

[4] See Francis Mulhern, *Culture/Metaculture* (Abingdon, 2000). Mulhern identifies metacultural discourse primarily—though by no means exclusively—with the European tradition of *Kulturkritik*, which he associates with Matthew Arnold, Julien Benda, José Ortega y Gasset, F. R. Leavis, T. S. Eliot, and others; his book makes an exceptionally acute diagnosis of the ways in which the terms of this discourse continue to permeate the work of many who have tried to escape its core assumptions.

does not simply flatten literature into politics. Coetzee tries to
conceive of writing instead as a type of serious, or to use the term
he borrows from Joyce, 'jocoserious' play with the rules and boundaries that govern political discourse. On a thematic level his fiction
repeatedly suggests that the condition of modernity is made up of
competing, equally important, and yet incommensurate ways of
imagining the good community; by way of response, the crucial
effect of Coetzee's prose lies in the way it tries to de-homogenize
the concepts that differently positioned readers bring to the text, and
thereby to hold open, and place in dialogue, divergent legacies of
political thinking. I will emphasize throughout that it is only by very
close attention to the reading experience that the special nature of
Coetzee's intervention into politics can be understood: namely, the
way in which his writing, to use his own words, not only 'tries to
please' the reader, but also 'tries continually though surreptitiously
to *revise and recreate* her'.[5]

The first chapter sets out the main lines of the debate over the
relation between writing and politics in the late twentieth-century
context in order to identify the questions, at once political and
literary, that animate Coetzee's work in their most general form.
This prepares the ground for the exploration of Coetzee's specific
interest in Beckett in the chapter that follows, in which I discuss
how the early fiction (especially *In the Heart of the Country* (1977)
and *Waiting for the Barbarians* (1980)) creatively assimilates aspects
of Beckett's prose style. Thereafter, individual chapters deal with
different aspects of, and questions raised by, Coetzee's ongoing and
ever more ambitious dialogue with the novel tradition. Chapter 3
extends the analysis of prose style begun with reference to Beckett by
considering *Life & Times of Michael K* (1983) in relation to debates
over the nature of literary truth and Kafka's handling of focalization
in 'A Hunger Artist'. Chapters 4 and 5 deal with the most explicitly
historicist phase of Coetzee's engagement with the form of the novel

---

[5] J. M. Coetzee, *Giving Offense* (1996) 38; my italics.

in *Foe* and *Age of Iron* (1990), while Chapter 6 considers his portrait of the artist in *The Master of Petersburg* (1994). Chapter 7, on *Disgrace* (1999), focuses in greater detail on the way in which Coetzee's serio-comic handling of tone and register relates to his special understanding of the demands made by South Africa's pluralist political ambitions. The last chapter considers the Australian fiction in relation to the longstanding debate over the nature and value of cultural criticism, and suggests that Coetzee's work as a whole should be understood as a substantive rethinking of the terms that structure this debate.

I should note that the argument I am making about Coetzee's handling of the form of the novel, and his subtle and innovative negotiation of the relation between writing and politics, emerges cumulatively through the different chapters. While the final chapter deals specifically with the Australian fiction, it is intended as a conclusion to the book as a whole: it places debates on the novel in particular in the context of debates on culture in the very broadest sense.

1

Writing and Politics: Contexts and Debates

I am not a herald of community or anything else...I am someone who has intimations of freedom (as every chained prisoner has) and constructs representations—which are shadows themselves—of people slipping their chains and turning their faces to the light. I do not imagine freedom, freedom *an sich*; I do not represent it.

J. M. Coetzee, *Doubling the Point.*[1]

I have chosen as the epigraph to this chapter one of the clearest statements Coetzee has made on the relationship between writing and politics. And yet, aside from his refusal to be a 'herald of community', it is not very clear at all. When he speaks of freedom, why does he use the continuous present tense to speak of people 'turning their faces to the light', and 'slipping their chains', rather than the perfective ('turned', 'slipped')? Is this just a mannerism left over from his novels—many of which are written in this tense? Whereas David Lurie, with his special interest in the perfective tense of verbs ('the perfective, signifying an action carried through to its conclusion') would have spoken of someone being 'freed', or

---

[1] J. M. Coetzee, *Doubling the Point: Essays and Interviews*, ed. David Attwell (Cambridge, Mass., 1992) 341. '*An sich*' is an allusion to the Kantian concept of 'Ding an sich', which translates as 'thing in itself': Kant used this term synonymously with 'noumenon' (the opposite of 'phenomenon') to indicate an actual object and its properties as it exists independent of any observer.

even 'freed up', Coetzee will not: freedom is something that must remain in a state of incompletion.[2]

Things only become more complicated when we return this quotation to its context. It comes in an interview in *Doubling the Point* at the conclusion of a series of questions posed by David Attwell about the relation of writing to politics, which had started with Attwell's observation that white South African writing 'has been better at subverting colonial traditions than at replacing them with the imaginative possibility of a moral community'. Coetzee agreed with this observation, albeit with some reservations about the implication that writers necessarily have a duty to imagine 'such a possibility'. However, accepting the concept of 'duty' in a provisional way, Coetzee then distinguished between two forms of political obligation, each of which amounts to a different idea about what makes for a good community. The first is a duty that emerges from a particular society's dominant self-understanding, and its consequent demand to find this understanding reproduced in art: it is 'an obligation imposed on the writer by society, by the soul of society, by society in its hopes and dreams'. The second is different in kind, and is a duty that Coetzee 'tentatively' calls a 'transcendental imperative': an imagining of community that moves past cultural particularity, presumably in the name of a universalist ideal. The 'tiny demurral' that Coetzee makes is that he does not want to privilege either type of duty: he explains that he 'would not want to favor the

---

[2] In his exile at the Eastern Cape, David Lurie starts to reflect on his role as a professor of communications: 'explaining to the bored youth of the country the distinction between *drink* and *drink up*, *burned* and *burnt*. The perfective, signifying an action carried through to its conclusion' (*Disgrace* 71). This interest in the perfective in fact predates the classroom: his first conspicuous use of it is in relation to his management of sexual desire: with the prostitute Soraya he achieves 'a moderate bliss, a moderated bliss' (6). It continues in his discussion of Wordsworth's *The Prelude* ('*Usurp*, to take over entirely,' he tells his students, 'is the perfective of *usurp upon*, usurping completes the act of usurping upon' (21)), and is driving his thinking right up to the last page of the novel, where he plans to 'wheel the bag into the flames and see that it is burnt, burnt up' (220).

first definition unhesitatingly over the second'. So as well as a freedom that remains incomplete, Coetzee puts in play two different notions of the 'moral community'—one culturally particular, the other universalist or 'transcendental'—the choice between which he evidently wishes to hold open, and place in a sustained state of deferral. Indeed, the specific terms in which Coetzee refuses to be a 'herald of community' relate to this desire to refuse the 'perfective' and to remain in a state of incompletion: 'To be a herald,' he explains, you would have to have slipped your chains for a while and wandered about in the real world.' The political question of what makes for a good community cannot, or at least should not, be decided by supposing that a perspective systematically beyond the fact of cultural situatedness is available to the writer.[3]

So to return to the epigraph, Coetzee's statement that he is not a 'herald of community' does not imply that his fiction refuses any kind of relation to politics. His broader suggestion seems to be that there may be other ways of imagining the political, ways that consist of holding open, rather than either perfecting or closing down, different ideas of what constitutes a good community, to which his writing is indeed amenable. This 'anti-foundational' approach to the question of how to think about community and freedom certainly goes along with the pressure Coetzee puts on the semantic foundations of the comments he delivers to Attwell, for one of the most unusual aspects of this interview, which was conducted in writing, is the very style of Coetzee's responses—the disconcerting comic edge he introduces into the exchange. While Attwell's questions are

---

[3] What Coetzee most especially wishes to avoid is the type of position taken by André Brink: 'Deep inside him [the writer] apprehends a welter and a whorl of truth, a great confounding darkness which he shapes into a word; surrounding him is the light of freedom into which his word is sent like a dove from the ark. In this way, through the act of writing, truth and liberty communicate.' 'Mapmakers', in *Mapmakers: Writing in a State of Siege* (London, 1983) 164. Contrast, though, Brink's later view, in which he calls for the 'deconstruction of the real', and argues that 'the very nature of each version or possibility of freedom, as it presents itself, will have to be interrogated'. 'Reimagining the Real', in *Reinventing a Continent: Writing and Politics in South Africa 1982–1995* (London, 1996) 157–8.

ingenuous, focused, and clear, Coetzee's responses are playful and disorienting. He structures his answer around an allusion to Plato's allegory of the cave—one of the most enduringly influential philosophical statements on the distinction between an embodied existence that is degraded and imprisoning and a rational life that is transcendent and free—but he does so with unmistakable irony. Recall what he says about being a 'herald': 'To be a herald you would have to have slipped your chains for a while and wandered about in the real world.' The comic note comes in the assumption of familiarity made by the pronoun, as if slipping 'your' chains and wandering in the realm of 'the real', seeing things (to paraphrase Matthew Arnold) as they really are, is something that, typically, 'you do' if you're a writer. (When? Every day? Every Monday morning?) The effect of this and other comparable moments is not just to mark his dissent from the Platonic identification of freedom with reason, for Coetzee has already made this dissent clear. Instead, the way in which he introduces this distinctively 'literary' effect into the otherwise well-grounded 'philosophical' discourse makes the very terms themselves start to slip and wobble. Perhaps, the reader starts to wonder, the whole framework of real versus ideal, responsibility versus irresponsibility, duty type one (particularist) versus duty type two (transcendental)—perhaps this whole framework of thinking is itself a construction we should treat with a certain circumspection; perhaps only beyond it, or at least in some radical complication of its central terms, is where the truth of things lies.

The questions we must ask are therefore as follows: Why, in the political climate of late twentieth-century South Africa, might it make sense to take the Coetzeean approach, and to discuss the relation between politics and writing through a series of partial disavowals and ironic qualifications? Why must concepts such as community and freedom be projected in terms of incompletion and unfoundedness, rather than in their 'perfective' form? Also, what stance must a writer adopt towards the form of the novel to make it amenable to this approach? In this chapter I will attempt to answer the first two of these questions in very general terms. I'm going to argue that intercultural democracies like South Africa are faced with a complex choice between two different ways of conceptualizing what makes for a good community. These different political ideals, I will suggest, are equally the product of modernity, and each possesses a different concept of what culture is and does (or what it should be and what it should do). What I will argue is that Coetzee's stance as a writer is driven by his appreciation of the necessity for, but inadequacy of, either of these political concepts—so his 'tiny demurral' in relation to which 'duty' should inform his writing will come to seem not so tiny after all.[4] In the chapter that follows I will go on to answer the latter question, and will show that Coetzee's assimilation of the comic energies of Beckett's prose style is crucial to his broader rethinking of the relationship between writing and politics.

In *Multiculturalism: Examining the Politics of Recognition* (1994) Charles Taylor argued that one of the most important political problems facing many late twentieth-century democracies is the experience of a collision between two competing and ultimately incommensurate legacies of political thinking, both of which have their roots in distinctively modern concepts of human identity. These he defines as, on the one hand, a universalist impulse towards a 'politics of equal dignity', and a countervailing particularist impulse towards a 'politics of difference'. Both derive in different ways from the general political ideal of 'equal recognition': drawing on a distinction first made by Peter Berger, he argues that the cultural and institutional transition most definitional of modernity is from a non-democratic politics based on the honour ethic, in which power is organized around rank and social hierarchy, to a politics based

---

[4] Although he writes about a markedly different context, Dipesh Chakrabarty's formulation conveys this stance well: teleological concepts of politics that derive from European modernity are, Chakrabarty argues, 'both indispensable and inadequate' for the political problems posed by Indian modernity. See *Provincialising Europe: Postcolonial Thought and Historical Difference* (Princeton, 2000) 6.

instead on equal human recognition.[5] However, as Taylor goes on to show, while there has always been debate over what is at stake in recognition, in the post-World War II period various different (though not entirely distinct) political phenomena—including decolonization, mass migration, and feminism—have raised the stakes in the debate, and have in many parts of the world hardened a long-standing tension between the universalist and particularist forms of the politics of equal recognition to the point of outright impasse.

The politics of equal dignity is based on the universalist ideal that all humans are equally worthy of respect. As Taylor argues:

> It is underpinned by a notion of what in human beings commands respect, however we may try to shy away from this 'metaphysical' background. For Kant, whose use of the term *dignity* was one of the earliest influential evocations of this idea, what commanded respect in us was our status as rational agents, capable of directing our lives through principles. Something like this has been the basis for our intuitions of equal dignity every since, though the detailed definition of it may have changed.[6]

Deriving from the Kantian account of rational agency, it is a vision of community that understands human dignity to 'consist largely in autonomy, that is, in the ability of each person to determine for himself or herself a view of the good life', and which regards the human agent as 'primarily a subject of self-determining or self-expressive choice' (56). The politics of difference, however, is based on a quite different intuition as to what a truly moral community should be. An important intellectual origin of this politics lies in Herder's reaction against Kant, and his concern that a community must be founded on the recognition, and active fostering of, cultural particularity.[7] This politics,

---

[5] See Peter Berger, 'On the Obsolescence of the Concept of Honour', in Stanley Hauerwas and Alasdair MacIntyre (eds.), *Revisions: Changing Perspectives in Moral Philosophy* (Notre Dame, Ind., 1983).

[6] Charles Taylor, *Multiculturalism: Examining the Politics of Recognition*, ed. Amy Gutman (Princeton, 1994) 41.

[7] See *Multiculturalism* 30–1. For a fuller account of Herder's reaction against Kant see in particular Charles Taylor, *Hegel and Modern Society* (Cambridge, 1979) 1–9.

Taylor argues, has found its clearest post-war articulation in Franz Fanon, especially Fanon's insistence that the misrecognition of cultural difference should be established as a genuine harm, and that the struggle for freedom and equality must therefore be centrally concerned with the revision of damaging cultural stereotypes.[8] Not all Fanon's followers have heeded his call for violence as part of this cultural contestation, but, as Taylor argues, 'the notion that there is a struggle for a changed self-image, which takes place both within the subjugated and against the dominator, has been very widely applied. The idea has become crucial to certain strands of feminism, and is also a very important element in the contemporary debate about multiculturalism' (65). Of particular importance in this debate is the strong form of the claim made by the politics of difference about the type of community a universalist politics purports to bring into being:

The claim is that the supposedly neutral set of difference-blind principles of the politics of equal dignity is in fact a reflection of one hegemonic culture. As it turns out, then, only the minority or suppressed cultures are being forced to take alien form. Consequently, the supposedly fair and difference-blind society is not only inhuman (because suppressing identities) but also, in a subtle and unconscious way, itself highly discriminatory... [T]he worrying thought is that this bias might not just be a contingent weakness of all hitherto proposed theories, that the very idea of such a liberalism may be a kind of pragmatic contradiction, a particularism masquerading as the universal. (43)

Before exploring the ways in which Coetzee's fiction addresses itself to this widely experienced political impasse, we need also to explore the cultural models that go along with these concepts. Only then will we be in a position to evaluate the way political problems play out at the level of literary form.

I am going to start with the politics of equal dignity, and will draw upon Jürgen Habermas's account of the ways in which the cultural institutions and literary forms that emerged with political

---

[8] See Franz Fanon, *The Wretched of the Earth*, trans. Constance Farrington (Harmondsworth, 1967).

modernity—most especially the form of the novel—aimed to create, and to sustain, the ideal of equal dignity itself. In *The Structural Transformation of the Public Sphere* (1962) Habermas argued that while the chief benefit deriving from the transition from a pre-modern politics based on the honour ethic to one based on equal recognition is the creation of a 'public sphere' in which rank and identity-difference are suspended in the name of 'rational-critical debate'; underpinning, and indeed preceding, this new political ideal were two equally new institutions—the 'intimate sphere' of the domestic bourgeois family, and the 'public sphere of the world of letters'. Habermas's case in outline is that the special forms of privacy and human intimacy cultivated in the intimate sphere were crucial both in generating the emotive conviction that humans are fundamentally autonomous in-dividuals, and in sustaining the kinds of sympathetic interpersonal identification that extend this recognition equally to others.[9] Inter-twined with, and supportive of, the intimate sphere was the public sphere of the world of letters, which encompassed two major changes. The first was a crucial shift in the meaning of the word 'culture': here Habermas follows Raymond Williams's argument in *Culture and Society* that with the rise of political modernity the term 'culture' started to designate an activity 'separate from the reproduction of social life' (37), and which related more exclusively to art; ultimately, Williams shows, the term 'culture' came to be used quite explicitly to designate a principle through which difference within the public sphere might be transcended and reconciled, at least in symbolic form.[10] Most crucial for our present concern is that this changing concept of culture was coextensive with the rise of the novel, not least due to the novel being a

---

[9] See Jürgen Habermas, *The Structural Transformation of the Public Sphere*, trans. Thomas Burger with the assistance of Frederick Lawrence (Oxford, 1989), 46. The text originally appeared in German as *Strukturwandel der Öffenlicheit* (Darmstadt and Neuweid, 1962).

[10] As an example, Williams points to Matthew Arnold's *Culture and Anarchy* (1867–8), which argues for a cultural principle, discovered predominantly, though by no means exclusively, within aesthetic experience, as that which elevates to a 'best self'—a self liberated from the narrowly factional pursuit of self-interest.

literary form most suited to commodity-style reproduction, and to mass consumption by a non-expert audience.[11] Habermas argues that the distinctively new kind of literary experience the novel offered was one that helped to rehearse and confirm the new form of reciprocal recognition first instilled in the intimate sphere:

On the one hand, the empathetic reader repeated within himself the private relationships displayed before him in literature; from his experience of real familiarity (*Intimität*), he gave life to the fictional one, and in the latter he prepared himself for the former. On the other hand, from the outset the familiarity (*Intimität*) whose vehicle was the written word, the subjectivity that had become fit to print, had in fact become the literature appealing to a wide public of readers. The privatised individuals coming together to form a public also reflected critically and in public on what they had read, thus contributing to the process of enlightenment which they together promoted.   (50)

The novel—read in private, and discussed in public—acts as bridge between the intimate and public spheres, a 'training ground' (29), as Habermas puts it, through which the emotive identifications begun in the intimate sphere are applied in relation to others, both within the reading experience itself and in the public discussion of how to interpret the moral lives of fictional characters.

Coetzee's novel *Foe*, set in Britain in the early stages of the emerging political formation that Habermas describes, is a more sceptical

---

[11] Williams does not explicitly connect the rise of the novel with the shift in the meaning of 'culture', though he does include the nineteenth-century 'industrial novel' as an example of this type of discourse. Williams locates the main origins of the modern idea of culture in romanticism, though would presumably have acknowledged a deep continuity with the rise of the novel through the shared (though continually transformed) cult of sensibility. For an argument that the rise of modern notions of aesthetic experience are indeed centrally related to the development of the novel, see Michael McKeon, 'Politics of Discourses and the Rise of the Aesthetic in Seventeenth-Century England', in Kevin Sharpe and Steven N. Zwicker (eds.), *Politics of Discourse: The Literature and History of Seventeenth-Century England* (London, 1987) 35–51. For Williams's views on Arnold and the industrial novel, see *Culture and Society 1780–1950* (London, 1958) 103–30.

presentation of these dramatic changes in the realm of both culture and politics. It portrays the early eighteenth-century novelist Daniel Defoe ('Foe') living by the skin of his teeth, and wresting Susan Barton's narrative into a shape that will have some chance of selling in the marketplace. Most notably, the rendering of her story into a novel in fact prevents Susan, as a woman (let alone Friday, as a colonized subject), from laying claim to the recognition of human equality she wants, and forces her instead into the type of story more amenable to the fiction-buying public's understanding of 'the feminine'. *Foe* therefore betrays little confidence that the cultural forms of the new politics of equal dignity actually succeed in living up to their ideal.[12] In *Doubling the Point* Coetzee is especially clear on the historic failure of this political ideal in South Africa: arguing that it arrives as part of 'British liberal culture'—a quite different cultural inheritance to Dutch Calvinism—he speaks not only of its failure to 'engender a literature of equal and reciprocal relations', but its failure to 'engender equal and reciprocal relations, period—[it] failed to persuade the colonists, British or Dutch, that equal and reciprocal relations were a good enough thing to make sacrifices for' (62).[13] Habermas's main example of how the novel helps to bring about, in theory at least, a reciprocal recognition of equal dignity is not Defoe, but the epistolary novel, or 'the novel of sensibility'—especially Samuel Richardson's *Pamela* (1740). I will return to Richardson in some detail in Chapter 5, with regard to Elizabeth Curren's enormous and ambivalently affective epistle to her daughter in *Age of Iron*. But before moving onto the cultural models favoured by the politics of difference, I must emphasize that the idea that the novel helps to generate a

[12] Though as I will argue in Ch. 4, neither does Coetzee wish wholly to negate this politics, and set it up as a 'foe'.

[13] While more overtly sympathetic than Coetzee to the politics he describes, Habermas also insists on separating the ideal of reciprocal recognition from the fact that in practice it has meant merely the enforcement of a particular cultural norm as 'universal'. In the eighteenth century, for instance, it tended to mean 'the identification of the public of "property owners" with that of "common human beings"' (*Structural Transformation* 56).

universalist type of recognition is by no means simply a peculiarity of the early enlightenment period, but constitutes an enduringly important way of understanding what the novel is and does. Perhaps the most influential defence of the novel's cultural value in these terms is George Eliot's claim that it brings about an 'extension of our sympathies' that can transcend difference, and thereby help bring about a truly 'moral community' based on the sentiment of a universally human identity. The realist novel does this, Eliot argues, regardless of the author's intentions, or even of the specific thematic content of the particular novel at stake: it is the 'mode of treatment', not the plot or the characters, that is 'really moral in its influence'.[14] Eliot is very specific about the way in which, by inviting the reader to share the thoughts and feelings of characters from different and unfamiliar social backgrounds, 'more is done towards linking the higher classes with the lower, [and] towards obliterating the vulgarity of exclusiveness' in what Habermas called the 'training ground' of a realist novel than in 'hundreds of sermons and philosophical dissertations' (110).[15] As evidence of the enduring power of these ideas compare the position taken by André Brink—a South African novelist contemporary with Coetzee, and indeed for a time one of his colleagues at the University of Cape Town. In 'The Arts in Society'

[14] As Eliot argues, this is because the realist style is emphatically not one that forces an abstract moral injunction upon the reader: instead, by portraying the human nature of ordinary people—that is to say, people who are 'mixed and erring, and self-deluding, but saved from utter corruption by the salt of some noble impulse, some disinterested effort, some beam of good nature' (309)—the reader is encouraged to recognize their equal humanness amidst the ostensive difference, and thus practise making the act of sympathetic identification that claims to cut through difference. See George Eliot, *Selected Essays, Poems and Other Writings*, ed. A. S. Byatt and Nicholas Warren (London, 1990) 309.

[15] As J. Hillis Miller has argued in *The Ethics of Reading: Kant, de Man, Eliot, Trollope, James and Benjamin* (New York, 1987), Eliot's own view of her novels does not necessarily correspond to the effects they actually generate. What I wish to emphasize, though, is that her understanding of the realist novel is a powerful and enduring construction both of the goals of novel-writing and of what is required in a readerly engagement with the novel.

(1987) Brink argued that literary 'meaning' is something that 'transcends political causes, treatises, pamphlets, however indispensable these may be in themselves', and that thereby uncovers a common humanity: the 'meaning' of literary experience 'has to do not only with the rights and wrongs of a given system or a struggle but with the good and evil of being human'.[16] Despite the considerable historical distance between them, what connects Eliot and Brink is a shared view that the form of the novel embodies the understanding of culture I have outlined, and as we shall see in later chapters, Coetzee's historicist interest in the origins of the novel derives from his concern both to contest and develop the legacies that remain at stake—whether writers acknowledge them or otherwise—in the very structure of the literary form he inherits from European modernity.[17]

As Habermas argued, the politics of equal dignity generates an understanding of culture as separate from the 'reproduction of social life', and regards the novel in particular as one of several institutions within the public sphere that helps to bring about, in a strongly affective way, an ideal of human community grounded in the transcendence of difference. By contrast, though, the major line of thinking within the politics of difference is based around a refusal of this distinction between culture and social reproduction, and the rejection of a transcendental function for culture in favour of a polemical one. As Charles Taylor suggested, Fanon is key to the post-war articulation of this line of thinking, and in South Africa the

---

[16] André Brink, *Reinventing a Continent: Writing and Politics in South Africa 1982–1995* (London, 1996) 57. Elaborating upon this point, Brink claims that writers are 'not agents of power, but campaigners for invisible values no human being can live without... Perhaps, in the final analysis, all art can really do is to help us formulate those questions on which our true survival as human beings depends. Only through questions can one hope to gain access to truth' (58).

[17] This is evident even among the very first of Coetzee's critical essays: see e.g. the article on Yvonne Burgess's novel *The Strike*, where Burgess is criticized for an unreflective use of the realist novel. To do so, Coetzee argues, is merely to reinforce forms of 'class solidarity', and thus unwittingly to promote and entrench misrecognition. See *Doubling the Point* 91–3.

most influential interpretation of Fanon's work came in the 'black consciousness' movement. I'm going to focus briefly on the policy manifesto of the South African Student's Organization (SASO): published in 1973 (the year before Coetzee's first novel, *Dusklands*), *SASO on the Attack*, edited by Ben Langa, is a major statement from one of the most important voices in this movement.[18]

The starting point of the SASO document is a rejection of the politics of equal dignity, which is branded as a political ideal that has failed to live up to its promise, and that has established only a narrowly 'white' idea of cultural value that masquerades as 'the universal'. The 'liberal institutions' in South Africa offer integration, but not 'the kind of integration that would be acceptable to the Black man. Their attempts are directed merely at relaxing certain oppressive legislations and to allow Blacks into a white-type society' (11).[19] Instead, SASO make a claim for a moral community founded on the politics of difference, whose primary goal is an intervention aimed at removing the inauthentic identity that has been instilled in Blacks through generations of misrecognition. This goal of achieving freedom through the recovery of authenticity even has priority over 'literal' liberation from the apartheid regime: 'SASO is ... working for the liberation of the Black man first from psychological oppression by themselves through inferiority complex and secondly from the physical one accruing out of living in a White racist society' (9).

---

[18] Black consciousness was not, of course, by any means the only black political movement in South Africa, but, as David Attwell has argued, it was, by 1974—the year Coetzee published his first novel—'the most volatile and visible of new political developments in opposition to the government' (138). He characterizes its intellectual flavour as a 'mélange of existentialism, politicised psychoanalysis, negritude, structuralism, Maoism, and cultural revolution', adding that while these where all 'rather different movements' in their own spheres, 'their cohesion is more than the sum of their parts, especially as they were received by South Africans at some remove from their sources'. *Rewriting Modernity: Studies in Black South African Literary History* (Scottsville, SA, 2005) 138, 141.

[19] *SASO on the Attack* is available online at the DISA website: www.disa.ukzn.ac.za/index.php?option=com_displaydc&recordID=pol19710709.032.009.746, accessed 14 Dec. 2009.

The document reiterates throughout that the effort of SASO is as much cultural as political—indeed, as I have already indicated, it respects no distinction between 'culture' and 'social reproduction'— and its political activism is directed towards cultural ends: 'the search for the black man's real identity and of his liberation' (6), and for the 'consistent search of the Black Truth' (9). The black man 'must build up his own values systems, see himself as self-defined and not defined by others' (10), as only then, by forcing his particular and authentic identity to be recognized, will his 'basic human dignity' be restored. Authenticity, however, is construed in a subtle twofold way: partly backward-looking, in relation to 'cultural tradition', but also based upon the fact of a 'common oppression', around which communities with different ethnicities and cultural traditions can rally. In an especially powerful phrase, the policy statement speaks of 'the acquisition of blackness by participation in a meaningful organisation': authenticity is being defined by no means simply through ethnicity, but as an existential choosing of the self within a general project of communal assertion.[20]

White South African intellectuals were not slow to perceive that one key effect of the culture-war initiated by the politics of difference was to throw inherited ideas of literary value—deeply intertwined as they were with the increasingly discredited politics of equal dignity—into crisis. In a 1979 essay titled 'Relevance and Commitment' Nadine Gordimer summarized the seeming redundance of her own position as a novelist in the wake of the black consciousness movement:

---

[20] It should be emphasized that one of the ambitions of the black consciousness movement in South Africa was a construction of 'blackness' that included the full range of racially oppressed ethnic groups; this differentiated it from (e.g.) the goals of black consciousness in the United States. As an example of this attempt to build a multi-ethnic solidarity see Strini Moodley's insistence in his open letter to the 'Fakir' of the *Leader* (dated 14 June 1971) that the Indian community must 'identify with the oppressed mass of South Africa', and recognize that 'We are all Black South Africans', or otherwise 'become the "priveleged" [*sic*] lackey of the white man'. See the DISA website: www. disa.ukzn.ac.za/index.php?option=com_displaydc&recordID=let19710614.032.009.745, accessed 14 Dec. 2009.

For a long time [the white writer] assumed the objective reality by which his relevance was to be measured was somewhere out there between and encompassing black and white. Now he finds that no such relevance exists; the black has withdrawn from a position where art, as he saw it, assumed the liberal role Nosipho Majeke defined as that of the 'conciliator between oppressor and oppressed'.[21]

Gordimer's essay revolves around the problem posed by this apparent impasse, placing a tentative hope in the possibility of a new 'sense of totality' (142), in which the recognition of equal dignity is genuinely achieved, though how this is to be brought about, and what concept of culture might be amenable to the bringing about of the new 'totality', remain unspecified.[22] By contrast, as the novelist and critic Es'kia Mphahlele indicated in 'African Writers and Commitment' (1968), the key influence on black writers was that of Sartre, and most especially Sartre's outright rejection of what Gordimer referred to as the 'liberal role' of the novel in *What is Literature?* (1948).[23] For Sartre the properly 'committed' novelist has 'given up the impossible dream

---

[21] Nadine Gordimer, *The Essential Gesture*, ed. Stephen Clingman (London, 1988) 138.

[22] Not all white intellectuals became cognizant of the problem in the same way: in contrast to Gordimer, André Brink retained a faith in the 'liberal role' of the writer. Abstracting black consciousness from its goal of cultural contestation, he continued at this time to regard culture as the site upon which difference might be transcended: 'What individual writers express is obviously determined primarily by private experience, temperament, hope and the frustration of hope: yet essentially all are involved in the same activity—not just of *opposing* a political regime, but of *affirming* lasting human values, and providing the open ends through which these can expand and continue to grow. All are involved in the articulation of cultural languages, different in syntax, identical in essence.' 'The Languages of Culture', in *Mapmakers* 229–30.

[23] 'After Sartre, several people have claimed that African literature is "functional", meaning, I believe, that this writing advocates the black man's cause and/or instructs its audience' (*Voices in the Whirlwind* (London, 1972) 188). Mphahlele himself regretted the influence of Sartre, believing his idea of the novel 'indicates a dangerous tendency, which is to draw a line of distinction between a function in which an author vindicates or asserts black pride or takes a socio-political stand and

of giving an impartial picture of Society and the human condition':
instead, the language of realism is now valued exclusively for its ability
to lend expressive weight to the assertion of a particular identity. The
writer, for Sartre, 'knows that he makes the word "love" and the word
"hate" *surge up* and with them love and hate between men who had
not yet decided upon their feelings. He knows that words . . . are
"loaded pistols". If he speaks, he fires'.[24] Sartre's writer expresses
himself in all the particularity of his identity, with particularity
being conceived in explicitly political terms: 'Whether he wants to
or not,' Sartre claims, 'and even if he has his eyes on eternal laurels, the
writer is speaking to his contemporaries and brothers of his class and
race' (49); 'each book,' he adds, 'proposes a concrete liberation on the
basis of a particular alienation' (51). And yet how, it must be asked,
does the Sartrean novel actually differ—except by assertion—from the
descriptions of the realist novel we encountered earlier? Whereas
George Eliot carefully described the ways in which the novel en-
courages the reader to recognize and sympathize with the characters
it portrays, Sartre makes no comparable account of the experience
of reading: his argument, unlike Eliot's, is generally confined to the
writer's intentions, and what they should and should not be if his act
of writing is to be authentic.[25] So in retort to Sartre it could be argued
that the novel itself—an invention, after all, of political modernity,
and coextensive with its concern for equal dignity—writes the writer,
so to speak, regardless of his intentions.[26]

a function in which he seeks to stir humanity as a whole'; he finds in several aspects
of African writing—especially the novel—a more labile interplay between polemical
assertion and stirring 'humanity as a whole'.

[24] Jean-Paul Sartre, *What is Literature?*, trans. Bernard Frechtman (London,
1967) 13.

[25] See especially her essay 'The Natural History of German Life', in *Selected
Essays*, ed. Byatt and Warren.

[26] Coetzee made this type of argument in his brief and rather acid 'Note on
Writing' (1984), where he warns of a 'particular kind of writing, writing in
stereotyped forms and genres and characterological systems and narrative orderings,
where the machine runs the operator'. *Doubling the Point* 95.

In order to understand the particular stance towards politics taken by Coetzee, it is important to emphasize that the attack on the universalist assumptions of the politics of equal dignity is by no means limited to active proponents of the politics of difference. Another type of critique is that made by a line of political philosophy that originates in the thinking of Martin Heidegger, and this has taken several different directions: perhaps the best known in the Francophone world is Jean-Luc Nancy's *The Inoperative Community* (1986); within Anglo-American political philosophy, Charles Taylor's work is certainly marked by Heidegger's influence, but the most avowedly Heideggerian approach is that taken by John Gray in *Enlightenment's Wake: Politics and Culture at the Close of the Modern Age* (1995). Gray rejects the totalizing ambitions of the politics of equal dignity, which he describes as 'the historical philosophy which the Enlightenment project incorporates, in which cultural difference must in the end yield to rationality and generic humanity as these are embodied in a universal human civilisation'.[27] Unlike Fanon, however, he grounds this rejection in a broader, Heidegger-inspired critique of 'logocentrism', by which he means 'the conception in which human reason mirrors the structure of the world', a 'central Western tradition' that extends back to Plato, and that is sustained most markedly by the Christian tradition. Gray argues that the fact that 'we find at the close of the modern age a renaissance of particularisms, ethnic and religious' is an unavoidable condition that we should not seek to overturn by making appeal to a 'view from nowhere' (162), as such a view is always illusory. Resigning ourselves to the fact that the logocentric presumption is an illusion (or, with Coetzee, accepting that the vantage offered by the 'herald of community' is unavailable) requires that we acknowledge that any given attempt to extend recognition on the basis of 'rationality and generic humanity' will indeed, to recall Charles Taylor's phrase, always issue merely in

---

[27] John Gray, *Enlightenment's Wake: Politics and Culture at the Close of the Modern Age* (London, 1995) 167.

'a particularism masquerading as a universal'. More precisely, he claims that the desire to extend recognition of human equality in this way fails to escape the limitations of what Heidegger calls 'calculative thinking'. In his late work *Gelassenheit* (Discourse on Thinking), upon which Gray draws extensively in *Enlightenment's Wake*, Heidegger described calculative thinking, which he considered dominant in and even characteristic of political modernity, as 'justified and needed in its own way', but limited in its ability to deal with difference: at best it reinforces and perpetuates, ever more efficiently, current understandings of human value; at worst it is sheer will to power, riding roughshod over anything that doesn't correlate with its own prerogatives.[28]

It is in this line of Heidegger-inspired thinking about the calculative limitations of the ideal of equal dignity that we should position Coetzee, and most especially his first work of fiction, *Dusklands*. While there is no evidence to suggest that Coetzee was reading Heidegger at this time he had certainly imbibed Heideggerian ideas from his reading of Sartre's *Being and Nothingness* (1943), and in a more direct and polemical way from his exposure to the French literary avant-garde of the 1950s, especially the Roland Barthes of *Writing Degree Zero* (1953).[29] *Dusklands* is an important

[28] Martin Heidegger, *Discourse on Thinking*, trans. John M. Anderson and E. Hans Freund (New York, 1966) 46.

[29] See in particular the chapter entitled 'Writing and the Novel', important to Coetzee for its criticism of the perfective past tense: Barthes argued that in deploying this tense (in literary French, the *passé simple*), the realist novel inevitably 'presupposes a world which is constructed, elaborated, self-sufficient, reduced to significant lines, and not one which has been sent sprawling before us, for us to take or leave . . . a slim and pure logos, without density, without volume, without spread' (*Writing Degree Zero*, trans. Annette Lavers and Colin Smith (New York, 1967) 30). In his doctoral thesis Coetzee quoted Alain Robbe-Grillet to similar effect: 'While essentialist conceptions of man met their destruction, the idea of "condition" henceforth replacing that of "nature", the *surface* of things ceased to be for us the mask of their heart . . . Thus it is the entire literary language which has to change— which has already changed.' 'The English Fiction of Samuel Beckett: An Essay in Stylistic Analysis'. Diss., University of Texas, 1969, 152.

early work primarily for what it reveals of Coetzee as a political thinker in this intellectual line, as in it he combines a polemical stance against the universalist ideal with an overt assault on the form of the novel.[30] Most especially, this rather schematic pair of fictions (or more accurately 'anti-novels') insist that the aspiration towards a single rational basis for human identity and political life is best understood as a 'white' tribal myth that enshrouds an essentially calculative will to power; this will to power is associated by Coetzee in equal measure with the history of early European colonialism and with the then contemporary American involvement in Vietnam.[31] Such a view is presented most overtly by the allegorical frame of the text, which situates the two protagonists, Eugene Dawn and Jacobus Coetzee, as representative of the era of modernity, whose 'dawn' was in the eighteenth century, coincidental with the expansion of colonialism in Africa, and whose 'dusk' is apparently now—symbolized by Dawn's insane scheming and his final neurosis. As in *Enlightenment's Wake*, Coetzee's text insists that the cultural and political ideas at stake in the outlook of these two men have their roots in the logocentric mythos of the Christian tradition. The second fiction begins with a passage describing Jacobus's anxiety that white folk are losing their differentiatedness with the 'Hottentot'. But, he affirms, it is the authentic possession of Christianity that ultimately grounds the racial distinction: 'The one gulf that divides us from the Hottentot is our Christianity. We are Christians, a folk with a destiny. They become Christians too, but their Christianity is an empty word' (57). His Christianity empowers his faith that he is the bearer of a higher form of autonomous and rational humanity, and this makes him quite unlike the 'Hottentot', who is 'locked into the present'. With the

---

[30] This association is, of course, made most overtly by the ancestry the novelist Coetzee claims with the colonialist 'Jacobus Coetzee' in the second fiction, and the naming of Eugene Dawn's manager as 'Coetzee' in the first.

[31] *Dusklands* is full of references to myth: Eugene Dawn works in a 'mythography' department; he is a scholar of the ways in which 'myths operate in human society' (4), though he chooses to remain unaware of the mythical thinking that empowers his own stance.

Eugene Dawn of the late 1960s, this specifically Christian idea has metamorphosed into different terms: Dawn now speaks in a more nationalist and technocratic style of 'the true myth of America' (9) which consists in a 'duty towards history' (29), involving an 'evolutionary duty toward the glory of consciousness' (28), but there is nonetheless a clear epistemic continuity between the two men. What *Dusklands* emphasizes throughout, not least through its repeated portrayal of Hegel's master and slave dialectic, is that while Eugene Dawn and Jacobus Coetzee masquerade as a higher historical realization of the human essence, their comportment towards the cultural 'others' they encounter is in fact remorselessly calculative, and utterly incapable of respecting their own self-justifying universalist rhetoric.[32]

This brief survey of the main concepts in politics and culture current in the late twentieth century helps us pose the questions we asked at the beginning of this chapter with greater clarity and precision. If the strongest, Heidegger-inspired, form of the critique of the politics of equal dignity is right, and the attempt to extend recognition on this basis is indissociable from a calculative will to power, then are we left with an identity-based assertion of difference as the only viable foundation for politics? Must we give up entirely on what Coetzee called the 'transcendental imperative'? And must we also therefore give up the idea that culture is 'higher' than, or even distinct from, social reproduction?

---

[32] For the master and slave dialectic, see G. W. F. Hegel, *Phenomenology of Spirit*, trans. A. V. Miller (Oxford, 1977) 178–96. Jacobus makes a telling distinction between the constrained type of relationship possible with Dutch girls, who fall within his conception of what counts as human (they are white, Christian, and so on), and that available with a 'Bushman girl': 'She is completely disposable. She is something for nothing, free. She can kick and scream but she knows she is lost. That is the freedom she offers, the freedom of the abandoned. She has no attachments, not even the well known attachment to life. She has given up the ghost, she is flooded in its stead with your will. Her response to you is absolutely congruent with your will' (61).

The striking fact about the politics of difference is that many of its most strident proponents refuse to answer a simple 'yes' to at least the first two of these questions (if not always to the third), most especially when they turn from the immediate prerogatives of the political struggle to address the question of the future. As just one example I will return to the 1973 SASO policy manifesto. The most complex part of this document is the section dealing with the medium to long term, in which there is an attempt to envisage the truly intercultural society of the future, in which 'both Black and White . . . continue to live together' (10). It is clear to SASO that due to generations of misrecognition, negative ethnic sterotyping, and political oppression, 'Whites have defined themselves as part of the problem', and therefore a line of 'anti-Whitism' must be taken—but not permanently, just as 'a more positive way of attaining a normal situation in South Africa'. Yet what is meant by a 'normal situation'? Further down the page the document refers instead to an 'open society': 'before the Black people should join the open society, they should first close their ranks, to form themselves into a solid group to oppose the definite racism that is meted out by the White society, to work out their direction clearly and bargain from a position of strength' (10). Again the question arises—what is meant by this 'open society'? What happens to the 'Black Truth' and authentically black 'values systems' [*sic*] in a society that is 'normal', or 'open'? Are they to take over from the 'white' values and truths? Or live alongside them, somehow? (But how? Both have their own distinctive conceptions of value.) The manifesto makes appeal to the concept of 'integration', and deploys this word in an unconventional way. 'Integration' does not here mean 'an assimilation of Blacks into an already established set of norms drawn up and motivated by white society'. It cannot mean a simple return to the politics of equal dignity, for this would involve the abandonment of a hard-won authenticity—the truths and values forged in cultural combat that played an essential, perhaps even constitutive, part of winning freedom from oppression—in favour of a 'universal' identity which, if the lessons of the past are heeded, will in fact be only a particularism in disguise. Yet the call for 'integration' cannot mean, either, a simple continuation of the politics of difference. The SASO document recognizes, when it looks to the future, that a community based exclusively on the assertion of politicized identity would be no community at all, but merely a territorial space featuring an ever-escalating hostility between increasingly hermetic political groups, each with their own occult preserve of truth and value. What, then, is this 'integration' that is, somehow, not an 'assimilation'? The SASO policy document is thought-provoking because it places a complex demand on the future, even though it doesn't itself work through the implications of this demand.[33] The implicit demand is for a community founded neither upon the assertion of difference, nor upon a reversion to the transcendence of difference, but instead on some yet-to-be-articulated exchange between the two.

I hope we have now come some way to understanding why it might make sense for Coetzee, in the political context of late twentieth-century South Africa, to respond to the idea of community in the highly equivocal way that he does, insisting on an anti-foundational approach. He refuses to position himself as a 'herald of community', but wishes to retain an 'awareness' of (not, he specifies, a 'faith' in) the 'transcendental imperative'; he distinguishes between the particularist and the universalist ideal of

---

[33] As David Attwell argues, this positing of 'a future in which black and white might co-exist on some yet-to-be-discovered, universal basis', is a common feature of the Black Consciousness form of the politics of difference (*Rewriting Modernity* 143). In *Speaking of Freedom: Philosophy, Politics, and the Struggle for Liberation* (Stanford, 2007), Diane Enns takes a pointedly critical stance towards the unanalysed utopianism of some forms of the politics of difference, arguing that 'a view of freedom as beyond power, beyond the forces that subjugate, classify, or organize along racialized or gendered bases, assumes an ideal realm that escapes the political' (71). Enns regards this 'desire [ultimately] to escape from the contingencies of power and politics', which she finds especially manifest in the writings of Biko and Memmi, as falsifying and unjustifiable, though admits the empowering hopefulness that such a vision can inspire.

community, and with a 'tiny demurral' refuses to choose the one over the other; when he speaks of freedom it is neither as an achieved state, nor as an impossible illusion, but as a becoming-free, or a freedom-in-process. In consequence, as I will go on to show, he tries to find a way of working with the medium of the novel that avoids the assumption that politics can be addressed from a 'view from nowhere', and that grants the 'perfective' to neither of the political concepts I have described. Instead of making itself amenable either to a society founded on a logocentric account of reason and human autonomy, or one founded instead on the assertion of difference and cultural distinctiveness, Coetzee's fiction is most amenable to what Jean-Luc Nancy speaks of as a democracy without foundations.[34] His writing seeks to hold open divergent ideas of what makes for a good community, and to place them, within the reading experience, in a continually disruptive dialogue with what each excludes and forgets.

I do not wish to substantiate these last points right now, as that will follow in the detailed readings I will give of Coetzee's texts, each of which intervenes in a quite singular way within the political culture it inhabits. In the next chapter I will start out by showing that it is chiefly through Coetzee's creative assimilation of Beckett's prose style that his fiction seeks to generate the type of political effect I describe. First, though, I will conclude this chapter on the debates and contexts that have played a part in shaping Coetzee's fiction by briefly clarifying what I mean by 'disruptive dialogue', as this will prepare the way for the next chapter on Beckett.

As part of his own answer to what a politics truly in the 'enlightenment's wake' might be like, John Gray draws upon the later Heidegger's concept of *Gelassenheit*, which translates loosely as 'releasement' or 'letting be'.[35] The term *Gelassenheit*

---

[34] 'Absence of foundation', Nancy argues, '*is* foundation for democracy.' See *The Experience of Freedom*, trans. Bridget McDonald (Stanford, 1993).

[35] Gray places an important caveat around his use of *Gelassenheit*, explaining that he is politicizing the concept in a way that Heidegger might not have

refers to an anti-foundational mode of thinking, upon which Heidegger draws as part of his response to calculative thinking. It is emphatically not the opposite of the calculative, and should not be read as shorthand for the 'altruistic'; instead, *Gelassenheit* is a type of comportment towards the world which is both like and unlike the calculative: as Heidegger says, it 'expresses "yes" and at the same time "no" to calculative thinking. It says "yes" in so far as it retains an "active" character—it is by no means a "kind of passivity", or a matter of outright rejection of the will, of "weakly allowing things to slide and drift along"' (61). It says 'yes' to the desire to know and understand within calculative thinking. But its 'no' relates to the manner in which knowledge is brought about, and there follows in Heidegger's text a long meditation on the nature of 'waiting', which is of course also a great theme of Beckett's. In waiting 'we always wait for something', but nonetheless, waiting can be distinguished from 'awaiting', which is rooted in a calculation of what we will discover. Heidegger develops a special sense of waiting in which 'we leave open what we are waiting for', a type of waiting that, as he puts it, 'releases itself into openness' (68), and that thereby imports a self-questioning anxiety into the striving for knowledge. Applied to the political question of recognition, *Gelassenheit* therefore suggests a form of dialogue in which the desire to recognize the other is engaged with a potentially transformative alertness to, or a 'waiting for', the difference the other might bring—a difference that might transform the terms upon which recognition is extended. In an earlier lecture Heidegger explained this process of engagement in a particularly felicitous way:

---

approved: 'the mode of *Gelassenheit* . . . in which we wean ourselves from willing and open ourselves to letting beings be, is most needful in our circumstances. Contrary to much in even the later Heidegger, however, it is not openness to 'Being' that is needed, but instead an openness to beings, to the things of the earth, in all their contingency and mortality.' *Enlightenment's Wake* 182.

To let be is to engage oneself with beings. On the other hand, to be sure, this is not to be understood only as the mere management, preservation, tending, and planning of the beings in each case encountered or sought out. To let be—that is, to let beings be as the beings which they are— means to engage oneself with the open region and its openness into which every being comes to stand, bringing that openness, as it were, along with itself.[36]

As well as emphasizing the element of unpredictable difference at stake in this encounter—the 'open region' with which one must engage—Heidegger's central emphasis is that *Gelassenheit* is necessarily a process without a conclusion: it will never culminate in a fully grounded knowledge, but is instead a sustained dialogue in which the 'yes' within the drive to knowledge is put in touch with the 'no' of waiting. The anti-foundational nature of *Gelassenheit*—its refusal of the 'perfective'—is emphasized when Heidegger touches on the implications for linguistic expression. 'A word', he suggests, 'does not and never can represent anything; but signifies something, that is, shows something as abiding into the range of its expressibility.' Words, that is to say, can register the difference at stake, but only that aspect that comes into the 'range of its expressibility': they have themselves to be subjected to a 'waiting', and must not be allowed to stand still and 'reify' (67) the otherness at stake into the terms provided by any given act of calculative thinking. True difference will bring about an interruption in the very terms used to gain knowledge of the other; sustained dialogue will therefore bring about a sustainedly unsettling 'churn of words', in which a given pattern of thinking is placed in transformative contact with that which it excludes.

The phrase 'churn of words' is my import, and is lifted from Beckett's novel *The Unnamable* (1953).[37] It is now—just as we

[36] Martin Heidegger, 'On the Essence of Truth', in *Basic Writings*, ed. David Farrell Krell, rev. edn. (New York, 1993) 125.
[37] Samuel Beckett, *The Unnamable*, in *The Beckett Trilogy* (London, 1979) 285. First published as *L'Innomable* (Paris, 1952).

begin to touch upon matters of prose style—that we can move to a more detailed consideration of the relation Coetzee tries to bring about between his work as a writer, and his concern for an anti-foundational imagining of freedom and community, through an analysis of his abiding interest in Beckett.

2

Writing and Politics After Beckett

What is missing from Beckett's account of life?

J. M. Coetzee, 'Eight Ways of Looking
at Samuel Beckett'.[1]

Coetzee posed the question cited in the epigraph in a lecture on Beckett given in September 2006 in Tokyo. It intrudes into the lecture all of a sudden, after a short account of Beckett's uneasily serio-comic presentation of the 'dualist' tradition in philosophy— the tradition that claims humans are in essence a 'body plus a mind' (19), and which normally regards the mind rather than the body as the genuine locus of the self. In answer to this question, Coetzee told his audience that 'many things' are missing from Beckett's account of life, 'of which the biggest is the whale' (21), and he then launched into an unusual comparison between Samuel Beckett and Herman Melville, centring on the novel *Moby Dick* (1851). The context of the lecture is important here, for the Japanese government had recently granted permission for whaling expeditions to resume, despite a global chorus of disapproval due to the scarcity of whales in the Pacific. One implication of the lecture is that the 'dualist' view of life can be one that eventuates in precisely this type of greedy and destructive behaviour: it gives free rein to what I have, following

---

[1] J. M. Coetzee, 'Eight Ways of Looking at Samuel Beckett', *in Borderless Beckett/ Beckett sans frontières*, ed. Minako Okamuro, Naoya Mori, Bruno Clément, Sjef Houppermans, Angela Moorjani, and Anthony Uhlmann (Amsterdam, New York, 2008) 21.

Heidegger, called 'calculative' forms of thinking, at the expense of a rightful care for the environment. But Coetzee's lecture is not confined to its polemical intervention within the debate on whaling. As he builds up an unexpectedly illuminating comparison between Beckett and Melville it becomes clear that he is making an important statement of his own mixed feelings about Beckett's legacy, and the terms on which it might be inherited and developed.

Coetzee chooses to focus on an overtly 'philosophical' moment in *Moby Dick*, which reveals Melville to be every bit as concerned with the dualist account of the self as Beckett. He quotes Captain Ahab's account of why he wants to seek revenge against the white whale that (in a previous encounter) cost him his leg:

'All visible objects [...] are but as pasteboard masks,' he says, offering a philosophical account of his vendetta against the white whale. 'But in each event—in the living act, the undoubted deed—there, some unknown but still reasoning thing puts forth the mouldings of its features from behind the unreasoning mask. If man will strike, strike through the mask! How can the prisoner reach outside except by thrusting through the wall? To me, the white whale is that wall, shoved near to me.' (21–2)

Most fundamentally, the 'philosophical' aspect of the Ahab story relates to how we deal with otherness, otherness here being construed very broadly indeed as that which is other to self-consciousness. Ahab perceives himself to be primarily a 'reasoning thing', an autonomous human agent, who has a craving to gain recognition of that true self in his embodied existence in the world: his wish is to 'put forth the mouldings of [his] features from behind the unreasoning mask' of his body. The otherness of the whale—its blithe independence from him, and the proof it offers that the world lived in by Ahab's body is not expressive of himself in the way he wants it to be—must, Ahab feels, be suppressed. 'How can the prisoner reach outside except by thrusting through the wall? To me, the white whale is that wall, shoved near to me'—and Ahab's metaphysical thrust will be made real by the literal thrust of his harpoon. In the calculative approach he takes to otherness, Ahab resembles the anti-heroes of

Dusklands: they too encountered the metaphorical 'whale' (in terms of the cultural otherness of the Vietnamese, and the native peoples of southern Africa, as well as the otherness of the natural world) with a violent desire to eliminate difference—and they too drew upon as much technology as possible to secure their dominance.

But as Coetzee points out, in Beckett's novels there is no whale. Whereas Melville's interest lay clearly in the life led by the body in the world, and the limitations placed on freedom by the existence of embodied otherness, 'Beckett's selves, his intelligences, his creatures, whatever one prefers to call them' have renounced their concern with embodied life—or had it renounced for them—in favour of solipsism. His characters are 'brains imprisoned in pots without arms or legs'; they are even 'worms' (23). The 'white wall' of otherness most at stake in Beckett is always within the self: an 'inner' wall in the consciousness that might conceivably contain 'the door that opens on my own story', as Beckett's Unnamable narrator puts it (382). Thus it is that the 'tool' possessed by a Beckett character is not Ahab's worldly 'harpoon', capable of piercing flesh, but 'pure thought': 'they and the intelligence behind them believe that the only tool that can pierce the white wall is the tool of pure thought'.

But as well as observing the limitations of Beckett's solipsism, Coetzee draws attention to the possibilities of his prose style. Whereas Melville imagined the encounter with otherness as tragedy—a tragic bloodbath—Beckett's style refuses this oversimplification at the level of literary mode:

To Melville, the one-legged man who trusts himself to the harpoon-thrust, though the harpoon fails him too (to the harpoon is knotted the rope that drags him to his death), is a figure of tragic folly and (maybe) tragic grandeur, *à la* Macbeth. To Beckett, the legless scribbler who believes in pure thought is a figure of comedy, or at least of that brand of anguished, teeth-gnashing, solipsistic intellectual comedy, with intimations of damnation behind it, that Beckett made his own. (23)

Coetzee makes the intriguing suggestion that Beckett's complex tragicomic way of handling the encounter with otherness is, despite his reservations about the drastic limitations placed by Beckett on the modes of otherness imagined, a much more compelling literary treatment than Melville's. He then squares up to literary history and poses a momentous 'what if':

> What if Beckett had had the imaginative courage to dream up the whale, the great flat white featureless front (front, from Latin *frons*, forehead) pressed up against the fragile bark in which you venture upon the deep; and behind that front, the great, scheming animal brain, the brain that comes from another universe of discourse, thinking thoughts according to its own nature, beyond malign, beyond benign, thoughts inconceivable, incommensurate with human thought? (24)

What if Beckett, or someone who were to write with Beckett's 'anguished, teeth-gnashing... comedy', had the 'imaginative courage' to take on Melville's great theme? What if someone who possessed Beckett's distinctively unsettling prose style were to move past his solipsism to take on the question of what it means to live an embodied life, and work through the problems of encountering the otherness out there in the world? If such a writer were to renounce the Melvillian 'tragic' mode, in which the encounter (culminating merely in a bloodbath) is styled with a tragic 'overreaching' grandeur, and embraces instead Beckett's 'serio-comic' treatment, what would happen then?

Coetzee is, I think, describing himself here. He is a writer deeply indebted to Beckett's prose, but has had the 'imaginative courage' to move it beyond solipsism, and reinterpret it in terms of the dynamics of embodied life: the life that has to confront not only the otherness of the self, but the otherness of the beings that one lives alongside, and thus the political question of what it means to live in a community. But while the Tokyo lecture gives us Coetzee's view of what is most at stake in his encounter with Beckett—his solipsism, the 'anguished... comedy' of his prose—it is short on detail. Why is this prose style of Beckett's so important to Coetzee? Can we give a fuller description of how it works and what it does? These are the two questions I will answer in the first half of this chapter. Then, turning to Coetzee's early fiction, I will describe the way in which he creatively assimilates the Beckettian novel in order to engage with the political problems that I outlined in Chapter 1.

BECKETT AND TEMPTATION

Coetzee's own account of the origin of his relationship with Beckett emphasizes his immediate and overwhelming pleasure in Beckett's prose. This is what he says in *Youth*:

> From the first page he knows he has hit on something. Propped up in bed with light pouring through the window, he reads and reads.
>
> *Watt* is quite unlike Beckett's plays. There is no clash, no conflict, just the flow of a voice telling a story, a flow continually checked by doubts and scruples, its pace fitted exactly to the pace of his own mind. *Watt* is also funny, so funny that he rolls about laughing. When he comes to the end he starts again at the beginning.
>
> Why did people not tell him Beckett wrote novels?[2]   (155)

Coetzee immediately recognizes in Beckett a kindred spirit: he has not only 'hit on something', but realizes he has found a prose 'fitted exactly to the pace of his own mind', the fit being most especially evident in Beckett's handling of comedy. The immediate product of this encounter with Beckett was doctoral research undertaken at the University of Texas, and as Coetzee explained in *Doubling the Point*, the research was designed to explain to himself why it was he found Beckett so stylistically compelling:

> Beckett's prose, up to and including *The Unnamable*, has given me a sensuous delight that hasn't dimmed over the years. The critical work I did on Beckett originated in that sensuous response, and was a grasping after ways in which to talk about it: to talk about delight.   (20)

This attempt to 'talk about delight' led to a thesis that Coetzee—rightly, in my view—described as a 'wrong turning' that 'didn't lead

---

[2] J. M. Coetzee, *Youth* (London, 2002) 155.

anywhere interesting' (22). It is a complex piece of work, and difficult to summarize, but its underlying aim was to use a positivist statistical methodology ('statistical stylistics') to describe the main features of Beckett's style. As such it was in hindsight doomed to fail, because, as Coetzee's first academic publications reveal, his 'sensuous response' to Beckett's prose could never be separated from history in the way that the positivist assumptions of his statistical method required. In his earliest published literary criticism Coetzee started to argue instead that Beckett's style only becomes meaningful when registered against a particular set of expectations and reading practices generated by the cultural phenomenon of the realist novel.

His 1970 article, 'The Comedy of Point of View in Beckett's *Murphy*', is an exposition of Beckett's 'attitude of reserve' towards the form of the novel, and what now most interests Coetzee is the way in which Beckett's self-reflexive comedy undermines what I spoke of in the previous chapter as the cultural principle presupposed both by the novel's conventions, and the reading experience those conventions invite. Most obviously, Beckett's 'attitude of reserve' is to be found in the ways in which *Murphy* makes play with the conventions that sustain the logocentric illusion of objectivity, or what Coetzee rather ironically calls 'the principle of the separation of the three estates of author, narrator, and character' (36). In a series of close analyses of randomly chosen sentences, Coetzee shows how Beckett violates this principle in a number of different ways: by foregrounding the narrator and the author, by foregrounding 'anomalies created by a convention of a preterite narrator of an imaginary history', by bringing about 'interplay between narrator and character in authorial roles', and even by initiating an 'interplay between narrator and author'. This 'comic antigrammar of point of view', which undercuts the feeling of having a disinterested gaze upon things, is, Coetzee argues, 'of a piece' with the way in which Beckett also interrupts the flow of sympathetic identification between reader and characters that takes place in the novel. He cites Beckett's flippant authorial asides, such as 'All the puppets in this book whinge sooner or later, except Murphy, who is not a puppet', noting that 'the comedy is ironic, and acts to keep sentiment at a distance: the bassoons of irony sound to drown the elegiac melodies that keep stealing over the piece' (37). As Coetzee goes on to suggest, this 'attitude of reserve' to the form of the novel grows ever more important to Beckett, such that

[...] by the time of *The Unnamable* (1953) [it] has become, in a fundamental sense, the subject of Beckett's work... 'The Unnamable' as a name is a token of an inability to attain the separation of creator and creature, namer and named, with which the act of creating, naming, begins ('To be an artist is to fail,' wrote Beckett in 1949). 'I seem to speak,' says The Unnamable, 'it is not I, about me, it is not about me.'

What most interests Coetzee, and also most disturbs him, is exactly where this assault on logocentric fictional conventions ends up. Finally unable, as Coetzee puts it, 'to arrive at a division between consciousness and the objects of consciousness', the demolition of the realist novel carried out in *The Unnamable* drives Beckett ever further into an imprisoning solipsistic impasse. For once the premise of objectivity falls away, he ultimately loses not only the possibility of intersubjective recognition, but even the possibility of self-knowledge: in the increasingly paranoid realm occupied by the Unnamable, 'consciousness of self can be only consciousness of consciousness. Fiction is the only subject of fiction. Therefore, fictions are closed systems, prisons' (38). Coetzee clearly has in mind the sense of escalating paranoia on display in *The Unnamable*, in which the narrator comes to fear that there is no way to transcend his situatedness in patterns of discourse always already constructed by others, and thus no way to gain access to his authentic self. 'All is a question of voices,' Beckett's narrator comes to believe, doubting whether there is 'a single word of mine in all I say' (317–19). The Unnamable increasingly alludes to a mysterious set of powerful 'others', collectively a 'they', who construct and imprison him at every turn: 'Do they believe it is

I who am speaking?' he asks. 'That's theirs too' (319). The self, he fears, is always already 'spoken' or 'written', by the various networks of representation that make up the cultural field: a 'they', who inhabit the self at every turn, and are bent on making the self into 'one of us' (289).[3]

As his remarks on its 'imprisoning' quality imply, Coetzee was not only fascinated with but also appalled by the sceptical and disintegrative energies of Beckett's prose. In another essay of this period, 'Samuel Beckett and the Temptations of Style' (1973), he tried to make sense of his profoundly mixed feelings by introducing an important distinction—a distinction which will in fact remain the basis of his approach to Beckett right up to, and including, the Tokyo lecture. His distinction is between Beckett the programmatic anti-realist (a Beckett he denigrates) and another, more compelling Beckett whose prose is poised unsettlingly between realism and anti-realism. The distinction turns around *The Unnamable*, which is now featured as a 'limit' text in Beckett's œuvre: after *The Unnamable*, in Coetzee's judgement, Beckett tips over into an automated programme-writing. As an example, Coetzee cites a line from *Imagination Dead Imagine* (1965): 'Islands, waters, azure, verdure, one glimpse and vanished, endlessly, omit.' Then follows his analysis of the Beckettian programme:

---

[3] I am following Derek Attridge's use of the term 'cultural field' to signify 'among other things, the artistic, scientific, moral, religious, economic, and political practices, institutions, norms, and beliefs that characterise a particular place and time'. An individual always apprehends the cultural field through his or her 'idioculture'—a term that refers to 'the way an individual's grasp on the world is mediated by a changing array of interlocking, overlapping, and often contradictory cultural systems absorbed in the course of his or her previous experience, a complex matrix of habits, cognitive models, representations, beliefs, expectations, prejudices, and preferences that operate intellectually, emotionally, and physically to produce a sense of at least relative continuity, coherence, and significance out of the manifold events of human living... Idioculture is the name for the totality of the cultural codes constituting a subject, at a given time, as an overdetermined, self-contradictory system.' See *The Singularity of Literature* (2004) 19, 21–2.

The first four words, flagrantly *composed* though they may be, leading associatively one to the next via even the bathos of rhyme, threaten to assert themselves as illusion, as The Word in all its magical autonomy. They are erased ('omit') and left like dead leaves against a wall. The sentence thus embodies neatly two opposing impulses that permit a fiction of net zero: the impulse toward conjuration, the impulse toward silence...Around the helix of ever-decreasing radius described by these conditions Beckett's art moves towards its apotheosis, the one-word text 'nothing' under the title 'fiction'. (43)

What he claims is that, while Beckett's characteristic negation of the cultural principle that informs the novel's conventions ('The Word in all its magical autonomy') had been designed as a refusal of the fake transcendence they offer, this process of negation contains a temptation towards its own variety of fakeness. In the texts that follow *The Unnamable*, such as *Imagination Dead Imagine*, *Ping* (1966), and *Lessness* (1969), Coetzee finds an increasing 'formalization or stylisation of autodestruction: that is, as the text becomes *nothing but* a destructive commentary upon itself by the encapsulating consciousness, it retreats into the trap of an automatism of which the invariant mechanical repetitions of *Lessness* are the most extreme example to date.' The danger of the 'stylisation of autodestruction', which he now also claims to find in the lulling 'rhythm of doubt' on display in the pages of *Watt*, is that it too becomes another false foundation, and another fake aesthetic release. It may be a different kind of falsification to that made by the realist novel—now an automated closing-down of illusion into 'the prison of empty style'—but the 'stylisation of the impasse of reflexive consciousness' is nonetheless an encounter with reality that is just as inauthentic as its simple opposite.

The Unnamable becomes a key text for Coetzee. Here, the argument now runs, is to be found a Beckett whose writing is at a point of maximally productive instability—a writing that has departed from the unwarrantable logocentrism of novelistic realism without yet becoming a stylized negation. It is a prose that unfounds the 'magical autonomy' of The Word, but without ending up in an alternative stylistic retreat—a prose that remains anxious, open, and unpredictable. Coetzee illustrates this by distinguishing *The Unnamable* from the later short text *Ping*. Both fictions, he shows, draw upon a similar device of parodic disruption—the 'ping' that keeps intruding into, and disrupting, the representational flow of the later text is parallel to the 'plop' to which the Unnamable resorts ('But let me complete my views, before I shit on them. For if I am Mahood, I am Worm too, plop'). But while the disruptive effect in *Ping* 'has evacuated itself of lexical content', its 'primitive forebear' in *The Unnamable* is 'yet heavy with content'. Furthermore, whereas the anti-illusionism of *Ping* is stylized and automated, the 'anti-illusionary reflexive consciousness' in *The Unnamable* is both 'celebrated and damned' (45). This distinction between a writing that is creatively and productively unbalanced ('celebrated *and* damned') and one that is stylized (either through its commitment to 'The Word in all its magical autonomy' or through a countervailing programme of parodic 'autodestruction') proves to be essential to Coetzee. Over thirty years later, in his Preface to the *Grove Centenary Edition* of Beckett's shorter fiction, he distinguishes again between the unresolved prose style of *The Unnamable*, and the 'increasingly mechanical stripping process' undertaken by the later fiction. His specific terms are interesting: 'By the eleventh text [of *Texts for Nothing* (1950–2)], that quest for finality—hopeless, as we know and Beckett knows—is in the process of being absorbed into a kind of verbal music, and the fierce comic anguish that accompanied it is in the process of being aestheticised too.'[4] As in the 'Temptations of Style' essay, what Coetzee values is that the parodic movement of Beckett's prose isn't allowed to take over in *The Unnamable*: in contrast to the 'verbal music' of the 11th of the *Texts for Nothing*, there is a 'fierce comic anguish', or (later) a 'comic energy, with [a] power to surprise' (p. xii), in the earlier novel—not simply a laughter but a pain; not a process that is simply celebrated, but one that is 'damned' too. In *Doubling the Point*

----

[4] J. M. Coetzee, Preface to *Samuel Beckett: the Grove Centenary Edition*, iv (New York, 2006) p. xi.

Coetzee phrases the same distinction between *The Unnamable* and the later work in a slightly different way:

Beckett's later short fictions have never really held my attention. They are, quite literally, disembodied. *Molloy* was still a very embodied work. Beckett's first after-death book was *The Unnamable*. But the after-death voice there still has body, and in that sense was only halfway to what he must have been feeling his way toward. The late pieces speak in post-mortem voices. I am not there yet. I am still interested in how the voice moves the body, moves in the body. (23)

Now he structures the same distinction around the collapse of a properly dialogical relation between Word and Body, which anticipates the Tokyo lecture's critique of Beckett's lack of 'imaginative courage' before the fact of embodied life.

What Coetzee is suggesting—time and again—is that while the conventions of the realist novel may indeed rely upon, and inculcate, an insupportable logocentrism and thus a deeply falsifying sense of objectivity and human recognition, parodic 'autodestruction' is an equally inauthentic alternative. Not only does it risk becoming an equally 'stylized' variety of aesthetic retreat, it automatically voids any attempt to engage with the problems posed by embodied life. In these scholarly essays Coetzee does not explicitly connect his interest in Beckett's prose style to questions of how literature should intervene in politics, though elsewhere, in contexts more amenable to this type of discussion, it is clear that he is thinking about this question very carefully indeed: in one essay of this period he adduces Beckett's style as one among several alternatives (none of which seem satisfactory) to the falsifying realism he finds in the contemporary South African novelist Yvonne Burgess.[5] But nonetheless, my suggestion is

---

[5] See *Doubling the Point* 91–3. The essay on *Murphy* was originally published in *Critique: Studies in Modern Fiction* 12/2 (1970); the 'temptations of style' essay in *Theoria* 41 (1973) 45–50. The more polemical piece on Yvonne Burgess was published in one of the early editions of *English in Africa* 3/1 (1976). Coetzee does not in fact produce an account of the relation between literature and politics that does justice to the effects his writing actually has until much later, when he writes about Erasmus in *Giving Offense*. See Ch. 5 for the relation of this essay to *Age of Iron* (1990) in particular.

that Coetzee's early and intuitive interest in a prose that avoids the temptations of both realism and anti-realism—that brings about a continual unfounding of the temptation to aesthetic autonomy—in fact becomes a core part of the way he tries to position his own writing in relation to politics. What Coetzee is looking towards— already—is a type of writing that can hold open divergent possibilities in such a way that maintains the 'power to surprise'.

'NOTHING TO DISCOVER': BECKETT AND THE NOVEL

We now understand the direction of Coetzee's thinking about Beckett's prose in broad terms, but only, as yet, in a negative way. Coetzee is clearly interested in *The Unnamable* because of its anti-foundational potential, but can we say more about what this text *is* doing, rather than what it is not? To answer this question we will have to turn, for a while, to Beckett himself in a more direct way. What I am going to suggest is that the Beckettian novel is designed to do 'nothing'. Not 'nothing at all', but nothing itself. Beckett's claim to a central position in the history of the novel rests on his development of an aesthetic model, whose risks are well described by Coetzee, based on the failure of expression, through which failure 'the nothing' is expressed.

Beckett set out his aesthetic theory in the 'Three Dialogues' about modern painters, written between *Malone Dies* and *The Unnamable*.[6] In the dialogue, a character called 'B' claims that Bram Van Velde is particularly distinguished among contemporary artists because he has realized that there is 'nothing to paint and nothing to paint with'; this recognition is what extricates him from 'the bosom of Saint Luke', the logocentric tradition upon which, according to 'B', all previous art has

---

[6] 'Three Dialogues: Samuel Beckett and Georges Duthuit' was first published in *Transition Forty-Nine* 5 (Dec. 1949) 97–103. The edition quoted from here is that reproduced in *Disjecta: Miscellaneous Writings and a Dramatic Fragment*, ed. Ruby Cohn (London, 1983).

been premised. Instead of expression itself, 'B' prefers the 'expression that there is nothing to express, nothing with which to express, nothing from which to express, no power to express, no desire to express, together with the obligation to express' (*Disjecta* 139). But if there is 'nothing to express', what is the 'nothing' that Beckett sets himself the task of expressing? By 'nothing', Beckett means something like the 'remainder'—that which is left over when any given act of representation takes place. As he puts it in the 'Three Dialogues': 'All that should concern us is the acute and increasing anxiety of the relation [between the artist and his occasion] itself, as though shadowed more and more darkly by a sense of invalidity, of inadequacy, of existence at the expense of all that it excludes, all that it blinds to' (145). Beckett is clearly taking the same kind of position on knowledge that we saw Heidegger take in *Gelassenheit*: if the logocentric premise is invalid, then any attempt to know made by the subject will be partial, and indissociable from the special ways that subject is situated in the cultural field—therefore a 'failure'. Any knowledge gained of the object will create a residual 'nothing'—that which the concept used in the act of knowing 'excludes' and 'blinds to'.[7] As the narrator of *The Unnamable* suggests, this attempt to express nothing does indeed emerge out of the realization that the self cannot transcend its situatedness, and that fictions are, as Coetzee had suggested, 'closed systems, prisons': 'Having nothing to say, no words but the words of others, I have to speak... Nothing can ever exempt me from it, there is nothing, nothing to discover, nothing to recover, nothing that can lessen what remains to say'

---

[7] See Heidegger's lecture 'What is Metaphysics?' for his own reflections on 'the question of the nothing', and the special type of perceptual comportment required to apprehend it. Heidegger underlines the 'formal impossibility' of an attempt to place thinking in touch with the nothing ('For thinking, which is always essentially thinking about something, must act in a way contrary to its own essence when it thinks of the nothing' (97)), and therefore emphasizes the importance of the emotion of anxiety in gaining an attunement towards nothingness (*Basic Writings* 89–110). For more on anxiety in this Heideggerian sense, see my discussion of Blanchot in Ch. 3.

(288). With 'no words but the words of others', the Unnamable is trapped: he has nothing truly his own to say. And yet his words don't quite say this, or at least only this. The words start to 'fail' to express one thing only, and begin to suggest an alternative possibility. Being trapped in the 'words of others', he has the task of 'nothing to say'— that is, he must endeavour to express the nothingness occluded by the concepts he has inherited. Being tasked with 'nothing to say' might therefore be liberating, rather than futile. 'Nothing can ever exempt me' from this task, the Unnamable says, meaning both that he is doomed to repeat inauthentic words, and also (this sense is half-expressed, as the words fail) that 'the nothing', if he apprehends it aright, can indeed 'exempt' him from being imprisoned in his con-structedness. Having 'nothing to discover, nothing to recover' cer-tainly describes a powerful sense of entrapment and futility. Yet the phrases fail sufficiently so as to glance in another direction, with a different prospect—towards a possible freedom, or (better put) a process of becoming-free through the 'churn of words'.

This slippery prose, in which no expression is safe from the nothing, inaugurates a distinctively different view of what animates the activity of writing from either of the views we considered in Chapter 1. This is a kind of fiction that 'wants for nothing' (275), that desires nothing, and hence (as this phrase encloses) lacks nothing. As the Unnamable puts it: 'I'm a big talking ball, talking about things that do not exist, or that exist perhaps, impossible to know, beside the point' (280).What the Unnamable wants to say is indeed 'beside the point': the 'nothing' is that which has been confined to the non-serious by the prerogatives of the 'they'; it exists 'perhaps' (if at all) in the shadow of the point, 'beside' it, so to speak. There is thus a deeply serious commitment to truth and freedom involved in this writing, as the Unnamable comes to realize when he pauses to reflect on a life spent writing (a life wasted, he believes, in 'an irresistible torment', governed by his 'vile mouth' spitting out 'vain inventions'): 'I have done nothing, unless what I am doing now is something, and nothing could give me greater satisfaction' (282). How satisfying to have truly 'done nothing'—made the nothing be—unless it turns out that the nothing done was a something all along, in which case nothing will not really have been 'done' at all.

That is Beckett 'in theory', at least: a prose style grounded in a continual 'churn of words' (285) that holds out, within the process of sustained linguistic rupture, the chance of encounter with the excluded 'nothing', which is a knowledge of self (and as Coetzee emphasized, in Beckett it is always solipsistic knowledge that is at stake) that is forever occluded by the 'words of others'. But in order to understand Coetzee's experience of sheer sensual delight in Beckett's prose, and also his particular estimation of its 'fierce comic anguish' in a fuller way, we will have to consider a longer passage of text, and in doing so pay attention to the more 'literary' aspects of Beckett's writing: in particular, to his handling of linguistic register.

As Bakhtin shows in *Discourse in the Novel*, the form of the novel invites readerly judgement through the control of tone: most especially, the author uses irony and parody to help the reader identify the right way to interpret a particular character or scene, and meaning emerges through a modulation of the relations between 'straight' and parodic representation.[8] However, in *The Unnamable* what we encounter is a continual disturbance of the novel's expressive devices that leads to a sustained disorientation of the interpretative process. As an example we will consider a passage near the beginning of the text. Here the Unnamable is describing the air that surrounds him as an ambivalent shade of grey: 'This grey, first murky, then frankly opaque, is luminous none the less.' Then the ambivalence starts to proliferate: is he in the open air, or in an enclosure? Equally, is the space he inhabits 'the old void, or a plenum'? If only he had a stick he could tell for sure:

---

[8] See 'Discourse in the Novel', in *The Dialogic Imagination*, trans. Caryl Emerson and Michael Holquist (Austin, 1981) 259–422. Also see in particular Mikhail Bakhtin, *Problems of Dostoevsky's Poetics*, trans. Caryl Emerson (Minneapolis, 1984) 199.

But the days of sticks are over, here I can count on my body alone, my body incapable of the smallest movement and whose very eyes can no longer close as they once could, accordance to Basil and his crew, to rest me from seeing, to rest me from waking, to darken me to sleep, and no longer look away, or down, or up open to heaven, but must remain forever fixed and staring on the narrow space before them where there is nothing to be seen, ninety-nine per cent of the time. They must be as red as live coals. I sometimes wonder if the two retinae are not facing each other. And come to think of it this grey is shot with rose, like the plumage of certain birds, among which I seem to remember the cockatoo.

In this text at least two incommensurate judgements on the nature of the Unnamable are kept in play: there a serious sense, in which he is symbolic of an alienated and imprisoned 'human condition', and there is also a lurking doubt about this reading, an 'other' sense (a 'nothing' or non-sense) that is hard or even impossible to take entirely seriously, pulling against the clear meaning of the words. This is what Coetzee spoke of as the 'fierce comic anguish' of the prose. We register the 'other' way of seeing chiefly through the uncanny feeling generated by the mixing of registers in the text.

On a first quick reading, it is the anguish of the scene—even a 'teeth-gnashing' anguish—that is most apparent. This seems to be a nightmarish description of entrapment: some sort of confined space, eyes fixed, body incapacitated, nothing to see or do. And yet, as we read more closely, pulling against this 'anguish', and the sympathetic feeling that flows with it, are a series of comic effects, each modulated in a different way. The opening phrase, 'the days of sticks are over', sits uncomfortably alongside the rather macho, Crusoe-like resolution to 'count on my body alone'. It strikes a comically nostalgic note—comic not only in the suggestion that the 'days of sticks' were somehow days of bygone hope and glory, suitable to be remembered with nostalgia, but also in the image of the Unnamable as a reflectively nostalgic person—rather than (say) a tormented or neurotic or despairing person. There is then an outright joke when, having told us that he relies on the body alone, the Unnamable adds that his body is 'incapable of the smallest movement'. (What is he relying on then? Nothing, of course.) But—before we actually laugh—the Unnamable shifts into a plangent register, redolent with pathos: his 'very eyes can no longer close as they once could, accordance to Basil and his crew, to rest me from seeing, to rest me from waking, to darken me to sleep, and no longer look away, or down, or up open to heaven, but must remain forever fixed and staring on the narrow space before them where there is nothing to be seen'. Instead of laughter these darker tones start to generate a flow of sentiment in the reader—until, that is, we get to the end of the phrase: 'ninety-nine per cent of the time'. Here the flow of sentiment that passes from reader to narrator, in which we identify the Unnamable as a tragic sufferer, is again cut short: this is far too akin to a salesman's glib pseudo-statistical patter—talk like this just doesn't go along with the expression of pathos.

The 'comic anguish' generated by this text is even more strikingly evident in the next two sentences: 'They [his eyes] must be red as live coals. I sometimes wonder if the two retinae are not facing each other.' Here we are given a truly horrific perspective on the Unnamable— eyes red as live coals is a genuinely 'fierce' anguish. But then he suddenly turns into a clown: he may have red eyes, but he is cross-eyed. Not just cross-eyed, in fact, but goggle-eyed—the retinae are 'facing each other'. The sentiment is once again given and then taken away: in the Unnamable's text full identification of the self within the 'words of others' (for that is what they instantly become) is always interrupted and deferred. He has told us that he is living in a grey void, a threatening, confining place. But 'come to think of it,' the Unnamable tells us (calmly, as if by the bye, during a quiet conversation, 'eyes red as live coals' now forgotten), 'this grey is shot with rose, like the plumage of certain birds, among which I seem to remember the cockatoo'. The place he is in, the confining 'void' (or was it a 'plenum'?) of grey in which he was trapped, now lights up with 'rose'. Is it then not a place of nightmare, but a place of beauty? But before we can take this intimation seriously—before we can turn this 'nothing' into a 'something'—it is smothered in bathos: hard to make the sudden sight of 'rose' in the grey stand for anything too serious when it is associated with a bird as remorselessly silly as the cockatoo.

In *The Unnamable* there is a continual oscillation between competing tonalities that brings about an ongoing rupture with the expressive devices of the novel—a 'comic energy... with a power to surprise', as Coetzee put it. As I have suggested, the most obvious way to read the passage is to regard the Unnamable as symbolic of an anguished human alienation, but there is always another way of knowing making itself felt in an uncanny way when the anguish is placed in touch with the text's corrosive comic experience. There is a non-serious, 'beside the point' view of the Unnamable, in which he is not trapped but free; he is not encased in an ugly grey light, but has visions of beauty; he is not in pain, but in ecstasy; he is not tragic, but comic. The text does not assert this alternative view from some kind of ontologically privileged vantage point—in fact, it is hard to take it seriously at all. Instead, it emerges only as a 'nothing' can: the 'fierce comic anguish' of the prose places pressure on each different judgement I make about the Unnamable. Each way of responding to him is put in play with another, and then another. Beckett's text therefore has a certain power: not a power to persuade me to a predetermined end, but rather to bring about a transformation of the rules and concepts I apply when I read the text, and thereby in the way I perceive more broadly.

This is a crucial point, and before turning back to Coetzee, I want to emphasize this remark on the 'power' of the Beckettian novel. I want to emphasize, as Beckett himself does, that the 'strength' of the text comes not from its assertive power: it makes no claim to any cultural principle from which it might set out the reality of things. Instead its strength, and its responsibility to the 'nothing', paradoxically relies upon its weakness: it does not rely on 'being clever', on outwitting and out-persuading me, but instead upon 'being stupid'—on making those discursive structures in which reader and writer are equally situated wobble and collapse. As the Unnamable puts it: 'They'll never get the better of my stupidity' (318). It is with this sense of the cleverness of stupidity that the Unnamable, clearly a

chess enthusiast, sends in 'Worm to play' (318) against the 'they'—
those unnamed and inchoate avatars of the cultural field that speak
through him and construct him. Worm is the last in a long line of the
Unnamable's 'delegates', each of which are increasingly alien to even
the minimal description of 'the human'. Worm is as close to sheer
organic matter, sheer 'stuff', as it is possible for a character in a novel
to be. He might be a sperm, or a foetus, or a phallus; perhaps, though,
he is just a 'shapeless heap, without a face capable of reflecting the
niceties of a torment' (328). But sending Worm in 'to play' has some
interesting effects. Once in play, the powers that be (the 'they')
inevitably set to work upon him, constructing him in their image,
'humanizing' him. But they have a problem:

> The rascal, he's getting humanized, he's going to lose if he doesn't watch
> out, if he doesn't take care, and with what could he take care, with what
> could he form the faintest conception of the condition they are decoying
> him into . . . That's his strength, his only strength, that he understands
> nothing, can't take thought, doesn't know what they want, doesn't know
> they are there, feels nothing.   (331)

Worm doesn't *outwit* the processes of hostile assimilation that start up
when he bumbles aimlessly into the cultural field. He just can't figure
out exactly what they want, quite what it would take for his behaviour
to come up to scratch, and so he makes for an uncanny, disturbing
presence. Poised unsettlingly on the boundary between human and
non-human, his stupidity, his inability to 'take thought', makes for a
curious condition, one which Beckett calls 'balls': 'What balls is going
on before this impotent crystalline, that's all that needs to be imagined' (333). Worm's 'balls' is (are?) an infuriating state, in which no
concept seems to be adequate; and yet, as the narrator says, it is 'all that
needs to be imagined'. The 'they' use their imagination and apply a
concept: 'A face, how encouraging that would be . . . Worth ten of
Saint Anthony's pig's arse' (333). And then another, when the first
face fails: 'It might even pause, open its mouth, raises its eyebrows,
bless its soul, stutter, mutter, howl, groan and finally shut up, the
chaps clenched to cracking point, or fallen, to let the dribble out. That

would be nice. A presence at last.' But confronted by Worm, all turns to 'balls', as his 'kingdom unknown' provokes a continual upheaval in the process of representation: 'For here there is no face, nor anything resembling one, nothing to reflect the joy of living and succedanea, nothing for it but to try something else' (334). With this stupid 'shapeless heap' there is in fact a continual need to 'try something else': he is neither 'a presence at last' nor an absence, but a creative kind of weakness. He makes a 'balls' of the concepts that are used to make sense of him, and introduces the possibility that his life will have 'changed nothing'. In all seriousness he will change nothing at all; but perhaps the impossible will come to pass, and that which the 'they' define as nothing will, through Worm's intervention, itself be changed.

The story of Worm might be read, I suggest, as Beckett's allegory for the way his fiction engages its readers—who are included in the 'they', that anonymous crowd of hostile others—and how it brings about freedom. As we saw in the previous chapter, the realist novel, in one account of it at least, purported to make us free by enabling an emotive intersubjective recognition of equal dignity; by contrast the Sartrean novel wills freedom by making a strong assertion of collective determination on behalf of a particular class or race. The Beckettian novel, though, follows neither of these well-worn paths to liberty. Without rejecting the realist ambition in a programmatic way, Beckett's novel behaves stupidly, like Worm. In the cockatoo passage we found the text becoming ever more stupid—brilliantly stupid, but stupid nonetheless. It was ever less able to pull itself together and express something; instead it kept falling apart. The text thereby tries to enter into what I have called a disruptive dialogue with otherness, through which it tries to make 'nothing happen'—not by any process of assertion, but by making a continual 'balls' of the way we read. The freedom it generates in this repeated contact with the nothing is never a 'perfective' freedom—never, as Coetzee put it, 'freedom *an sich*' (in itself)—but instead an ongoing process: continually slipping the chains, a continued action of turning the face to the light.

'MORE THAN MERELY PEBBLES': *IN THE HEART OF THE COUNTRY*

Coetzee's response to Beckett is a complex process of critical assimilation in which the prose style of *The Unnamable* is brought together with a more expansive and politicized definition of what is at stake in the 'nothing' I have just described. Beckett's category of 'nothingness' becomes, in Coetzee's early fiction, staged primarily as the socio-cultural other who lies outside the normal kinds of recognition produced by the available traditions of 'white writing'.[9] In the later work, though, it is expanded to include what Derrida mischievously called 'other others'—that is to say, it includes not only racially marked groups, but whatever modalities of feeling or thought that are becoming unfeelable, or unthinkable, within a given cultural field. This is an important difference, and is especially evident in Coetzee's later South African novels (*Age of Iron* and *Disgrace*) and in the Australian fiction: the way Beckett's writing places the reader in touch with the nothing becomes, in Coetzee, a matter of holding open, and creatively disorienting, those notions of moral and political value that a given cultural field is making 'beside the point'. But to remain for now with the early fiction, the key transition at stake is from a Beckettian novel rooted in solipsism towards a novel that takes in the political life—the life lived by the body in a community—and which envisages that life as a perpetual dialogue with, or 'waiting for', socio-cultural forms of otherness. In this section I am going to trace the ways in which Coetzee reflects upon the problem of how to inherit the Beckettian novel in *In the Heart of the Country*. Then to conclude this chapter I will make a fuller description of the

---

[9] In *White Writing: On the Culture of Letters in South Africa* (New Haven, 1988), Coetzee defines a mode of writing as white 'only insofar as it is generated by the concerns of people no longer European, not yet African' (11); the particular mode of white writing addressed by *In the Heart of the Country* is discussed in ch. 3 of his monograph, 'Farm Novel and Plaasroman'.

distinctively Beckettian reading experience involved in *Waiting for the Barbarians*: at this point we will return specifically to the political problems outlined in Chapter 1.

The main point I am going to make about *In the Heart of the Country* is that it is not just a novel 'after Beckett' that deploys the same 'anti-illusionary reflexive consciousness', although it does indeed do that. More importantly it is simultaneously a text that stages the Beckettian novel as a problem in its own right. 'What's next,' it asks, in an overt and explicit way, in the 'history of the novel'?[10]

The novel's monologist, Magda (another in a long line of Beckettian 'M's, including Murphy, Molloy, Moran, and Malone) has recognizably the same 'anti-illusionary reflexive consciousness' as the Unnamable. Like Beckett's narrator, she too is struggling for her freedom from the 'they' by taking up a parodic stance towards the cultural constructions that enshroud her identity in misrecognition: she too is trying to place herself in touch with the occluded 'nothing', where her self more truly lies. Magda is particularly conscious of the way in which she, and people like her, are socially constructed by patterns of thinking most obviously incarnate in the sub-genre of the 'farm novel'—she feels the pull of its powerful 'babble of words within . . . that fabricate and refabricate me as something else' (53). The first paragraph describes her father bringing home his new bride in a beginning typical of one of these sort of novels, and then refers to herself as a counter in its conventions: 'I am the one who stays in her room reading or writing or fighting migraines. The colonies are full of girls like that, but none, I think, so extreme as I. My father is the one who paces the floorboards back and forth, back and forth in his slow black boots.' Note 'the one'—she and father are described as if fulfilling token 'roles' in a pattern of representation always already

---

[10] 'Anti-illusionism—displaying the tricks you are using instead of hiding them—is a common ploy of postmodernism. But in the end there is only so much mileage to be got out of the ploy. Anti-illusionism is, I suspect, only a marking of time, a phase of recuperation, in the history of the novel. The question is, what's next?' *Doubling the Point* 27.

constructed by the 'they'. Magda cannot simply transcend the fact of her constructedness, but she can, as a Beckettian 'narrator–narrated', subject this story to parody. In another passage she dives into the 'farthest oubliettes of memory' and finds an image of her dead mother—'the image of a faith grey frail gentle loving mother huddled on the floor'. But—and here comes the Unnamable's 'plop'—this is the sort of image that 'any girl in my position would be likely to make up for herself' (2). For Magda, as for the Unnamable, it is in the writing of herself, in the restless 'churn of words' she initiates, that she is carried from the 'mundane of being' into the fascinating 'doubleness of signification' (4), where she might 'get beyond myself ' (5) into some 'other tale' (5); she might 'let go the real for the deep darkdown desired' (9).

The parodic energies unleashed by Magda's drive to gain freedom (though always an equivocal, 'unnamable' freedom—'what liberation is it going to bring me, and without liberation what is the point of my story?' (5)) lead, as in *The Unnamable*, to an increasing solipsism. But as I have suggested, there is an extra level of metafictionality in Coetzee's text—one that reflects upon the process of anti-illusionism as a concept and indeed as a problem. This first begins to emerge just after Magda has her first murderous fantasy, in which she kills her father and his new wife. Why, she asks of herself, did she need to subject the portrayal of her relationship with her stepmother to such drastic textual cancellation?

Is it possible that I am a prisoner not of the lonely farmhouse and the stone desert but of my stony monologue? Have my blows been aimed at shutting those knowing eyes or at silencing her voice? Might we not, bent over our teacups, have learned to coo to each other, or, drifting past each other in the dark corridor, hot and sleepless in the siesta hour, have touched, embraced, and clung? (13)

Just as for Coetzee in the Tokyo lecture, the solipsistic state is not enough for Magda: she longs for some relationship that will 'liberate me into the world' (10), and that will thereby place her in contact with the others that inhabit that world—though she is of course hyperconscious of the perils of misrecognition this involves for the 'true deepdown I beyond words' (17). In another passage, this time about her relations with her father's black farm-hand, Hendrik, she expresses a similar concern with regard to the power of anti-illusionism, described this time in terms of its curtailment of the flow of sympathetic emotion. 'Poor Hendrik,' she reflects, sharing in his feeling of desolation consequent upon losing his wife to her father, 'undone, undone. I weep drunken weeping':

> Then I screw my eyes tight against the pain and wait for the three figures [Hendrik, Anna, and her father] to dissolve into streaks and pulses and whorls ... There is finally only I, drifting into sleep, beyond the reach of pain. Acting on myself I change the world. Where does this power end? Perhaps that is what I am trying to find out.   (39)

As these passages suggest, Magda comes to distrust the corrosive and solipsistic energies of her anti-illusionistic self-consciousness. It just doesn't seem capable of measuring up to her need for community; more pointedly, it also seems another way of exercising power over subject people like Hendrik—a convenient way of shutting off the powerful emotions the body generates when human suffering is witnessed.

This distrust of her Beckettian self is compounded by the series of jarring bodily encounters around which the text revolves: encounters with the metaphorical 'whale', to recall the Tokyo lecture again. These are at times invited by her and at times thrust upon her, but in each case, the act of being forced into or against the body—sometimes her own, sometimes that of another—has a profoundly disturbing impact. The first comes in a physical confrontation with her father, where we read three different versions of Magda interrupting him in his bed-room with Anna: 'I have spoken and been spoken to, touched and been touched,' Magda realizes; 'Therefore I am more than just the trace of these words passing through my head on their way from nowhere to nowhere,' she concludes (61). Other important moments where the body breaks in upon her are when she is 'hit' twice in the corridor (63), when she is shaken by Hendrik ('I smell his heat, not without distaste' (82)), when she witnesses the sexual encounter between Hendrik and Anna and sees Hendrik's erect penis (83), and of course when she experiences the appalling stench of her father's dying body (83), and the clumsy digging and shoving of the burial (99). Among these different moments of bodily intrusion—and each in its own way constitutes a turning-point in Magda's regard for her anti-illusionistic self-consciousness—the most important is the sexual scene that takes place between her and Hendrik. This scene is often thought of as a rape, but to conceptualize it securely in this way is in fact to miss what is, for Magda, the most important thing about it, namely its ability to disrupt and transform the patterns of thinking that structure her imagination of love across the colour bar. Magda herself wants to hold off as long as possible from placing a meaning on the scene, relaying it to us in several different versions, in each one of which the event is reinterpreted. She is patient enough to undergo what I spoke of in the previous chapter as a process of 'waiting'—an anxious alertness to difference in which her self-understanding is slowly transformed. This may seem a strange, or even downright perverse, way to think of this violent encounter, but we must not forget that it is an encounter about which Magda has already fanta-sized. In paragraph 167 she imagined Hendrik talking in bed to Anna about visiting her, Magda, one night, and the question she poses through him is whether she would be willing and ready for sex, or whether Hendrik will have to use force: 'Would she pretend it was a dream and let it happen, or would it be necessary to force her?'

The rape scene is uncomfortably poised between these two alter-natives. The first description (para. 205) is of a violent exchange, and not of a rape: she defends herself with a fork; Hendrik kicks her. The second (206) is also a scene of violence, this time clearly of a rape, in which she feels 'something is dying' within her, and sheer 'despair'. In the third (207) the rape is not described, but a new description is featured in which Magda protests in a humanistic way that Hendrik shouldn't 'hate me so': 'What have I done to you?' she asks. 'It is not my fault that everything is going so badly.' It is an important addition, and one of the first signs that Magda is at least preparing for a view of herself from Hendrik's perspective, this being a perspective in which she might appear other than the powerless and oppressed farmer's daughter she perceives herself to be. The fourth description (208) takes place in the bedroom rather than on the kitchen floor, and enlarges upon Magda's protest that Hendrik won't treat her as equally human: 'You do nothing but shout at me, you never talk to me, you hate me.' Now, though, she seems to accept the sexual encounter as something strangely inevitable, and something to be endured—something that will 'disarrang[e]' her life, and cause her to 'rediscover who I am'. This sense of the transformation she is undergoing is enlarged in the fifth passage (209), in which she presents herself in a more self-critical light, and Hendrik as in some respects a caring lover. Magda is critical of her own reserve ('I am cold . . . I clench everything together, I have nothing to give him, I am beyond being persuaded . . . he will have to break me open, I am as hard as a shell, I cannot help him'); Hendrik in turn reassures her that the sex 'won't hurt', and that she shouldn't be 'afraid'. Whatever is going on now seems much less like a rape, though there is still hostility and violence breaking through: 'Open up', Hendrik harshly commands at one point, quite at odds with the more caring persona he had started to take on.

Through these repeated encounters with the event, each one an uncanny repetition-with-difference, Magda is pushing against the frameworks of response that the 'words of others' have generated to govern racially transgressive relationships. She is trying to place herself in touch with ways of feeling about a man like Hendrik that are, as yet, 'nothing' to her—that she cannot seriously credit. The encounter hovers between a traumatic 'invasion and possession', in which she is wholly subjugated ('A body lies on top of a body pushing and pushing, trying to find a way in . . . What will he leave me of myself?') (117), and an alternative way of registering the experience, one that is gradually flickering into life. The key point is that this bodily encounter—inseparable from, but perhaps not merely confined to, physical violence—also brings about a process of rupture with Magda's solipsistic Beckettian self-consciousness. It brings about in her a desire for new ways of recognizing Hendrik that are free of the old frameworks of racial domination, and in fact Magda now sets about trying to engender this in a classic novelistic form through the shared flow of sentiment that takes place in a romantic plot. Opening herself to the relationship, which consists of Hendrik arriving sporadically at night for sex, Magda struggles to imagine forms of reciprocity: despite her 'shame' (121), and the 'humiliation' she feels (and suspects Hendrik of wishing to engender in her) she tries to find ways of gaining intimacy with him. 'I do not know what pleases him,' she worries, 'whether he wants me to move or lie still when he takes me. I stroke his skin but feel no response from it' (121). However, this desire eventuates in 'no transfiguration' (124): the process of encounter never rises to any-thing like the reciprocal recognition for which Magda now yearns. Frustrated with Hendrik's suspicion, bitterness, and reserve, her departure from solipsism tips right over into a quite straightforwardly liberal demand: 'I am not simply one of the whites, I am *I*!' she claims. 'I am I, not a people. Why have I to pay for other people's sins?' (128). During this discourse on the theme of transcending difference Hendrik walks out on her, never again return to the farm.

What *has* happened, then? What, if anything, is actually gener-ated by this encounter? Magda is conscious that 'the story took a wrong turn somewhere', and that her yearning for a 'someone else' to lead her out of the 'monologue of self' has not brought about a reciprocal recognition that transcends the painful facts of their historical situatedness. But as she suggests, perhaps we should see it as a 'start': 'In the heart of nowhere, in this dead place, I am making a start; or, if not that, making a gesture' (120). It is indeed 'a start', for above all it has convinced her that she cannot follow straightforwardly in the line of Beckett's solipsistic heroes. Recal-ling the famous stone-sucking passage in *Molloy*, Magda is now sure that she needs 'more than merely pebbles to permute' (130), and that she needs to account for the ways in which her body is

situated in a world with others:[11] 'I need people to talk to, brothers
and sisters or fathers and mothers, I need history and a culture,
I need hopes and aspirations, I need a moral sense and a teleology
before I will be happy, not to mention food and drink' (131). It is,
of course, impossible to take all of this new talk entirely seriously.
There is an unmistakable bathos in the last two of these clauses:
the placement of the need for food and drink *after* the need for
a 'moral sense and a teleology' is frankly comic, and the way in
which Magda links her need for a teleology merely to the desire
to be happy is also comic, though in a more quietly corrosive way
(not many philosophers would be impressed by this hedonistic
justification of teleology). In her newfound drive for an embodied
life, Magda is therefore by no means abandoning the sceptical
energies of her Beckettian forebears. Indeed, large doses of parody
wash around in the final pages of the text at the expense of her new
hopes, most especially in her moving but undeniably cracked desire
for a language of 'pure meanings' sent down by the gods. *In the
Heart of the Country* leaves Magda's discourse with 'nothing': no
grand interracial bridges are built in which 'the contraries should
be reconciled'. But in doing so, neither she nor Coetzee are left
with 'nothing at all'.

'QUESTIONABLE DESIRES': *WAITING FOR THE BARBARIANS*

Having followed the inner debate Coetzee conducts in the pages of
In the Heart of the Country about the nature and value of Beckett's
legacy, we now need to focus more intently on the question of
prose style. Missing from our understanding of the relationship
between Coetzee and Beckett is some account of the reading

---

[11] For the stone-sucking see Samuel Beckett, *Molloy*, in *The Beckett Trilogy*
(London, 1979) 66–9.

experience generated by Coetzee's novels equivalent to the account that I made of *The Unnamable*. What, above all, does the Coetzeean text *do* to its readers? And how does this experience of reading bear out my claim that Coetzee's fiction tries to hold open, and destabilize, divergent ideas of what makes for a 'moral community'?

In order to evaluate what goes on in the experience of reading *Waiting for the Barbarians*, I must first outline the broader structural ways in which this novel has expanded, and thereby politicized, Beckett's horizon of concern. Most obviously, while Coetzee's novel continues with the monologue form, though it is the last of his texts to do so, the otherness at stake in the novel is now, from the very start, explicitly politicized—most broadly around the distinction between 'Empire' and 'Barbarian', but more pressingly around the figure known in the text only as the 'barbarian girl'. The 'unnamability' in the novel has shifted from being exclusively within the self-consciousness of the monologist, and is now allegorized through a highly politicized character with whom the monologist (here a man known only as the 'Magistrate'), tries to develop a relationship. Most daringly, though, Coetzee makes the barbarian girl closely equivalent to the figure of 'Worm' in *The Unnamable*. Recall that the Unnamable sent in 'Worm to play' against the 'they', and also recall that the sheer ungiving materiality of Worm (the way in which he seemed poised between the human and the non-human) bedevilled the attempts of the 'they' to assimilate him. His very dumbness generated a transformative anxiety of interpretation— a pushing at the boundary of what we recognize as human. Likewise, in *Waiting for the Barbarians*, Coetzee sends the barbarian girl in 'to play' against the Magistrate, and his sympathetic and enquiring liberal conscience thereby meets with a baffling unreadability. She is to him an 'alien body' (45) that doesn't respond to his touch. While recognizably human, she also seems disturbingly non-human: 'I have a vision of her closed eyes and closed face filming over with skin. Blank, like a fist beneath a black wig, the face grows out of the throat and out of the blank body beneath it, without aperture, without entry' (45). The Magistrate feels increasingly 'enslaved' to this body (46), finding it to be a 'surface across which I hunt back and forth seeking entry'. She seems to have come from nowhere, or at least from outside his horizon of thinking: 'something has fallen in upon me from the sky, at random, from nowhere: this body in my bed, for which I am responsible, or so it seems, otherwise why do I keep it?' (47). Her strange absence-in-presence pushes against the way he conceives of humanness itself: reflecting on her 'incomplete body', the Magistrate feels that 'if I took a pencil to sketch her face I would not know where to start' (50); above all, this is a body that both ignites and blocks the flow of sentiment that the (always partial) recognition generates: 'With a rush of feeling I stretch out to touch her hair, her face. There is no answering life. It is like caressing an urn or a ball, something which is all surface' (52). Even after the girl has left to rejoin the barbarians, her image lives on in a hauntingly aporetic afterlife: 'From her empty eyes there always seemed to be a haze spreading, a blankness that overtook all of her' (94). Like Worm in *The Unnamable*, the barbarian girl generates a powerful sense of crisis in the Magistrate: she makes a 'balls' of his desire to know her, and (now to draw upon the truly Beckettian sense of the novel's title) she sends him into what I have described as the anxious and productive state of 'waiting'. The fruits of this waiting emerge in a series of baffling dreams, whose common theme is their portrayal of children constructing a snow-fort (which resembles the town itself) and finally—not now in the dream—a snowman. The last of these visions brings the Magistrate a strange sense of release, and he is 'inexplicably joyful'. The implication is surely that his concept of what counts as 'the community' (the snow-fort) and 'the human' (the snowman) are being placed in a creative transmogrification through his repeated encounters, both in the flesh and in his memory, with the Worm-like barbarian girl. He feels ever more 'lost' and even 'stupid' in this process—but these feelings of increased weakness may also suggest that the Magistrate has become one of those people who are—as Coetzee put it—'slipping their chains and turning their faces to the light'.

This outline of how the text relates to the Beckettian novel in structural terms must, however, rank a crude second to a grasp of how Coetzee's prose actually works. The main point I want to make is that just as the barbarian girl makes a productive 'balls' of the Magistrate's ways of perceiving, so does the text itself make a 'balls' of the interpretative frameworks differently positioned readers bring to it. I'm going to focus in detail on a scene that has already been much discussed in Coetzee criticism: the Magistrate's first encounter with the girl, in which he discovers her begging in the town square, and invites her back to his lodgings.[12] The Magistrate can be read as a liberal-minded person, who understands politics chiefly in terms of equal dignity and the extension of sympathy: indeed, his responsiveness to the tug of sentimental identification has already drawn him, at no small personal cost, into an opposition to Colonel Joll, the high-ranking official from the Imperial capital, who has come to the

---

[12] I have chosen this passage for analysis most especially because it is the one chosen by Derek Attridge for scrutiny in the chapter entitled 'Against Allegory' in *J. M. Coetzee and the Ethics of Reading*, and thus will mark the affinities and differences in our respective understandings of Coetzee's handling of form. Arguing rightly that 'the experience of such passages complicates any process of allegorical transfer by questioning the rational procedures on which this type of interpretation itself depends', Attridge's reading in fact tends to emphasize the ways in which Coetzee's text surpasses rather than 'complicates' the act of political judgement. Most notably, he claims that the 'complex of feelings' the reader experiences through the Magistrate's encounter with the barbarian girl, 'that momentary complicity with something dark and destructive, as something that happens to the reader, is more significant testimony to the power and distinctiveness of literature, and to the brilliance of Coetzee's art, than any extracted moral about the errors of liberal humanism', adding that in his experience most readers value the text 'for itself, not because it point[s] to some truths about the world in general or South Africa in the 1970s in particular' (45). My reading will suggest instead that what is at stake in the text is precisely this political question as to what status should be granted to an 'extracted moral about the errors of liberal humanism': that is to say, I will argue that the literariness of Coetzee's text inheres not in any absolute distinctiveness (a value 'for itself') but in the way it brings about, within the act of reading, a play of difference and deferral within the act of moral and political judgement.

town to discover the truth about the barbarians by torturing them.[13] The scene we will now focus on revolves around the question of the Magistrate's feelings—feelings that seem both to generate sympathetic recognition of the girl, and charitable action on her behalf, yet also to have a potentially darker hue. Staying within the terms of the political concepts of 'equal dignity' and 'difference' we considered in the previous chapter, I want to suggest two alternative ways of reading the Magistrate. On the one hand, let us imagine a liberal-minded reader who would instinctively identify with him, would praise his responsiveness to the tug of sentiment, and his attempts to transcend racial difference in the name of social justice.[14] On the other hand, let us also imagine a reader who would attack the Magistrate's implicit belief that despite his 'white skin' he can know a 'black soul', and who would argue that his humanism is a self-serving myth that should be 'cracked and killed'.[15] What I'm going to suggest is that this Worm-like text makes a 'balls' of both these readers: it refuses to confirm either of their foundationalist understandings of politics, and places both in a productive dialogue with the 'nothing' they exclude.

[13] The tug of sentiment felt by the Magistrate when he sees the tortured boy in the first chapter is an important political impulse: 'I feel my heart grow heavy. I never wished to be drawn into this,' he complains, but is unable to resist the powerful moral feeling: 'I ought never to have taken my lantern to see what was going on in the hut by the granary. On the other hand, there was no way, once I had picked up the lantern, for me to put it down again' (8).

[14] For an example of such a reader in action, see the response of the censor Reginald Lighton, who regarded the Magistrate as a 'compassionate, sincere man, a loner who has gone "semi-native," to the extent that he antagonizes the police & military authorities—for he reveals some sympathy with the barbarians', and the novel as a whole as a 'sombre, tragic book' that ends 'with the bloody but always unbowed Magistrate heading the dispirited remnants of the populace "waiting for the barbarians"'. These references from Lighton's censor's report are taken from Peter D. McDonald, 'The Writer, the Critic and the Censor: J. M. Coetzee and the Question of Literature', in *Book History* 7 (2004) 287–8.

[15] To portray the second of these readers I have used some phrases of Steve Biko's. See Steve Biko, *I Write What I Like*, ed. Aelred Stubbs (London, 1978) 20–2.

We pick the scene up on the day after the Magistrate first offered the girl residence in his apartment as a cleaner—which, perhaps suspicious of the Magistrate's intentions, she did not accept.

A day passes. I stare out over the square where the wind chases flurries of dust. Two little boys are playing with a hoop. They bowl it into the wind. It rolls forward, slows, teeters, rides back, falls. The boys lift their faces and run after it, the hair whipped back from their clean brows.

I find the girl and stand before her. She sits with her back against the trunk of one of the great walnut trees: it is hard to see whether she is even awake. 'Come,' I say, and touch her shoulder. She shakes her head. 'Come,' I say, 'everyone is indoors.' I beat the dust from her cap and hand it to her, help her to her feet, walk slowly beside her across the square, empty now save for the gatekeeper, who shades his eyes to stare at us. (29)

The text hovers between different interpretations of the Magistrate's desire to know the girl—his ostensible desire to grant her equal recognition, and extend charity to her. First, why is the Magistrate interested in the children? Perhaps their vulnerability arouses a protective sentiment?—or do they represent something rather darker in the Magistrate's desires? (Notice that he is watched suspiciously by the 'gatekeeper', guarding the allegorical boundaries of Empire, no doubt making his own reading of the Magistrate's intentions.) When he approaches the girl, the language he uses strains towards an extremely elevated register, one that evokes nothing less than Jesus in the Gospels. 'Let the little children come to me, and do not hinder them, for the kingdom of God belongs to such as these' (Luke 18: 16). Following the biblical resonance, the Magistrate's interest in the children and 'the girl' could be interpreted as a Christlike charitableness, a genuine good-heartedness, that wants to recognize in her the sufferings of another equally human individual.[16] Or alternatively,

---

[16] As we saw in the analysis of *Dusklands* in the previous chapter, Coetzee identifies the type of recognition sought by the politics of equal dignity very closely with the Christian tradition. Here, however, there is a more complex judgement—a deferral of judgement—upon that tradition.

perhaps the fact that his desire to approach 'the girl' was stimulated by his lingering gaze from the vantage of his rooms upon the children at play grants a counter-suggestion that, at the very root of his motivations, he is using his power to prey on the innocent. Elsewhere in the text we are told that he enjoys sex with very young women—not only with young prostitutes, but with the girls of the town; later in the novel he will give voice to his fear that his lust will turn to 'little boys' (49).[17] Whatever political assumptions the reader has about a man like the Magistrate, this text immediately starts to cause problems, pulling as it does into two competing moral evaluations. Then, inside his lodgings, things become even more troubling:

The fire is lit. I draw the curtains, light the lamp. She refuses the stool, but yields up her sticks and kneels in the centre of the carpet.

'This is not what you think it is,' I say. The words come reluctantly. Can I really be about to excuse myself? Her lips are clenched shut, her ears too no doubt, she wants nothing of old men and their bleating consciences. I prowl around her, talking about our vagrancy ordinances, sick at myself. Her skin begins to glow in the warmth of the close room. She tugs at her coat, opens her throat to the fire. The distance between myself and the torturers, I realize, is negligible; I shudder.

'Show me your feet,' I say in the new thick voice that seems to be mine. 'Show me what they have done to your feet.'

She neither helps nor hinders me. I work at the thongs and eyelets of the coat, throw it open, pull the boots off. They are a man's boots, far too large for her. Inside them her feet are swaddled, shapeless.

'Let me see,' I say.

'The distance between myself and the torturers, I realise, is negligible': a chilling thought for the Magistrate to have, but one he finds hard to avoid. He cuts a strange figure: his movements around her are a 'prowl', predatory and sexual; he is 'sick at [himself]', even while asserting that his behaviour is 'not what you think it is'. Both

---

[17] The Magistrate recalls how he 'would fall into conversation with young girls promenading in twos and threes, buy them sherbet, then perhaps lead one away into the darkness to the old granary and a bed of sacks'. *Waiting for the Barbarians* 48.

he and Colonel Joll have the girl entirely in their power: she is quite literally powerless to resist, and both are (albeit with ostensibly different motivations) trying to interpret her. Realizing how little distance stands between him and the torturers, he 'shudders': this is what Bakhtin has called a 'double voiced' word—a word that carries not a single referential meaning, but a word in which two meanings, possibly two incommensurate meanings, are enclosed.[18] In the most obvious sense, the Magistrate shudders because he is horrified at the thought that what he is doing has a kind of moral equivalence with what Colonel Joll and the torturers did: that he might be dominating and abusing the girl in the very impulse of his charitableness. But it also looks another way, for as well as carrying the moral meaning of an instinctive repugnance, a shudder carries sexual overtones of a quivering anticipation.[19] Could this be an excited shudder, a shudder that reveals the Magistrate's sadism—his stimulation at being so close to the barbarian girl's tortured body? He is certainly fascinated by what the torturers have done to the girl, and perhaps what the Magistrate wants, however subconsciously, is to take sadistic pleasure in replaying to himself the violence that Colonel Joll had enacted upon her body. Again, the text seems to hover between these different patterns of evaluation, deferring the finalizing judgement that each brings to bear.

It is at this point—this dubiously double-voiced shudder—that he asks to see the girl's feet. He speaks in a 'new thick voice' that only 'seems to be mine': it would seem that this is the first invitation to undress in readiness for sex, and to start with the girl's wretchedly

---

[18] See *The Dialogic Imagination* 360.

[19] This second sense of the word is used by Coetzee in 'The Novel in Africa', when the Russian singer tries to explain the sexual appeal of Emmanuel Egudu: '*Shaudern*. Shudder. The voice makes one shudder. Probably does, when one is breast to breast with it' (*Elizabeth Costello* 57). The word is used in its more obvious sense as an affective moral response in the previous lesson, 'Realism', when John Costello beholds a very fat woman eating popcorn in the airport: 'He thinks of the cud of mashed corn and saliva in her mouth and shudders. Where does it all end?' (33).

disfigured feet would appear to confirm a reading that aligns his sexual desire with the most degraded fascination with torture. The text allows this critical evaluation of the Magistrate's desire to take hold, even as it simultaneously looks in another direction. Because the Magistrate now does something rather surprising:

She begins to unwrap the dirty bandages. I leave the room, go downstairs to the kitchen, come back with a basin and a pitcher of warm water. She sits waiting on the carpet, her feet bare. They are broad, the toes stubbly, the nails crusted with dirt.

She runs a finger across the outside of her ankle. 'That is where it was broken. The other one too.' She leans back on her hands and stretches her legs.

'Does it hurt?' I say. I pass my finger along the line, feeling nothing.

'Not any more. It has healed. But perhaps when the cold comes.'

'You should sit,' I say. I help her off with the coat, seat her on the stool, pour the water into the basin, and begin to wash her feet. For a while her legs remain tense; then they relax.

I wash slowly, working up a lather, gripping her firm-fleshed calves, manipulating the bones and tendons of her feet, running my fingers between her toes. I change my position to kneel not in front of her but beside her, so that, holding a leg between elbow and side, I can caress the foot with both hands.   (30)

In a language that is suddenly simple and crystal-clear—not double voiced at all—he tells us, 'I leave the room, go downstairs to the kitchen, come back with a basin and a pitcher of warm water' (30). They talk, and then, as he kneels before her with her feet in the water, he washes her feet. One of the resonances is now towards another biblical scene, in which Jesus washes the feet of his disciples in an act of humility (John 13). Yet this most elevated interpretation of what the Magistrate is doing—his charity, through which he humbles himself before the wrecked body of the girl—is conjoined with a cruder suggestion. Fascinated by the girl's physicality, her 'firm-fleshed calves', which way does his 'caress' turn? Towards a redeeming charity or a self-serving lust?

I lose myself in the rhythm of what I am doing. I lose awareness of the girl herself. There is a space of time which is blank to me: perhaps I am not even present. When I come to, my fingers have slackened, the foot rests in the basin, my head droops.

I dry the right foot, shuffle to the other side, lift the leg of the wide drawers above her knee, and, fighting against drowsiness, begin to wash the left foot. 'Sometimes this room gets very hot,' I say. The pressure of her leg against my side does not lessen. I go on. 'I will find clean bandages for your feet,' I say, 'but not now.' I push the basin aside and dry the foot. I am aware of the girl struggling to stand up; but now, I think she must take care of herself. My eyes close. It becomes an intense pleasure to keep them closed, to savour the blissful giddiness. I stretch out on the carpet. In an instant I am asleep. In the middle of the night I wake up cold and stiff. The fire is out, the girl is gone.

In the washing he falls asleep. Perhaps he is overcome by the effort of self-abasement before the girl—this would be the charitable inter-pretation, the one that takes him seriously.[20] For years the Magis-trate has run the town complacently, taking prostitutes and young girls on a casual basis as his due; but in humbly kneeling before the barbarian girl and washing her feet he is placing this identity in doubt, making this the exhausted sleep of someone who has been challenging himself to the utmost. Yet it is a 'blissful giddiness', an 'intense pleasure': perhaps it is instead the sleep of a complacent conscience, the type of sleep granted to a man who believes he is 'doing his bit' to remedy injustice, and can now rest more easily. And then another even less forgiving judgement comes into view. Perhaps it is a 'post-coital' kind of sleep: the erotic charge of running his hands over the feet that Joll has mangled has sufficed to satisfy him sexually and send him into a slaked exhaustion. There is an undeniable sexual charge in the encounter, and a reading that would criticize the Magistrate as someone who has a merely calculative

---

[20] As David Attwell was the first to observe, the Magistrate's different encounters with the barbarian girl and the prostitute could relate to Barthes's distinction between the 'writerly' and 'readerly' text: one resists comprehensibility and can lead the reader into both extreme bliss and boredom (thus the sleep); the other gives an easier pleasure merely (*J. M. Coetzee: South Africa and the Politics of Writing* 79).

interest in the girl would seem quite a persuasive one, for as soon as he works himself into a drowsy state he loses interest in the girl herself ('I am aware of the girl struggling to stand up; but now, I think, she must take care of herself'), and surrenders entirely to the 'blissful giddiness'. There are therefore at least three ways of reading the Magistrate's sleep: one that takes him seriously on his own terms, and two others that make an increasingly severe judgement of what he is doing. The text oscillates between these alternatives, keeping them in play.[21]

Just as in *The Unnamable*, Coetzee's text brings about a crisis in, or makes a 'balls' of, the reading experience, its aim being to bring about in the reader a disorienting spell of 'waiting', through which he or she becomes open to other ways of perceiving—ways that had hitherto been felt to be 'nothing', or 'beside the point'. It is possible to regard the Magistrate's desire to open up a channel of sympathy with the girl, and thereby to extend human recognition to her, as a self-deluding stance that masks a merely calculative will to power— an essentially sadistic drive to dominate and humiliate the 'other'. But this interpretative framework never takes hold of the text: the prose is too slippery, too akin to the infuriatingly unreadable body of Beckett's Worm for that to happen. 'That's its strength,' we might say of the text, as the Unnamable said of his 'delegate', 'its only strength, that it understands nothing, can't take thought.' Like *The Unnamable*, *Waiting for the Barbarians* is an art of failure; unlike the Beckettian novel, though, it makes that failure central to the imag-

---

[21] The homodiegetic simultaneous present of the narrative stance in *Waiting for the Barbarians* helps sustain this ambivalence: as James Phelan has argued, this approach 'takes teleology away from the Magistrate's narrative acts: since he does not know how events will turn out, he cannot be shaping the narrative according to his knowledge of the end ... we habitually make tentative inferences about that [teleology] as we read, inferences that remain subject to radical revision as the Magistrate's narrative moves in its necessarily unpredictable direction' ('Present Tense Narration, Mimesis, the Narrative Norm, and the Positioning of the Reader in *Waiting for the Barbarians*', *Understanding Narrative*, ed. James Phelan and Peter J. Rabinowitz (Columbus, 1994) 223.

ining of a 'moral community'. Amenable to neither of the competing visions of community furnished by the politics of recognition in their 'perfective' form, it offers instead to bring about a continual rupture in the patterns of evaluation differently situated readers necessarily bring to the text, and to place them in touch with what they exclude and forget. To return to the formulations made in Chapter 1: it is thereby a writing that is most truly amenable to an anti-foundational imagining of moral community—one that, like the Magistrate himself, is placed in a sustained condition of 'waiting', and that experiences freedom as a continued slipping of the chains.

3

'JOEY RULES': Telling the Truth in *Life & Times of Michael K*

> Whoever reads Kafka is . . . forcibly transformed into a liar, but
> not a complete liar. That is the anxiety peculiar to his art, an
> anxiety undoubtedly more profound than the anguish over our
> fate, which often seems to be its theme.
>
> Maurice Blanchot, 'Reading Kafka'.[1]

In the previous chapter we saw how Coetzee assimilates the destabilizing energies of Beckett's prose style: while he moves Beckett into very
different territory, this style remains crucial to the way he negotiates
the conventions of the novel. In this chapter I am going to focus very
closely on the question of prose style, dealing not only with Coetzee's
control of tone and register but also with his distinctive handling of
focalization. What I am going to emphasize is the central importance
of comic experience within Coetzee's prose—indeed, my claim will be
that the particular prose style he develops is designed to bring about an
alternative way of apprehending truth in literary narrative. As the K
suggests, *Life & Times of Michael K* is Coetzee's homage to Kafka, and
I am going to start on the subject of truth-telling with Maurice
Blanchot's remarks on the challenge Kafka poses to the way we read.

   In the epigraph above, Blanchot suggests that any given attempt to
interpret Kafka will fail to encompass the truth of the text, though it

---

[1] Maurice Blanchot, 'Reading Kafka', in *The Work of Fire*, trans. Charlotte
Mandell (Stanford, 1995) 4. Originally published as *La Part du feu* (Paris, 1949).

will not necessarily, if made in good faith, be a total lie either. The feeling of interpretative inadequacy that Kafka's prose generates—that feeling of being caught between a truth and a lie—produces in the reader a special sort of 'anxiety', and this is for Blanchot a 'more profound' feeling than any that can be generated by Kafka's themes, however angst-ridden they may be. In fact, Blanchot's chief complaint about the reception of Kafka was that altogether too much energy has been poured into the extraction of 'Kafka's philosophy', at the expense of an engagement with the special anxiety produced by the reading experience. Here is Blanchot's rather acid summary of Kafka scholarship:

The commentators are not fundamentally in disagreement. They use almost the same words: the absurd, contingency, the will to make a place for oneself in the world, the impossibility of keeping oneself there, the desire for God, the absence of God, despair, anguish. And yet of whom are they speaking? For some, it is a religious thinker who believes in the absolute, who hopes for it, who struggles endlessly to attain it. For others, it is a humanist who lives in a world without remedy and, in order not to increase the disorder in it, stays as much as possible in repose. According to Max Brod, Kafka found many paths to God. According to Mme. Magny, Kafka finds his main consolation in atheism. (5)

Of whom are these commentators speaking? asks Blanchot. Always themselves. The humanist atheist Mme. Magny uncovers in Kafka a humanist atheist; the religious Max Brod discovers in him 'a sort of superior Max Brod', as Blanchot puts it. The quest for the truth of the text always seems to eventuate merely in the truth of the self. Instead of following these commentators in demanding that Kafka's prose tell an extractable truth, Blanchot claims that Kafka's writing can instead do something the reader will not be able to predict. With Kafka, 'our reading revolves anxiously around a misunderstanding', and that anxiety can be a creative state—one that has a transforming rather than a reinforcing effect on the self.

Despite the substantive differences of historical situation between Kafka and Coetzee, there is nonetheless a certain similarity in the way their writing has been received. Like Kafka, Coetzee's fiction has been thrust into a vibrant debate on truth and lies; unlike Kafka, that debate has been generally phrased in political rather than existential terms.[2] Instead of a Max Brod claiming him as a source of religious truth, Coetzee was sent Nadine Gordimer, who publicly attacked him in the *New York Review of Books* as a source of political lies. Gordimer's review of *Life & Times of Michael K* accused Coetzee of making a false portrayal of black heroic identity: in choosing as the hero of the novel a man who opts out of a revolutionary role in troubled times and elects instead to concern himself with the cultivation of the land, Gordimer felt that the text made a clear statement that 'Coetzee's heroes are those who ignore history, not make it.'[3] This is the main thrust of Gordimer's attack:

No one in this novel has any sense of taking part in determining [the] course [of history]; no one is shown to believe he knows what that course should be. The sense is of the ultimate malaise: of destruction. Not even the oppressor really believes in what he is doing anymore, let alone the revolutionary.

This is a challengingly questionable position for a writer to take up in South Africa, make no mistake about it. The presentation of the truth and meaning of what white has done to black stands out on every page, celebrating its writer's superb, unafraid creative energy as it does; yet it denies the energy of the will to resist evil. That *this* superb energy exists with indefatigable and undefeatable persistence among the black people of

---

[2] Does this fact signify an impoverishment of literary debate? Elizabeth Costello seems to think so: in 'At the Gate' she finds herself in a rather tawdry version of the situation in which Josef K found himself in 'Before the Law': 'the wall, the gate, the sentry, are straight out of Kafka. So is the demand for a confession, so is the courtroom ... Kafka, but only the superficies of Kafka; Kafka reduced and flattened to a parody' (209). Instead of Kafka's grand concerns with the nature of justice itself, she is asked a set of almost comically banal questions about her 'beliefs' (200).

[3] Nadine Gordimer, 'The Idea of Gardening', *New York Review of Books* (2 Feb. 1984) 3.

South Africa—Michael K's people—is made evident, yes, heroically, every grinding day. It is not present in the novel. (6)[4]

The reason Coetzee is telling such lies about black heroic identity is because of his own 'stately fastidiousness': the 'revulsion against all political and revolutionary solutions' that *Life & Times* expresses is emphatically Coetzee's 'own revulsion' towards a revolutionary identity politics. His own definition of freedom, Gordimer claims, refuses any role for a properly political form of heroism rooted in 'the energy of the will', for Coetzeean freedom is merely 'to be "out of all the camps at the same time"'. Unlike most novels, which merely 'explore questions', 'this book,' Gordimer believes, 'is unusual in positing its answer', and the 'answer' Coetzee gives is this: 'Beyond all creeds and moralities, this work of art asserts, there is only one: to keep the earth alive, and only one salvation, the survival that comes from her' (6).

Just as Max Brod was contradicted by Mme Magny, so has Gordimer been contradicted by a range of commentators, mostly writing after the very worst years of apartheid had passed. Generally agreeing with Gordimer's main perception that Coetzee's text asserts its own truth about heroism, commentators have instead found ways of revaluing her values: they portray Michael K as a true, rather than a false, portrayal of the heroic, and in doing so they effectively reverse the two main strands of Gordimer's attack.

---

[4] Gordimer is here drawing upon Georg Lukács's theory of the realist novel, but is doing so in a highly selective way. Lukács's theory is underpinned by a model of history as a totality, such that, for example, a certain character in an effective realist novel will be recognizable as a 'world historical individual' (*The Historical Novel*, trans. Hannah and Stanley Mitchell (Harmondsworth: Penguin, 1962) 146); however, what would be for Lukács the extremely complex question as to whether, or to what extent, the particular circumstances of the South African situation might be extrapolated into 'world history' does not emerge as a theoretical concern for Gordimer—though, in broader terms, she explores the relevance of Marxist ideas of history to the anti-apartheid movement through the portrait of Lionel Burger in *Burger's Daughter* (London, 1979).

On the one hand it is argued that Michael is a genuine hero because he 'resists meaning'—most notably, the symbolic frameworks of apartheid race-description, but also more broadly any kind of 'binary' thinking. While, as we have just seen, Gordimer had little patience with this merely negative and individualistic concept of freedom, Laura Wright elevates it into the chief value of all of Coetzee's work, arguing that his writing is characterized by 'the space established by [the] character of Michael K, who discovers "that it is enough to be ... out of all the camps at the same time"'.[5] The other strand of criticism revalues what Gordimer perjoratively called the 'idea of gardening', and discovers instead what Rita Barnard calls 'a utopian vision: a dream of rural life without patriarchal or colonial domination' in Michael's attempts to develop a new style of relationship with the land.[6] David Attwell makes a carefully guarded articulation of this view: reluctant to attribute a strong symbolic status to K's interest in gardening, he nonetheless allows 'a certain scope to symbolism' (98) in the novel. But Michela Canepari-Labib takes it to the extreme: 'even though Coetzee is very careful not to turn Michael into an angel or a saint,' she argues,

by becoming the one left with the duty of saving the seeds that will permit the regeneration of human society after the holocaust, the protagonist emerges as a shining symbol even in the middle of war, chaos and oppression ... Throughout the novel we see him becoming a sort of mythical figure, a prophet ... Michael also seems to take on Christ-like qualities, therefore assuming, in spite of his deformity and 'slowness', an almost divine role.[7]

As Blanchot said: 'The commentators are not fundamentally in disagreement. They use almost the same words'—albeit with

[5] Laura Wright, *Writing 'Out of All the Camps': J. M. Coetzee's Narratives of Displacement* (New York, 2006) 10.

[6] Rita Barnard, *Apartheid and Beyond: South African Writers and the Politics of Place* (New York; Oxford, 2007) 34.

[7] Michela Canepari-Labib, *Old Myths—Modern Empires: Power, Language and Identity in J. M. Coetzee's Work* (Oxford, 2005) 275–6.

different valuations underpinning the words. As with Kafka the commentators, with few exceptions, do not focus on *how* Coetzee's novel tells the truth, and the anxieties it thereby generates, but instead attempt to acquit the author from the charge of lying by claiming the behaviours Gordimer condemned are properly heroic virtues.[8] What I'm going to argue is that both the Gordimer and the anti-Gordimer stance towards the text are lies—partial lies, but lies nonetheless. To get anywhere with *Life & Times of Michael K* we have to think more carefully about how Coetzee's novel conducts the act of truth-telling.

'JOEY RULES'

In 1987, at the height of the political unrest in South Africa, Coetzee gave a lecture at the Weekly Mail Book Week in Cape Town, entitled 'The Novel Today': in this lecture, published in the journal *Upstream*, but not collected in *Doubling the Point*, or indeed ever republished elsewhere, Coetzee set out two distinctive ways of understanding the type of truth the novel tells. The first idea is 'supplementarity'—the view that the novel gives an affective embodiment to truths that another discourse has already defined, and uppermost in Coetzee's mind was the discourse of 'history': 'There are some novels,' he argued, 'that fit better in the history classroom than others, some novels that *supplement* the history text better than others. Why is the point crucial? Because at certain times and in certain places—and this is one of those times and places—the novel that supplements the history text has attributed to it a greater truth than one that does not.'[9] Coetzee may have been thinking, no doubt

---

[8] One exception is Derek Attridge's account of Michael K in *J. M. Coetzee and the Ethics of Reading* (Chicago, 2004).

[9] J. M. Coetzee, 'The Novel Today,' *Upstream* 6/1 (1988) 2.

among other cultural events,[10] of the favourable reception afforded
to Stephen Clingman's influential *The Novels of Nadine Gordimer:
History From the Inside* (1986): this work had drawn on formulations
made by the later Georg Lukács in *The Historical Novel* in order to
claim that Gordimer's novels were of value for the way in which, to
quote Lukács, they represent 'the way society moves'.[11] In contrast
to this idea of the novel as a supplement to 'history', with 'history'
here acting as a term that designates several very loosely post-Marxist
political concepts, is what Coetzee calls 'a novel that occupies an
autonomous place', and is positioned as a 'rival to history'. Such a
novel 'operates in terms of its own procedures and issues in its own
conclusions', and it is emphatically not one that 'operates in terms of
the procedures of history and eventuates in conclusions that are
checkable by history (as a child's schoolwork is checked by a school-
mistress)' (3). Unlike the novel of supplementarity, the novel of
rivalry 'is prepared to work itself out outside the terms of class
conflict, race conflict, gender conflict or any other of the oppositions
out of which history and the historical disciplines erect themselves'
(3). The truth this novel tells transcends other discourses: it speaks
on its own terms, in its own way.

This concept of the novel as 'rival', which is the concept Coetzee
here appears to be advocating, should give us pause. In the previous
two chapters I have argued that Coetzee's engagement with the
tradition of the novel, and especially with Beckett, was rooted in a
desire to work out an alternative to two equally unattractive ways of

---

[10] In contextualizing 'The Novel Today' David Attwell emphasizes the 'People's
Culture' campaign of the United Democratic Front (UDF), with its concern with
the accessibility of art, the construction through art of a symbolic framework to
support a national culture, an emphasis on documentary realism, and an insistence
that artists submit themselves to alliance with the mass democratic movement
(*J. M. Coetzee: South Africa and the Politics of Writing* (Berkeley, 1993) 16).

[11] Clingman uses Lukács's definition of 'critical realism', in which 'social and
private life are seen as integrally related' in the allegorization of history as 'a fair
encapsulation of the perspective of most of Gordimer's writing' (*The Novels of
Nadine Gordimer* (London, 1986) 8).

handling narrative. Recall that Coetzee's interest was in the way the prose of *The Unnamable* not only refuses an illusory faith in what he called 'The Word in all its magical autonomy', but that it did so without succumbing to a 'formalisation or stylisation of autodestruction'. Yet here, in upholding the idea of 'rivalry', Coetzee appears to be positioning the novel as a form of thinking that does indeed rely upon some kind of 'magical autonomy': the novel of rivalry is one that can somehow de-situate itself from the terms of the cultural field, and escape the pervasive cultural constructions of what the narrator of *The Unnamable* called the 'they'. It claims to be able to bypass the conceptual frameworks that 'history' has constructed (and what more potent aggregation of Beckett's 'they' could there be than 'history' itself?) in order to address politics from an 'autonomous place'. Has Coetzee suddenly forgotten the lessons he drew from Beckett?

In advocating 'rivalry' in this irascible and, as I have already noted, unrepublished lecture, Coetzee does indeed position his writing in a way that belies his own long-held quarrel with forms of thinking grounded in logocentric premises.[12] I am going to argue, though, that Coetzee's idea of 'rivalry' actually belies the stance towards literary truth taken by *Life & Times of Michael K* itself. However, I want to start by noting that this idea is equally at odds with certain alternative formulations of literary distinctiveness also present in 'The Novel Today', most especially the crucial idea of 'difference'. Having set out the alternatives of supplementarity and rivalry, Coetzee goes on to suggest another one: a story, he explains, is 'not made up of

---

[12] Peter McDonald has argued that Coetzee's advocacy of 'rivalry' in this lecture is rather ironically akin to the concept of literariness held by certain of his erstwhile censors: 'Coetzee's formalist appeal to the literary as a discourse with its own distinct or, more strongly, rivalrous mode of existence looks like a version of the censor's privileged aesthetic space . . . Far from being patriarchal monsters determined to usurp the position of the beloved reader, it seems that the unexpectedly literary censors, not the politicized critics, were Coetzee's closest allies in the 1980s.' See 'The Writer, the Critic and the Censor: J. M. Coetzee and the Question of Literature', in *Book History* 7 (2004) 294.

one thing plus another thing, message plus vehicle, substructure plus superstructure. On the keyboard on which they are written, the plus key does not work. There is always a difference; and the difference is not a part, the part left behind after the subtraction. The minus key does not work either: the difference is everything' (4). These terms are taken from Stanley Fish's critique of the different, and competing, versions of literary essentialism, and far from upholding literature as an 'autonomous' space that can transcend the political, Fish's essay collapses the distinction between 'ordinary' and 'literary' language.[13] What, then, does it mean to say of a 'story' that 'the difference is everything'? Claiming that 'storytelling... is another, an other mode of thinking', Coetzee tells a parable about a cockroach: stories are like cockroaches, even though 'in the end there is still the difference between a cockroach and a story, and the difference remains everything'. As Coetzee indicates, Kafka featured cockroaches, or at least insects, in his stories: so Kafka would seem important to any answer we might give.[14] The presence of Derrida also looms large in this lecture: not only with terms such as 'supplement' (which evokes Derrida's now famous thoughts on the logic of the supplement in *Of Grammatology*) and *différance*, but also with Derrida's enduring interest in Kafka himself in mind.[15] Before

---

[13] In 'How Ordinary is Ordinary Language?' Fish argued that 'A message-minus definition [of literature] is one in which the separation of literature from the normative centre of ordinary language is celebrated; while in a message-plus definition, literature is reunited with the centre by declaring it to be a more effective conveyor of the messages ordinary language transmits' (*Is There a Text in This Class? The Authority of Interpretive Communities* (Cambridge, Mass., 1980) 103). Coetzee's allusion to Fish's essay was first remarked upon by McDonald, 'The Writer, the Critic and the Censor' 294–5.

[14] The story is, of course, 'The Transformation' ('Die Verwandlung'), and in fact Gregor Samsa is not quite an 'insect', let alone precisely a cockroach: he is an 'Ungeziefer', a vaguer term meaning 'vermin' or 'pest', connoting harmfulness and nastiness rather than identifying any actual creature.

[15] Jacques Derrida, *Of Grammatology*, trans. Gayatri Chakravorty Spivak (Baltimore, 1974; corrected edn., 1997) 141–57.

exploring *Life & Times of Michael K* itself, I will therefore briefly outline a account of literary truth that avoids the pitfalls of both 'rivalry' and 'supplementarity', and to do so will draw upon Derrida's essay on Kafka. We know from a literary-critical essay of this period, 'Time, Tense and Aspect in Kafka's "The Burrow"' (1981), that Coetzee was reading interpretations of Kafka rooted in Derridean conceptions of literariness while *Life & Times of Michael K* was being composed.[16] In 'Before the Law' Derrida gives a reading of the famous parable in the Cathedral from *The Trial*, in which an individual's access to 'the law' is perpetually deferred, to define the special nature of literary truth. While Derrida's subject in the essay is the longstanding debate on how to think about the categorical distinctiveness of the literary, the Heideggerian inflection Derrida brings to that debate will help us come to terms with the understanding of truth-telling that, as I will show, the prose style of *Life & Times of Michael K* tries to generate.

Kafka's parable runs as follows: inside the cathedral, itself an image of truth incarnate, Josef K is told by a priest the story of a man 'from the country' who spends his life waiting to be admitted by a gatekeeper to an unmediated access to the law, which, he feels, 'should be accessible to every man and at all times'; at the end of his life, tantalizingly 'aware of a radiance that streams inextinguishably from the gateway of the Law', the gatekeeper finally closes the gate, mysteriously observing that it was made only for the petitioner himself.[17] Derrida reads Kafka's text as a meditation on the way in which literature is necessarily a type of discursive non-self-presence, situated on the boundary of the particular and the universal, an

---

[16] Coetzee's footnotes in the essay refer us to Henry Sussman, 'The All-Embracing Metaphor: Reflections on Kafka's "The Burrow"', *Glyph* 1 (1977) 100–31, which draws heavily upon Derrida's *Speech and Phenomena*, trans. David B. Allison (Evanston, 1973); this journal published a substantial number of Derrida's articles in the 1970s and 1980s (indeed, the seminal essay 'Signature Event Context' appears in the same issue as Sussman's article.)

[17] Franz Kafka, *The Trial*, trans. Willa and Edwin Muir (London, 1953) 235–6.

event through which 'the categorical engages the idiomatic' (*Acts of Literature*, 213):

It seems that the law as such should never give rise to any story. To be invested with its categorical authority, the law must be without history, genesis, or any possible derivation. That would be *the law of the law*... And when one tells stories on this subject, they can concern only circumstances, events external to the law, and, at best, the modes of its revelation. Like the man from the country in Kafka's story, narrative accounts would try to approach the law and make it present, to enter into a relation with it, indeed, to enter it and become *intrinsic* to it, but none of these things can be accomplished. The story of these manoeuvres would be merely an account of that which escapes the story and which remains finally inaccessible to it. (191)

Like the man from the country, literature stands before the law, attempting to access it through a door that is wholly unique (designed only for the petitioner himself), ever hoping for a glimpse of its radiance; yet any embodiment of law will only constitute another deferral, 'an interminable *différance*... As the doorkeeper represents it, the discourse of the law does not say "no" but "not yet", indefinitely' (204). In the act of serving the law as one of its 'modes of its revelation' (191), literature always does something 'other' to the law: it has the potential to make otherness felt by interrupting the law in the act of serving it—by saying 'not yet' to its decision upon the truth of the matter. Derrrida is quite specific about how literature brings about a state of 'subversive juridicity': 'Under certain linguistic conditions, [literature] can exercise the legislative power of linguistic performativity to sidestep existing laws... This is owing to the referential equivocation of certain linguistic structures. Under these conditions literature can *play the law*, repeating it while diverting or circumventing it' (216). The italicized 'play the law' reads in French *jouer la loi*, which also implies both 'playing at being the law' and 'deceiving the law', and the aspect of literary experience that enables this play is 'referential equivocation' within language. The distinctive truth that literature tells comes not because it plays *by* the rules of other discourses (the idea of supplementarity), or by any claim it might make to transcend those rules (the idea of rivalry) but by the way it equivocates with the rules those discourses set, including the rules internalized by readers of literature. As Coetzee put it in an interview with Dick Penner, literature plays 'the game of the rules', and a successful text may, he went on to say, not only have a chance of changing the rules, but might 'change the game'.[18] Literary truth-telling emerges, in this account, through the process of interpretative anxiety that occurs within any given act of reading, an experience that equivocates with and bends the rules different readers apply to the text when they read. This is why Blanchot felt that the anxiety 'peculiar to [Kafka's] art' was 'undoubtedly more profound' than his overt thematics.

All this talk of playing with the rules makes literature sound like a rather hedonistic affair—disseminative, to use Derrida's metaphor, rather than intently inseminative (or to use Barthes's, not only pleasurable but orgasmic)—and this hedonistic resonance is by no means disconfirmed by *Life & Times of Michael K*. At the beginning of part III we leave the Medical Officer behind and resume the type of focalization that characterized part I, for K has escaped from the hospital: 'Weak at the knees after his long walk, screwing up his eyes against the brilliant morning light, Michael K sat on a bench beside the miniature golf course on the Sea Point esplanade, facing the sea, resting, gathering his strength' (171). In this passage there is—to return to the overarching question of heroism—an equivocal play between the purposefully heroic and the indolently hedonistic. 'Gathering his strength' suggests K is on some kind of mission—that he is someone who needs to gather strength for special purposes. But 'gathering his strength' to what ends? The notion of a serious purpose is delicately offset against the hedonistic pleasure-park milieu that surrounds him, a 'miniature golf course' being an unlikely site for anything of much

---

[18] Dick Penner, *Countries of the Mind: the Fiction of J. M. Coetzee* (New York, 1989).

seriousness.[19] Then there rises a powerful sense of expectancy: 'The air was still. He could hear the slap of waves on the rocks below and the hiss of retreating water.' But this is again punctured by simple pleasures of various kinds:

> A dog stopped to sniff his feet, then peed against the bench. A trio of girls in shorts and singlets passed, running elbow to elbow, murmuring together, leaving a sweet smell in their wake. From Beach Road came the tinkle of an ice-cream vendor's bell, first approaching, then receding. At peace, on familiar ground, grateful for the warmth of the day, K sighed and slowly let his head sag sideways. (171)

The various hedonisms—the dog's sniffing and peeing, the 'trio of girls in shorts and singlets', the ice-cream van, the warmth of the day—seem to pull K away from any serious purpose associable with 'gathering his strength'. But then to round the paragraph off: 'Whether he slept or not he did not know; but when he opened his eyes he was well enough again to go on.' We are back where we started, restored to a sense of purpose: K is 'well enough again to go on'. (But to what?)

This paragraph, with its minute shifts of tone and resonance, has moved between the suggestion of a serious purpose for Michael, and a non-serious non-signification, which in each case is pleasurable. Here we find precisely what Derrida spoke of as 'referential equivocation', through which Coetzee's text is playing the 'game of the rules': it lets us start to see Michael K in a heroic light, as someone with a serious purpose, and then this truth flickers out, pushed up against, in this case, the decidedly non-serious hedonistic milieu of the seaside. This last section in fact introduces a good deal of hedonism into the text, qualifying a number of assumptions we might have made about Michael K, and thus compounding the 'anxiety' we come to feel as readers: by the end of part III we cannot think of him as saintly (he is fellated in a public convenience—an 'orgasmic' text indeed), or abstemious (he boozes not just once, but

---

[19] It is worth stressing Coetzee's realism here: there is indeed a miniature golf course on the Sea Point esplanade in Cape Town.

whenever offered a drink), or as someone making an 'escape' (he returns to his mother's room), or 'abandoned' in any principled sense (he admires December's capacity for taking care of himself, unlike his own experience of living on a mountain (178)), or especially open to 'mystical' intuitions (the brandy brings as much 'peace' as the fasting ever did (179)). This beachside hedonism takes place within a setting that is now devastated by war: K, 'conscious of being naked inside the blue overalls', walks through a scene of burnt-out cars, 'scorched grass', 'broken glass and charred garbage', and having picked his way across the lawn, 'crossed the road, and passed out of sunlight into the gloom of the unlit entrance of the Côte d'Azur, where along a wall in looping black spraypaint he read JOEY RULES' (172). Why is 'JOEY' ruling in this scene of devastation? Who is this Joey, anyway? Joey could be a proper name; or given all the hedonism of the last part of the text it could morph into 'joy'; alternatively (given the French setting—we are in the Côte d'Azur apartments here) it could become *jouer*. Recall Derrida's notion that literature, unlike other discourses, can *'jouer la loi'* (215), which translates variously as 'to play at being the law (or the rules)'; 'deceiving the law/rules'; 'playing the law/rules'. What I'm going to spend the rest of the chapter showing is that the sort of play with linguistic register that we have just witnessed, and the 'referential equivocation' it engenders, is central to the way *Life & Times of Michael K* plays with the rules: this text playfully reorients the established truths of what counts as the properly heroic through the anxiety it creates in readers who try not to lie about what they read.

'A WRONG STORY, ALWAYS WRONG': NARRATIVE IN *LIFE & TIMES OF MICHAEL K*

I'm now going to make two different close readings of the element of comic play in the narrative, each of which will, I hope, differently enrich our sense for the way 'JOEY RULES'. The first rule I will start with is Gordimer's 'idea of gardening': 'Beyond all creeds and moralities, this work of art asserts, there is only one: to keep the earth alive, and only one salvation, the survival that comes from her.' In this view Coetzee's text takes a 'challengingly questionable position', or what we might call a 'rival' position, against South African cultural politics as Gordimer perceived it. To see whether Gordimer is telling the truth, we will consider the very last pages of the text, in which K is back in his mother's room under the stairs in the Côte d'Azur apartments in Sea Point, waiting for the return of the person who seems now to be inhabiting the room. We are told that he starts thinking again of 'the farm': inspired by the thought, or perhaps 'vision', that, among the desolate wilderness of the veld, 'if you looked carefully you suddenly saw a tip of vivid green, pumpkin leaf or carrot-bush', he begins to project a return visit, in which the as-yet undiscovered occupant of his mother's room will fill the role his mother played on the first trip:

It did not seem impossible that whoever it was who disregarded the curfew and came when it suited him to sleep in this smelly corner (K imagined him as a little old man with a stoop and a bottle in his side pocket who muttered all the time into his beard, the kind of old man the police ignored) might be tired of life at the seaside and want to take a holiday in the country if he could find a guide who knew the roads.   (183)

Ignoring the war going on around him, Michael longs to embark on a new journey back to his cherished garden. But in order to decide what kind of status to grant to his intuition that the 'idea of gardening' counts for more than joining in with the political struggle, we must consider the peculiar texture of this writing. The person he imagines to be 'a little old man', but who could, for all he knows, be a young revolutionary, 'might be tired of life at the seaside'. 'Life at the seaside?' Is this really the right term for the life offered at Sea Point—with its 'scorched grass', its 'broken glass and charred garbage' (182), its boarded-up windows and burnt-out cars? The 'little old man' is surely at best 'living by the beach', not participating in 'life at the seaside': while 'seaside' summons up a cheery holiday optimism hardly warranted by the war-torn reality of the beach itself, the phrase 'life at the seaside' conjures a rather genteel round of holiday activities and social gatherings (keep in mind that we are supposedly dealing with a 'little old man') that is at a quite absurd remove from the smelly cardboard-box bed in an air-conditioning cupboard under the stairs in a devastated city. Note that the 'little old man . . . *might be tired* of life at the seaside': this is an interesting note to savour, with its suggestion that the genteel variety of a seaside life could nonetheless (perhaps the 'little old man' retired early?) become a little dull, leaving mild ennui to set in. If this is so, Michael speculates (or so we are told), the old man might 'want to take a holiday in the country if he could find a guide who knew the roads'. If only the 'old man' could fathom the sort of 'holiday' he would be letting himself in for with Michael K: not, he would quickly realize, the sort of 'holiday' on which one dines well and enjoys the finer things of life (no 'life at the seaside' this!); rather, the sort of holiday where one eats insects, then pumpkins, then nothing at all, and lives in a small hole in the ground beneath a shelter that leaks. Nor, he would realize perhaps even more quickly, is Michael exactly a 'guide who knew the roads', for he does not know 'the roads' at all: his first expedition with his mother along the highway failed due to his ignorance of the restrictions on travel; the second ended when he was picked up outside Stellenbosch having walked into the very first checkpoint he encountered, promptly to be removed from the 'roads' and put on a train, later to be returned to Cape Town courtesy of the South African army.[20]

Yet in contrast to the plunging bathos that accrues to Michael's projected journey back to his 'idea of gardening', the register and tone of the narration also elevate and dignify his situation, even to an

---

[20] It is of course very much open to doubt whether K ever did find his mother's farm—the Visagie farm was simply the one that sounded most like the names his mother had mumbled, nor was she clear that Prince Albert was indeed the town she had in mind.

almost absurd degree: the text *also* grants the possibility of seeing Michael K as purposefully heroic. Consider the effect generated by the elaborate conditionality of the above sentence: 'It did not seem impossible', it begins, with a delicately reserved double negative, before unfolding in a series of conditional clauses, including a speculative parenthesis (in fact we remain in the conditional tense until the very end of the text). The sense of a reticent civility this implies ('It did not seem impossible') is coupled with what would appear to be Michael's own superfine sense of sexual delicacy: 'They could share a bed tonight,' the narrative continues, 'it had been done before.' This in turn combines with a boy's-own optimism in the vision of Michael K and the old man finding an abandoned barrow 'if they were lucky', and then 'spinning along the high road', making good time on their journey. In each moment of the text there is embedded a contradictory movement: a pull upwards that attributes a sense of dignity and purpose, and a bathetic fall downwards, towards an implied reality that is always much cruder and dumber.

The account of the trip continues with an encouraging nudge '(things were gathering pace now)', as the narrative voice continues to drum up excitement and a sense of purpose, and they reach a projected situation in which the source of water at the farm has been blocked by rocks from an explosion. Michael K, we are told, would not despair even at this eventuality:

He would clear the rubble from the mouth of the shaft, he would bend the handle of the teaspoon in a loop and tie the string to it, he would lower it down the shaft deep into the earth, and when he brought it up there would be water in the bowl of the spoon; and in that way, he would say, one can live. (184)

How to read this without lying? It would be possible, or at least, it would 'not seem impossible', to imagine a reading that sides with the tenor and style of the narration, in which Michael is an almost visionary figure, sustained by the continual hope of new life ('you suddenly saw a tip of vivid green') through the trials of his journey into the promised land of the farm, keeping up standards of human decency in a world gone mad ('They could share a bed tonight, it had been done before,' as he humbly serves the 'little old man'), surviving on nothing but a holy-man's skill, simplicity, and grace (note the *politesse* of the impersonal pronoun, and the restrained pedagogy of 'in that way, he would say, one can live'). Alternatively, it would 'not seem impossible' to read against the grain of the narration, to produce a dumb or even idiotic Michael K, comically at odds with the way the story is told: he has not even met the man (or woman) he is travelling with, though this has not stopped him from absurdly, and narcissistically, fantasizing him into an image partaking both of himself (as 'the kind of old man the police ignored', or equally, Michael is described as 'a little old man' by the medical officer (129)) and his mother (for whom, despite his mature years, he still hankers). The return to the farm, symbolically elevated into a search for a promised land, could easily be seen merely as a nonsensical idea, rooted in a fetishization of his mother's dying whim; the spiritual profundity of his interest in growing vegetables could be explained psychologically by reference to the fact that he was allocated the job of 'Gardener, grade 3(b)' (4) at a formative stage in his youth (though gardening has remained a skill at which he is nonetheless singularly inept); the closing image of the survival-by-teaspoon, which might elevate upwards into a sense of miraculous survival-by-grace, could instead be the moment at which we are most truly back where we started, with Michael K being fed in infancy by teaspoon because his hare lip prevented him from taking sustenance either from the breast or the bottle.[21] The gardening, the 'voyage home', the teaspoon: all rise upwards into significance at the same time as they are naggingly brought back down as mere fantasies derived from formative—even infantile—psychological experiences that are stubbornly insignificant. There is a tendency, in the tone and register of the text, to elevate Michael's aspirations into a seriousness and dignity and meaningfulness

[21] See *Life & Times of Michael K* 3.

worthy of a hero (of a certain kind); there is also an observable, and frequently observed, reality that pulls him back down with a thud. Whoever reads Coetzee is forcibly transformed into a liar, but not a complete liar: the 'referential equivocation' of the text plays with both the attempt to elevate Michael into a hero, and the attempt to dismiss him as a false icon. It suspends the reader in what Blanchot called a state of anxiety—and what (to recall the previous chapter) we saw Beckett speak of as the 'acute and increasing anxiety' that should properly surround representation, such that the writing is 'shadowed more and more darkly by a sense of invalidity, of inadequacy, of existence at the expense of all that it excludes, all that it blinds to' (*Disjecta* 145).

Moving on from the idea of gardening, let us now consider a moment in *Life & Times of Michael K* that has attained an iconic status as a marker of the idea of heroism that Michael is often felt to embody: his decision to stop plundering the Visagie's house for useful things to help with the construction of his burrow: 'The worst mistake, he told himself, would be to try to found a new house, a rival line, on his small beginnings out at the dam. Even his tools should be of wood and leather and gut, materials the insects would eat when one day he no longer needed them' (104). The iconic status of this passage began with Gordimer's review, which seized upon it as 'the concrete expression, through the creative imagination, of political debate about the future of South Africa under black majority rule: whether or not it should take over what has been the white South African version of the capitalist system' (3). But what truth does it really tell us about this debate on political economy?

The passage seems to suggest a reversal of the 'capitalist' Robinson Crusoe, who of course plundered the shipwreck for all it was worth in order to re-enact for himself on the island a colonial version of English civilization. It is indeed possible, or again, would 'not seem impossible', to seize hold of K at this moment as an icon for some new anti-capitalist and (presumably) pro-ecologist style of living, and there is indeed a certain lyricism granted by the narration that leads the reader to this impulse: the sudden realization of an unforeseen virtuousness at the beginning of the second sentence, 'Even his tools should be of wood and leather and gut', with its satisfying falling cadence onto 'gut'; the level-headed and sober acknowledgement of eventual death ('when one day he no longer needed them') that closes the paragraph; the general resistance to the corrosive processes of commodification that all this suggests. But any idealization must be offset against the formulations made by the previous sentence: its presumption that his burrow—this hole in the ground in which Michael will gradually and unwittingly starve himself to death—could conceivably, even *with* the help of the Visagie's tools and possessions, be construed to constitute the founding of a 'new house', or ('things were gathering pace now') 'a rival line', capable of competing with the colonial lineage of the Visagie clan, wobbles on the edge of foolishness, especially when capped off by the beguiling idiot's modesty of referring to the existing construction as 'his small beginnings'. The reader becomes aware of the constructedness of these formulations, of a distinctive consciousness motivating them, pushing the impulse to give an iconic meaning just a little too far. This passage by no means reaches the heady heights of near-absurdity we found in the closing dream of a 'holiday' for the 'little old man': the anti-capitalist 'meaning', which dignifies and elevates K's decision to stop plundering into an ethically compelling gesture, is not totally dispersed by the comic, but nor is it granted the full seriousness it demands. Instead, the text keeps making us anxious, keeps pushing us towards some other way of reading Michael—the truth he represents is something we can't quite name (unless we lie).

NARRATORS IN COETZEE AND KAFKA

The way I have been reading Coetzee's text raises the question of its implied narrator—an identifiable presence that is responsible for elevating and dignifying what happens to Michael, even to the point of near-absurdity. It is clear that the narration is not focalized exclusively through Michael from the moment we begin to compare his own effort to tell his story (a masterpiece of compression: 'I didn't always get enough to eat,' he tells his expectant audience on the upper slopes of Signal Hill, before frustratedly lapsing into silence (176)) with the continually engaging account of his movements given to us by the text itself. In order to think about the role and identity of the narrator in Coetzee's text it will help first to consider the Kafka text that is the most likely literary model for *Life & Times of Michael K*—'A Hunger Artist'.[22] I will draw upon Roy Pascal's reading of that text in 'The Identifiable Narrator of "A Hunger Artist"': this account takes issue with the hitherto most influential view of the text, which had presented the narration as 'impersonal' and 'authoritative and factual', and which had attributed to the hunger artist himself 'an allegory of either the artist in the modern world or the saint'. Instead, Pascal's reading of Kafka uncovers 'a rich vein, almost a riot, of humour', in which the narrator comes into view as a rather crass impresario figure, intent on 'bigging-up' (to use the register most appropriate to the man) the performance of the hunger artist himself.[23]

'A Hunger Artist' cultivates an unsettlingly comic disjunctiveness between the tone of the narration and the occasional insights we have into the experience of the 'artist', beginning with the title itself. 'Hungerkünstler' is a deeply unusual term for what is, after all, not much of an art—hunger is only a lack, only a state to be endured, not something created, and we are even told at the end by the artist

---

[22] Although Coetzee was obviously very interested in Kafka's handling of the tense and aspect of German verbs in 'The Burrow' (see *Doubling the Point* 210–32), much of the art of *Life & Times of Michael K* lies instead in its handling of the narrator—and as I will show, 'A Hunger Artist' is thus the more likely model.

[23] See Roy Pascal, *Kafka's Narrators: A Study of his Stories and Sketches* (Cambridge, 1982) 105–7. It is unlikely, though not impossible, that Coetzee himself read Pascal's influential account prior to composition of *Life & Times of Michael K*. But given the linguistic attentiveness with which Coetzee had studied 'The Burrow', we can be sure he would have studied 'A Hunger Artist' closely in German.

himself that there is nothing to admire in the fast. Yet the rather blasé manner in which the term is introduced, as if hunger artistry were a well-established cultural norm, is striking. The character of the narrator then proceeds to reveal itself rapidly over the first few sentences of this highly compressed text: 'During these last decades the interest in professional fasting has markedly diminished. It used to pay very well to stage such great performances under one's own management, but today that is quite impossible. We live in a different world now.'[24] Although the Muirs' translation (quoted here), which is committed to a view of the narration as impersonal and objective, renders Kafka's effects hard to perceive, a German reader would immediately notice a range of oddities. First there are the crude emphases: what the Muirs translate as 'to pay very well' is in German the mildly oafish 'gut lohnte', more accurately 'well worth your [one's] while', in which 'gut' marks the oafishness. Then there are numerous clumsy contractions, such as 'grosse derartige Vorführungen', which the Muirs render as 'such great performances', but which Pascal corrects as the clumsier 'great performances of that kind'. This is coupled with an insistent usage of the showy business jargon of 'in eigner Regie' (under one's own management), and later on the same page, 'Abonnenten' ('those with subscription booking'), and 'Besichtigungen' ('tours'), very much of a piece with the sentimental tautology of the closing sentence of the extract, 'We live in a different world now.' Immediately the text generates a unsettling comic effect through the gap between a reality that is strange and disturbing (an art of starvation), and a discourse that is homogenizing and nudgingly familiar. The character of Kafka's narrator here is that of an insider, a showman himself, a personality close to the impresario who actually manages the affairs of the 'hunger artist': the man who, as will be recalled, insists on ending each fast, much to the artist's chagrin and resentment, at forty-day intervals, as 'Experience had proved that for about

---

[24] Kafka, *The Complete Short Stories*, ed. Nahum N. Glatzer (London, 1999) 268.

forty days the interest of the public could be stimulated by a steadily increasing pressure of advertisement, but after that the town began to lose interest, sympathetic support began notably to fall off' (270). In sum, Pascal argues that Kafka's text generates a 'massive grotesque comedy' by presenting a tortured, reticent, and opaque man through the discourse of a hustling, cliché-ridden raconteur.

What is the 'character' of the narrator in *Life & Times of Michael K*? Recall that the very title of Kafka's story, 'A Hunger Artist', immediately offered to render the opaque motivation possessed by the man in the cage to starve himself to death into something familiar and consumable as entertainment. The title of Coetzee's text promises to render Michael K's life not into entertainment, but as consumable instead in a political way: it conjures up that sense of officiality and importance due to a heroic 'national figure'—someone, at any rate, whose 'life' was of sufficient importance to illuminate the 'times' themselves. Coetzee's narrator is not a commercial raconteur, but is more akin to someone who has been appointed to write by a political committee: not, of course, the sort of committee that a Nadine Gordimer would sit on, but a committee of (let's say) ecologically minded individualist pacifists.

Consider, for instance, the gush of committee-writing officialese that greets us at the very beginning of the novel: 'At the age of fifteen he passed out of Huis Norenius and joined the Parks and Gardens division of the municipal services of the City of Cape Town as Gardener, grade 3(b)' (4). Do we really need to be told the full title possessed by Cape Town ('City of Cape Town')? Is there another 'Cape Town' that is, crucially, not a city, that might at this juncture confuse the meaning? Of course not: this is the argot of an official report, along with the stacked genitive clauses (of . . . of the . . . of the . . . of), careless of literary elegance, betraying a jobsworth anxiety to set down all the facts properly and in order. Such details are only interesting if we are considering the life of a great and important figure, whose every move is interesting to his admirers. And thus following the rule of reverse attribution (by which if a story is reported frequently enough it will become news) *because* we are given these official-sounding details, we assume this Michael K must be someone important: a mere idiot, a dolt incapable of looking after himself (the narrator smooths over his mental denseness with the clipped carefulness of 'his mind was not quick') would hardly merit an official 'Life & Times' biography, let alone the extraordinary degree of specificity this one delivers. The passage continues: 'Three years later he left Parks and Gardens and, after a spell of unemployment which he spent lying on his bed looking at his hands, took a job as night attendant at the public lavatories on Greenmarket Square.' In one sense, this continues the idealizing elevation of Michael K, now extending it into the realm of the symbolic. Michael's 'spell of unemployment which he spent lying on his bed looking at his hands' rises into an invitation to consider K in a moment of self-assessment, asking himself what kind of labour belongs to him, probing the meaning of his existence. This thread of symbolic importance is the one that will lead, later in the text, into a narration that will edge us ever closer into an attribution of visionary near-holiness to Michael as a cultivator of the earth— which Gordimer denigrates, and (as we have seen) others have celebrated. But already in the text there is a tug of bathos that pulls down these creeping allegorical tendrils. Consider the image: did Michael K, who needs (and indeed loves) to eat and sleep really spend this whole 'spell' 'lying on his bed looking at his hands'? The insistently elevating narration is rendered briefly comic. Carrying on with the passage:

On his way home from work late one Friday he was set upon in a subway by two men who beat him, took his watch, his money and his shoes, and left him lying stunned with a slash across his arm, a dislocated thumb and two broken ribs. After this incident he quit night work and returned to Parks and Gardens, where he rose slowly in the service to become Gardener, grade 1.

The return to 'Gardener, grade 1' clearly represents a satisfying end to the paragraph for this narrator: it is thereby well-rounded as a narration of Michael's rise from grade 3(b) to grade 1, through the

unfortunate deviation of 'a job as night attendant at the public
lavatories on Greenmarket Square'; furthermore, it has located his
life for us squarely in the role of gardener, most especially through
the symbolic moment of soul-searching (or at least hand-searching)
woven into the officialese. It thereby establishes at the very outset the
type of story the narrator will tell: that of Michael's near-mystical
affinity for gardening, which will underpin and motivate his quest
into the wilderness: to 'find Canaan' (his mother's home); then to
enter into a meaningful relationship with the earth. But there is a
nagging (and deeply bathetic) doubt here: what about the story of
the lavatories, Michael K's alternative career? This makes a brief but
brilliant comeback right at the end, along with the teaspoon: he
wanders into the public conveniences at Sea Point, noting inwardly
(with a professional's eye) that they are so unkempt as to be full of
driftsand; it is here that the pimp and prostitutes find him not once
but twice (172, 178). As far as they are concerned, 'Mister Treefeller'
(174) may as well be 'Mister Lavatory Attendant'—a thought to
conjure with. Perhaps Michael's true utopian vision was not the 'idea
of gardening' after all, but the distinctively less resonant 'idea of
lavatory cleaning'?

   Leaving this decidedly bathetic thought to one side, I have built
up this picture of a narrator with an 'official' character, eager to
dignify and lend prestige to a bumbling, meaninglessly particular
Michael K, in order to clarify certain qualities in the narration that
are not normally perceived. But in doing so I have been involved in
a partial misrepresentation of my own—both of *Life & Times of
Michael K* and of 'A Hunger Artist'. My reading is beginning to
suggest that there is indeed a completed (or 'perfective') truth that
can be extracted from these texts: that there is a 'misrepresenting'
narrator whose discourse might be penetrated by irony so as to arrive
at the truth of the text. But this is not so. We will return briefly to
Kafka's 'A Hunger Artist', and to certain suggestions in that text that
the distinction between the aggrandizing narrator, and the opaque
asceticism of the 'artist', are not as stable as I suggested earlier. For
the fact is that, notwithstanding the cage he sits in, the artist is not in

any sense the prisoner of the impresario, but a free agent who employs the man, and is quite able to leave him: it is of his own volition that, when times grow hard for hunger-artistry, 'he took leave of the impresario, his partner in an unparalleled career, and hired himself to a large circus' (273). The reason the artist is prepared to work with the impresario is that as well as desiring the removal of himself from all things consumable, he also *wants* to be consumed by the public: in fact he has a substantial vanity of his own to appease. When times grow hard we are told that he joins the circus because 'He had been applauded by thousands in his time and could hardly come down to showing himself in a street booth at village fairs'; when the circus take him on, 'in order to spare his own feelings he avoided reading the conditions of the contract', so careful is he of his own wounded vanity (273). We then learn that one motive for his desire to fast for more than forty days was that of publicity: he would 'astound the world by establishing a record never yet achieved'; at the circus his attitude to public consumption is quite different to that towards eating: 'it was exhilarating to watch the crowds come streaming his way' (274). Pascal argues that the hunger artist can even be read as actively participating in the grotesquely inappropriate symbolic constructions of the 'emergence from fasting' spectacle that we had previously attributed solely to the impresario. For this spectacle does not just happen once only—in which case we could perceive the artist as being caught unawares by the impresario. Instead Kafka carefully qualifies the controlling verbs with an iterative aspect, using the auxiliary 'immer' (always).[25] The impresario *always* stops proceedings at forty days, *always* raises his hands in an appeal to the divine, *always* picks him up roughly to make his legs wobble; the women are *always* disgusted (do they feign disgust?) to the point of sickness; the artist *always* accepts this charade, and actively participates in it, as the cutting 'as if' clauses of this passage suggest:

[25] The iterative aspect is an especially important use of the verb for Kafka, as Coetzee argues in 'Time, Tense and Aspect in Kafka's "The Burrow"', *Doubling the Point* 211–20.

The artist now submitted completely; his head lolled on his breast *as if* it had landed there by chance; his body was hollowed out; his legs in a spasm of self-preservation clung close to each other at the knees, yet scraped on the ground *as if* it were not really solid ground, *as if* they were only trying to find solid ground.   (271, my italics)

If this 'always' happens, and the artist 'always' ends up participating in this appropriation of himself, as is suggested here, there is no originary and authentic 'true artist' in Kafka's text: he is always-already participating in his own misrepresentation.

The same applies for *Life & Times of Michael K*. As much as Michael, at times, seems to want to 'resist' symbolic status, or resists it *de facto* by his sheer dumbness, there is much in his behaviour to suggest that the narrator does not misrepresent him, but that Michael participates, as did the hunger artist, in aspects of his own iconic assimilation. I'll begin with the queer sense of dignity and high civility that we have already witnessed the narrative producing: 'K made a journey to Oliphant Road in Green Point, to St Joseph's Mission, where in earlier times one had been able to find a cup of soup and a bed for the night, no questions asked' (13). To say he 'made a journey' is a strangely elevated way of putting it: there has been a riot and a downpour of rain; when people are back on the streets and it has stopped raining, K peeps out of hiding and then wanders off to a church (do we need to know *precisely* where it is?—'Oliphant Road in Green Point, to St Joseph's Mission') to get the free soup. There is then the odd dignity of the impersonal pronoun: to say that 'in earlier times one had been able' to do something resonates, for a moment, with a sophisticated withdrawal from a world gone mad: *après moi le deluge*. This resonance is clinched with the closing 'no questions asked'—a phrase, I believe, normally associated with higher net worth individuals than the ant-like Michael K: in times of national crisis like these, money and valuables have been known to change hands with 'no questions asked'. The soup-kitchen workers at St Joseph's Mission for a moment become refined models of tact: ex-empla of how to live decently when, so to speak, the rabble rise and times grow hard. All this may seem to be entirely the effect of 'the narrator': his punctilious observation of detail, his high civility, his continual dignifying of Michael K's undignified situation. But Michael's own observable behaviour prevents us from making such an easy distinction. We have already witnessed his sense of propriety with regard to matters of the bedchamber ('They could share a bed tonight, it had been done before' (183)). But we also know that when Michael and his mother left Sea Point, they left it decently, despite the chaos around them: 'The room was as they had left it, neatly swept for the next occupant' (23)—exactly how one should behave, war or no war. Michael also displays a refined sensibility at the picnic on Signal Hill: when told, with little delicacy, that the polony produced by December is very valuable ('"Gold!' he said, wagging the sausage in K's direction. 'For this you pay gold!'"), we learn that 'K ate of the bread and condensed milk, even ate half a banana, but refused the sausage.' (Note the sudden religious resonance of 'ate *of* the bread'—the preposition makes all the difference.) Even when being robbed by December Michael displays a fastidious politeness in his reluctance to embarrass his host: 'The packet of seed emerged so noisily that K was ashamed to pretend not to hear. So he groaned and stirred' (176). Each of these incidents are actual reported actions of K's—the tidy room, the refusal of the polony, the well-timed groan—independent of the narration's subtly aggrandizing resonances.

Perhaps more important than the civility is Michael's own abiding search for a grand meaning to his life. Far from wanting to escape from 'meaning' and 'binary thinking', as some commentators have suggested, Michael is in fact profoundly concerned to arrive at a distinctively metaphysical understanding of himself. Near the beginning of the text there is a quietly placed joke on this matter: 'The problem that had exercised him years ago behind the bicycle shed at Huis Norenius, namely why he had been brought into the world, had received its answer: he had been brought into the world to look after his mother' (7). The joke here is that behind the bike sheds most children would not be discovered asking the metaphysical question (the 'why'), they are asking the empirical question (the 'how'): not the why of generation, its meaning, but 'how can I', or, more to the point, 'will you let me?'. Michael K himself continually searches for meaning, and keeps trying to determine what his proper purpose is. When no one on the road offers him a lift, he draws a little lesson from the experience: 'Perhaps, he thought, it was better when one did not have to rely on other people' (24). When he is on the farm for the first time he kills a goat, then begins to regret it: 'The lesson, if there was a lesson, if there were lessons embedded in events, seemed to be not to kill such large animals' (57). When he finds pleasure in watering the earth at sunset he immediately reaches for a metaphysical explanation: 'It is because I am a gardener, he thought, because that is my nature' (59). Watching the girl in the camp who has lost a baby he even starts to project himself into the passage of a *Bildungsroman*:

Is this my education? he wondered. Am I at last learning about life here in a camp? It seemed to him that scene after scene of life was playing itself out before him and that the sense all cohered. He had a presentiment of a single meaning upon which they were converging or threatening to converge, though he did not know yet what that might be.   (89)

Even to the last Michael K is still, just like Josef K in *The Trial*, standing perpetually before the law, waiting for it to descend and announce its arrival: 'Is that the moral of it all, he thought, the moral of the whole story: that there is time enough for everything? Is that how morals come, unbidden, in the course of events, when you least expect them?' (183). I do not, of course, wish to deny that there is also a tendency in Michael K, as in the Hunger Artist, to retreat from the official-sounding, symbol-generating tendencies that we find most insistently in the narration and which build him up into heroic status. He climbs up the mountain at Prince Albert to get away from the Visagie grandson for precisely this reason: 'surely now that in all the world only I know where I am, I can think of myself as lost' (66). But he climbs back down from the mountain again with the explicit fear that 'my story might end' (69) in the chastening air of its complete withdrawal from significance—in which there is nothing but starvation.

As Josef K could have told him, 'there is no mode of living completely outside the jurisdiction of the court'.[26] Instead of setting out its own truth in a rivalrous fashion, Coetzee's text generates an equivocal and playful movement between the serious and the non-serious: it won't play the game any given reader wants it to play, but makes its own 'subversive juridicity', pushing back against the different rules different readers bring to it, trying 'continually though surreptitiously to *revise and recreate*' the reader.[27] To describe the text as telling the truth in its own way is specifically not—in these terms—to make an aestheticist argument for its autonomy: my emphasis has instead been on the complex ways in which Coetzee's writing both evokes and defers finalizing affective constructions upon reality, and opens those constructions to an unsettling contact with otherness. Indeed, when a reader engages with the full anxiety of this experience of 'JOEY RULES' the hope is that the game itself—in this case the alternatives currently available within the cultural field for how we think about heroism—may be changed.

GORDIMER'S 'LASHING'

Recall that Gordimer coupled her attack on the perceived political untruthfulness of *Life & Times of Michael K* with an *ad hominem* attack on Coetzee's 'stately fastidiousness'—his wish, which she deduced from his earlier fiction, 'to hold himself clear of events and their daily, grubby, tragic consequences in which, like everyone else in South Africa, he is up to his neck'. I have suggested that this is at best a limited way of reading the text, and at worst one that holds back, in a self-protective gesture, from its most distinctive and

---

[26] Franz Kafka, *The Trial*, trans. Willa and Edwin Muir (London, 1953), 234.

[27] See J. M. Coetzee, *Giving Offense: Essays on Censorship* (Chicago, 1996) 38.

challenging effects. But what I want to consider is the extent to which the *ad hominem* side of the attack rankled with Coetzee. Compare the attack launched by Milton Appel upon Nathan Zuckerman's fiction, also due to its perceived lack of respect for the affective claims of community, in Philip Roth's *The Anatomy Lesson* (1983): 'Sooner or later there comes to every writer the two-thousand-, three-thousand-, five-thousand-word lashing that doesn't just sting for the regulation seventy-two hours but rankles all his life. Zuckerman now had his: to treasure in his quotable storehouse till he died.'[28] Twelve years after the review of *Life & Times of Michael K*, in an essay that returns to and revises the concept of the novel as 'rival' we find Coetzee discussing the life of Desiderius Erasmus in terms that distinctly recall the terms of Gordimer's 'lashing'. In a section entitled 'Choosing Sides', he explains the following:

Though he first made his name as a critic of clerical worldliness, Desiderius Erasmus found it hard to commit himself to the side of the Lutheran radicals in their conflict with the Papacy. Sympathetic to many of the ideals of reform, he was nevertheless disturbed by the intolerance and inflexibility of the actual reform movement; generally he tried to maintain a distance between his critique of the Church's and Luther's. To the extent that he became involved in the rivalry between the Pope and Luther, his involvement was unwilling. At a personal level he found conflict uncongenial

---

[28] Philip Roth, *The Anatomy Lesson*, in *Zuckerman Bound* (London, 1998) 351. The hostile reading given by Milton Appel to Zuckerman's novel *Carnovsky* in this text bears more than a passing resemblance to Irving Howe's polemical article, 'Philip Roth Reconsidered' (1972), which responded to Roth's *Portnoy's Complaint* (1969). Howe was critical of Roth's failure to remain recognizable as the serious writer his early work promised, and regarded *Portnoy's Complaint* as a betrayal of the Jewish community: 'their history is invoked for the passing of adverse judgement . . . but their history is not allowed to emerge so as to make them understandable as human beings' ('Philip Roth Reconsidered', in Harold Bloom (ed.), *Modern Critical Views: Philip Roth* (New York, 1986) 73). Astonished, dismayed, and hurt that such an intelligent critic could make such a hostile assimilation of his work, the terrible truth eventually dawns on Zuckerman: '*He doesn't find me funny*' (345).

(which is not to say that his reluctance to take sides was merely a matter of temperament: in a deep sense it was political too).[29]

If we grant the parallel between Coetzee and Erasmus, Coetzee here goes so far as to grant the *ad hominem* side to Gordimer's critique, admitting that 'at a personal level he found conflict uncongenial', but adding that the 'reluctance to take sides' was not simply temperamental, but in a 'deep sense . . . political too'. I have already argued in previous chapters that this reluctance to 'take sides' in relation to the different concepts of community important to South Africa's political modernity might be seen as in itself a valuable intervention, and it is not difficult to see how this case for the defence can be argued in relation to heroism too. In a South Africa dominated by powerful political constructions of black identity in heroic struggle, Coetzee's text tentatively opens out onto other ways of perceiving what a hero might be, and does so in a way that is worthwhile and important. After all, is there not a price to pay in understanding the heroic in *exclusively* political terms as (to use Gordimer's phrase) 'the energy of the will'? Is there not a future risk, as well as a high present human cost, in constructing identity around this will-based ideal?[30] Equally, though, it is wrong to suggest that politics in general, and the potent constructions of identity demanded by certain important political formations in 1980s South Africa in particular, should be bypassed in the name of the purely negative freedom that some readers have tried to value as the heroic goal of Michael's life. Truly political 'in a deep sense', Coetzee's equivocal text is opening differently positioned readers to the complex demands of the future: it is a seriously playful response to the demand for national icons.

---

[29] J. M. Coetzee, 'Erasmus: Madness and Rivalry', in *Giving Offense* 83. For more on how this essay informs the way Coetzee tries to position literary discourse, see Ch. 5.

[30] Njabulo Ndebele's short story 'The Test', in *Fools and Other Stories* (Braamfontein, 1983), poses these questions about black political identity in an equally subtle and ironic way.

Why, then, if this is a sound case for the defence, did Gordimer's attack so rankle with Coetzee?

Possibly for the same reasons that Milton Appel's attack on Nathan Zuckerman so infuriated him. While Zuckerman could easily point to the ways in which Appel had travestied his novel *Carnovsky* by tearing particular statements (such as, 'the Jews can stick their historical suffering up their ass') from the carefully qualified literary context they occupy (in this instance, the words were spoken by the angry 14-year-old Carnovsky to his older sister), he also privately doubted whether the text was sufficiently artistically achieved: that is to say, he doubted how successful the text really was at playing the rules—at evoking, yet simultaneously displacing, his readership's inevitable attempts at assimilating it to more familiar patterns of evaluation.[31] How much resistance does *Life & Times of Michael K* really generate to an allegorical reading that regards it as construing the 'truth about heroism' as, for example, a resistance to all ideology, a negative and individualistic ideal of freedom, and a utopian drive back to the land? What if the elaborate attempt to avoid 'taking sides' in the writing actually only masked the mere advocacy of a particular position—a fastidious revulsion towards the black politics of heroism—that everyone but the writer himself could perceive? These are precisely the doubts and fears that inform the explorations made by Coetzee's later work—especially, as I will argue in Chapter 6, *The Master of Petersburg*. As Coetzee describes it through the figure of Erasmus, the act of writing is necessarily vulnerable to this sort of reading, and these self-doubts. The text's exposure to hostile assimilation is even, paradoxically, increased by its success (*Life & Times of Michael K* won the Booker Prize, and established Coetzee's international reputation):

The claims of the little phallus to dubiousness and provisionality dissolve: the little phallus grows, threatens the big phallus, threatens to become a figure of law itself. The more of a success *The Praise of Folly* becomes, the more Erasmus has to disown or play at disowning it: his friend Thomas

---

[31] *The Anatomy Lesson* (London, 1983) 356.

More egged him on to write it, he protests, it is out of keeping with his own real character, it is anyhow a silly book. His attempts fail, or succeed, it is hard knowing which: the more the book amuses some, the more it angers others; the more it is condemned, the more it is read; the more successful Erasmus is at defining a position from which he can comment on power from the outside, the more he is caught up in the play of resentful powers.   (100)

As its international reputation grows, the text grows in importance; interpretations start to accrue to it; it becomes used as evidence for the claims of this side or that. Inevitably, some respond only to the comic side ('the book amuses some'), but others take it deadly seriously, finding in it only the affirmation of already-existing law. If 'JOEY RULES' it does so in a very fragile way indeed, as the critical reception of *Life & Times of Michael K* would appear to suggest. It is necessarily and productively exposed to being read into the terms formulated by other discourses: 'What truth is it telling? What is it saying about how we should live?'—these are after all the fundamental questions that bring readers to the novel.

4

'An author I have not read': *Foe, Crime and Punishment,* and the Problem of the Novel

We have so far considered some of the ways in which Coetzee's writing puts pressure on the novel's processes of representation, and I have placed special emphasis on how the comic energies of his prose are inseparable from the particular type of intervention he aims to make in political debate. But Coetzee's engagement with the form of the novel is not limited to questions of prose style: his next work, *Foe,* deepens his exploration of the origins and legacies of the form, and does so most obviously through its allusive relationship with Defoe's *Robinson Crusoe* and *Roxana.* Due to this co-textuality, *Foe* has often been showcased in the range of commentaries it has attracted as a postcolonial 'writing back' to the canonical works of an imperialist European culture.[1] But before we can even begin to consider the ways in which *Foe* reflects upon how the form of the

---

[1] For instance, Helen Tiffin used *Foe* as an example of what she calls 'post-colonial counter-discourse', whose 'strategies involve a mapping of the dominant discourse, a reading and exposing of its underlying assumptions, and the disman-tling of these assumptions from the cross-cultural standpoint of the imperially subjectified "local"'. Coetzee, she argues, is not 'simply "writing back" to an English canonical text, but to the whole of the discursive field within which such a text operated and continues to operate in post-colonial worlds'. Bill Ashcroft, Gareth Griffiths, and Helen Tiffin (eds.), *The Post-Colonial Studies Reader* (London, 1995) 94–6.

novel intersects with colonialism, we must address a further problem of literary allusion. Despite the substantial body of commentary devoted to examining this novel's relationship to Defoe, the allusions it makes to Dostoevsky's *Crime and Punishment*, at crucial moments in the narrative, have not so far been spotted. The presence of *Crime and Punishment* derives most proximately from Coetzee's contemporaneous literary-critical study of Dostoevsky—another novelist for whom the form of the novel is part of a dubious cultural inheritance from Western Europe.[2]

At the beginning of the third section of *Foe*, when Susan at last rediscovers the elusive novelist 'Mr. Foe', she greets him with the remarks:

'Life is never as we expect it to be. I recall an author reflecting that after death we may find ourselves not among choirs of angels but in some quite ordinary place, as for instance a bath-house on a hot afternoon, with spiders dozing in the corners; at the time it will seem like any Sunday in the country; only later will it come home to us that we are in eternity.'

'It is an author I have not read.'[3]

The author that Mr Foe has 'not read' is Dostoevsky, the novel is *Crime and Punishment*, and the scene alluded to features a character called Svidrigailov taunting Raskolnikov with an ugly glimpse into the nihilistic heart of things:

'You see, we always think of eternity as an idea that can't be comprehended, as something enormous, gigantic! But why does it have to be so very large? I mean, instead of thinking of it that way, try supposing that all there will

---

[2] In *Dostoevsky and the Novel* (Princeton, 1977), Michael Holquist argues that 'Because Russians laboured so long under the fear and shame of not possessing what Sartre called "that proprietor's luxury, a past," they experienced modernity as a state forced upon them by West European historical models that excluded their presence. . . .Dostoevsky is the inheritor of a particular historical tradition, a tradition of radical doubt about history itself' (34). Coetzee's major essay on Dostoevsky is 'Confession and Double Thoughts: Tolstoy, Rousseau, Dostoevsky,' written during 1982–3.

[3] J. M. Coetzee, *Foe* (London, 1986) 113–14.

be is one little room, something akin to a country bath-house, with soot on the walls and spiders in every corner, and there's your eternity for you. You know, I sometimes see it that way.'

'Can you really, really not imagine anything more just and consoling than that?' Raskolnikov exclaimed with a feeling of pain.[4]

What does this vision of a 'bath-house', or 'country bath-house' in Svidrigailov's words, have to do with Susan and Foe, and Defoe for that matter? Of course Dostoevsky is an author Defoe has 'not read': *Crime and Punishment* was published well over a century after his death. It is tempting to pass quietly over this bizarre allusion.

But it won't let itself be forgotten: the allusion reappears at the end of the text in a particularly prominent place—the closing paragraphs of the mysterious section IV. In the first part of this final section an unnamed narrator enters Foe's room, which seems preserved in a timeless stasis, and makes his way over to Friday. At first nothing happens, but then, without further effort, Friday's 'teeth part' and, with mystical resonance, the impossible comes to pass: 'without a breath, issue the sounds of the island' (154). In the second part, the narrator (the same one?) returns to Foe's house in the present day—again mysteriously preserved in a timeless stasis— and finds Susan's account of her time on the island. When he (is it a he?) begins to read he literally descends into her story, and suddenly we are not in Foe's house but in Susan's boat, slipping overboard into the sea. He tries to swim for the island, but is dragged underwater, down to the ocean's floor where lies a wrecked ship: at last we will discover the truth about Friday's origins, the real 'eye of the story' (142). The narrator passes through the sea's preserving dankness, which again seems to be beyond the corrosive processes of time, and presses on into the ship. One door is closed, but with some force 'the wall of water yields', and we gird ourselves for the long-awaited revelation. But our discovery of Susan and Friday is prefaced by an odd and completely uncontextualized remark: this strange

[4] Fyodor Dostoevsky, *Crime and Punishment*, trans. David McDuff (Harmondsworth, 1991) 346.

place, we are told, 'is not a country bath-house'. The ending of *Foe* remains one of the biggest interpretative conundrums of all of Coetzee's writing: we seem to leave the carefully documented world familiar to readers of novels, in which Friday is tongue-less, story-less, and silent, and enter a type of storytelling that operates according to altogether different rules, where Friday mysteriously takes on an expressive power—this is some sort of literary genre in which 'bodies are their own signs'. Any meaningful response will have to take into account the massive and sudden shift in narrative technique; it will also have to ask what is meant by the 'country bath-house'. Dostoevsky is clearly central to whatever is going on at the end of this book about the origins of the English novel.

Coetzee began the composition of *Foe* in 1983; he had worked on a long and extensively researched essay, 'Confession and Double Thoughts: Tolstoy, Rousseau, Dostoevsky,' over 1982–3, and in the extended autobiographical reminiscence that closes *Doubling the Point* Coetzee chose to emphasize the centrality of the 'Confession' essay to his personal development.[5] We are asked to regard the essay as staging an implied debate between 'cynicism' and 'grace': 'Cynicism: the denial of any ultimate basis for values. Grace: a condition in which the truth can be told clearly, without blindness. The debate is staged by Dostoevsky; the interlocutors are called Stavrogin and Tikhon.' In the 'submerged dialogue between two persons' that is said to take place in the essay, Coetzee positions himself in transition between a Stavrogin figure, the cynic who considers 'there is no ultimate truth about oneself, there is no point in trying to reach it, what we call the truth is only a shifting self-reappraisal whose function is to make one feel good', and Tikhon, 'the person I desired to be and was feeling my way toward', whose position is less clearly defined, but which by implication encompasses the 'grace' and faith that Stavrogin lacks. The staging of the debate between these two characters from Dostoevsky's *The*

---

[5] These dates are provided by Coetzee in *Doubling the Point* 392.

Possessed marked, Coetzee claims, a 'pivotal' moment in his career: 'the beginning of a more broadly philosophical engagement with a situation in the world' (*Doubling the Point* 392–4).

Despite this advice, it is hard to read the essay as a debate between 'Stavrogin and Tikhon': to the extent that these terms have any hold at all, the essay would seem more straightforwardly to embody the sort of position Stavrogin might take. Structured as a series of explorations into what it means to tell the truth in autobiographical writing, it focuses on authors who, according to Coetzee, are increasingly dubious about the possibility of ever doing so, or who use means of vouchsafing that truth which now defy credulity. For instance, while Tolstoy is said to have been able to sidestep the labyrinth of sceptical questioning opened up by the self-doubting individual by virtue of having 'acquired the credentials, amassed the authority' to set down the truth without equivocation, the unspoken thought is that no such credentials and authority are available to a white South African writer in the latter half of the twentieth century (293). Rousseau is denigrated as a writer who is largely ignorant of the problems of 'regression to infinity of self-awareness and self-doubt' that beset confessional narrative (274). The high value the essay places on Dostoevsky derives chiefly from the respect earned by the searchingness of his scepticism, and the passages that deal with his novels are chiefly devoted to spotting the few moments where he has fallen back upon unwarrantably metaphysical groundings. For instance, in the reading of *Notes from Underground* Coetzee's interest lies in revealing the 'moments at which the narrator does not understand himself', which catch Dostoevsky short-circuiting his own scepticism by making artistic recourse to the truth-telling powers of the subconscious self.[6]

For all the importance that Coetzee grants the essay, it is therefore difficult to regard it as anything more than a restatement of well-established ground. As we have already seen, Coetzee's early essays

---

[6] The novel is ultimately 'disappointing', Coetzee tells us, 'if we think of it as an exploration of confession and truth', because it unwarrantably introduces a 'lack of *subsequent* censorship at the level of the narrating subject' (278, 281).

on Beckett, especially 'The Comedy of Point of View in Beckett's *Murphy*' (1970), had specifically likened Beckett's scepticism towards the logocentric illusions of the realist novel to the experience undergone by Dostoevsky's Underground Man: Coetzee noted back in 1970 that in both Beckett's *The Unnamable* and Dostoevsky's *Notes from Underground*, 'consciousness of self can be only consciousness of consciousness. Fiction is the only subject of fiction. Therefore, fictions are closed systems, prisons' (38). Curious, then, for him to place such 'pivotal' importance upon this essay, which seems only to take us back to the debates on metafiction and solipsism staged in his early novels. But there is an odd moment in the 'Confession' essay that invites closer scrutiny. Having spelled out the type of narrative impasse *Notes* writes itself into, Coetzee remarks that 'Dostoevsky in *Notes from Underground* has not found a solution to the problem of *how to end the story*, the problem whose solution Michael Holquist rightly identifies as the great achievement of his mature years' (281; Coetzee's italics). A momentous claim: if Dostoevsky is to be admired as a writer properly sceptical of the falsifying illusions of the novel, *how*—without simply reinstalling the novel's unwarrantably logocentric conventions—has he found a way of bringing the regress of self-doubt and misrecognition to a halt? In Coetzee's essay we never actually get the answer—we only get an explanation of how in *The Idiot* even the 'Christlike man', Prince Myshkin, is finally unable to save himself from the sceptical processes Dostoevsky's novel has unleashed upon him (287).

Turning therefore to Michael Holquist's book, *Dostoevsky and the Novel*, we find the first text Holquist singles out as an example of how, in Coetzee's phrase, the mature Dostoevsky finds 'a solution to the problem of *how to end the story*', is *Crime and Punishment*— a novel not discussed in the 'Confession' essay. Holquist's account focuses upon the main interpretative hurdle Dostoevsky's novel poses: the fact that the text explores, for over six hundred pages, the complexities of Raskolnikov's search for the truth of himself and his actions—a search which, by relying exclusively on Raskolnikov's own secular rationalism, opens onto an ever-deeper sceptical regress—only to end with an epilogue that cuts short this process with a mystical revelation. This is Holquist's useful plot-summary:

It is divided into six parts (or books) and an epilogue. In the first part Raskolnikov murders two women; then, in the next five parts, everyone (including Raskolnikov) tries to figure out the crime; in the sixth part Raskolnikov confesses, is tried, and sent to Siberia. In the epilogue he repents of the crime (but only in the second part of the epilogue) and has a mystical experience; the novel ends with the narrator's assertion that 'here begins a new story'.[7]

What Holquist argues is that *Crime and Punishment* has a highly self-conscious metafictional structure: its epilogue, he suggests, brings the novel to a halt not only literally but figuratively, by deploying a fundamentally different literary genre—the wisdom tale—whose origins lie instead deep in the pre-enlightenment past, in religious tradition. It is set outside time, among the 'yurts of the nomad tribesmen', in a place where 'time itself seemed to have stopped, as though the days of Abraham and his flocks had never passed' (628). Whatever it is that happens to Raskolnikov comes to pass in some realm of experience beyond the model of subjectivity hitherto assumed by the novel: there is no self-doubt in this sphere, no time-bound search for cause and effect, no rationalist voice questioning its own motives, but instead a suddenly granted mystical unity of the body and its meaning:

They tried to speak, but were unable to. There were tears in their eyes. Both of them looked pale and thin; but in these ill, pale faces there now gleamed the dawn of a renewed future, a complete recovery to a new life . . . even if he had been able to, he would not have found his way to a solution of these questions in a conscious manner; now he could only feel. In place of dialectics life had arrived, and in his consciousness something of a wholly different nature must now work towards fruition.   (629–30)

Unlike the novel, the wisdom tale does not 'demonstrate a gradual unfolding in horizontal time', but seeks instead to remind us 'of the

---

[7] Michael Holquist, *Dostoevsky and the Novel* (Evanston, Ill., 1977) 75.

cut-off between vertical levels of temporality, man's change and the Gods' stasis' (*Dostoevsky and the Novel* 81–2). Its narrative structure is quite different to that of the novel: hinting at the disparity between the secular type of knowledge available to human reason through causal explanations, it suggests there is a special type of perception that lies beyond this sphere—one that is of necessity mysterious, pointed-towards rather than grasped by the reasoning individual. Dostoevsky's purpose, Holquist argues, is to highlight the limits of the novel's secular realism by juxtaposing it with this pre-modern genre—and his juxtaposition certainly has a powerful effect.[8] In the course of the six 'novelistic' books of *Crime and Punishment*, each attempt Raskolnikov makes to submit himself to interpretation, or to relate himself to other people—particularly his family and his faithful friend Razumikhin—fails. He becomes haunted in the text by a ghostly double, Svidrigailov, the nihilistic image of what he might become. Through a series of frightening encounters with Svidrigailov, of which the vision of eternal emptiness in the country bath-house alluded to in *Foe* by Susan Barton is possibly the most decisive, Raskolnikov comes to realize that he will never be able to reach the truth through his own will and reason: the implication is that all novels end in a version of the hollowed-out Svidrigailov, unless they lie about the type of truth secular reason can tell. Raskolnikov's saga of self-doubt could (the implication runs) continue for another six hundred pages of text, were it not brought to a halt by the wisdom-tale epilogue.[9]

[8] 'All readers of the novel have sensed this disjunction,' Holquist argues, 'many objecting to the forced or tacked-on quality of the ending, usually because they assume Dostoevsky was striving for a conventional narrative homogeneity. But if we assume on the contrary that he seeks to accentuate, to dramatise, the differences between the two parts of the book, the shape of the text assumes another unity' (96).

[9] 'The whole novel is an account of Raskolnikov's various attempts to forge an identity for himself with which he can live... It is only in the epilogue that he discovers the kind of narrative that is properly his own to live: it is not a secular history to which he belongs, but a wisdom tale' (97). Later Holquist suggests, with rhetorical flourish, that 'All of Dostoevsky's mature work would seem... to have

The narrative movement of *Foe* clearly echoes that of *Crime and Punishment*: Susan falls from her initial confidence that the story of herself, Cruso, and Friday can be enclosed in a realist novel, and enters into a state of self-doubt that is truly Svidrigailovian in its nightmarish intensity:

I thought I was myself and this girl a creature from another order speaking words you made up for her. But now I am full of doubt. Nothing is left to me but doubt. I am doubt itself. Who is speaking me? Am I a phantom too? To what order do I belong? And you: who are you? (133).[10]

We pass from this spiralling emptiness, in which—despite Susan's best efforts—Friday remains mute, subject to the infinite regress of fictionality ('I say he is a cannibal and he becomes a cannibal; I say he is a laundryman and he becomes a laundryman. What is the truth of Friday?' (121)) to a different form of literary knowing, one that is 'not a country bath-house'—a very different eternity to that of Svidrigailov's ghostly imaginings. As in *Crime and Punishment*, this is a place where there is a mystical unity between the body and its meaning ('where bodies are their own signs'), and where Friday appears to find a voice distinctively his own. So given all the connections I have now elaborated, what Coetzee is doing with the epilogue would therefore seem clear enough: he is replacing Dostoevsky's essentially religious critique of the novel with a political one. Like Dostoevsky he breaks decisively with the corrosive impasse of the novel, whose method of representation is inadequate to tell the truth of the distinctively 'other' Friday, and he accepts the 'grace' of a new wisdom-tale ending. This is an act of faith for Coetzee: not faith in a higher divine reality, but in the higher political reality of Friday,

been written for no other purpose than to illustrate Lukács's thesis that the novel essentially narrates a search for an autonomous self that ends in failure' (170).

[10] The connection between Susan and the characters from *Crime and Punishment* is reinforced in *Foe* through patterns of imagery around ghosts (38, 51, 59, 64, 87, 132, 139) and spiders (48, 59, 120, 139)—recalling the 'spiders in every corner' of Svidrigailov's eternal bath-house.

the occluded colonial subject. Like Dostoevsky, Coetzee is breaking
with his enlightenment inheritance—an inheritance as alien to South
African soil as to Russian—with a faith in the hermetic difference of
the other.

Such a reading of the ending of *Foe*, while perhaps going some
way to clarifying the mystery of the ending and the puzzle of the
'Confession' essay, in fact aligns tidily with well-established readings
of the text. As we turn to address these readings, it is important
to notice a certain historical irony in the relationship with *Crime
and Punishment*, as from this irony a more disconcerting reading—a
fuller 'anxiety', to recall Blanchot—will start to emerge.[11]

Although, as Michael Holquist argued, Dostoevsky was himself
dubious about the value of the historicist exploration of self and
motive Raskolnikov undergoes prior to his exile in Siberia, in the
critical reception of *Crime and Punishment* it was the six hundred
pages of dissonant self-doubt that won the book its acclaim, while
the ending, in which the generic norms of the novel are both literally
and figuratively brought to an end, was almost universally denigrated—especially by Bakhtin.[12] Holquist draws attention to the
history of discontent with the 'discontinuity' of the epilogue, citing
Philip Rahv's verdict as exemplary of the trend: 'We as critical
readers,' Rahv advised, 'cannot overmuch concern ourselves with
such intimations of ultimate reconcilement and salvation' (96). But
in the literary-critical discussion of Coetzee's *Foe* we find quite the
reverse: the wisdom tale ending of section IV, which explicitly

---

[11] It is worth bearing in mind that in the autobiographical sketch Coetzee is
careful to point out that he has not completed the transition from 'cynicism' to
'grace': this remains, with him, a transition that refuses the 'perfective': 'One is a
person I desired to be and was feeling my way toward. The other is more shadowy:
let us call him the person I then was, though he may be the person I still am'
(*Doubling the Point* 392).

[12] 'We will say only that almost all of Dostoevsky's novels have a *conventionally
literary, conventionally monologic* ending (especially characteristic in this respect is
Crime and Punishment).' M. M. Bakhtin, *Problems of Dostoevsky's Poetics*, trans.
Caryl Emerson (Minneapolis, 1984) 40; see also 92.

parallels that of Dostoevsky's novel, sometimes seems the only thing relevant to literary-critical discussion. Even commentators as distrustful of the metaphysics of presence as Gayatri Chakravorty Spivak celebrate the place 'where bodies are their own signs': 'In this end, the staging of the wish to invade the margin, the seaweeds seem to sigh: if only there were no texts. The end is written lovingly, we will not give it up.'[13] David Attwell goes further: relating the ending of *Foe* to the problems raised by the 'Confession' essay, he argues it represents Coetzee staging an act of authorial self-surrender: 'Friday possesses the key to the closure of the narrative... The ending amounts to a deferral of authority to the body of history, to the political world in which the voice of the body politic of the future resides' (*J. M. Coetzee South Africa and the Politics of Writing* 112–16). In doing so we note that he is reading the ending in precisely the terms of aesthetic judgement Dostoevsky might well have wished for *Crime and Punishment*—albeit in political rather than spiritual terms. The novel is being discarded as a form that leads only to a metafictional sceptical regress—a prison house of fictionality—and a distinctively pre-enlightenment literary genre is held up as the basis of literary value.

I have been suggesting that one important aspect of the intelligence of Coetzee's texts is their ability to predict, elicit, and creatively disorient the assumptions that patterns of literary evaluation bring to bear upon them—and the narrative structure of *Foe* is set up to engender just this kind of creative 'anxiety'. Surely conscious of how the *Crime and Punishment* structure of *Foe* would be read in a contemporary critical climate overtly and overwhelmingly, in South Africa at least, preoccupied with the politics of difference, Coetzee invites readings that affirm 'the home of Friday', but simultaneously introduces an important complication to the Dostoevskian structure that, like the allusion to Dostoevsky himself, critics have

---

[13] Gayatri Chakravorty Spivak, 'Theory in the Margin: Coetzee's *Foe* reading Defoe's Crusoe/Roxana', in Jonathan Arac and Barbara Johnson (eds.), *Consequences of Theory* (Baltimore, 1991) 174.

'not read'. This complication relates to the person being 'saved'. In *Crime and Punishment* the hero of the novel, Raskolnikov, went to Siberia without family or friends—except for the 'holy fool' Sonya—and was, as we have seen, redeemed by a 'new narrative' (630). However in *Foe*, the heroine of the main body of the novel—Susan Barton—is not the one who is saved. From being a bold, self-confident woman pursuing liberty and self-determination in unpropitious circumstances at the beginning of the text, when we discover her in section IV, she—and indeed everyone else but Friday—is deathly silent. The unidentified narrator of the final section makes considerable effort to disguise the fact that 'the home of Friday' is the graveyard of the other characters: 'They lie side by side in bed, not touching. The skin, dry as paper, is stretched tight over their bones. Their lips have receded, uncovering their teeth, so that they seem to be smiling. Their eyes are closed' (153). They may 'seem to be smiling', but look again and see not the smile of living, embodied happiness, but the empty grin of a death's-head: 'the lips have receded, uncovering their teeth'. Read through the lens of literary realism, it is the fake smile of a decomposed skull. Or again in the second part of IV: 'Susan Barton and her dead captain, fat as pigs in their white nightclothes, their limbs extending stiffly from their trunks, their hands, puckered from long immersion, held out in blessing, float like stars against the low roof' (157). It is possible to see only the benediction that Susan appears to be giving; but the 'blessing' she is said to send to Friday, who sits below, is not, again reading through the lens of realism, properly Susan's at all: it is no more than the effect of rigor mortis, the 'limbs extending stiffly' after death. So powerful is the moral and political impulse to extend 'blessing' to Friday, to 'seem to be smiling' in the place that is his 'home', that we easily overlook the reduction of the heroine of the novel—herself a compelling and sympathetic character—to a deathly silence. An awkward thought: the monological 'wisdom tale' narrative processes that give life to Friday are those that put an end to Susan.

What to make of this awkward thought? Let us follow the leads provided by the text itself. Section IV sends us back in a quite literal way to the start of Susan's story and the beginning of *Foe*: we discover her again as she slips out of her boat, 'with a sigh, making barely a splash', to swim for the island; the narrative sends us down into the ship from which she was cast away to find a year's refuge on the island with Cruso (155). In sending us back, it invites comparison to be drawn between the 'home of Friday' in IV and the home of Cruso in I: like the eternal stasis we find in IV, the island is also a place without history, or at least seems so to Susan. 'Wind, rain, wind, rain, such was the pattern of days in that place, and had been, for all I knew, since the beginning of time,' she complains; the flock of sparrows she sees have likewise 'known no harm from man since the beginning of time'; when Friday fails to respond to the death of Cruso she reflects that 'No man had died on his island since the beginning of time' (14, 30, 35). This eternal scene combines with the type of extra-linguistic self-presence that we find in section IV. On the island, when Susan attempts to express herself she is treated as if she were already dead by a self-enraptured Cruso: 'I would have told him more about myself too, about my quest for my stolen daughter, about the mutiny. But he asked nothing, gazing out instead into the setting sun, nodding to himself as though a voice spoke privately inside him that he was listening to' (13). As in IV, there is again a situation in which others (here Cruso) reside in a quasi-mystical embodiment, while Susan's voice goes unheard (here it is self-censored). Likewise we notice that on the island, the 'eternal' is not only something that is found, but something that is maintained, perhaps even produced, to someone's advantage and someone else's cost. When Susan wonders whether it might be possible to make 'a lamp or a candle so that we should not have to retire when darkness fell, like brutes', Cruso bluntly rules out the possibility. She reflects: 'There were many tart retorts I might have made; but, remembering my vow, I held my tongue. The simple truth was, Cruso would brook no change on his island' (27). The aspects of Susan's character readers tend to find most compelling include her determination, her intelligence, and precisely the quick-witted 'tart retorts' we find her self-censoring here: anything that interrupts the stasis of pure, unquestioned being that Cruso has established on the island is silenced with tyrannical force. He is furious when Susan leaves the compound without permission ('While you live under my roof you will do as I instruct!'), and again enraged when Susan dares to make her own pair of shoes (20). She has good cause to speak of his 'unquestioned and solitary mastery' that demands a 'slavish obedience', for Cruso is himself quite clear about her utter irrelevance both to himself and the life of the island: 'I do not wish to hear of your desire', he tells her (25, 20, 36). Just as in section IV, which is 'not a place of words', so is a silence produced on the island, not only through Cruso's own wordless self-communing, but through a deliberate curtailment of the possibilities of language: 'This is not England, we have no need for a great stock of words' (157, 21). Susan's 'bold words' are treated as deviations from an ideal of silence that quite nakedly serves another interest (48).

A disturbing comparison, then—one that troubles a wholeheartedly favourable literary-critical judgement of section IV. Even if the broad parallels I have enumerated between the home of Friday and the home of Cruso were not explicitly written into *Foe*, are we not now, as readers, sufficiently sensitized to the long tradition of appeals for women to be silenced in the name of a greater good to be suspicious of this particular one? 'I would not rob you of your tongue for anything, Susan', Mr Foe assures her (150). But *Foe* does end by robbing Susan of her tongue, in the same moment that it takes leave of the processes of the novel.

We saw in the first chapter, with reference to Habermas's account of the origins of the politics of equal dignity, that there are a cluster of important political and ethical legacies at stake in the form of the realist novel. What I'm going to suggest is that, in its exploration of the origins of the English novel, *Foe* does not let us forget that fact, or the enduring importance of these legacies. As I have begun to suggest, part of the resistance the text makes to a positive valuation of the anti-novelistic epilogue is by presenting an image of an anti-rationalist politics—by characterizing the organization of Cruso's island, and the ethics of Cruso himself, as distinctively anti-enlightenment in their character, and thus hostile to Susan's desire for speech and self-dramatization. Cruso is not only uninterested in deriving a rational understanding of things in general ('he had come to be persuaded he knew all there was to know about the world'), but acts like a tyrant: 'King of his tiny realm', he warns Susan 'not to venture from his castle', and is 'the true king of the island' (13, 14, 15, 37). Defoe's Robinson Crusoe of course jokes to himself about his lordship of the desert island, but such thoughts remain at the level of jest—he is in fact continually engaged in consulting the abstract dictates of rationality (which he thinks of as Divine Providence) in a way that Coetzee's Cruso would not permit for a moment.[14] As an enlightened subject, Susan wants to know what the laws of the island are, and how they are enforced upon recalcitrant individuals through systems of discipline ('How do you punish Friday, when you punish him?' she asks of Cruso (37)). But the island is not governed by a system of law, in which difference can be resolved rationally in the public sphere; rather, it is one in which power is embodied symbolically in an individual: 'One evening, seeing him as he stood on the Bluff with the sun behind him all red and purple, staring out to sea, his staff in his hand and his great conical hat on his head, I thought: He is a truly kingly figure' (37). This lack of rational governance horrifies Susan ('It seemed to me that all things were possible on the island, all tyrannies and cruelties, though in small'), her objection to Cruso's mystique of power mirroring that made by John Locke, just under thirty years before the publication of *Robinson Crusoe,* in *Two Treatises of Government* (1690). In this seminal formulation of the enlightenment state, political governance is grounded in a set of abstract rational principals based on individual rights, instead of the traditional symbolic orders of Church, family, and King.

The importance of Susan's politics within *Foe* lies in the way that her ideals of rationality and rights for the individual are bound

---

[14] See John J. Richetti, *Defoe's Narratives: Situations and Structures* (Oxford, 1975) for an account of how *Robinson Crusoe* sets about blending the empirical with the Providential.

up with the form of the novel itself. As Ian Watt argues in *The Rise of the Novel*:

The modern novel is closely allied on the one hand to the realist epistemology of the modern period, and on the other to the individualism of its social structure... Defoe, whose philosophical outlook has much in common with that of the English empiricists of the seventeenth century, expressed the diverse elements of individualism more completely than any other previous writer, and his work offers a unique demonstration of the connection between the rise of individualism in its many forms and the rise of the novel.[15]

Clearly these are contentious claims, but for present purposes it suffices to know that in a 1997 interview, Coetzee affirmed, *en passant*, that he was in broad agreement with Watt's account:

There's a good deal of truth in the account of realism—in England, at any rate—that situates it within the rise of the middle class. As you know, the famous book is the one by Ian Watt, *The Rise of the Novel*. It dates from the 1950s, and has been queried on details, sometimes large details, but as long as one doesn't generalize too far from the group of novelists Watt was writing about, I think its outlines remain very firm.[16]

Watt states the issue in the broadest terms, but we can phrase it more precisely by examining Susan's own ideas on how stories should be told. She is appalled by Cruso's style of storytelling, which, in contrast to her own meticulous observance of detail, reeks of old fireside romance adventure. His tales of his past life have so little respect for detail, and are so contradictory, that Susan is forced to conclude that they have no literary value at all: 'in the end I did not know what was truth, and what was lies, and what was mere rambling' (12). In the name of the sanctity of the individual, she urges him to reconstruct the story of his life in the manner the literary tradition later came to call 'realism' and associate with the novel:

---

[15] Ian Watt, *The Rise of the Novel* (London, 1957) 62.
[16] Joanna Scott, 'Voice and Trajectory: An Interview with J. M. Coetzee', *Salmagundi* 114–15 (Spring/Summer, 1997) 97–8.

Seen from too remote a vantage, life begins to lose its particularity. All shipwrecks become the same shipwreck, all castaways become the same castaway, sunburnt, lonely, clad in the skins of the beasts he has slain. The truth that makes your story yours alone, that sets you apart from the old mariner by the fireside spinning yarns of sea-monsters and mermaids, resides in a thousand touches which today seem of no importance.

As well as another denigration of the romance mode we have here the demand that in good storytelling there must be some kind of movement between any allegorical 'meaning' the story might seek to enclose (in which 'all castaways become the same castaway') and the concrete experience that marks out Cruso's particular truth.[17] We might also note that this variety of storytelling produces, in Susan's evangelizing at least, a more active and individualist Cruso than the one she discovers on the island—one who lives in history with an eye on the future, who 'paced about in his apeskin clothes, scanning the horizon for a sail' (18).

Susan's notion of storytelling is thus quite clearly at once a politics and an aesthetics: her enlightenment politics of an abstract rational law to which the particular individual must submit is mirrored in her realist aesthetics of an abstract universalizing meaning being continually verified by, or embodied within, the individual instance: 'a thousand touches which today seem of no importance'. The aesthetic process of the literary genre she advocates—a process that combines together the rational and the sensual, the abstract and the concrete—will (she hopes) issue in a Cruso that, as we can surmise, would be much more akin to Defoe's realist hero than the man we find in the pages of *Foe*, one more intent on finding the abstract dictates of reason working its way through what seem the most resolutely empirical facts. Accordingly it is a genre that the tyrannical and unenlightened Cruso in *Foe* rejects with 'a look full of defiance',

---

[17] Recall the two divergent descriptions of the relationship between materiality and allegory in 'Realism'. Susan's is closer to the first: 'Supply the particulars, allow the significations to emerge of themselves. A procedure pioneered by Daniel Defoe' (*Elizabeth Costello* 4).

the same type of look with which he will continue to refuse Susan's desires (18). With so much of the political and ethical legacy of the enlightenment at stake in Susan, or at least in the idea of storytelling that Susan represents and advocates, it is, I suggest, at least with increased reluctance and doubt that we might celebrate the ending of *Foe*—in which the chief literary form of the politics of equal dignity is cast aside in a sweeping gesture towards difference. In fact, regardless of whether any given reader shares these reservations on an intellectual level, they are enforced by the emotive schema of the novel—for Coetzee has rather mischievously linked the enlightenment story of individualistic self-determination *not* (as one might expect from prior knowledge of *Robinson Crusoe*) with the white male but with the 'more sympathetic' feminine subjectivity of Susan. Although we have many reasons to distrust the realist novel's metaphysical underpinnings, *Foe* in fact challenges us, through the sympathetic character of Susan, to register the value of, and the values of, the novel: its commitment to a sphere in which the individual can emerge to insist upon the equal value of her own humanity against those who wish to silence her: 'I am a free woman,' as Susan claims, 'who asserts her freedom by telling her story according to her own desire' (131). To put this same thought in another way: as Coetzee argued in a later essay, there may be certain 'fictions of dignity'— fictions of human rationality, fictions that recognize the equal freedom of all individuals—that are so constitutively important that a truly just society would be unimaginable without them.[18] And as *Foe* reminds us, the novel, as a cultural artefact, has played, and continues to play, its part in instilling these necessary fictions.

---

[18] 'Affronts... to the dignity of our persons are attacks not upon our essential being but upon constructs—constructs by which we live, but constructs nevertheless. This is not to say that affronts to innocence or dignity are not real affronts, or that the outrage with which we respond to them is not real, in the sense of not being sincerely felt. The infringements are real; what is infringed, however, is not our essence but a foundational fiction to which we more or less wholeheartedly subcribe, a fiction that may well be indispensable for a just society, namely, that human beings have a dignity that sets them apart from animals and consequently protects them from being treated like animals'. *Giving Offense* 14.

But before we get carried away in praise of the realist novel, let us bring Friday back to mind. We still haven't answered the question as to why Susan and Friday appear to be so at odds: why does Friday seem to stand in the way of Susan's attempt to tell her story as a 'free woman'? I'm going to answer this question by paying close attention to the opening pages of *Foe*. What I want to suggest now is that, as the story of *Foe* unfolds, what it unfolds is a more nuanced judgement of the novel as a literary genre both deeply compelling and deeply dubious.

On the first page of the text, Susan describes how she 'lay sprawled on the hot sand', exposed somewhat erotically to the sun ('my petticoat (which was all I had escaped with) baking dry upon me'), but above all 'grateful, like all the saved' (5). Susan's claim here is important: to say she is 'saved' is surely to imply not only that she has been washed up on the island by wholly empirical tidal forces, but that some higher force—like the Providence that Defoe's Crusoe is so eager to attribute to the details of island life—has 'saved' her. This is, to say the least, an interpretation of events— an allegory that sits on top of them, as yet rather uncomfortably. In the paragraph that follows, the allegory of Providence tries to implicate itself more subtly within the mere facts of what happens: 'A dark shadow fell upon me, not of a cloud but of a man with a dazzling halo about him. "Castaway," I said with my thick dry tongue. "I am cast away. I am all alone." And I held out my sore hands.' It is a well-worked piece of literary realism—characteristic of the best effects of this genre. At the level of sheer fact it is crystalline: the man's head moves in front of the sun, thus making his own features invisible to Susan, who is looking up into brightness: all she can see, looking into the 'orange blaze' of the bright sunlight, is a blankness where the man's head is assumed to be, and a shimmer of light around it: 'dazzling halo' is perfect. Even more perfect when we appreciate how tactfully 'dazzling halo' enforces the allegory of Providence that is trying to weave its way into the fabric of things: the man who has at the level of fact simply stepped in front of the sun to get a better look at Susan is at the level of value subtly elevated into one of Providence's angels, sent to rescue her. But then we have a shock, and an interpretative crisis. The man 'squatted down beside me', and now out of the sun's glare (again, the meticulous observance of 'a thousand touches' at the level of fact) he is suddenly not an angel but noticeably 'black: a Negro with a head of fuzzy wool'. This face does not glide easily into the allegory of Providence, but calls for a more considered interpretation: 'I lifted myself and studied the flat face, the small dull eyes, the broad nose.' Providence dissolves on the surface of Friday's face and is replaced by another allegory—an equally well-worn set of meanings centring on race: 'At his side he had a spear. I have come to the wrong island, I thought, and let my head sink: I have come to an island of cannibals.'

As Susan and Friday walk away from the beach, she treads on a thorn and cannot walk. Friday (here as yet only 'the Negro') offers to take her on his back: 'So part-way skipping on one leg, part-way riding on his back, with my petticoat gathered up and my chin brushing his springy hair, I ascended the hillside, my fear of him abating in this strange backwards embrace' (6). What now is the meaning working its way into these strange facts? Friday slips out of the cannibal allegory ('my fear of him abating') and tantalizingly evokes another allegory relating to the 'white man's burden'—but with the terms outrageously reversed! And what are we to make of the sexual frisson of the encounter—the 'petticoat gathered up', the 'embrace'? In fact Friday never settles into any of the interpretative models that Susan's realist storytelling extends to him. A couple of pages later the Friday of the disturbingly indeterminate 'strange embrace' has become, more safely, 'my porter', but only after an equally disturbing aesthetic mis-encounter with the island itself (8). As she is carried by Friday to the top of the island, Susan is dismayed that what she sees does not resemble the kind of place produced by the genre of 'traveller's tales', stories which conjure up 'soft sands and shady trees where brooks run to quench the castaway's thirst and ripe fruit falls into his hand, where no more is asked of him than to drowse the days away till a ship calls to fetch him home' (7). Whereas in 'traveller's tales' the castaway finds a benign island, whose every detail seems to bespeak the destined character of his experience in the fulfilment of the higher workings of reason, the island on which Susan finds herself is 'quite another place'. It will be only by an act of willed interpretative violence that this unpropitious place—'dotted with drab bushes', giving off 'a noisome stench', full of 'swarms of large pale fleas', literally covered in excrement ('the rocks were white' with guano)—might be made to bespeak a meaning. This problem of bringing Friday and the island into a broader interpretative framework that can be recognized as rational and benign only intensifies during Susan's year as a castaway. For a time, when she sees Friday rowing out to sea to perform his mysterious scattering of the petals, she is overjoyed, as he seems at a stroke to become more amenable to the model of her narrative: 'This casting of the petals was the first sign I had that a spirit or a soul—call it what you will—stirred beneath that dull and unpleasing exterior' (32). But later, in the second part of *Foe*, she is forced to admit that the mystery of the scattering of the petals, along with the mystery of Cruso's bizarre terraces, the mystery of Friday's mutilated mouth, the mystery of his 'submission', and finally the mystery of why Friday appears not to desire her sexually all resist the meaningfulness she wishes to bring to them (83–6).

What is it that is stopping the very style of the realist novel in its tracks, preventing its narrative processes from building up an embodiment of the truth, and making it seem an ever more dubious endeavour? In *Foe* there is no mistaking that the recalcitrance of these elements of Susan's experience, most especially the figure of Friday himself, is due to material forces—the blunt and crude workings of money, violence, and power: '"It is a terrible story," I said. A silence fell. Friday took up our utensils and retired into the darkness. "Where is the justice in it? First a slave and now a castaway too. Robbed of his childhood and consigned to a life of silence. Was Providence sleeping?"' (23). Cruso sardonically observes that Providence appears to be awake only in certain parts of the world: 'If Providence were to watch over all of us . . . who would be left to pick the cotton and cut the sugar cane?' Susan has frequent cause to draw contrast between the England she knows and Cruso's island: a Patagonian would be comfortable on the island, an Englishwoman certainly is not; Britain is an island, but a geographically stable one, unlike Cruso's; Cruso would be 'tight-lipped and sullen in an alien England' (15, 26, 35). In an England with a developed (or, in Susan's day, developing) bourgeois public sphere, the bodies of its subjects are more easily reconciled to a benign rational order—although the lack of major working-class heroes in the history of the novel testifies to the limits of the English novel's socio-political reach.[19] But out in the colonies, as literary realism sets to work on the opaque body of Friday, and the stubbornly hostile geography of the island, it seems either destined to fail, or to become more and more nakedly the exercise of power—a falsifying transcendence of material inequalities that require political redress. Susan describes her story as a 'relation' (12), and it is certainly an attempt to 'relate' herself to Friday, to fashion him into a novelistic subjectivity like herself; but as her writing lapses into 'long issueless colloquies', she becomes ever more conscious of the power she may unwittingly be serving (78). Even at the end of part I, when she is confident that the sailors who come to take them back to England are 'friends, not foes', she acknowledges that Cruso, who 'struggled to be free' as the sailors hauled him onto the ship, 'was a prisoner, and I, despite myself, his gaoler'; later she will be forced to face the uncomfortable notion that 'he has the last word who disposes over the greatest force' (41, 43, 124). It is, however, to her credit, a force she is never prepared to use: 'I will not have any lies told', she demands, and remains true to that demand, even at enormous personal cost (40).

Susan herself quite explicitly comes to see that no one, not even Mr Foe with his superior artistry, can aestheticize the mute

---

[19] See Bruce Robbins, *The Servant's Hand: English Fiction from Below* (New York, 1986) for an analysis of the disruptive effects of working-class subjects in the novel.

and enslaved body of Friday into a shared rational vision of things. Or at least, that to do so would be a lie, the crude exercise of power: 'I ask myself what past historians of the castaway state have done—whether in despair they have not begun to make up lies' (88). In fact, Susan's own view as to what it is that constrains the telling of 'The Female Castaway' changes over the course of *Foe* as her appreciation of the problems of the novelist grows in sophistication. At first she considers these problems to be merely stylistic, and related to her own lack of literary technique; later on she realizes that the style of the realist novel itself, in its continual attempt to reconcile the particular with the universal, itself constitutes a problem of content, as far as Friday is concerned. His mutilated body and the enslaved geographies of the colonial world are what most resist the novel, driving Susan's story ever further into the ghostly depths of fictionality, and she comes to recognize that the fault is not Foe's: 'Might not Foe be a kind of captive too?', she asks (151).

The main energies of *Foe* are therefore devoted to complicating, both in literary and political terms, what we mean by 'the foe'. The text won't let us join together as 'friends' to decide the issue—instead, it hunts out ways of tripping up our judgement, and in so doing, of keeping divergent political impulses, and divergent sympathies, in a productive tension. Mr Foe tells Susan that 'In a life of writing books, I have often, believe me, been lost in a maze of doubting' (135): Coetzee complicates the problem of narrative posed by *Crime and Punishment* by splitting the heroes of the novel and the wisdom tale into the occluded female subject and the occluded racial subject respectively, thereby restricting the power of political imperatives to decide where literary value lies, and leading readers into the problem the novel itself poses. How might the realist tradition respond when confronted by Friday? What conviction can it carry? What would be lost in political and ethical terms if the cultural processes engendered by the novel were to be discarded? Or perhaps most tellingly—what kind of status can Susan's literary genre find in a world in which it is ever harder to pretend its story can be told without also telling the story of Friday? By creating a text through which these questions must be kept in play, *Foe* refuses to allow its readers to 'sail across the surface and come ashore none the wiser, and resume our old lives, and sleep without dreaming, like babes' (141).

5

Genre and Countergenre: *Age of Iron,* *Pamela,* and *Don Quixote*

> A fool introduced by the author for purposes of 'making strange' the world of conventional pathos may himself, as a fool, be the object of the author's scorn. The author need not necessarily express a complete solidarity with such a character. Mocking these figures as fools may even become paramount. But the author needs the fool.
>
> Mikhail Bakhtin, 'Discourse in the Novel'.[1]

One of the central claims I have been making about Coetzee's fiction is that it tries to hold open, and bring about dialogue between divergent ideas about what makes for a good community. Moreover, I have argued that this stance towards politics is incommensurate with the stance towards literary truth-telling that Coetzee defined as 'rivalry': a text that tries to cultivate an anti-foundational form of thinking cannot also be one that is 'prepared to work itself out outside the terms of class conflict, race conflict, gender conflict, or any other of the oppositions out of which history and the historical disciplines erect themselves', or that lays claim to the cultural privilege of what Coetzee called an 'autonomous place' in doing so.[2] Instead, if we recall our discussion of *Life & Times of Michael K,* it must be a text in which 'JOEY RULES': I have argued that the

---

[1] M. M. Bakhtin, *The Dialogic Imagination,* ed. Michael Holquist, trans. Caryl Emerson and Michael Holquist (Austin, 1981) 404.

[2] See Ch. 3.

disorienting serio-comic movement of Coetzee's prose style attempts to create a space of difference and deferral that plays with the different 'rules' readers bring to the text, and that tests the limits of what those rules have defined as, to use Beckett's phrase, 'beside the point'.

In the texts we have considered so far, the alterity at stake in this serious play has often been staged in racially marked terms: recall the Barbarian Girl, or Friday himself, who both possessed an 'unreadable' body, and who both generated an effect akin to Beckett's Worm upon characters who wished to draw them into some form of equal recognition. But this is not the case in *Age of Iron*. This text portrays a historical situation dominated by two competing forms of a difference-based politics: there is the apartheid regime, whose thin veneer of enlightenment institutions masks a radical refusal of equal recognition to the majority of the population. On the other hand, the text portrays a fractured black family whose lives are dominated by the need to resist this regime, and who have developed a strong and exclusionary form of communal identity to do so. Taking a lonely stand against both these forms of politics is the protagonist, Elizabeth Curren. Saving her strongest criticism for the apartheid state itself, she is nonetheless also critical of the black revolutionaries on grounds that can be described most broadly as liberal and humanitarian. She thinks they are wrong to use children in the struggle, wrong to rule out any recognition of her own sympathetic identification with their situation, and wrong to violate what she regards as the normal forms of privacy and human civility. Yet for a liberal-minded reader one of the most discomfiting aspects of the novel is the way in which Elizabeth's voice is pointedly ignored, both by the South African police she encounters and by the black people she knows, and is without any practical influence at all on the events that unfold around her. As Coetzee put it in an interview, Elizabeth 'speak[s] from a totally untenable historical position'; in the South Africa of the 1980s, she is truly 'beside the point'.[3] Moreover, unlike Friday or the Barbarian Girl Elizabeth doesn't even have the virtue

---

[3] *Doubling the Point* 250.

of being *compellingly* or *interestingly* 'other'. To most of the characters in *Age of Iron* she is just an old woman who can't be taken seriously.

What, then, are we as readers being asked to make of Elizabeth's 'totally untenable historical position'? Coetzee is obviously sufficiently interested in this 'position' to write about it at length—so is he suggesting that Elizabeth is telling important truths we ought in fact take seriously, and which the other characters in the novel are wrong to ignore? Several commentators have suggested we should take Elizabeth very seriously indeed, and have tended to base this judgement on a quite different assessment of the nature of Elizabeth's 'position', and also on a particular feeling for how she is presented in Coetzee's text. Derek Attridge's reading, for instance, emphasizes her heroism: not her physical heroism, for she does not join in the political struggle in any literal way, but the seriousness with which her ethical response to the otherness of Vercueil and the political commitment of the black revolutionaries is presented by Coetzee. Defining the ethical in Levinasian terms as an 'always contextualised responsiveness, and responsibility, to the other', in contrast to the 'generalisations, programs, and predictions' that constitute the political (105), Attridge argues that 'For Mrs Curren, and by implication for J. M. Coetzee...the ethical appears...as the difficult task of responding with full justice to the moment, with a trust in the other and the future that is ultimately beyond measure' (110). However, in reading *Age of Iron* in this way, it is important to notice that Attridge effectively puts the text in the position of what Coetzee called aesthetic 'rivalry'. His claim is that *Age of Iron* affirms, through its portrayal of Elizabeth Curren, a set of values and behaviours that are marked as 'the ethical', and that are implicitly superior to 'the political', which Attridge describes as a predominantly instrumental discourse of 'generalisations, programs and predictions'.

In this chapter I will make two main points, both of which will suggest different ways of approaching this complex text. First I will argue that we should not regard Elizabeth as an allegorical figure for an ethical position that can be identified with Coetzee himself, or that otherwise has authority. Instead, I will show that the text invites us to regard her as a character that is giving voice, most literally, to a politics—to the core assumptions and values of a universalistic politics of equal dignity. I will emphasize this point by showing that Coetzee's text allusively links Elizabeth to the origins of the English novel, most especially to the epistolary novel of Samuel Richardson (she is writing a rather grandiose epistle herself, which makes up the text of *Age of Iron*), and that Elizabeth thereby embodies the intellectual and emotive legacies closely intertwined with the 'novel of sensibility' that Richardson pioneered for English letters. My second point will relate to the particular way Elizabeth is presented in Coetzee's text, and will thereby bring us to the question of how seriously to take her 'totally untenable historical position'. In line with my broader ongoing argument, I will show that *Age of Iron* is neither asserting Elizabeth's position as superior to that of the politics of difference, nor suggesting that she should be ignored: instead the main energies of this text are devoted to a creatively 'jocoserious' play with the rules and boundaries put in place by each of these forms of politics. The term 'jocoserious', which Coetzee borrows from Joyce, appears in his 1992 essay 'Erasmus: Madness and Rivalry'—an essay deeply connected to the spirit and purpose of *Age of Iron*.[4] Reflecting upon the complex ways in which *The Praise of Folly* negotiates its own historical situatedness, Coetzee here attempts to outline the seemingly impossible idea of a 'nonposition', which involves the elaboration of a series of unstable ironies around the figure of the fool. The 'power' of such a text, Coetzee explains, lies not in the strength of any alternative it is asserting, but 'in its weakness—its jocoserious abnegation of big-phallus status, its evasive (non)position inside/outside the play' (103).[5]

---

[4] See *Ulysses: the 1922 Text*, ed. Jeri Johnson (Oxford, 1993) 629.

[5] Although Coetzee is now formulating these ideas about the creative 'weakness' of the literary in his own critical discourse, they have long been implicit in his

Likewise, *Age of Iron* makes no 'big-phallus' assertion of the political values that Elizabeth Curren (and thus the 'novel of sensibility') brings to bear upon South Africa of the 1980s. The text refuses to position itself as a 'rival' form of truth-telling, but instead offers itself jocoseriously as a disorienting and anti-foundational type of play within the cultural field. In fact, what I am going to suggest more specifically is that Coetzee's presentation of Elizabeth explicitly parallels the way in which another great Erasmian, Miguel de Cervantes, presented what was in his day the equally 'untenable' genre of the chivalric romance. Both Elizabeth Curren and Don Quixote are old-fashioned fools confronting a reality that, conceived metafictionally in terms of literary genre, has no time for them and their assumptions; both texts are a site upon which one outdated and untenable genre collides with what Claudio Guillen, with *Don Quixote* in mind, refers to as a 'countergenre'.[6] It is by playing with the Quixotic figure of the fool, in a continual movement between the comic and the serious, that Coetzee's text makes its own quite singular negotiation of the demands made upon the genre of the novel by the age of iron it occupies.

---

fiction: recall the discussion of Beckett's Worm in Ch. 2, whose 'only strength, that he understands nothing, can't take thought, doesn't know what they want, doesn't know they are there, feels nothing'—and the particular ways in which Coetzee incorporated the silence and vulnerability of Worm into his presentation of cultural difference.

[6] With regard to the relation between picaresque and romance in *Don Quixote*, Guillen argues that '"negative" impacts or *influences à rebours*, through which a norm is dialectically surpassed (and assimilated) by another, or a genre by a countergenre, constitute one of the main ways in which a literary model acts upon a writer' ('Genre and Countergenre: The Discovery of the Picaresque', *Literature as System: Essays Toward the Theory of Literary History* (Princeton, 1977) 146–7). I do not want to describe Coetzee's text in terms of a dialectical surpassing, but Guillen's terms (and his analysis of *Don Quixote*) are nonetheless very helpful in considering the conflict over the genre of the novel in *Age of Iron*—a self-consciously Cervantian text.

ELIZABETH CURREN AND THE CURREN(T)
STATUS OF THE NOVEL

We know Coetzee was thinking about *Don Quixote* around the time he began composition of *Age of Iron*. His Jerusalem Prize Lecture (1987) draws attention to the address given two years previously by Milan Kundera, which 'gave tribute to the first of all novelists, Miguel Cervantes' (98), and emphasized the value of the novel as a form able to challenge the intolerant certainties of history. Kundera, of course, had the totalizing political systems of Central and Eastern Europe in the Cold War years very much in mind; Coetzee, however, complained that he was constrained from joining Kundera in an equivalent tribute to the legacy of Cervantes. The writer in Africa, he adverted, unlike the writer in Europe, cannot draw upon those resources at once aesthetic and ethical that are, as Kundera put it, 'being held safe as in a treasure chest in the history of the novel' (164). The precise terms of the reasons he gives are interesting: Coetzee described the form of the novel as 'too slow, too old-fashioned, too indirect to have any but the slightest and most belated effect on the life of the community or the course of history,' implying that for the writer in South Africa, the type of truths the novel might be able to tell are as old-fashioned and irrelevant as the chivalric romance was in the days of Alonso Quixano. For a South African writer to embrace the novel as a serious alternative to 'history' is just as fantastical and doomed to ignominious failure as Alonso's embrace of the chivalric romance.

The relation of this address to *Age of Iron* will become clear if we reflect for a moment upon Cervantes' comic masterpiece. Alonso read many romances before madness overcame him, but took as his main literary model *Amadís de Gaula* (1508) by Garcí Rodriguez de Montalvo. According to Stephen Gilman, while the chivalric romance form of the *Amadís* was still popular by the beginning of the seventeenth century, when Cervantes began to compose *Don*

Quixote, its popularity 'resembled that of western romances shortly after the disappearance of [the US] frontier' (4), which is to say that it spoke, in grandest terms, of the values and imperatives of the Spain of the *reconquista*, completed by the conquest of Granada in 1492, over a hundred years before. Changed times had produced a literary reaction to romance in the form of the picaresque, first with the anonymous novella *Lazarillo de Tormes* (1554), and then with the instant success and wide publication of Mateo Aleman's *Guzman de Alfarache* (1599): this genre effectively turned the idealism of romance on its head by replacing the questing knight with a base-born observer, whose role was to portray everything that was hateful and dismaying about humankind from his 'dog's-eye' view of the world.[7] Gilman emphasizes the ways in which *Don Quixote* invites a metafictional reading as a 'collision of genres' between the Quixotic idealism of the old romance form, and the cruder, more prosaic realism of the new picaresque, which the deluded and hapless Alonso repeatedly encounters, and which defeats him every time: Cervantes requires the reader to recognize his hero as the parodic incarnation of a moribund (if still much loved) literary genre. Both Amadís de Gaula and Don Quixote are advanced in years, but whereas Amadís is miraculously free from the effects of ageing, Quixote is a worn-out old man; instead of Amadís's fair and noble steed, Quixote has an old nag, Rocinante (which translates roughly as 'workhorse previously'); instead of his deeds winning respect and admiration, Quixote is forced to observe that he does not occupy the age of chivalry, or as he terms it, quoting Hesiod, the 'golden age', but is instead faced with an 'age of iron', an age in which his values and his genre have no hold: 'Friend Sancho, you must know, that, by the will of heaven, I was born in this age of iron, to revive in it that of gold, or, as people usually express it, "the golden age".' If the reference to Rocinante did not suggest the

---

[7] Cervantes was later to write a parody of the genre, *Dialogue of the Dogs*, literalizing this metaphor by featuring two dogs as *picaros*, worrying about whether the fact of their 'dogness' was affecting their good judgement of the social scene they observed.

relation between the Cervantes' *Don Quixote* and Coetzee's *Age of Iron* (Elizabeth jokingly describes her decrepit Hillman car as 'willing but old, like Rocinante' (18)), then Quixote's repeated invocations of the 'age of iron' he occupies of course must.[8] Elizabeth drives out in her own 'Rocinante' to confront the new reality that by turns ignores and despises her, just as Quixote sallies out on Rocinante to confront his 'age of iron', the new and crudely material world of the picaresque, which mocks and bewilders him. Like Quixote, Elizabeth is not only a 'fossil from the past' (72), but 'a dodo'—moreover, by her own reckoning 'the last of the dodos' (28). The difference between these two dodos is that whereas Quixote wished to return the present age of iron to an age of gold, the age in which his genre of chivalric romance was more meaningful, Elizabeth wishes to return to a newer age, an age in fact opened up by the story of Alonso Quixano himself in 1605. This is what she calls 'the age of clay' or 'the age of earth' (50), an age in which things are not fixed and certain, but malleable and open to doubt. It is the age in which individuals and the importance of their ethical experience rose to pre-eminence in literature: Kundera's age of the novel.

Just as any reading of *Don Quixote* that aims to appreciate Cervantes' Erasmian play with the institution of literature in seventeenth-century Spain depends upon the reader's skill in being able to recognize the hero as the embodiment of a moribund and old-fashioned—if nonetheless much loved—literary genre, so does a reading that wishes truly to take the measure of *Age of Iron* depend upon the reader's ability to recognize Elizabeth Curren as a throwback, a fool stuck in a bygone age, a museum piece, or even 'a museum that ought to be in a museum' (190)—not 'Curren(t)' at all. Coetzee fashions her as a heroine from the form of the epistolary novel, 'a fossil from the past' (72) if ever there was one, which is as soft a target for critics of the novel's claim to cultural authority as was the chivalric romance for Cervantes: 'too slow,

---

[8] There are repeated references to Alonso Quixano's regret that he occupies an 'age of iron': see especially 77, 142, 151, 481.

too old-fashioned, too indirect' to be considered a serious rival to the ways of knowing and being now in the ascendant.

But before exploring why Coetzee and Cervantes choose to make fools of their heroes, and pair them up with clowns, it is important to take the measure of just how truly Quixotic Elizabeth Curren is, how rich in patent absurdity her discourse can at times be in its African context. I am not simply referring to the more comic aspects of her nostalgia, although this certainly does include the downright absurd:

> I have a vision of Esther Williams, of plump girls in flowered bathing costumes swimming in effortless backstroke formation through sky-blue, rippling waters, smiling and singing. Invisible guitars strum; the mouths of the girls, bows of vivid scarlet lipstick, form words. What are they singing? Sunset... Farewell... Tahiti. Longing sweeps through me for the old Savoy bioscope, for tickets at one and four pence in a currency gone forever, melted down save for a few last farthings in my desk drawer. (27)[9]

But this hankering after the gaudiest cultural vestiges of a bygone age, comparable to Quixote's mooning after the days when scantily clad aristocratic ladies played at being shepherdesses in the pastures, is only the tip of the iceberg. The foundationary *Amadís de Gaula* of the epistolary novel is Samuel Richardson's *Pamela* (1740), and a great many outdated ideas are carried over from this 'old fossil' of high sensibility straight into Elizabeth's letters. Perhaps primary amongst the follies is her mystified belief in the privileged status of epistolary communication as an especially direct and honest form, capable of literally embodying the heroine's feelings. Pamela claims she can vouch for the truth of her writing unproblematically, because 'tho' I don't remember all I wrote, yet I know I wrote my Heart', and can maintain to her parents that the presence of her letters literally

---

[9] Just as Alonso's historical loss coincides with the end of the age of the *reconquista* and the decline of Spain's overseas empire (see *The Novel According to Cervantes* 77), so does Elizabeth's with the decline of the era of English liberalism.

make up for her absence: 'I know you divert yourselves at Nights with what I write,' she claims, for no other reason than 'because it is mine'. Symbolically, she keeps her letters hidden on her body, either stuffed into her bosom or sewn into her clothes, as if they really were a physical part of her.[10] Such a faith in the privileged status of epistolary discourse is maintained by 'J.B.D.F.', the author of the epistle dedicatory, who claims that the form deployed grants an unmediated access to 'the fair Writer's most secret Thoughts', and that as such, 'the several Passions of the Mind must, of course, be more affectingly described, and Nature may be traced in her undisguised Inclinations with much more Propriety and Exactness, than can possibly be found in a Detail of Actions long past' (5). Disconcerting to find Elizabeth maintaining exactly the same mystified nonsense: 'day by day', she claims, 'I render myself into words and pack the words into the page like sweets... Words out of my body, drops of myself, for her to unpack in her own time, to take in, to suck, to absorb' (9). These words certainly are 'old-fashioned drops', and this outdated idea of incarnate language, spread on thickly with a gluti-nous sentimentality, is never surrendered by Elizabeth: long after the crisis of self-doubt she undergoes in her traumatic drive to the township of Guguletu, Elizabeth is still talking about 'this letter from elsewhere (so long a letter!), truth and love together at last' in which in 'every *you* that I pen love flickers and trembles like Saint Elmo's fire' (129), or insisting that 'these words, as you read them, enter you and draw breath again' (131).

But this sentimental faith in a language of the heart is by no means the only fossilized ideology Elizabeth Curren Quixotically preserves. As I suggested in Chapter 1, the type of emotive interpersonal recog-nition fostered by the novel of sensibility is coextensive with, and supportive of, other radical changes in social institutions in the mod-ern period—most especially the new importance of the intimate

[10] Samuel Richardson, *Pamela* (1740), ed. Thomas Keymer and Alice Wakely (Oxford, 1999) 230, 54.

sphere of the home. In this distinctively bourgeois space, 'privatised individuals', as Habermas puts it, could learn to perceive themselves 'as persons capable of entering into "purely human" relations with each other'.[11] As with Pamela herself, the violation of the intimate sphere of Elizabeth's home—even though this core institution of sensibility has already been emptied of its conjugal family—leads to some of her greatest exasperation. The return of Bheki and then the addition of John to the house leads to an irritable questioning of who is staying where, to which Bheki's taunt, 'Must we have a pass to come in here?' (47) truly finds the mark. She is later enraged upon discovering that John has been sleeping in her car, another cherished private space:

'I hear you and your friend have been sleeping in my car. Why didn't you ask my permission?'
    Silence fell. Bheki did not look up. Florence went on cutting bread.
    'Why didn't you ask my permission? Answer me!'
    The little girl stopped chewing, stared at me.
    Why was I behaving in this ridiculous fashion?   (58)

As was the case with Elizabeth's feeling that her faith in a language of the heart is 'old-fashioned', so is her judgement here a true one—she does cut a rather 'ridiculous' figure in this politically charged situation by insisting on the type of privacy and personal space that it was Pamela's fight to win from Mrs Jewkes and Mr B. But it is surely not more ridiculous than the floods of tears she continually sheds, again in common with Pamela's own outpourings of sensibility. Few are the scenes of confrontation with Mr B when Pamela does not trump his verbal power by 'a deep Sigh' or a burst of remonstrative tears, and Mr B becomes so used to the expressive power of these tears he starts referring to her 'speaking Eyes' (186), whose flow is so vast and repetitive that he is moved to joke with Pamela that 'I suppose I shall have some of your Tears in my Wine!' (185). Likewise, Elizabeth has no reticence in abandoning herself 'first to a quiet, decent sobbing, then to long wails without articulation, emptyings of the lungs,

---

[11] *The Structural Transformation of the Public Sphere* 48.

emptyings of the heart' (19)—in which the different grades of emotional disturbance are distinguished with real connoisseurship. Later, again with Vercueil, she begins to feel 'a welling up of tears' and admits that 'I cry more and more easily' (70); she cries a few pages later ('Tears came again, easy tears' (72)), and again in the same conversation, 'tears came to the eyes' (76). Passing over several floods of tears, by the time Elizabeth is stranded under the overpass she has been crying so much that the dog is attracted to 'lick up the salt of my tears' (160); near the end of her story again 'my eyes swam with tears' (185) when Vercueil makes his seductive offer to do away with her.

Perhaps even more telling is Pamela and Elizabeth's shared commitment to what Ruth Perry refers to as 'the agonised individual consciousness' (116) as the basis for ethical action.[12] What continually surprises Mr B about Pamela is her lack of recognition for the imperatives of his essentially feudal schema of ownership and obligation, and her reliance instead upon the truth told by her own heart, as evidenced by her letters' continual investigation into how to behave. Over time this inwardness of Pamela's, and indeed its physical incarnation in her letters grows to fascinate him until he is 'awaken'd to see more Worthiness in you than ever I saw in any Lady in the World' (84). Equally, even in the most pressing situations, Elizabeth characteristically refuses to accept ready-made moral formulae: at Guguletu, when she is asked by Thabane to pronounce upon what she has seen, she falters and refuses, explaining that while these are 'terrible sights' that 'are to be condemned', she 'cannot denounce them in other people's words. I must find my own words, from myself. Otherwise it is not the truth. That is all I can say now' (98–9). Like Pamela, the real truth lies in Elizabeth's heart, not in communally agreed formulae. But as with her 'old-fashioned words', her 'ridiculous' insistence upon privacy, and her 'easy tears', it is hard to resist the force of the denunciation coming from 'the man in

---

[12] Ruth Perry, *Women, Letters and the Novel* (New York, 1980) 116.

the crowd': '"Shit", he said. No one contradicted him'—least of all Elizabeth herself.

However, this last example is just as revealing of the differences between Pamela and Elizabeth as it is of their continuity. To those familiar with the conventions of the epistolary novel, it is ludicrous to feature a mother as the heroine: from the *Five Love-Letters from a Nun to a Cavalier* (1678) through to Clarissa herself, the heroine is invariably a nubile young girl, often of uncertain social status, but, crucially, vulnerable to the wiles and ruses of rogue sexual desire. There are no mothers as heroines (as far as I am aware) in the history of the genre until *Age of Iron*, where, in as grotesque a parody of the epistolary heroine as 'the knight of the sad countenance' was of the chivalric, the heroine is not only a mother, but is possessed of a decaying and disease-ridden body. She is the foolish, lingering terminus of her tradition, a Pamela grown old, sexless and hopeless. (Is it a mere coincidence that Pamela's mother was also called Elizabeth?) Ruth Perry emphasizes the centrality of sexual desire as a motive force in the literary innovativeness of the genre:

Most early epistolary novels duplicate a woman's consciousness by providing her letters, and then allowing the audience to get inside it by reading those letters. The fact that the climax of the plot generally also had to do with 'getting inside' a woman suggests that the sexual act works as a metaphor for the more important literary innovation— the getting inside of a woman's consciousness by the writer and by the reader. (*Women, Letters and the Novel* 131)

This is especially the case in *Pamela*: recall the famous scene in which Mr B tries to undress Pamela ostensibly to get to the letters she has sewn into her clothes and stuffed into her bosom. As Perry puts it, 'Her body and her consciousness are all that she possesses in the world and Mr. B. wants them both. The way they are combined in the plot is made evident by the way Mr. B. marries Pamela shortly after he takes possession of her letters and, therefore, her conscious-ness' (133). Elizabeth's cancer-ridden old body is as undesirable as Pamela's beautiful young body (she is between 15 and 16 years old) is compelling; by extension, her words—the whole inner drama of the 'agonised individual conscience'—are as undesired in South Africa as Pamela's were treasured, sought for, and fought over. Elizabeth comes to recognize that 'Mr. Thabane does not weigh what I say. It has no weight to him. Florence does not even hear me. To Florence what goes on in my head is a matter of complete indifference' (163)—but quite the opposite was the case with Pamela Andrews's words, which could not have become more powerful over the course of her story, as she reforms Mr B and ineluctably progresses into the higher echelons of society.

So the power-dynamic of a rising literary form based on the emotive recognition of equal dignity confronting the vestiges of an old order based on the remnants of an honour ethic—an order that has no time for the individual and his or her subjective experience—are reversed in *Age of Iron*. Elizabeth's class and ethnicity associate her with the reactionary order of the book, and her opposition to the clear political imperatives of the day is at best dubious ('my dubious discourse', she calls her letter). Whereas in *Pamela*, Mr B's words were the ones continually placed in doubt, and he is left insisting with ever greater peremptoriness that he be trusted and believed ('May I not have my word taken?' (96); 'Place some confidence in me' (205)), often in the same moment that the text has exposed the crudely disingenuous quality of his words and deeds, in *Age of Iron* it is the cracked old voice of the novel that has no weight. As Mr Thabane tells her on the telephone, 'Your voice is very tiny, very tiny and very far away' (149). Elizabeth's insistence upon the value of the individual soul over the group bond, and upon the innocence of childhood over the urge to commit, and upon the truth of the heart over the truth of the community—all this simply passes unweighed, has no more truck with proceedings than Quixote's insistence that 'master Andres' not be beaten by his cruel employer.[13]

---

[13] See *Don Quixote* 38–40.

GENRE AND COUNTERGENRE

Having now established the parodic, or 'jocose', side of this joco-serious text, we must now join it with the serious, and again *Don Quixote* comes to our aid. In the closing words of the Jerusalem prize address Coetzee drops a hint: 'The story of Alonso Quixano or Don Quixote—though not, I add, Cervantes' subtle and enigmatic book—ends with the capitulation of the imagination to reality, with a return to La Mancha and death' (99). What is it, then, about a 'subtle and enigmatic book' that might allow the Quixotic fool to evade this fate?

As I have already suggested, *Don Quixote* stands in a tradition of writing about folly, or even writing by Folly, beginning with Erasmus's *The Praise of Folly* (1509), in which the position of the fool is exploited within a series of textual processes that create a particularly unstable irony—one which playfully troubles prevalent rules and boundaries around what counts as the serious. By choosing to stage the politics of equal dignity in the guise of a recognizably old-fashioned fool, Coetzee seeks to decline for his text what the Erasmus essay called a 'big-phallus status': *Age of Iron* aims to steer away from 'the scene of rivalry' and the self-assertiveness of 'taking sides'. Indeed, a reading of *Age of Iron* that emphasized the allegorical thrust of the story would be hard pressed indeed to discover any 'big-phallus' assertion of the ongoing value of the novel of sensibility and the emotive form of 'purely human' identity it projects. However, Quixote's great fortune was to pass through the world with the clownish figure of Sancho Panza by his side, and I want to consider the figure of Sancho for a while before returning to the 'countergenre' at stake in Coetzee's text, and finally to Verceuil—Coetzee's own version of Sancho.[14]

---

[14] The name Verceuil sounds like Virgil in some pronunciations (especially the Afrikaaner), and it is therefore tempting to connect him not with Cervantes' comic epic, but with Dante's serious one, in which Virgil is Dante's guide to the underworld. As part of her own quest for seriousness Elizabeth certainly wants to cast him

In *The Novel According to Cervantes* Stephen Gilman argues for the crucial importance of Sancho to the very highest ambitions of Cervantes' text: namely, the attempt it makes to intervene in, and creatively disorient, those habitual rules of perception that are reinforced by the patterns of literary genre. As I have already suggested, *Don Quixote* stages a confrontation between incommensurate countergenres—the romance and the picaresque. This is what Gilman says:

> By bringing them [the chivalric romance and the picaresque] together in a single narrative, he would 'invent' not only 'in' the innumerable printed romances he himself had read but, more importantly, 'in' the very minds of his readers. Then as each reader came to appreciate and laugh at Cervantes's play with generic rigidity—his delightful tangle of fictional expectations— mass identification would no longer be possible.
>
> (*The Novel According to Cervantes* 91)

In staging the conflict of rival genres, Cervantes mirrored the confrontation that takes place in *The Praise of Folly* between Folly's Epicureanism and a merely silent and assumed Stoicism: in confronting the extreme of Quixote's absolute sense of value with a world absolutely lacking in any value whatsoever, the caricatural nature of both genres would be exposed for the reader's playful Erasmian laughter, such that the text becomes a site in which *invención* (invention)—a favourite Cervantian word—can take place. But in order to sustain the creative interplay between a romance hero and an unforgivingly picaresque world, Cervantes needed not only a fool (Quixote) but also a clown.

The importance of Sancho is that he is not simply placed in the text to mock Don Quixote—although laughing at his master's folly is certainly one of his functions. Instead, he is more like a companion in folly, being foolish enough himself to believe, at least in part,

in this role, but Verceuil is no Virgil: in fact he pointedly refuses to escort her to the 'underworld' of Guguletu ('Fuck off ', he tells her when she asks (88)), just as Sancho, in Cervantes' parody of the epic motif, refuses to escort Don Quixote into the Cave of Montesinos.

though with growing dubiousness, aspects of Quixote's illusion. He also helps Quixote, being in his own way quite clever and practical— his ass Dapple carries provisions and some money, which they do turn out to need in the Age of Iron they occupy, so little respectful are modern Innkeepers of the privileges due to chivalry. He quite literally enables the quest to carry on. He takes Quixote seriously, talks to him and provides someone for Quixote to talk to, and it is in these conversations the book generates a continuing and indeed abiding interest in its foolish adventures. When his master loses badly, as after the confrontation with the windmills at the beginning or the herd of pigs at the end, Sancho is there to listen credulously to his master's explanation of what happened and allow him the space in the book to regain a sense of dignity, or at least to restore himself to the reader through a gentler type of laughter. When he wins, Sancho is at hand with a ready measure of scepticism to pull Quixote back down to earth. Erich Auerbach has pointed to the sheer formal brilliance of Quixote's speeches in their command of rhetorical elegance and literary allusion, and the presence of Sancho, to whom these speeches are at least addressed (if never quite understood), allows this eloquence to restore something at least of the dignity and nobility of the battered and beaten romance form.[15] As Gilman puts it, Sancho is 'a sort of human buffer state between his master and the stony implacability of what was out there in the world' (93). If there is one idiotic extreme in the text called 'romance', and another intolerantly serious extreme called variously 'picaresque' or (more authoritatively) 'reality', Sancho and his beloved Dapple seem to hover between, forever changing shape to suit the moment, keeping the play going by shifting the boundaries between seriousness and non-seriousness.

Elizabeth Curren's countergenre is not the picaresque, but the historical fate of being situated in a cultural field dominated by the politics of difference. Coetzee gives this anti-novelistic counter-

---

[15] See 'The Enchanted Dulcinea' in *Mimesis* (Berne, 1946; Princeton, 2003) 339–58.

genre literary embodiment as a mythical narrative—a narrative akin
to the story Freud described as that of the patriarch and the primal
horde.[16] From the outset of Coetzee's novel the patriarch, here the
South African state, lours in the most horrific and depraving way:
'The disgrace of the life one lives under them: to open a newspaper,
to switch on the television, like kneeling and being urinated on.
Under them: under their meaty bellies, their full bladders' (10). The
political father keeps coming back into view: 'Huge bull testicles
pressing down on their wives, their children, pressing the spark
out of them' (29). Florence's family is without a father, properly
conceived—he does not form part of the home but is stranded on the
chicken farm, not fully an adult in his own right but an economic
function of the will of the overweening patriarch; Elizabeth is left
vainly attempting to fantasize a normal family life for them (43). In
response, 'group psychology' has formed among the oppressed: to the
band of brothers, announces Florence, there are 'no more mothers and
fathers' (49); John and Bheki are only the most proximate examples of
a whole people, including adults like Florence and Thabane as well as
literal children like John and Bheki, trapped in the liminality between
childhood and adulthood, unable to progress, locked in rivalry with
the father.

Needless to say, Elizabeth's relation to the seemingly unassailable
moral force of this countergenre is tortured and problematic. The
true sons in the novel (John and Bheki) merely feel patronized by
her, and pointedly ignore her, clearly regarding her as complicit with
their enemy. Page after page of *Age of Iron* is filled with Elizabeth's
thoughts on motherhood, on her daughter, on her own mother, on
herself as a child and teenager, on Florence as a mother, on John and

---

[16] See Sigmund Freud, *Group Psychology and the Analysis of the Ego*, trans.
James Strachey (1922) 90–121. This idea of the primal horde countergenre will be
explored in more detail in the next chapter: Freud derived this narrative from *The
Brothers Karamazov*, a text that has an integral relationship to *The Master of
Petersburg*. Reference to the primal horde myth appears in Coetzee's work as
early as *Dusklands*, in Eugene Dawn's report on the psychic relationship between
the Americans and the Vietnamese (24).

Bheki as children. She is incapable of apprehending a situation without wishing to see in it some sort of normative family context, a habit that repeatedly brings pain and uncertainty to herself, at the same time that it leads to her being resented, dismissed, and ignored by the other characters. The story she wishes to tell is of a stable world of parents and children, in which the former are responsible for keeping the latter in an innocent 'time of wonder, the growing time of the soul' (7). As Lawrence Stone has observed in *The Family, Sex and Marriage* (1977), this idea itself has a quite specific material history: the construction of childhood as a stage of life to be marked off as a sentimental time of innocence and nurturing, coupled with a new cultural emphasis on child-rearing that featured motherhood as a kind of profession, emerged most clearly in European culture towards the end of the seventeenth century, doing so out of the social dysfunction relating to the role (or, better put, the lack of a role) of city-dwelling women in the new mercantile classes. Of course, it is no coincidence that it was at this time, and with precisely this type of woman as its subject, that the epistolary novel emerged.[17] Coetzee's text confronts the 'old-fashioned' story that Elizabeth's genre insists on telling with another story with quite different conditions of narrative truth, in which the family is not a stable unit, and the development of the soul is irrelevant when compared to the brotherly bond of comradeship, in which, in Mr Thabane's definition, 'you are prepared to lay down your lives for each other without question . . . [and] a bond grows up that is stronger than any bond you will know again' (149).

The full significance of the conflict between genre and counter-genre is brought out in part III, in what is literally the middle of Coetzee's text, the expedition to Guguletu. One study of the Guguletu episode in *Age of Iron* has shown how Elizabeth narrates her trip to the hellish site of conflict as a version of the 'descent to the underworld' trope in classical literature with the aid of literary

---

[17] Lawrence Stone, *The Family, Sex, and Marriage in England, 1500–1800* (London, 1977) 405–49.

allusions largely from Dante's *Commedia*.[18] While it is indeed
characteristic of Elizabeth to present her experience in the most
elevated terms available, just as Quixote himself was anxious to
align his experience with his own elevated (though outdated)
models of literary knowing, this particular trip to the underworld
issues in a collision of generic modes that owes rather more to
Cervantes than to Dante—in particular to the 'Cave of Montesinos' episode in *Don Quixote*. This episode is Cervantes' parody of
the 'descent to the underworld' motif, and is the lowest point
Quixote reaches in his text: the point at which his noble illusion
is at its most fragile, and most distrusted by his faithful Sancho.[19]
As we have already seen, at Guguletu Elizabeth's insistence on the
truth-telling powers of her own heart is here made to seem deeply
dubious: refusing to adopt ready-made political slogans she finds
herself unable to 'bear witness', and acknowledges that what she
says is 'shit'. At first this inability to speak seems simply because she
is so overwhelmed: she tells us that the scene is so violent and
appalling it requires 'the tongue of a God' to narrate (99). But in
fact what is at stake is the way in which she is confronted by the
divergent forms of sociability asserted by the countergenre that is
unfolding around her. First, Thabane renames Florence: '*My sister*
he called her, not Florence. Perhaps I alone in all the world called
her Florence.' Then, inside the school hall as she stares at the
corpses, a little girl asks her if she is a 'sister'. The girl means to
ask if she is a sister of the Catholic Church, thus here to help, but
the scene carries a far greater weight of significance. "No,' she [the
girl's mother] went on, speaking to the child in English, 'she is not
one of the sisters.' Gently she unlocked the child's fingers from my
sleeve' (101–2). Twice in rapid succession Elizabeth is excluded
from *being sister* to the people around her: they are in a different
type of story, one in which moral prerogatives founded in history

---

[18] David E. Hoegberg, '"Where is Hope?" Coetzee's Rewriting of Dante in *Age
of Iron*', *English in Africa* 25/1 (1998) 27–42.

[19] See *Don Quixote* pt. II, chs. 22 and 23.

and identity tell the whole truth of the situation. Furthermore, while she had previously thought her status as mother and her mother's love was what might save her ('That thought is the pillar I cling to when the storms hit me' (72)), now it is clear that in fact her familial identity represents everything that stands between her and the people around her. If whatever she might say is simply 'shit', and the language of the heart counts for nothing, this is because the power of the genre she faces is such that she is inevitably read into its terms: she is positioned on the side of the patriarch, just as Quixote, upon emerging from the Cave of Montesinos full of fantasies about what he had seen, was inevitably positioned as mad. This is the decisive moment of guilt-acknowledgement in her story—coming at the point where the two narrative modes collide. Elizabeth pauses in her letter to instruct her daughter to distrust the creeping tendrils of her own emotive discourse: 'If lies and pleas and excuses weave among the words, listen for them . . . Do not read in sympathy with me. Let your heart not beat with mine' (103–4).

'HOW SILLY ONE LOOKS FENDING OFF A DOG!': THE COMIC AND THE SERIOUS

However, we must not decontextualize the descent to Guguletu, and present its crushing dismissal of Elizabeth as the sum total of the text's generic play. Above all, we should not ignore Vercueil. Elizabeth had asked Vercueil to accompany her to Guguletu, not least because he is rather handy at getting 'Rocinante' going. But he refused point blank:

The dog lay at Vercueil's side. It tapped its tail on the floor when I came in but did not get up.

'Mr. Vercueil!' I said loudly. He opened his eyes; I held the light away. He broke wind. 'I have to take Florence to Guguletu. It is urgent, we have to leave at once. Will you come along?'

He made no reply, but curled up on his side. The dog rearranged itself.

'Mr. Vercueil!' I said, pointing the light at him.
'Fuck off,' he mumbled.   (88)

Vercueil won't go near Guguletu, any more than Sancho would go
down into the Cave of Montesinos. He gives two answers: a fart, and
a 'fuck off'. His dog seems pleased with the decision: concerned
when Elizabeth comes in ('it tapped its tail'), it swiftly rearranges
itself around Vercueil's curled-up body. When Elizabeth comes back
from Guguletu she is truly harrowed by the experience: a series of
self-lacerating questions culminate in the desolate feeling that she
'will never be warm again' (108); she comes home and falls asleep,
but upon waking her sense of total desolation remains: 'I woke up
haggard. It was night again. Where had the day gone?' (108). Then
she walks to the toilet:

Sitting on the seat, his trousers around his knees, his hat on his head, fast
asleep, was Vercueil. I stared in astonishment.

He did not wake; on the contrary, though his head lolled and his jaw
hung open, he slept as sweetly as a babe. His long lean thigh was quite
hairless.   (108)

It is Vercueil at his most clownish—a literally astonishing interruption of her serious mood (all Elizabeth can do is stare 'in astonishment'). Vercueil has the inevitable hat on his head, which stays put
despite the fact his head 'lolled' in this fully grown baby's easy, open-
jawed sleep. Of course the funny hat is a comic device as old as the
clown itself, and featured in modern clowns too—from Vladimir
and Estragon to Leopold Bloom's 'high grade ha'. But it is not only
Vercueil who interrupts Elizabeth's seriousness. When she goes
down to the kitchen she finds another scene of devastation:

The kitchen door stood open and garbage from the overturned bucket was
strewn all over the floor. Worrying at an old wrapping paper was the dog.
When it saw me it hung its ears guiltily and thumped its tail. 'Too much!'
I murmured. 'Too much!' The dog slunk out.

Wherever Vercueil and his dog go they make a mess: tripping up,
spilling things over ('As he left he bumped against the cat tray,

spilling litter all over the veranda' (12)), wallowing in rubbish. And note that this is not a morose and tetchy old dog, but a silly young thing, 'little more than a pup' (6), always fooling around and getting into trouble. Here we have the mildly ludicrous spectacle of the dog accepting his disgrace, assuming the role of guilty pariah, knowing it has (again) gone too far, and sloping off-stage. For Elizabeth it is exasperating and even astonishing that such clownish goings-on should interrupt her ethical temper—but their presence in the narrative has a complex effect. Vercueil and the dog break into the emotional flow of Elizabeth's discourse, making it indeed seem less serious: so in one sense they diminish the emotive hold her letter has on the reader. But in another sense, their comic interruption 'saves' her—saves her, that is, from getting swallowed up in an orgy of despair, and losing the reader's patience entirely.

I will return to the question as to why Vercueil and his dog so pointedly refuse to go near Guguletu. But we must first explore the broader range of effects these two have in the novel, and I will begin with the dog. 'Is it possible that the dog is the one sent'? Elizabeth asks (193); the question that arises is surely: sent for what? While this may seem to be a merely rhetorical question, it actually has a surprisingly clear answer in *Age of Iron*: the dog was sent to chase away the cats. We learn at the end of the book that Elizabeth's house was chosen by Vercueil for two reasons: because she 'wouldn't make trouble' and because she 'didn't have a dog' (184). Hers was a 'house of cats' (12), and as soon as the dog arrives it starts making characteristically 'playful dashes' at the cats (12), who are 'unsettled by these newcomers'. Elizabeth is unsettled by them too, but she immediately warms to the dog (it is 'no doubt stolen from a good family' (19); later she goes further, saying it is a 'nice dog: a bright presence, star-born, as some people are' (114)) and starts to agree with it that her cats are undesirable things. Put off their food by the dog and refusing to eat, Elizabeth becomes swiftly enraged at their prickly dignity, at the way one raises 'a finicky paw to avoid being touched', and how they contemptuously 'spurned the food'. ' "Go to hell, then!" I screamed, and flung the fork wildly in their direction—

"I am sick of feeding you!"' (12). This seems at first most safely interpreted as a transference of resentment (she has just been diagnosed with cancer) to the seemingly ungrateful cats, but as *Age of Iron* develops it becomes increasingly clear that the cats themselves are indeed the target. Twenty pages later the cats are again on the wrong side of a valuation with the dog: when Vercueil, truly a 'Dog-man' (56) (quite unlike the 'Cat-woman' Elizabeth (85)) refuses Elizabeth's request to come in and feed the cats after she is dead, an image springs to her mind of the absurd dignity of an Egyptian burial: 'In Egypt they bricked in their cats with their dead masters. Is that what I want: yellow eyes padding back and forth, searching for a way out of the dark cave?' (32). It is not: she decides to have them 'put down' rather than found a new home. Again, the strained and somewhat ludicrous dignity of the cats, and the hyperbole of the cattish burial of the Egyptians, is contrasted with the low comedy of its doggish equivalent: '[Vercueil] will die in a doorway or an alley with his arms hugged across his chest; they will find him with this dog or some other dog by his side, whimpering, licking his face' (33). She recalls another cat later on, 'an old ginger tom', who she nursed back to health; Elizabeth resents this cat its stupid pride, its stubborn inability to accept the vulnerability of its position: 'Even when he was at his weakest his body was hard, tense, resistant under my hand' (79). Later, and much to her regret, she is forced to observe that 'the dog has not warmed to me. Too much cat smell' (85), and in the midst of her grand, self-searching lament after returning from Guguletu ('I am hollow, I am a shell') comes the resentful accusation that 'the cats, if the truth be told, have never really loved me' (112). This cattish absence of love contrasts to the fluency of love between Vercueil and the dog ('His hand moved restfully over the dog's fur, back and forth. The dog blinked, closed its eyes. Love, I thought: however unlikely, it is love I witness here' (114)), and which is unhesitatingly extended to her under the overpass, when the dog comes to find her and starts licking the tears off her face: 'Kisses, if one wanted to look at them that way' (160). By the end of the text, Elizabeth is just as bound by the prerogatives of her foolish old genre as ever before, and still preoccupied in an attempt to convince Mr Thabane that his assumptions are wrong, but she has made a definite transition as a lover of animals: 'I asked him whether he was still feeding the cats. "Yes," he said, lying. For the cats are gone, chased out. Do I care? No, not anymore. After I have cared for you, for him, there is little space left in my heart. The rest must, as they say, go to pot' (197). By the end of her story, the cats—again somehow tied in with an idea of dignity, of things *not* having gone 'to pot'—are gone, and the dog and the 'Dog-man' have taken possession of the house to the extent that both of them sleep in her bed (Elizabeth at first only asks for the dog to sleep with her, but apparently the dog does not come without Vercueil). Then in *Giving Offense* Coetzee himself caps it all off by making his own rather negative judgement of cats, observing that we 'see enough of animals concerned for their dignity (cats, for instance) to know how comical pretensions to dignity can be' (14).

What is the point of all this talk of dogs and cats? While cats strut around, taking everything deadly seriously, dogs—especially young dogs like the one in Coetzee's text—seem to be rather more foolish creatures who stop things from getting too serious by their inadvertent clowning. Recall the episode to which I referred in our earlier discussion of Elizabeth's persistence in the assumptions of the novel of sensibility, where the demand for privacy had led her into the tone of a prison-guard:

'Why didn't you ask my permission? Answer me!'
    The little girl stopped chewing, stared at me.
    Why was I behaving in this ridiculous fashion?   (58)

It is a Quixotic moment, in which the impulses of Elizabeth seem thoroughly crushed by the dignified silence of the black characters. But before we can draw a line under things and simply condemn the folly of her genre, in come Vercueil and the dog: 'immediately the tension was broken' and Elizabeth is rescued from her slide into an attitude that, given the wider situation, is hardly tenable. 'The dog was leaping up at him, bounding, frisking, full of joy. It leapt at me too, streaking my skirt with its wet paws. How silly one looks fending off a dog!' (59). A small incident perhaps, but what the dog has done is effectively to keep the play of the text going: the bounding and frisking and general silliness places an Erasmian boundary around Elizabeth at the moment she needs it most, marking her off from the serious judgement about to be remorselessly applied: she becomes too 'silly' to be worth condemning, the judgement upon her slips off in the presence of the clown. And inconsequent though she has just become, she does not merely remain so: she has survived the scene, and her presence in the text, her story, carries on.

'Dogs, which sniff out what is good, what evil: patrollers of boundaries: sentries' (85). In 'Erasmus: Madness and Rivalry' Coetzee tells us that Erasmus chose Terminus, the god of boundaries, as his emblem. The dog, as the patroller of boundaries is (like the 'Dogman' Vercueil) also a blurrer of boundaries and a spirit of playfulness: both Vercueil and his young dog love to play (and Vercueil hates working), although their play is continually in danger of being curtailed.[20] This is never more clear than at the beginning of part II, when the black characters have just returned to the house only to discover Vercueil lurking there, unsteadying things with his games:

As I watched, the baby advanced upon Vercueil, her arms held out wide, her fists clenched. As she was about to stumble over the lawn mower he caught her and led her by the chubby little arm to a safe distance. Again, on unsteady feet, she bore down on him. Again he caught her and led her away. It was on the verge of becoming a game. But would dour Vercueil play?

Once more Beauty lunged towards him; once more he saved her. Then, wonder of wonders, he wheeled the half-dismantled lawn mower to one

---

[20] Another great Erasmian, Johan Huizinga, argued that play is a pre-cultural phenomenon, common to humans and animals alike: 'Animals play just like men. We have only to watch young dogs to see that all the essentials of human play are present in their merry gambols' (*Homo Ludens: A Study of the Play-Element in Culture*, trans. R. F. C. Hull (London, 1944) 19).

side and, offering one hand to the baby, one hand to Hope, began to turn in circles, first slowly, then faster. Hope, in her red sandals, had to run to keep her footing; as for the baby, she spun in the air, giving shrieks of pleasure; while the dog, closed off behind the gate, leaped and barked. Such noise! Such excitement!

At that point Florence must have come on the scene, for the spinning slowed and stopped. A few soft words, and Hope let go of Vercueil's hand, coaxed her sister away, disappeared from my sight. The dog, full of regret, whined. Vercueil returned to the lawn mower. Half an hour later it began to rain (38).

Vercueil's playfulness contrasts with Florence's termination of the game and Bheki's apparent inability to play: his pastime of bouncing the ball against the garage wall is no game, only a 'remorseless thudding' (38) that has no variability and no interaction. It compares to the false play in Guguletu, where Elizabeth tells of how 'a girl in an apple-green school tunic advanced on me, her hand raised as if to give me a slap. I flinched, but it was only in play. Or perhaps I should say: she forbore from actually striking' (101). To return to the question I posed earlier regarding Vercueil's reluctance to squire Mrs Curren to Guguletu: the fact is that the war-torn township is an area too absolutely and remorselessly serious for Vercueil—with his playful blurring of boundaries—to enter, as are other especially stark aspects of the political. Likewise, when Bheki and John are knocked down by the police (cruelly, they are for once out playing together on John's bike) and injured, the boundary separating the serious from the foolish hardens, and the dogs are shut out: 'Vercueil's dog tried to lick him. "Go away!" I whispered, and gave it a push with my foot. It wagged its tail . . . Vercueil's dog came pushing in again. "Get that dog away," I snapped. The plumber gave it a kick. It yelped and sidled away' (63). There are clear limits, Coetzee's text suggests, to the *invención* being staged: the resolutely serious moral demands of the politics of difference have certain limits that are resolutely closed off to the complicating and unsettling processes of play. Recall the *ad hominem* attack made by Gordimer upon Coetzee's supposed 'revulsion' towards politics: Vercueil's curt refusal and the kicked dog clearly signify the seriousness and humility with which Coetzee responds to this attack.

But it is not only the counter-genre that resists being played with: its old-fashioned and 'untenable' competitor is also wary of protecting her boundaries and claims to seriousness, even in the act of condemning her rivals as 'dour little puritans, despising laughter, despising play' (125). Like Quixote, quite unable to recognize the complex way in which Sancho's clowning and fellowship-in-folly provides the ballast and rebound that keeps him in play, Elizabeth is and remains to the end rather cattish (despite the expulsion of the cats themselves) and touchy about the seriousness of her status:

'I have a favor to ask of you,' I said. 'Please don't make fun of me.'
  'Is that the favor?'
  'Yes. Now or in the future.'
  He shrugged.   (120)[21]

Even at the end of her story, when the cats are all chased out of the house, and the claim to dignity would seem particularly strained, Elizabeth is still Quixotically resisting the incursion of the comic. When Vercueil installs the television, and turns it on to the national anthem, she angrily commands him to switch it off. In response, he begins to play around: 'Swaying his hips, holding his hands out, clicking his fingers, he danced, unmistakably danced, to music I never thought could be danced to' (180). But 'despising laughter, despising play' herself, determined to the end on holding a wholly serious status in the text, she again commands Vercueil to turn the set off and demands of him to stop playing: 'don't be silly, Vercueil. And don't make fun of me. Don't trivialise me' (181). (His answer is another non-answer that corrodes her seriousness and tries to salvage the play: 'Still, why get in a state?')

---

[21] Quixote detested being laughed at, whether by the whores that stand on duty at the inn in the first sally (28); or when Sancho mocks him after the truly cringe-worthy episode of the fulling mills: '"Pray, Sir, be pacified; by the living God, I did but jest." "Though you jest, I do not," answered Don Quixote' (151).

The effect of all this horsing around (Vercueil's face is repeatedly compared to the funny face of a horse) can at times act to corrode the status of Elizabeth's strong sensibility and ethical intensity. But what I am suggesting is that it can also work in different ways. When in outright confrontation with the unqualified seriousness of her countergenre, Elizabeth's insistence on the enduring value of her own assumptions often seems entirely foolish—as we have seen, she can't be taken at all seriously in Guguletu. But with Vercueil and his dog the boundaries separating the serious from the non-serious slip and slide in an unpredictable manner, at times allowing Elizabeth's discourse to find a seriousness it would otherwise be straightforwardly denied. Right at the end of part II, just after Elizabeth hesitantly invites Vercueil to sleep in the house, thus opening up the boundary of her private space (although Vercueil refuses, insisting that the dog must be let in too or it will 'carry on' (84)), she tells him about her quest to the police station in Caledon Square in order to lay charges against the policemen who knocked down John and Bheki. Of course, as she pathetically recognizes, in the cold air of the police station, where the conditions of the countergenre prevail most resolutely, her words seem merely a piece of 'liberal-humanist posturing' (85), an opportunity to give a grand discourse ('"You make me feel ashamed," I told them') that falls flat and makes her look 'such a fool'. And she does look like a fool: what are the value and weight of her words, now that she is 'suddenly on the edge of tears again' (yet again)? Nonetheless, back in the car with Vercueil her discourse escalates, drawing upon some of the most powerful resources of ethical description that the tradition of the novel has at its disposal:

'Perhaps I should simply accept that that is how one must live from now on: in a state of shame. Perhaps shame is nothing more than the name for the way I feel all the time. The name for the way in which people live who would prefer to be dead.'

   Shame. Mortification. Death in life.

   There was a long silence.

   'Can I borrow ten rand?' said Vercueil. 'My disability comes through on Thursday. I'll pay you back then.   (86)

I quote at length, here and elsewhere, because of the particularly protean nature of this text, and the complex back-and-forth between, or interplay among, the serious and the foolish. For here Elizabeth's words are all spoken in report to Vercueil, who sits in the parked car on Buitenkant Street. *Buitekant* is the Afrikaans word for 'outside', literally made up of *buite* (out) and *kant* (side), and Buitenkant Street—Outside Street—on which is situated the Castle, is so named because it formerly marked the boundary between what was then the Cape Colony and the rest of Africa. Typical of Vercueil to be patrolling the boundary: but upon which side do Elizabeth's words fall—the foolish or the serious? We cannot quite say, for within the shifting boundaries of Vercueil's play, nothing is easy to arbitrate. Across the road, in Caledon Square, Elizabeth's words made a total 'fool' of her. But here in the car with Vercueil they sit differently. The grand self-condemnations ('Shame. Mortification. Death in life') pass into one of Vercueil's long silences. But does the silence only mean he is not listening—that Elizabeth is simply irrelevant? He then asks to borrow money, which is of course quite amusing coming so hard upon the high seriousness claimed by (if not quite granted to) Elizabeth's speech. But there are two things to notice: first, that Vercueil's request does indeed make the scene mildly funny, and not merely risible (which it had been, according to Elizabeth, in Caledon Square) and that whereas something that is risible is simply dismissed, something that is funny is not necessarily wholly untrue; secondly, that this peculiar transition into Vercueil's comic request comes after a silence, which may well be a respectful silence that allows Elizabeth's words space to breathe and settle, to find some weight. Vercueil from time to time actually seems to be quite interested in Elizabeth's words, not least when she begins to talk about the classical literary tradition (upon which her rhetoric freely draws), and thus one of the rules we must respect if we are to play the game of this text is not to prejudge the meaning of his many silences. This is a complicated thought, but what is happening in the text is indeed complex: Elizabeth's words, the cracked old voice of a particularly moribund form of the novel, clearly do not hold centre-stage in the text, as she would wish them to, but neither—like Quixote's fine speeches—are they simply shunted off-stage. In the car with Vercueil it is much harder to decide how Elizabeth's discourse should be judged.

But what is it that we do see then, if this text grants full weight neither to the novel of sensibility, with its prizing of the ethical, the truth of the heart, and the individual conscience, nor its resolutely adversarial countergenre? What is next, as Coetzee asked in a different context, 'in the history of the novel' (*Doubling the Point* 27)? Whereas in *Don Quixote* the interplay of the romance and the picaresque brought out a new interest in the psyche of the questing individual, here the collision and interplay between the novelistic psyche of Elizabeth and the iron-like hardness of the countergenre deflects the interest of the narrative in a different direction—one that keeps these different foundations for human identity and community in play. We do not lose interest in Elizabeth's feelings and her ethical wrangling, but these do have less importance in themselves; she has a claim on our attention, but not the sole claim; her story is not the only one in the book, but neither is it completely nugatory. With Elizabeth's growing sense of herself as a character forever doomed to wait 'for someone to show me the way across' (179), with her continuing cattishness ('Don't make fun of me. Don't trivialise me') despite her lack of cats, and with her persistence in clinging to the role of mother right until the end ('As you see, I still believe in your love' (197)) we should not look to her as a new 'type' of hero any more than we did to Alonso Quixano: she begins and ends within the foolish discourse of the epistolary novel. But a fool, bound up in a playful text, is not necessarily doomed to be merely irrelevant, and this is by no means a story that ends in a crushing defeat.

I will conclude by considering the ending of *Age of Iron*—an ending that is set in train by a spectacular bout of folly on Elizabeth's part. Late in the text the police arrive at her home and end up killing John—who has taken up residence there. This brings about a crisis of identity: while it is clear to the police that she is on their side, and equally clear to the distrustful John, Elizabeth is nonetheless determined to claim she transcends her identity, and that she can sympathetically identify with John. '"*Ek staan jie aan jou kant jie*," I said. "*Ek staan aan die teenkant.*" I stand on the other side.' (153–4). This assertion of course convinces nobody, but she pushes her assertion of the heart's truth (rather than the skin's truth) to a higher and higher pitch, throwing herself in the way of the proceedings, dropping her blanket, denouncing the scene in transcendental terms ('God forgive us!') and generally getting in a 'fury'. 'What did it matter if they thought me dotty?' she reflects—and they do, quite literally: '*Sy's van haar kop af*' (she's off her head) remarks the policewoman. Perceived, like Quixote in his darkest moments, as merely mad, there is nothing left for her but to amble down to Buitenkant Street again, to sit under the overpass. As we have seen, Buitenkant Street, the boundary, is the special residence of Vercueil: from the very beginning of the book Elizabeth saw him here as one of the 'derelicts... drinking under the overpass' (4). It is the dog that finds her, possibly attracted over by nothing more than the saltiness of her face from the plentiful tears that have poured down it. Then: 'A match flared. Yes, it was Vercueil, hat and all.' And down on the boundary this clownish man—her ever-faithful squire—does something quite remarkable:

With his high shoulder blades and his chest narrow as a gull's, I would not have guessed that Vercueil could be so strong. But he lifted me, wet patch and all, and carried me. I thought: forty years since I was last carried by a man. The misfortune of a tall woman. Will this be how the story ends: with being carried in strong arms across the sands, through the shallows, past the breakers, into the darker depths?   (160)

The ending of the story comes into sight for Elizabeth in this bathetic yet strangely moving image of romantic love: the grand old hackneyed scene of the man carrying the woman into the sunset, 'up Buitenkant Street he bore me, across Vrede Street, street of peace' (161)—although in this version, so carefully poised on the boundary of the utterly ludicrous, the woman's 'wet patch' results more from incontinence than from sexual stimulation. She clasps to

Vercueil, and feels him replacing her daughter in her affections: 'Him, not you. Because he is here, beside me, now' (162).

Recall that one of the main structural features of the epistolary novel was sexual desire: we saw that the desirableness of Pamela's body and the weight carried by her words were in a special way, within the controlling symbolism of her book, made equivalent, and that Mr B seemed to hunger as much after her letters as after her. As Perry put it, 'The fact that the climax of the plot generally also had to do with 'getting inside' a woman suggests that the sexual act works as a metaphor for the more important literary innovation—the getting inside of a woman's consciousness by the writer and by the reader' (131). We noted that this was obviously the main difference separating Pamela and Elizabeth, the way in which the cold air of parody in Coetzee's text was at its most frosty: old mothers cannot be desirable young girls, and as such Elizabeth's words carry no weight, her consciousness is irrelevant. And yet here, patrolling the boundary on Buitenkant Street, always at risk of tumbling down into sheer bathos, Elizabeth's story does seem to have a chance at fulfilment, her words do stand a chance of being desired. 'Do you mind if I talk?' she asks Vercueil. 'Talk,' he tells her (162).

Easy to have missed in this 'subtle and enigmatic' book, but the love between Vercueil and Elizabeth has in fact been building up for some time. Recall, for example, Elizabeth's strange 'fury' at the woman Vercueil introduced into the house: '*This country!* I thought. And then: *Thank God she is out!*' (60). I will not list the numerous references to this oddball relationship, which is in itself perhaps confined to Elizabeth's fantasy; suffice to say that the theme reaches a crescendo at the end of the book, when Elizabeth and Vercueil (and the dog, who keeps them 'honest') 'share a bed, folded one upon the other like a page folded in two, like two wings folded: old mates, bunkmates, conjoined, conjugal'; Vercueil has become her 'shadow husband'; she is 'Mrs. V.' (189–90). Although she loves him foolishly, 'as a dog loves', dogs are for her by no means asexual: she imagines a dog who 'sniffs at one's crotch, wagging its tail, its tongue hanging out red and stupid as a penis' (197). They then finally embrace with a 'mighty force' (198). But not everyone in the text goes along with the happy ending. '"*In Godsnaam,*"' a detective exclaims when he comes upon the two of them in Elizabeth's wrecked house: as Elizabeth lovingly clutches Vercueil's hand 'with the numb, clawlike grip of the old,' it is tempting to share the detective's judgement and turn away in disgust (173). This love-affair can seem almost ridiculous—like the idiotic sort of display put on by one of the old women Erasmus's Folly delights in: 'old women in the last stages of senility and so cadaverous that you'd think they'd been pulled out of the grave', yet who persist in claiming 'life is good', and carry on with the ludicrous spectacle of love-making, 'showing off their withered and pendulous breasts' and scribbling 'billets-doux' (*The Praise of Folly* 31). And yet if we play along with the two lovers, 'like two fools' grinning 'each at the other' (181), something rather interesting happens. In loving the man who is close 'to hand, as a dog loves' rather than focusing all her love upon her absent daughter, she is not condemned to die a 'death without illumination'. Instead, the plotline of the novel of sensibility is fulfilled, and *Age of Iron* ends, so to speak, happily ever after in 'marriage' between 'Mrs. V.' and her 'shadow husband'. (And yet—Vercueil 'does not know how to love . . . He does not know how to love as a boy does not know how to love. Does not know what zips and buttons and clasps to expect. Does not know what goes where' (196). Like the text itself, Vercueil makes no claim to 'big-phallus status'.)

'What matters,' Coetzee explained in interview, 'is that the contest is staged, that the dead have their say, even those who speak from a totally untenable historical position' (250). In *Age of Iron* there are clear limits on the extent to which Elizabeth's voice might stake its claim, and Vercueil's crude refusal to squire her to Guguletu is the most obvious of these limits. Without her Sancho, Elizabeth staggers from Guguletu harried, close to defeat, and with the front window of 'Rocinante' (her Hillman car) now smashed in. But as I have suggested, while she is certainly forced into a weaker status in Coetzee's text than the 'age of clay' would have granted her, this 'subtle and enigmatic' book also finds ways in which her discourse might survive. Confronted by a changed historical condition in which the literary form at the centre of their respective cultures was thrown into doubt, both Cervantes and Coetzee look for 'joco-serious' ways of mediating the conflict: of accepting the challenge of the new, while salvaging and reusing what might remain of the old. As Coetzee put it, 'the task becomes imagining this unimaginable, imagining a form of address that permits the play of writing to start taking place' (*Doubling the Point* 68).

6

'Redemption' or 'Delegitimization'? The Artist on Trial in *The Master of Petersburg*

Seriousness is, for a certain kind of artist, an imperative uniting the aesthetic and the ethical. It is also deconstructible as a feature of the ideology of so-called high art and the drive to power of the high artist.

J. M. Coetzee, *Giving Offense*[1]

I have now emphasized several of the ways in which Coetzee's writing attempts to break with what he calls in the above epigraph 'the ideology of so-called high art'. One of his earliest concerns was to depart from what he saw as the realist novel's logocentric commitment to 'The Word in all its magical autonomy' without falling back into other forms of stylistic temptation, and while Coetzee thereby refuses the stance of what he called 'herald of community', I have argued that this refusal is not part of an attempt to transcend or bypass politics, but that it derives instead from an attempt to find ways of respecting and negotiating heterogeneous political demands. In making this argument I have been defending the fundamental 'seriousness' of Coetzee's writing, even—in fact especially—when it draws upon the comic: the type of 'aesthetic' experience generated by

---

[1] J. M. Coetzee, 'The Harms of Pornography', *Giving Offense: Essays on Censorship* (Chicago, 1996). 73.

his prose might well be described as 'ethical', as Coetzee puts it, because of the openness to alterity enjoined by its disorienting play with the reading experience. But how seriously can we take this claim to seriousness? This was the question I posed at the end of our consideration of *Life & Times of Michael K* in Chapter 3. What is the guarantee that all the elaborate linguistic play I have been emphasizing isn't itself 'deconstructible' as a superfine 'literary' type of behaviour that masks a secret revulsion towards the political— a revulsion itself constitutive of the 'drive to power of the high artist'? Can we ever—in short—make a strong and categorical defence of the value of Coetzeean art?

While the protagonists of previous novels have always had something of the artist about them—think of the Magistrate's 'literary ambitions', Susan Barton's desire to write her own realist novel, and Elizabeth Curren's immense letter—in *The Master of Petersburg* Coetzee places the Master himself at the centre of the text, and the question of literary seriousness at the centre of his concerns. Given the particular importance of Dostoevsky to Coetzee, much is at stake in the question as to how we are being asked to judge this writer: it would be gratifying to discover in the figure of Dostoevsky a reassuring image of the genuine 'seriousness' of the artist. But this is not what Coetzee gives us.

By way of introduction to the problems Coetzee's portrait of the artist confronts us with, consider one of the more caustic of the novel's many intertextual ironies. In *Problems of Dostoevsky's Poetics*, Bakhtin famously remarked that 'Dostoevsky the artist always triumphs over Dostoevsky the journalist'.[2] But in *The Master of Petersburg* it is far from clear whether such a 'triumph'—one that neatly distinguishes serious 'high art' from low journalistic motives—actually comes to pass. Dostoevsky is invited by Nechaev to write a journalistic 'pamphlet' (200) denouncing the police for murdering his stepson, Pavel; in a moment of weakness he agrees, but uses it

---

[2] *Problems of Dostoevsky's Poetics* 92.

instead to accuse Nechaev of his murder, and clear the police of blame. As soon as he does so, however, he realizes he has 'fallen into a trap': Nechaev, who 'has him by the throat' (203), will use the pamphlet as he pleases. 'He has lost, and he knows it' (201), and it does indeed appear that 'Dostoevsky the artist' loses this exchange when two chapters later we learn that, fuelled by the pamphlet, Petersburg has begun to slide into anarchy. So Coetzee represents the Master as anything but masterful: Dostoevsky is caught up in, and manipulated by, events he cannot foresee and people he does not understand. More pressingly in this fiction, he is also caught up in a network of rogue sexual desires that belie the ethical ambitions of serious art—never more so than at the text's dismaying finale when he at last begins his novel, and out pours a truly vile stream of writing that combines together the pornographic and the sadistic around the figure of a child. What I am going to argue is that Coetzee's portrait of the Master pointedly refuses to accept any account of literary value grounded in notions of the artist's aesthetic distance, his privileged relation to the truth, or his access to higher values. Coetzee's interest lies instead in portraying literature as an equivocal and even marginal kind of discourse that emerges only in an unsettling way from a deeply compromised position of weakness. Recall our reading of *The Unnamable*: 'That's his strength,' Beckett's narrator said of his character Worm, 'his only strength, that he understands nothing, can't take thought, doesn't know what they want.' Or equally, recall the essay on Erasmus from the previous chapter, and its interest in defending the literary specifically as a condition of discursive 'weakness', as a sustained 'abnegation of big-phallus status' (103). Coetzee portrays Dostoevsky as often blind to his own motives, possessed of the most contemptible desires, and deeply implicated, in ways he can barely fathom, in political systems he can little comprehend: he is in no sense portrayed as someone who can outwit, or transcend, the powers and desires that shape and even animate him. As in *The Unnamable*, Coetzee's novel suggests that our understanding of literary value must start from 'nothing': from a full acknowledgement of the contingent and compromised position from which literature emerges.

THE DOSTOEVSKIAN PROJECT

Either during or just after the composition of *The Master of Petersburg* Coetzee wrote an essay called 'The Harms of Pornography: Catherine MacKinnon', collected in *Giving Offense* (1996), that deals with precisely the question of the status and value of art, and it is to this essay that we shall first turn.[3]

What interests Coetzee is MacKinnon's feminist attack on pornography, and in particular the totalizing ambition of the claims she makes. MacKinnon targets not only those publications most obviously recognizable as pornography, but the very idea that there might be a 'sacrosanct category for works of art' that exempts aesthetic experience from the critique she levels at blatantly pornographic images. I quote the passage of MacKinnon that Coetzee cites in *Giving Offense*:

Taking the work 'as a whole' ignores that which the victims of pornography have long known: legitimate settings diminish the perceptions of injury done to those whose trivialisation and objectification they contextualise. Besides . . . if a woman is subjected, why should it matter that the work has other value? *Maybe what redeems the work's value is what enhances its injury to women*, not to mention that existing standards of literature, art, science, and politics, examined in a feminist light, are remarkably consonant with pornography's mode, meaning and message.   (65; my italics)

Coetzee argues that these strictures on representation are animated by a Foucaultian impulse to 'recognize the master force, male power, operating behind its various conceptual masks' (68), coupled with a Sartrean analysis of the gaze, in which 'The relation between the one who looks and the one looked at is . . . fundamentally nonreciprocal because part of a power struggle' (70). As Coetzee points out, Sartre

---

[3] 'The Harms of Pornography' was one of the few chapters written specifically for *Giving Offense*, and not pre-published; it is therefore most likely to have been written after composition of *The Master of Petersburg* in 1994.

himself did in fact argue, principally with film in mind, for the possibility of an aesthetic space in which there was not only an 'obscene extreme', in which 'under the assaults of sadistic pain the subjecthood of the Other retreats, annihilated, into the facticity of flesh', but also a 'positive extreme', in which 'the body moves in a state of freedom, its every next movement unpredictable yet immediately in retrospect recognized as aesthetically necessary'. But unlike Sartre, MacKinnon refuses to concede 'the possibility of aesthetic redemption', as she 'clearly regards it as more urgent to address the politics of male hegemony than to affirm the freedom of artists to explore, for instance, the perverse' (65). Coetzee then raises an interesting hypothesis: say a 'male writer-pornographer' were to outline a project that aimed to explore the perverse in an open-ended fashion (without *a priori* assumptions about the intersection of gender identity with power) and that shared 'a thematics with pornography (including perhaps torture, abasement, acts of cruelty)'. 'If this project', Coetzee asks, 'were carried through and offered to the world, what would protect it from suffering the same fate—"delegitimisation"—as any work of pornography, except perhaps its *seriousness* (if that were recognised) as a philosophical project?' (73) Such a project is 'not fanciful', Coetzee insists, as 'to a reader sensitive to their implications, the twists and turns of erotic abasement in the novels of Dostoevsky are far more disturbing than anything likely to be encountered in commercial pornography' (73).

The project of the 'male writer-pornographer' is thus Dostoevsky's project, and given these remarks, it is possible to regard *The Master of Petersburg* as a text that tests the viability of such a project, for Coetzee's novel exposes Dostoevsky to the very strongest of these strictures on representation. Whereas MacKinnon was tempted to make a categorical distinction between print and visual media, arguing that film and photography, unlike literature, feature real people engaged in actual degrading acts, *The Master of Petersburg* allows no such exemption to Dostoevsky's writing, choosing to focus on the process through which the novelist gathers 'material' for his new book from real people going about their real lives. This involves, in Dostoevsky's case, an attempt to make some sort of artistic engagement with Pavel, his dead son, who will become in some shape or form the hero, or perhaps the anti-hero, of his next novel: the route to Pavel seems to involve Dostoevsky developing relationships with both a woman and a child that MacKinnon, and for that matter almost anyone else, would certainly, at times, find contemptible and degrading.

But the 'Dostoevskian project' that is at stake in *The Master of Petersburg* is indeed one that holds out at least the theoretical possibility of 'aesthetic redemption' for the 'writer-pornographer'. It was in large part through his encounter with Dostoevsky's writing that Bakhtin worked out the concept of dialogism, and Coetzee was thinking intensively about Bakhtin just prior to the composition of *The Master of Petersburg*.[4] While, as we have already seen, one aspect of Bakhtin's theory of dialogism was an analysis of 'double-voiced' language, equally important for Coetzee is his related theory of the artist. Most particularly, Bakhtin proposed the concept of a 'new authorial position', a new type of non-objectifying relationship between the novelist and his characters, and this he found best embodied in the novels of Dostoevksy.[5] Dostoevsky had his own rather pithy way of describing this 'new artistic position': as he put it in a letter of 1 February 1846 to his brother Mikhail, 'They [the public and the critics] have grown used to seeing in everything the author's mug; I didn't show mine.'[6] But the author in Bakhtin's theory has a more complex role, not reducible simply to the withdrawal of his 'mug':

---

[4] This is clear from his 1991 essay, 'Breyten Breytenbach and the Reader in the Mirror', where, writing about the complexity of Breytenbach's relation to his South African censors, he deployed the concepts of 'hidden polemic' and 'hidden dialogue'—ideas Bakhtin had defined as constitutive elements of dialogical discourse in Dostoevsky (*Giving Offense* 225).

[5] It is in this conception of the author–hero relationship, as pioneered by Dostoevsky, that Galin Tihanov finds most clearly 'the deep ethical layer in Bakhtin's aesthetics'. Galin Tihanov, *The Master and the Slave: Lukács, Bakhtin, and the Ideas of Their Time* (Oxford, 2000) 45.

[6] *Problems of Dostoevsky's Poetics*, 204.

The new artistic position of the author with regard to the hero in Dostoevsky's polyphonic novel is a *fully realized and thoroughly consistent dialogic position,* one that affirms the independence, internal freedom, unfinalizability, and indeterminacy of the hero. For the author the hero is not 'he' and not 'I' but a fully valid 'thou', that is, another and autonomous 'I' ('thou art'). The hero is the subject of a deeply serious, *real* dialogic mode of address, not the subject of a rhetorically *performed* or *conventionally* literary one.

(Problems of Dostoevsky's Poetics 63)

As Michael Holquist and Katerina Clark have argued, the Dostoevskian author resides in a state of 'extralocality', 'a position which can be known only through the most complex triangulation of interpersonal relations. It is a relationship and an activity more than a place, a location that has no existence in physical space'.[7] The activity is a process in which, to use the Dostoevskian metaphor, the author becomes possessed by the otherness of the hero: 'The author of a polyphonic novel is not required to renounce himself or his own consciousness, but he must to an extraordinary extent broaden, deepen and rearrange this consciousness...in order to be able to accommodate the autonomous consciousness of others' (68). Bakhtin also theorizes the moment of creation in terms that ground the aesthetic process in terms of a properly ethical comportment towards alterity:

Every creative act is determined by its object and by the structure of its object, and therefore permits no arbitrariness; in essence it invents nothing, but only reveals what is already present in the object itself... Once he has chosen a hero and the dominant of his hero's representation, the author is already bound by the inner logic of what he has chosen, and he must reveal it in his representation... Thus the freedom of the character is an aspect of the author's design. *(Problems of Dostoevsky's Poetics* 65)

Later, in the 'Notes Toward a Reworking of the Dostoevsky Book' (1961), Bakhtin would place even more emphasis on dialogism as

---

[7] Katerina Clark and Michael Holquist, *Mikhail Bakhtin* (Cambridge, Mass., 1984) 246.

the guarantor of a non-objectifying mode of engagement with otherness, through which both author and character experience a process of becoming free: for Bakhtin, the artist's special engagement with the hero is a heightened and idealized version of the ethics of everyday life (ibid. 290).

The disagreement between MacKinnon and Bakhtin over the nature of literary creativity is played out explicitly in *The Master of Petersburg* through the rivalrous relationship between Dostoevsky and Sergei Nechaev—a radical St Peterburg political activist. Dostoevsky is hostile to Nechaev's political extremism, telling him outright that 'the game you are playing is a game I cannot enter' (97), and privately condemning him in what are for Dostoevsky the strongest possible terms: 'Impossible to imagine Sergei Nechaev as a writer,' he thinks. 'An egoist and worse. A poor lover too, for sure…A pope of ideas, dull ideas' (196). Ultimately what distinguishes these rivals is not determinable at the level of rational principle (neither are exactly 'martinet[s] for principles' (36)) but instead their reliance upon different guarantees of seriousness. For Nechaev, 'If you do not kill you are not taken seriously. It is the only proof of seriousness that counts' (195). But for Dostoevsky, the '*Master of life*', the guarantee is ethical: in Bakhtin's terms, the artist's relation to his hero must be 'a deeply serious, *real* dialogic mode of address'. In 'The Harms of Pornography' Coetzee argued that the Dostoevskian project 'must enter the lists in an adversarial relation to MacKinnon's enterprise' (74). As Dostoevsky and Nechaev, Bakhtin and MacKinnon 'enter the lists' against each other in Coetzee's text, who emerges as the winner?

'VILENESS, OBSCENITY, PAGE AFTER PAGE OF IT'

The answer Coetzee makes to this question is one that, most fundamentally, wishes to avoid 'taking sides' in the rivalry at stake between the 'literary' and 'political' ways of knowing posed by Dostoevsky and Nechaev. Instead, *The Master of Petersburg* tries to open up anti-foundational ways of thinking about the nature of the literary, and this thinking cannot be extracted from the anti-foundational processes at work in the text itself: to come to a judgement about how Dostoevsky is presented in this fiction will therefore require detailed close reading.[8] However, whereas in the close readings made in previous chapters I have shown that the destabilizing energies of Coetzee's writing often derive from a 'jocoserious' movement between pathos and bathos, or the serious and the non-serious, *The Master of Petersburg* draws on different stylistic resources. The characteristic effects of this fiction derive instead from a sustained textual play with two different ways of judging Dostoevsky—and following Coetzee, I will name these as the perspectives of 'delegitimation' and 'redemption'.

The question of how to judge Dostoevsky dominates our encounter with the text from the very opening pages, in which he is ostensibly grieving for Pavel—for from the outset his thoughts and actions are troubled by some awkward suspicions. When he arrives at 'Sixty-three Svechnoi Street' (1) looking for Anna Sergeyevna, Pavel's landlady, he singles out from a group of children a particularly 'striking' girl (2). It turns out that the girl is no less than Anna's daughter—a remarkable coincidence in these crowded circumstances, where people live on top of each other in 'rickety wooden structures of two or even three storeys, warrens of rooms and cubicles' (1). Is it mere coincidence

---

[8] In literary-theoretical terms, this is because *The Master of Petersburg* in particular, and Coetzee's writing in general, is intertextual in the strong sense of that word—which is to say, as Kristeva puts it, productive of a condition of ambivalence between the literary and the political: 'The term "ambivalence" implies the insertion of history (society) into a text and of this text into history; for the writer, they are one and the same' (Julia Kristeva, 'Word, Dialogue and Novel,' *The Kristeva Reader*, ed. Toril Moi (Oxford, 1986) 39). In this essay Kristeva argues that Bakhtin's restructuring of the idea of the author—precisely the idea at stake in *The Master of Petersburg*—is pivotal to an intertextual handling of the novel: 'Bakhtinian dialogism identifies writing as both subjectivity and communication, or better, as intertextuality. Confronted with this dialogism, the notion of a 'person-subject of writing' becomes blurred, yielding to that of "ambivalence of writing"' (39).

that Dostoevsky singles out the girl? He will swiftly come to believe that she contains some spiritual residue of Pavel ('Somewhere in her he still lives' (14)), so perhaps, in a charitable explanation, it was a writer's intuition that guided him to her. Having paid for Pavel's room he enquires of her mother, 'You don't mind if I come now and then in the afternoons? Is there someone at home during the day?' He surely surmises that Anna, in this poverty-stricken area (these are 'the homes of the very poorest' (1)), will spend her days working, and therefore if anyone is at home in the afternoons it will be Matryona. (Perhaps Anna's muted reply already expresses concern about the nature of Dostoevsky's interest in residing in her apartment: "Matryosha is at home in the afternoons," she says quietly' (4).) When the exchange is over, the single word, 'Matryona' (5), is granted a paragraph to itself in the free indirect style that relays Dostoevsky's consciousness to us. Are we to read this interest in Matryona, an interest that immediately starts to dominate Dostoevsky's thoughts, as part of the writer's attempt to encounter his hero—to 'cast a spell' that will bring Pavel back to life in art (5)? Or should darker aspersions be cast upon the way she was singled out by the 'male writer-pornographer' as 'a girl with fair hair and striking dark eyes' from a group of boys before Dostoevsky could possibly have known she had anything to do with Pavel? Is the text offering to 'delegitimize' or to 'redeem' the 'Dostoevskian project'?

I am going to consider a long passage from the beginning of the third chapter, titled simply 'Pavel', as it is here that the artist starts to engage with the hero more fully, and also where the interplay between Dostoevsky's redemption and his delegitimation, already evident in the discordant nuances of the very beginning, starts to become especially complex. The previous chapter, 'The Cemetery', had ended with a vow made by Dostoevsky to Pavel: 'I will come again tomorrow, he promises: I will come alone, and you and I will speak. In the thought of returning, of crossing the river, finding his way to his son's bed, being alone with him in the mist, there is a muted promise of adventure' (11). These dubious thoughts establish the dynamic of the chapter. By 'his son's bed' Dostoevsky ostensibly refers to Pavel's grave, but this he never does get around to revisiting. What he will 'find his way' to is a much more literal conception of Pavel's bed—the one he slept in while alive. What is the nature of the 'promise of adventure'? Is it purely the adventure of writing, of becoming possessed by his son in the most intimate of his private spaces? Or is it an adventure of quite another kind—that of possessing the women who made up 'Pavel's erotic surround' (98) in Pavel's own bed?

It is the first type of 'adventure' that would seem to be suggested by the opening of the 'Pavel' chapter, as we find him sitting in his stepson's room with his white suit, trying to open himself to the sheer otherness of Pavel's experience in just the way Bakhtin's account of authorship required: 'breathing softly, trying to lose himself, trying to evoke a spirit that can surely not yet have left these surroundings' (12). He is then invited to have supper with Anna and Matryona, and while they are eating a rather different type of 'adventure' seems to begin. Dostoevsky's thoughts unpredictably turn to Anna, and take flight in an extraordinary paragraph: 'She strikes him as dry, dry as a butterfly's wing. As if between her skin and her petticoat, between her skin and the black stockings she no doubt wears, there is a film of fine white ash, so that, loosened from her shoulders, her clothes would slip to the floor without any coaxing' (13). 'She strikes him as dry, dry as a butterfly's wing,' he reflects, perhaps primarily out of impatience with the emotional dryness of her over-fastidious reluctance to pronounce his dead son's name; yet this impatience seems coupled with a sense of her beauty and refinement. 'As if', he continues, 'between her skin and her petticoat, between her skin and the black stockings she no doubt wears, there is a film of white ash': with the repeated focus on 'skin' we sense the rising current of desire, that seems to take over, yet further motivate, the writer's insight into the woman; this combines with irritation at an assumed prudishness in the 'black stockings she no doubt wears'. He goes on: 'so that, loosened from her shoulders, her clothes would slip to the floor' (and here desire seems more nakedly to take over from the writerly concern with Anna in herself), 'without any coaxing'. These last words, which round off the paragraph, come as a shock: Dostoevsky's desire seems now to have seized the reins from his engagement with Anna, fantasizing instead a scenario in which, like a prostitute, she would silently submit to him without any 'dialogism', even a dialogism most literally conceived as 'dialogue'—a category of verbal exchange he seems inclined to dismiss as mere 'coaxing'. Difficult to track the workings of desire here: it is never absent, and as I have suggested, even seems to provide the motivation for the extraordinary passage of description (the 'film of fine white ash' between her petticoat and skin, suggesting in the same moment a vivid sensuality and a morbid encasement in death—a masterful insight into the lived reality of Anna's situation); but his desire is unruly, and by the end of the paragraph seems to take over, deflating the vivid aesthetic apprehension of Anna into a pornographer's model, or a prostitute—someone who doesn't need to be 'coaxed' into doing exactly what he wants. Lest it be thought this is to read too much into the passage, consider Dostoevsky's thoughts about Anna in the previous chapter: 'Where does his desire come from? It is acute, fiery: he wants to take this woman by the arm, drag her behind the gatekeeper's hut, lift her dress, couple with her' (11). Note the 'take', 'drag', and 'couple': Dostoevsky's imagination is certainly coloured by aggression, and is alarmingly close to rape. But to return to the 'Pavel' chapter: in the lines following the paragraph quoted, whose conclusion seemed to obliterate Anna herself in the rising motion of Dostoevsky's desire, his apprehension of her modulates again:

He would like to see her naked, this woman in the last flowering of her youth.

Not what one would call an educated woman; but will one ever hear Russian spoken more beautifully? Her tongue like a bird fluttering in her mouth: soft feathers, soft wing-beats. (13)

We return to a form of engagement that can be more readily defended: to 'see her naked' in this context is to see Anna in a particular emotional state, one that carries a certain pathos ('this woman in the last flowering of her youth'), and above all one whose emotional colouring comes from herself. Dostoevsky now apprehends and renders the beguiling prettiness of Anna's voice: we are suddenly restored to the peaceful singing of her conversation after the currents of objectifying desire had seemed to have taken over and silenced her. So this is a complex portrait of the artist: his desire for the other seems tangled up with, and perhaps dependent upon, an objectifying desire—an unruly current of rogue energy that sustains and drives, but can also override, the ethical.

As the text advances, Coetzee's portrayal of Dostoevsky becomes ever more chromatic in its description of how desire is interwoven with representation. His thoughts turn to Matryona, who comes to him now with a sense of innocence, 'something of the young doe, trusting yet nervous, stretching its neck to sniff the stranger's hand, tensed to leap away', with none of her mother's 'soft dryness'; yet, he adds, 'the telltale signs are all there'. 'Telltale'? This seems to suggest a little more than the literal comparison with Anna's physical features (fingers, eyes, brow) that follows: is there not something rather leering in 'telltale'—perhaps envisioning in the young girl a kernel of the mother's sexuality, or even sexual availability? This is then coupled with a judgement that prefers the younger 'version' ('Strange how in a child a feature can take its perfect form while in the parent it seems a copy!'), a thought that even more frankly objectifies the people before him into the carriers of 'features'. Then his apprehension of the doe-like innocence of Matryosha darkens: 'The girl raises her eyes for an instant, encounters his gaze exploring her, and turns away in confusion. An angry impulse rises in him. He wants to grip her arm and shake her. Look at me, child! he wants to say: Look at me and learn!' (13). What is the nature of this 'gaze'? Is it 'delegitimized' as the 'male gaze' of the 'Harms of Pornography' essay—or is there, tangled up in here, some more dialogical apprehension that might offer to redeem it? Dostoevsky's reaction seems strange, as he has already conceived of Matryona as a 'young doe, trusting yet nervous, stretching its neck to sniff the stranger's hand, tensed to leap away'. But when she behaves in just that doe-like fashion upon discovering not the 'stranger's hand' but the stranger's 'gaze' upon her, an 'angry impulse rises in him'. It compares to the scene at Pavel's graveside, where Matryona was again involved in Dostoevsky's gaze, and where his response was equally loaded with violence: 'Let her see there are no bounds!... Herod, he thinks: now I understand Herod!' (9). Could it be that apprehending her as an innocent doe has less to do with her individuality, and rather more to do with a transference of some of the more corrupt of his own sexual desires? This is certainly the reading MacKinnon would give, and that Nechaev does indeed give to Dostoevsky later in 'The Printing Press' chapter: '"I know about your sentimentalising. You do it to women too, I'm sure. Women and little girls." He turns to the girl. "You know all about it, don't you? How men of that type drop tears when they hurt you, to lubricate their consciences and give themselves thrills"' (193). Nor is this analysis of his behaviour dismissed by Dostoevsky. 'For someone of his age,' he reflects to himself (albeit rather patronizingly), 'extraordinary how much he has picked up!' (194). 'Look at me and learn!' he silently voices to Matryona: is it only the depth of his grief for Pavel he wants to 'teach' her?

The scene calms when Dostoevsky drops his knife, and Anna intervenes in the conversation, speaking of the friendship between Pavel and Matryona. Dostoevsky makes a kindly offer to the girl: 'I would like you to have something of his,' he tells her. Then Matryona again starts to seem uncomfortable beneath his persistent gaze, returning a 'baffled look' in her eyes. The first thought comes: 'She cannot imagine me as Pavel's father,' no doubt because Pavel was not Dostoevsky's son by birth. But then a more complex thought emerges: 'And he thinks further: To her Pavel is not yet dead. Somewhere in her he still lives, breathing the warm, sweet breath of youth. Whereas this blackness of mine, this beardedness, this boniness, must be as repugnant as death the reaper himself' (14). Dostoevsky will later start to believe that Pavel is also living in Anna, and that through sexual intercourse with her he might find him. But what are we to make of this sudden intuition, following so quickly upon his sudden fantasies of sexual aggression? Are daughter and mother a way to Pavel, or is Pavel a way to the daughter and the mother? In a still darker twist, the writer's hope that Pavel survives in Matryona, and thus might be reached in a form that 'still lives', is coupled together with a truly wretched sexual jealousy. Entwined in the hope that through these women Pavel might be brought back from death into a new life in art is surely a sense of bitterness and envy that while the youthful Pavel is attractive to Matryona, and 'breathing the warm, sweet breath' of her youth, his own age and appearance can only make him an object of disgust, and can only exclude him from the richer sexual life she appears to offer. This opens a streak of sheer malice towards Pavel that is sustained, albeit sporadically, until the end of the book: not only do we encounter his 'envious imaginings' of Pavel's sexual experiences with Katri, made especially acute by his fantasy of her childlike body ('He resists the thought, then yields. He sees the Finn naked, enthroned on a bed of scarlet cushions, her bulky legs apart, her arms held wide to display her breasts and a belly rotund, hairless, barely mature. And Pavel on his knees, ready to be covered and consumed' (107)), but even after his own lovemaking with Anna Sergeyevna, his thoughts turn to his son: 'Poor child! The festival of the senses that would have been his inheritance stolen away from him!' Lying in Pavel's bed, whose iconic status for Dostoevsky we have already noted, 'he cannot refrain from a quiver of dark triumph' (135). Dostoevsky's apprehensions veer in an unruly fashion between protestations of love for Pavel, of responsibility towards him, and what appear to be sexually motivated assaults on his memory, combined with fantasies of sexual violence enacted on those his son knew best. 'From the depths of his throat, where he can no longer stifle it, a sound breaks out, a groan' (16). Does the groan express his grief for Pavel? Or is it for himself?

Following the text in such detail, we find that the gaze of this Orphic artist, committed to bringing his lost Eurydice back to life, can never be weeded out from the objectifying gaze of the 'male writer-pornographer': any movement towards 'otherness' is deeply intertwined—perhaps even constitutively so—with a calculative and objectifying intent. The next morning he sits at his desk waiting to write, 'but the writing, he fears, would be that of a madman—vileness, obscenity, page after page of it, untameable' (18). The chapter concludes with a thought that seems to extend an authorial love to Pavel, and find the impulse delegitimized, in the very same moment:

He cannot pretend he is writing. His mind is running to the moment of Pavel's death. What he cannot bear is the thought that, for the last fraction of the last instant of his fall, Pavel knew that nothing could save him, that he was dead. He wants to believe Pavel was protected from that certainty, more terrible than annihilation itself, by the hurry and confusion of the fall, by the mind's way of etherizing itself against whatever is too enormous to be borne. With all his heart he wants to believe this. At the same time he knows that he wants to believe in order to etherize himself against the knowledge that Pavel, falling, knew everything.   (21)

This sense of a gathering of incommensurabilities, a continual gathering and dispersing of Dostoevsky's seriousness (even, in passages like this, almost in the same instant) is woven into the very grain of the text. The insistent duplicity—the *weak* status that Coetzee's novel insists on attributing to the position of the author—is further enforced by the way the text picks up and transforms a motif specific to Bakhtin's theory of dialogism. Consider Bakhtin on the relationship between artist and hero:

Self-consciousness, as the artistic dominant in the construction of the hero's image, is by itself sufficient to break down the monologic unity of an artistic world—but only on condition that the hero, as self-consciousness, is really represented and not merely expressed, that is, does not fuse with the author, does not become the mouthpiece for his voice; only on condition, consequently, that accents of the hero's self-consciousness are really objectified and that the work itself observes a distance between the hero and the author. *If the umbilical cord uniting the hero to his creator is not cut*, then what we have is not a work of art but a personal document.
                              (*Problems of Dostoevsky's Poetics* 51, my italics)

Compare this passage from *The Master of Petersburg*, from the fourth chapter, 'The White Suit':

He is sitting on the bed with the white suit in his lap. There is no one to see him. Nothing has changed. He feels the cord of love that goes from his heart to his son's as physically as if it were a rope. He feels the rope twist and wring his heart. He groans aloud. 'Yes!' he whispers, welcoming the pain; he reaches out and gives the rope another twist. (23)

The 'cord of love' seems at first to suggest a dedication to Pavel, a pained responsibility to his otherness. But perhaps it does not require Bakhtin's strictures on the need to cut 'the umbilical cord uniting the hero to his creator' to apprehend a more dubious logic in this scene, one that pulls in quite a different direction. We are situated in the highly charged setting of Pavel's bed: the cord binds him to Pavel, but is it loving him, allowing Pavel to possess him, or is it capturing and possessing Pavel? And what lies in the groan, and the whispered 'Yes!'? Another comparable passage, from a later chapter titled 'Matryona', will cast its own light back on this scene:

He opens Pavel's suitcase and dons the white suit. Hitherto he has worn it as a gesture to the dead boy, a gesture of defiance and love. But now, looking in the mirror, he sees only a seedy imposture and, beyond that, something surreptitious and obscene, something that belongs behind the locked doors and curtained windows of rooms where men in wigs and skirts bare their rumps to be flogged. (71)

Catching sight of himself in the mirror, Dostoevsky is more inclined to doubt the nature of his interest in Pavel: from the idea it is an expression of love, from the sense that it is an attempt to engage with the alterity of the hero, it is suddenly traduced into a sado-masochistic fantasy (the groan, the extra twist, the 'Yes!') enacted on Pavel's bed. Unlike Bakhtin, in Coetzee's portrayal of the artist there is no claim that the ethical relation hoped for in aesthetic experience can ever fully transcend the situated and desiring self—that the 'umbilical cord' can ever be truly cut. The text (and author) always remain highly vulnerable to, though never—and this is the key point—simply *reducible* to, the same type of moral and political evaluation a reader would naturally bring to any other kind of writing.

Another Bakhtinian metaphor that Coetzee picks up and transforms is the 'mirror'. In 'Notes Toward a Reworking of the Dostoevsky Book' he argues that Dostoevsky was the first to reveal 'the complexity of the simple phenomenon of looking at oneself in the mirror: with one's own and with others' eyes simultaneously, a meeting and interaction between the others' and one's own eyes, an intersection of worldviews (one's own and the other's), an intersection of two consciousnesses' (*Problems of Dostoevsky's Poetics* 289). But here in *The Master of Petersburg* it is the very activity of Dostoevskian art itself that is required to encounter the gaze of the other in the mirror—the gaze of the censor, as Coetzee analyses it in his account of *Mouroir*, in 'Breyten Breytenbach and the Reader in the Mirror'. It is the idea of dialogism itself that is being made subject to the processes of a self-doubting 'dialogical frenzy' (*Giving Offense* 227). Return to the scene in which Dostoevsky is sitting on Pavel's bed, communing (as a charitable reading would have it) with the dead boy. Directly after he 'gives the rope another twist' the door opens and Matryona enters. 'Startled, he turns, bent and ugly, tears in his eyes, the suit bunched in his hands' (23). The view changes suddenly and cruelly from a passage that at least holds out the idea, however compromised, of a loving intensity of engagement, into the seediness that Matryona witnesses in him as his 'reader in the mirror'. Always teetering on the brink of the grotesque, he falls into the purely sordid, an old man, 'bent and ugly', moaning to himself. This is followed by a passage in which Dostoevsky's attentions turn to Matryona: his desire again starts to take flight when he is struck by her beauty, by 'the fine line of her temple and cheekbone, the dark, liquid eyes, the dark brows, the hair blonde as corn'. Then he is confronted by a sudden apprehension of the delegitimized version of himself in the mirror:

There is a rush of feeling in him, contradictory, like two waves slapping against each other: an urge to protect her, an urge to lash out at her because she is alive.

Good that I am shut away, he thinks. As I am now, I am not fit for humankind. (23)

Now his gaze returns to Matryona:

He raises his eyes to her. Nothing is veiled. He stares at her with what can only be nakedness.

For a moment she meets his gaze. Then she averts her eyes, steps back uncertainly, makes a strange, awkward kind of curtsy, and flees the room.

He is aware, even as it unfolds, that this is a passage he will not forget and may even one day rework into his writing. (24)

It is at this dubious moment that Dostoevsky's creativity starts to ignite: but from what sources does his inspiration come? Does it come because in this moment he has, in Bakhtin's terms, entered into a 'deeply serious, *real* dialogic mode of address'? In one sense it could be: he is there with the suit, trying to reach out to Pavel, or the Pavel he feels to be in Matryona ('He waits for her to say something. He wants her to speak. It is an outrageous demand to make on a child, but he makes it nonetheless' (23)). And yet such a view is plainly open to debunking: his desire for Pavel is, as we have seen, at least as strongly marked by sadism and possessiveness; his encounter with Matryona is entwined with an equally objectifying sexual violence. To say it is 'poised' between the one and the other is to bring a register of organization and control that the text does not invite: instead it lurches between mutually exclusive possibilities, now one, now the other—often focused together in the same paragraph, sentence, or even word. It is hard entirely to discount Dostoevsky's sincerity and seriousness, given the immense pain and self-loathing this process has engendered within him; yet it is equally hard to ignore, as he is the first to recognize, the shamefulness of the desires that compromise him and, more disturbingly, perhaps even animate his encounter with others.

SAVING DOSTOEVSKY?

Through this close reading I have tried to make evident Coetzee's determined refusal of any foundational way of perceiving the artist: the text continually prevents us from judging the Dostoevskian project either as an absolute 'redemption', or as an absolute 'delegitimation'. But before we can draw any conclusions on what the novel is saying about the nature of artistic inspiration, we must consider the ending of the text, in which Dostoevsky actually starts to set pen to paper. What I am going to suggest is that the ending pointedly refuses to grant a positive resolution to these questions: in fact it strongly tempts us to dismiss the possibility of 'redemption' altogether. As *The Master of Petersburg* progresses, the presentation of Dostoevsky increasingly narrows and darkens, such that by the end there seems to be almost nothing at all to hope for.[9]

It is in the concluding 'Stavrogin' chapter that Dostoevsky actually begins to write, and this is preceded by a 'fall' that finds him listening 'for the moment which may or may not arrive—it is not in his power to force it—when from being a body plunging into darkness he shall become a body within whose core a plunge into darkness is taking place, a body which contains its own falling and its own darkness' (234). This is a complex passage, and one that again seems to suggest the divergent possibilities with which we have engaged: either it is a delegitimized 'shameful fall' (234), in which the only body involved is his own, or it is a purer experience, resounding more closely with Pavel's fall from the tower, in which his son's

---

[9] Arguing that Coetzee's text demands of the reader a 'willingness to wait, to keep alternatives open', Derek Attridge has argued that the final chapter of Coetzee's novel fulfils 'the promise implicit in such demands: that there will be an end of waiting, that the time in the wilderness will be redeemed. Reader and character, perhaps writer too, are at last able to welcome the *arrivant*, even though the path to this moment remains obscure' (126). I am going to argue for a different reading of the ending of *The Master of Petersburg*—one that I think is closer both in spirit and detail to the text's broader presentation of authorship as weak, vulnerable, and divided.

experience is included within, but not assimilated to ('a body which contains its own falling and its own darkness') his own. But the actual writing that emerges indisputably belongs to our first interpretation of the fall—the 'shameful fall'. Dostoevsky writes two stories: the first, called 'The Apartment', is a revised version of a scene that has already happened: this story replays a scene in which Dostoevsky delighted in violating Matryosha's innocence by having intercourse with her mother while she looked on. The second, called simply 'The Child', is a nihilistic reworking of a story Dostoevsky had earlier told Matryosha about Pavel's white suit, in which the interest again lies in the sadistic violation of a child. The first 'act of writing' produces in Dostoevsky 'an exceptional sensual pleasure' (245); the second story he leaves exposed on his desk in the sure knowledge that Matryosha will come and read it, and become sexually corrupted in the process: 'It is an assault on the innocence of a child,' he reflects; 'It is an act for which he can expect no forgiveness' (249). The stories are in fact most proximate to a book Dostoevsky had earlier envisioned, to be called *Memoirs of a Russian Nobleman*.

A book of the night, in which every excess would be represented and no bounds respected. A book that would never be linked to him . . . With a chapter in which the noble memoirist reads aloud to the young daughter of his mistress a story of the seduction of a young girl in which he himself emerges more and more clearly as having been the seducer. A story full of intimate detail and innuendo which by no means seduces the daughter but on the contrary frightens her and disturbs her sleep and makes her so doubtful of her own purity that three days later she gives herself up to him in despair, in the most shameful of ways, in a way of which no child could conceive were the history of her own seduction and surrender and the manner of its doing not deeply impressed on her beforehand.   (134)

There is clearly no 'aesthetic redemption' in these stories, pieced together as they are from Dostoevsky's own sadistic and paedophilic lusts: they are a total betrayal of Pavel, not a true apprehension of him. In actual fact the stories at the end of *The Master of Petersburg* are very akin to the stories told in the chapter that was (in historical actuality, now) excised from Dostoevsky's novel *The Possessed*—the chapter known to most readers as 'Stavrogin's Confession'.[10] This is what Bakhtin had to say about it:

> No one else's word, no one else's accent forces its way into the fabric. There is not a single reservation, not a single repetition, not a single ellipsis. No external signs of the overwhelming influence of another's word appear to register here at all...The style is determined above all by a cynical ignoring of the other person, an ignoring that is pointedly deliberate. (*Problems of Dostoevsky's Poetics* 245)

Stavrogin's confession is for Bakhtin the epitome of anti-dialogical discourse: it is sheer objectification, a truly calculative 'male gaze' that is pornographic in both content and style.

But do these two pornographic texts tell the whole truth about Dostoevsky as a 'Master' novelist? Having reversed the hope of redemption in this emphatic way, we must now 'reverse the reversal too' (83), for *The Possessed* is not in fact the only Dostoevsky novel coming to life in *The Master of Petersburg*. We first encounter suggestions of another novel in the 'Maximov' chapter, where Dostoevsky is shown an excerpt of Pavel's writing. Pavel's story is about a 'landowner, who is portrayed as a gross sensualist' (40), who goes by the name of 'Karamzin' (41): Karamzin is a bully, a veritable embodiment of 'age and ugliness pawing maiden beauty', who attempts to rape a young woman called Marfa, but is prevented and then murdered by a man called Sergei, who is young enough to be his son. The allusions could hardly be clearer, especially when Dostoevsky muddles the name a few pages later—'Karamzin or Karamzov or whatever his name is' (47). Pavel's story is the seed for what will become *The Brothers Karamazov*—Fyodor Dostoevsky's late masterpiece, in which a tyrannical and sexually uncontrolled father,

---

[10] Most editions of *The Possessed* feature the excised chapter, 'Stavrogin's Confession', as an appendix to the novel. Having excised the chapter, Dostoevsky never attempted to reintegrate it in later editions—even though the gap it leaves in the completed text is discernible.

named Fyodor Karamazov, is murdered by his son Smerdyakov. (It is worth knowing that Smerdyakov is the son's 'familiar' name, but his Christian name is Pavel.[11]) Throughout the course of the novel, Dostoevsky becomes ever more intrigued by Pavel's story about doing away with his father: 'There was more real life', he recalls, 'in the filthy, waddling old bear in his story—what was his name? Karamzin?—than in the priggish hero he so painfully constructed. Slaughtered too soon—a bad mistake' (194). (The joke here is that in the novel the historical Dostoevsky would go on to write the 'filthy, waddling old bear' would not be 'slaughtered too soon': five hundred agonizingly tense pages would pass until Fyodor Karamazov is finally murdered.) Dostoevsky keeps thinking about Pavel's story, and by the end of *The Master of Petersburg* he is truly gripped by the creative possibilities it offers: 'He cannot pretend that the writing itself is not juvenile and derivative. Yet it would take so little to breathe life into it! He itches to take his pen to it, to cross out the long passages of sentiment and doctrine and add the lifegiving touches it cries out for' (216).

What is the significance of all these allusions to *The Brothers Karamazov*? Why is it important that the seeds of Pavel's story seem to be falling on such fertile ground? The answer relates to the particular type of story *The Brothers Karamazov* tells, and how this story itself informs Bakhtin's ideas about authorship. In *Dostoevsky and the Novel*, a commentary we know Coetzee studied closely, Michael Holquist stresses the similarities between the plot of *The Brothers Karamazov* and Freud's account of the primal horde myth,

---

[11] There are allusions to *The Brothers Karamazov* throughout Coetzee's text, of which the following are some important examples. The scene in the cellar with Nechaev provides the main elements of 'The Grand Inquisitor' story: Ivan Karamazov's phrase that 'everything is permitted', which is the basis for his legend, is employed by both Dostoevsky and Nechaev; Ivan's story, 'The Virgin Among the Damned', is told by Nechaev as the 'Pilgrimage of the Mother of God'. The great silent hug with which Christ answers the Grand Inquisitor's long disquisition, and which is copied by Alyosha as a response to Ivan's seemingly unanswerable arguments, finds its way into Coetzee's text when Dostoevsky hugs Nechaev as a riposte to his energetic and audacious assertions (190).

in which, as we have already seen, the sons band together to kill the oppressive father.[12] In the myth, the formation of the primal horde is occasioned by the unbridled exercise of the father's power at the financial and sexual expense of the sons; upon the death of the father a new order is instituted in which the acceptance of universal guilt for the murder is offset by the possibility of freedom, and a transcendence of the sharp antinomies of this psycho-political impasse. Holquist's analysis of the plot of *The Brothers Karamazov* makes it clear that Dostoevsky invites the reader to draw a parallel between the Karamazov family story and the Christian story of redemption, which also represents a passage from the unassailable (though not, in the strictly Christian context, tyrannical) law of God the Father to the transcendental freedom and grace brought by God the Son, who enacts in his body the Father's death, and brings the promise of the New Covenant. With the coming of the Son the binary oppositions between human and divine authority collapse: there is no longer a patriarchal mediation of grace.[13] Holquist argues that the plot of *The Brothers Karamazov* is a human enactment of this mythical narrative: it revolves around the capacity of different characters to place trust in the freedom of the 'time of Christ'—a leap of faith that not all the characters (for example Smerdyakov, who cannot overcome his subconscious craving for patriarchal domina-

---

[12] *Dostoevsky and the Novel* 177–81. As we have seen, Coetzee also uses the family drama of the primal horde story to characterize the 'countergenre' in *Age of Iron*.

[13] In line with his broader argument about Dostoevsky as a critic of the form of the novel, Holquist argues that the primal horde story has significance as a non-novelistic approach to storytelling: 'The liberating story Alyosha comes to tell is, of course, the life of Christ, not as a theological consolation (or not merely as such) but as a—literally—*viable* model of biography, a narrative that rationalises, mediates the transition from son to father' (189). By calling it 'viable', Holquist means to draw a contrast with the biographical model of narrative most familiar in the realist novel: instead of a narrative that seeks to discover at its ending a form of 'self-realization', the passage envisaged by *The Brothers Karamazov* centres instead upon transition in subject position, achieved through a process of gaining trust in what is necessarily unknowable.

tion) are capable of making, and which only Alyosha out of all the brothers is fully able to complete. The transition requires a trust in the future covenant of a radically free state—in the time without fathers, or at least without the father-position of power and authority—but along with Smerdyakov, Ivan has no faith in this possibility, and embodies his fears in the famous 'Grand Inquisitor' story, the tale of a man who cannot come to a moral acceptance of Christ's gift of radical freedom, and who therefore wishes to keep the whole of humanity in a state of primal childhood. The similarity between Bakhtin's 'dialogic' ideal and the story of displaced authority told in *The Brothers Karamazov* is not accidental. In their book on Bakhtin, Holquist and Clark in fact specifically trace Bakhtin's conception of the dialogical novelist to Dostoevsky's presentation of Christ in the 'Grand Inquisitor' legend, where Christ is presented 'a loving deity, who is silent so that others may speak and, in speaking, enact their freedom' (249).[14]

In *The Master of Petersburg* one of the most troubling thoughts for any reading that wishes to legitimize Dostoevsky as an artist is the thought that Pavel's story, which positions him as the tyrannical old father Karamzin or Karamazov is essentially correct in its allegory. This was certainly one way of reading Dostoevsky's interest in Matryona, Pavel's young friend, and his jealousy of Pavel's assumed sexual relationship with Katri—and this 'old matter of fathers and sons' (45) gradually insinuates its way into almost every relationship in Coetzee's text, casting ever darker doubts on the figure of the artist. Dostoevsky is insistent upon his assertion of a fatherly status

---

[14] Coetzee has himself pointed to the religious affiliations of Bakhtin's dialogism: 'I have a growing suspicion that Bakhtin attached a deep and specifically religious meaning to the notion which, I suspect, escapes many who have taken it over.' Eleanor Wachtel, 'The Sympathetic Imagination: A Conversation with J. M. Coetzee', *Brick* 67 (2001) 44. In *Diary of a Bad Year*, 'J.C.' declares himself out of sympathy with Ivan's 'rather vengeful views', even though they move him to tears: 'Contrary to him,' he says, 'I believe that the greatest of all contributions to political ethics was made by Jesus when he urged the injured and offended among us to turn the other cheek, thereby breaking the cycle of revenge and reprisal' (224).

with regard to Pavel, a status to which, as many are quick to observe, he has only a dubious claim: as Maximov reminds him, 'a man of twenty-one is his own master, is he not?' (34). Or as Nechaev tells him, albeit with some exaggeration: 'Do you know what you remind me of? Of a distant relative turning up at the graveside with his carpet-bag, come out of nowhere to claim an inheritance from someone he has never laid eyes on. You are fourth cousin, fifth cousin to Pavel Alexandrovich, not father, not even stepfather' (119). Like Fyodor Karamazov, who pursued a young woman called Grushenka (who was also his son Dmitry's lover), Fyodor Dostoevsky has not only pursued but married a woman 'much the same age' as Pavel (64), a marriage which, he is forced to recognize, fundamentally changed Pavel's attitude towards him (107). He comes to believe that the conflict of fathers and sons underlies the whole situation in which he finds himself: 'Not the People's Vengeance but the vengeance of the Sons: is that what underlies revolution—fathers envying their sons their women, sons scheming to rob their fathers' cashboxes? He shakes his head wearily' (108). Nechaev proudly vows that he will 'never be a father' (188), and Dostoevsky muses as to whether Nechaev's rage derives from the fact that his eyes have been opened to 'the fathers naked, the band of fathers, their appetites bared' (125). Increasingly to his mind it is 'A war: the old against the young, the young against the old' (247).

Even within the terms of *The Brothers Karamazov*, then, Dostoevsky would appear to be damned, not saved, by Coetzee's text. However, with this network of allusions in mind, we are now ready to appreciate the way in which the 'Stavrogin' chapter maintains, right up to the very end of the text, what I have called Coetzee's 'weak' defence of authorship and the literary. The ending of *The Master of Petersburg* in fact pulls in two directions: one direction, as we have already seen, assimilates Dostoevsky to the delegitimizing strictures on representation, and stalls upon Stavrogin's monologic confession; another direction, though, leads to the redeeming fulfilment of the Karamazov plot, and will lead Dostoevsky towards the creation of *The Brothers Karamazov*.

There is a scene towards the end of Coetzee's novel that takes place between Dostoevsky and Nechaev in a forgotten St Petersburg cellar. Here, Dostoevsky begins to feel he is losing the argument to Nechaev—that he is running out of responses in the face of Nechaev's awesome energy and moral force: 'he no longer knows where the mastery lies . . . All barriers seem to be crumbling at once: the barrier on tears, the barrier on laughter.' At this moment he claims that, if Anna were present, he would 'be able to speak the words to her that have been lacking all this time' (190). We have to turn back to 'The Shot Tower' chapter to discover what words Dostoevsky has in mind. Here, Dostoevsky tells himself that 'To make her understand he would have to speak in a voice from under the waters, a boy's clear bell-voice pleading out of the deep dark' (110). The boy's voice is that of Pavel, confined to a condition of childhood. Now, he feels—now that he, Dostoevsky, has reached a position of weakness and defeat—Pavel can speak. But instead of words, Dostoevsky steps forward and hugs and kisses Nechaev, thereby recalling (or anticipating) two important moments in *The Brothers Karamazov*: Christ's embrace of the Grand Inquisitor and Alyosha's copycat embrace of Ivan. In Dostoevsky's novel, both embraces are given as a response to an apparently unassailable logical argument, and in both cases the embrace is symbolic of a willingness to give a type of unconditional loving acceptance that the interlocutor cannot. But is this the meaning of Dostoevsky's embrace of Nechaev? While it is perhaps evidence of his emergent wish to become a Karamazov character (a Christ, or an Alyosha), and as we have seen is associated with a growth in Pavel's independence (perhaps Pavel now *can* speak), the embrace is altered in detail from Alyosha's. '*Trapping* his arms at his sides . . . he stands *locked* against him' (my italics). The gift of trust is far from being unconditional: he wishes to become Alyosha, so to speak ('breathing in the sour smell of his carbuncular flesh, sobbing, laughing'), but cannot quite do so as he retains the Grand Inquisitor's urge to control ('trapping . . . locked'). He is still, as the next chapter will show, in the scene of rivalry with Nechaev: the terms of father versus son still apply (190).

The question emerges: is our redescribed Dostoevsky actually able to fulfil the passage outlined in Holquist's reading of *The Brothers Karamazov*, and make an embrace like Alyosha's—one that is not that of a father trapping his son, but a genuinely open embrace of the other? Clearly what is of importance to the Karamazov narrative we are giving here is the extent to which Dostoevsky ceases to occupy his subject-position as father and as master, and this question, as Dostoevsky realizes, comes to a crisis in the final chapter: 'Either Pavel remains within him, a child walled up in the crypt of his grief, weeping without cease, or he lets Pavel loose in all his rage against the rule of the fathers.' One possibility open at the end of the novel is that Dostoevsky chooses this latter path—the path of self-abnegation, in which the father 'Fyodor' will be killed off: he starts to conceive of himself not as a father but as a mother ('must he give himself to being fathered by it?'); he also feels he is dying, losing all trace of himself ('Is he required,' he asks, 'to put aside all that he himself is, all that he has become, down to his very features, and become as a babe again?' (238–40)). But the crucial moment in Coetzee's text—the paragraph that precedes the one in which Dostoevsky starts writing ('Then at last the time arrives')—leaves open the two divergent possibilities. Rather fittingly for a text so concerned with the objectifying effects of pornography, it is the genitalia of the 'other' that is most at stake: Dostoevsky gazes on Pavel's genitals, 'the body-parts without which there can be no fatherhood', and he reflects that 'nothing is private any more'. There is a certain rather wry irony here. 'Nothing is private' is a line of Nechaev's: does this mean that delegitimization has triumphed—that the hostile gaze of Nechaev is present even here, at the moment of artistic creation? If so, the irony is caustic. Pavel's 'privates', his private parts, are no longer private to him, because they are objectified into Dostoevsky's pornographic text. In this reading there is no dialogism, no Karamazov narrative: it is the old story of merely calculative thinking. But an alternative reading would suggest that by forcing himself to stare at his stepson's genitals, Dostoevsky is making a recognition, 'as unblinkingly as he can', of Pavel's claim to paternity: he is trying to bring about his own displacement as father by putting Pavel's seed before his own. It is this act of 'saving' Pavel's 'seed' that brings 'aesthetic redemption'—that saves the Dostoevskian project (241). As an act of hospitality it constitutes a transition away from patriarchal control through the leap of trust—that leap which only Alyosha of all the Karamazov brothers was finally able to make.

In *The Master of Petersburg* the 'redemptive' text is, to recall Beckett's phrase, almost entirely 'beside the point': it is always only on the verge of being written, and it is readable only in the margins of its hostile assimilation. By fulfilling the Karamazov plotline to the extent of dying as father and trusting in the new world of the son, Dostoevsky goes on to have new life in writing *The Brothers Karamazov*, which, according to Bakhtin, is the dialogical novel *par excellence*; in the other version of events, he writes out the monologic pornography of Stavrogin's confession. The ending of the text, as with the continual semantic oscillation of the narrative, is anxiously poised between two competing outcomes—with, it hardly needs now to be stressed, the delegitimizing critique being by far the more obvious, and the redemptive version all but buried in a dense thicket of literary allusions. Instead of making a claim for the transcendent power of the artist, Coetzee's fiction insists upon his weakness and his vulnerability to hostile interpretation. Yet to be vulnerable and weak is not to be utterly devoid of power. *The Master of Petersburg* presents literature in anti-foundational terms as a practice necessarily subject to delegitimizing interpretations which themselves, in turn, necessarily risk illegitimacy.

7

'Is this the right image of our nation?' *Disgrace* and the Seriousness of the Novel

> It was not the erotic that was calling to him after all, nor the elegiac, but the comic.
>
> J. M. Coetzee, *Disgrace*.[1]

As John Gray has argued in *Two Faces of Liberalism* (2002), while there is no difficulty in accepting in an abstract sense that 'incompatible value-judgements need not be contradictory when the differing moral practices are distant from one another in time or place,' late twentieth-century politics has often posed the more challenging problem of how competing and incommensurate judgements of what constitutes the good might coexist.[2] It is precisely this problem of value pluralism that is raised by the constitution of post-apartheid South Africa. This is the Preamble to the constitution:

We, the people of South Africa, Recognise the injustices of our past; Honour those who suffered for justice and freedom in our land; Respect those who have worked to build and develop our country; and Believe that South Africa belongs to all who live in it, united in our diversity. We therefore, through our freely elected representatives, adopt this Constitution as the supreme law of the Republic so as to

---

[1] J. M. Coetzee, *Disgrace* (London, 1999) 185.
[2] John Gray, *Two Faces of Liberalism* (Cambridge, 2002) 55.

- Heal the divisions of the past and establish a society based on democratic values, social justice and fundamental human rights
- Lay the foundations for a democratic and open society in which government is based on the will of the people and every citizen is equally protected by law;
- Improve the quality of life of all citizens and free the potential of each person; and
- Build a united and democratic South Africa able to take its rightful place as a sovereign state in the family of nations.[3]

The aspiration of the constitution is to hold together what amount to two divergent ideas of the goal of the state, and at the level of the individual, two divergent ideas of subjectivity. On the one hand, there is a commitment to 'democratic values' and 'fundamental human rights', ideas deriving from what I have been calling the politics of equal dignity—a universalistic politics that regards citizens as abstractly equal and autonomous individuals. On the other hand, there is a commitment to the achievement of 'social justice', and to not only recognizing but healing 'the injustices . . . [and] divisions of the past', a commitment which of necessity puts aside the concept of the abstract individual in favour of some form of the politics of difference. A post-apartheid government in South Africa that did not attempt to redress the centuries-old economic and cultural oppression of the majority ethnic groups would be inconceivable; equally, though, there are values in the universalist strand of the enlightenment political legacy—freedom, human equality, respect for the value of the individual—that are important for any approach to a truly 'moral community'.

Yet for those who wish to see the divergent goals of the constitution prevail in a pluralist form of statecraft in South Africa, *Disgrace* has been the cause of much dismay.[4] The problem most readers

---

[3] See the South African constitution website: http://www.info.gov.za/documents/constitution/1996/96preamble.htm, accessed 21 Dec. 2009.

[4] *Disgrace* has more frequently been read in the context of the Truth and Reconciliation Commission (TRC) rather than the Constitution: while this resonance is undeniable, it does not restrict an appreciation of the broader intervention

encounter at the level of character and storyline derives from the
novel's portrayal of a collision between what I defined in Chapter 1
as the two forms of the politics of equal recognition that suggests no
form of accommodation is possible. The text seems to produce, or
even flaunt, a dismaying political allegory in which the universalistic
liberal ideals that David Lurie defends seem to have no future at all
in the new South Africa. Lurie's refusal to accept that his relationship
with Melanie had any wider relation to the 'long history of exploitation' between white and non-white, or male and female ('there are
no overtones in this case', he angrily insists (50)) costs him his job at
the university, and it is hard not to agree with the assessment of one
of his colleagues that he is 'a hangover from the past, the sooner
swept aside, the better' (40). Far from moving towards some sort of
compromise with the demands of the politics of difference, as
Disgrace progresses Lurie becomes ever more single-minded and
incapable of change. He is unable to give up his interest in Melanie,
and towards the end of *Disgrace* he is once again hounded out of
Cape Town by her friend Ryan, who tells him, again using the
language of 'overtones', to 'Stay with your own kind' (194). When
his daughter Lucy refuses to report her rape—regarding her father's
talk of equal rights as an irrelevance 'in this place, at this time'
(112)—he responds with such a monotone of horror and disgust
that she is ultimately forced to show him the door. He continues to
criticize Lucy's choice, with escalating urgency, right until the novel's closing pages:

'Lucy, your situation is becoming ridiculous, worse than ridiculous, sinis-
ter. I don't know how you can fail to see it. I plead with you, leave the farm

Coetzee's text is making in the South African cultural field, which, as we will see, the
most astute critics of the novel within the public sphere (especially Jakes Gerwel)
were quick to apprehend. For *Disgrace* in relation to the TRC see Rosemary Jolly,
'Going to the Dogs: Humanity in J. M. Coetzee's *Disgrace, The Lives of Animals*,
and South Africa's Truth and Reconciliation Commission', *J. M. Coetzee and the
Idea of the Public Intellectual* 148–71; Rebecca Sanders, '*Disgrace* in the Time of a
Truth Commission', *Parallax* 11/3 (2005) 99–106.

before it is too late. It's the only sane thing left to do.' . . . He goes to bed with a heavy heart. Nothing has changed between Lucy and himself, nothing has healed.   (201)

Then, right at the end of the novel, in almost the very last scene he will have with Lucy, he lets loose the following thoughts about Pollux, Lucy's black neighbour: 'The word still rings in the air: *Swine!* Never has he felt such elemental rage. He would like to give the boy what he deserves: a sound thrashing. Phrases that all his life he has avoided seem suddenly just and right: *Teach him a lesson, Show him his place*' (206). Nothing changes, nothing heals. As the text progresses, David Lurie becomes ever more the image that his adversaries hold of him: not only is he evasive of his situatedness in the 'long history of exploitation', he becomes well and truly tarred with the brush of explicit racism. He ends up living alone in a rather grim boarding house, along with another lost soul: 'a retired school-teacher' (211), in fact—possibly someone who has undergone a similar process of ostracization.

   Professor Jakes Gerwel, Director-General of the President's Office under Nelson Mandela, and himself an influence in the shaping of the South African constitution, responded to the problems, at once political and literary, that *Disgrace* poses in two useful newspaper articles. In the first, 'Is this the right image of our nation?', Gerwel praised Coetzee as a faithful chronicler of 'the dislocation of the white-in-Africa', but found himself dismayed by *Disgrace* as a whole, particularly its portrayal of the 'almost barbaric post-colonial claims of black Africans'; its representation of 'mixed-race charac-ters' as 'whores, seducers, complainers, conceited abusers'; most importantly, its apparent 'exclusion of the possibility of civilised reconciliation'.[5] David Lurie himself was regarded as an especially dismaying character, most pointedly because, as Gerwel perceived, the genre of the novel typically enjoins us to treat its hero as in some

---

[5] Jakes Gerwel, 'Perspektief: Is *dit* die regte beeld van ons nasie?' ('Perspective: Is *this* the right image of our nation?'), trans. Peter McDonald, *Rapport* (13 Feb. 2000) 2.

way representative: 'That such racists exist, is no surprise; that the nation can be typified thereby, is a question.' However, for all these reservations about *Disgrace*, as the title of Gerwel's follow-up article asserted, 'It is nonetheless better than Roodt's lightness of spirit.' Here he suggested that while Coetzee's text may indeed provide a dismaying picture of the new South Africa, it is at least a serious novel, and should be credited as such by its readers—unlike 'the stylised wispiness of, for example, Dan Roodt'. The novels of Dan Roodt are, for Gerwel, capable only of a 'parodying lightness of spirit', and thus lacking in the serious ambition of Coetzee's fiction.[6]

The way in which Gerwel couples a general sense of the high purpose of the form of the novel in mediating the conflicts of national life, with a view that *Disgrace* in particular is unacceptably bleak and dismaying, is perfectly logical. If the novel is to be taken seriously as a literary genre for the special way in which it allows us imaginatively to experience and reflect upon the most telling of our shared political and moral dilemmas, then David Lurie's isolated ending will quite logically be read into a series of extremely pessimistic meanings for the new South Africa, and the hopes expressed by its constitution.[7] But we might ask our own question of Gerwel. What would it mean for *Disgrace*, as a novel, to produce a 'right

[6] Jakes Gerwel, 'Perspektief: Dís tog beter as Roodt se ligsinnigheid' ('Perspective: It is nonetheless better than Roodt's lightness of spirit'), trans. Charl Engela, *Rapport* (9 Apr. 2000) 6. Dan Roodt is an Afrikaans-speaking writer and activist, perhaps best known for his strong views on the preservation of Afrikaans, and his trenchant criticism of the ANC.

[7] As a further measure of the dismay that *Disgrace* has elicited as an image of post-apartheid South Africa, consider Athol Fugard's disgust that 'we've got to accept the rape of a white woman as a gesture to all of the evil that we did in the past. That's a load of bloody bullshit. That white women are going to accept being raped as penance for what was done in the past? Jesus. It's an expression of a very morbid phenomenon, very morbid.' Fugard, however, had not read *Disgrace* at the time of making these remarks. See Christopher Goodwin, 'White Man without the Burden,' *Sunday Times News Review*, 16 Jan. 2000.

image of our nation'? The classic realist novel displayed a good deal of confidence in producing such images. For example, like *Disgrace*, Elizabeth Gaskell's *North and South* (1854–5) also created an image of a nation divided between radically divergent ideologies: on the one hand, a rationalist utilitarianism, embodied allegorically in 'the North', its industrialists, and its new forms of human relationship; on the other hand 'the South', rooted in more traditional and hierarchical cultural practices. But Gaskell's novel suggests that these divergent ideas, cultures, and geographies might indeed be brought to what Gerwel called a 'civilised reconciliation': the industrialist Mr Thorton is gradually won over by Margaret Hale's 'southern' values (as in turn is she by some of his) and starts to reform some of the most deleteriously utilitarian aspects of his business enterprise; ultimately they marry, and in a nice twist that crowns the symbolic union, Margaret provides the capital for Thornton's next business enterprise. Underpinning the form of *North and South* are two important assumptions. First, that the author can make recourse to the position Coetzee referred to as 'herald of community', in which the novel implicitly claims to address politics from a position assumed to be somehow systematically beyond the conflict at stake in the nation. Secondly, that the conflict might be resolved not through politics itself but on a 'human level' through a transcendent form of recognition: while Thornton and Margaret may differ ideologically, they share a common humanity that, through love, is capable of bringing those differences to a creative sublation. But a novel that would seek to typify and reconcile post-apartheid South Africa has to deal with the fact that a more complex demand is now being placed on the politics of recognition than was the case in nineteenth-century England. With regard to the first assumption, it is precisely the idea of a disinterested perspective upon the world that is being challenged by David Lurie's opponents in *Disgrace*: in the more extreme instances, these adversaries completely distrust the idea of a discourse that claims to rise above the general political situatedness of the subject. (It is of course Lurie himself who is the novel's main advocate of 'equal dignity': after Lucy's rape, he persistently tries to sympathize with her and to share her perspective, but Lucy insists any such attempt is not only an impossibility, but is also a particular kind of invasiveness.[8]) The second assumption underpinning *North and South*—the resolution 'at the human level'—is again one that Lurie's critics reject, once more through the lens of the politics of difference: such would be to obfuscate the 'long history of oppression' that Farodia Rassool invokes. (Again, while Lurie wants to believe his encounter with Melanie is a unique intersubjective encounter, his critics regard this as merely delusional: human relationships, especially the romantic, are instead the site upon which power relations intersect.) To write the kind of novel that Gerwel projects would be to place a falsifying bias on the complex demand that the South African constitution makes upon the future, for as we have seen, this future is explicitly one that refuses to choose between the competing legacies within the politics of equal recognition.

In what sense, then, might *Disgrace* be the 'right image of our nation'? Recall that Gerwel was dismissive of Dan Roodt's pernicious 'lightness of spirit', and was glad, despite his reservations, that *Disgrace* was by contrast serious writing. The rest of this chapter will argue that Coetzee's text engages with the political condition of value-pluralism within the constitution of post-apartheid South Africa by taking a more circumspect stance towards its own seriousness than has generally been realized. While *Disgrace* may appear to submit a remorselessly clear political allegory in which Lurie and all he stands for have no future, it in fact complicates its own act of truth-telling through a creatively disorienting variety of comic experience. In Chapter 3 I spoke of Coetzee's approach to literary truth as the cultivation of a 'subversive juridicity' whose interest lies in playing with the rules ('JOEY RULES') of different ways of thinking. Essential to

---

[8] Lucy suggests that as a man, Lurie is only able to take the rapist's perspective: 'Maybe, for men, hating the woman makes sex more exciting. You are a man, you ought to know' (158). Lucy also tells her father that, unlike him, she doesn't 'act in terms of abstractions' (112).

this process is what Coetzee, referring to Beckett, spoke of as a 'comic energy' that has the 'power to surprise'. Although David Lurie seems to become 'little enough' in the course of the story *Disgrace* tells—or perhaps 'less than little', and even 'nothing' (220)—this is a text written distinctively 'after Beckett' that is deeply interested in the 'nothing', and in what it means to give voice to that which has been made 'beside the point'.

Disgrace includes its own metafictional commentary on the place of comic experience in the work of art, and it is with this that we shall begin. David Lurie has from the beginning of the text been at work on an opera, *Byron in Italy*. It started life as a passionate *ménage-a-trois* between the youthful Teresa, her husband, and the adulterous Byron, with a lush musical setting, probably to be borrowed from Strauss. However, back in his wrecked flat near the end of *Disgrace*, Lurie starts to reconceive it: 'A woman complaining to the stars that the spying of the servants forces her and her lover to relieve their desires in a broom-closet—who cares?' (181). Trying 'another track', and 'abandoning the pages of notes he has written', he drops the husband entirely, and 'tries to pick Teresa up in middle age'. Byron's voice returns, but only falteringly, as if from the underworld. In a further reconception, 'it becomes clear that purloined songs will not be good enough, that the two will demand a music of their own', and setting to work on a score he never imagined writing, he finds, 'astonishingly, in dribs and drabs, the music comes'. But even more astonishing is how the music comes: the piano sound is 'too rounded, too physical, too rich', and instead Lurie goes up to the attic and 'from a crate full of old books and toys of Lucy's, he recovers the odd little seven-stringed banjo that he bought for her on the streets of KwaMashu when she was a child'. Now, 'to his surprise', the 'silly plink-plonk' of the banjo becomes utterly inseparable from the composition—indeed, Teresa is to carry and play the banjo on stage, 'on which she accompanies herself in her lyric flights; while to one side a discreet trio in knee breeches (cello, flute, bassoon) fill in the entr'acts'. The passage that follows must be quoted in full:

Seated at his own desk looking out over the overgrown garden, he marvels at what the little banjo is teaching him. Six months ago he had thought his own ghostly place in *Byron in Italy* would be somewhere between Teresa's and Byron's: between a yearning to prolong the summer of the passionate body and a reluctant recall from the long sleep of oblivion. But he was wrong. It is not the erotic that is calling to him after all, nor the elegiac, but the comic. He is in the opera neither as Teresa nor as Byron nor even as some blending of the two: he is held in the music itself, in the flat, tinny slap of the banjo strings, the voice that strains to soar away from the ludicrous instrument but is continually reined back, like a fish on a line.

So this is art, he thinks, and this is how it does its work! How strange! How fascinating!   (185)

In his account of *Disgrace*, Derek Attridge cites this passage as part of an argument that, like my own, seeks to complicate the apparently remorseless conclusions of the novel's political allegory. He argues that while Coetzee's novel may seem to be producing an overpoweringly dark image of South Africa, through the character of David Lurie the text makes its own counter-affirmation of ethical values: Attridge interprets his composition of the opera as an act of 'other-directed toil' (182), suggestive of the beginnings of a redemptive relation with alterity that is equally evident in Lurie's growing relationship with animals.[9] However, in referring to this passage Attridge does not consider two important aspects of the mysterious moment of composition.[10] The first is the role of the comic: 'It was

---

[9] In Attridge's reading, Lurie comes to embody the 'obstinate assertion of values more fundamental, if more enigmatic, than those embodied in the discourses of reason, politics, emotion, ethics, or religion—those discourses that govern the new South Africa and much else besides' (186). He is a character who moves away from the rationalist and humanistic position he defended before the committee, and indeed before his daughter Lucy, in ways that he barely understands and that he certainly cannot predict. While I agree that Coetzee's novel is placing the discourses that govern the cultural field of South Africa in doubt, I will argue that Lurie should not himself be regarded as an allegorical embodiment of that process, but a figure within it.

[10] See *J. M. Coetzee and the Ethics of Reading* 183.

not the erotic that was calling to him after all, nor the elegiac, *but the comic.*' The second is what happens to David when the comic enters his work of art, and the verb *Disgrace* used here is crucial: 'He is in the opera neither as Teresa nor as Byron nor even as some blending of the two: he is *held* in the music itself, in the flat, tinny slap of the banjo strings.' 'Held' implies that the comic sound of the banjo holds him back, as indeed Lurie recognizes, in his 'voice that strains to soar away from the ludicrous instrument but is continually reined back, like a fish on a line'. But 'held in' also suggests 'preserved', or 'protected', or at the very least, 'retained': it suggests, strangely, that the disruptively comic element is what keeps him going, albeit with an assuredly different status than the one his straining, soaring voice would wish to have. It makes no suggestion that he changes or develops, or that he becomes more compellingly ethical. To be precise, he is 'held'.

In order to explore how the comic movement in *Disgrace* works, and how it has the effect of preserving or protecting David Lurie—'holding' him, not simply letting him be 'swept aside'—we must consider the various types of comic experience to which the text alludes, as comedy in fact makes a number of appearances in different shapes and forms in this serious text. The first type is 'bourgeois comedy', upon which David reflects when he suggests, jokingly, that Melanie marry a man who cooks: 'Together they contemplate the picture: the young wife with the daring clothes and gaudy jewellery striding through the front door, impatiently sniffing the air; the husband, colourless Mr Right, aproned, stirring a pot in the steaming kitchen. Reversals: the stuff of bourgeois comedy' (14). There is a certain unwitting prescience here into his own 'reversal', but as well as bourgeois comedy we have the type of comedy in which Melanie herself performs, *Sunset at the Globe Salon*: 'A comedy of the new South Africa set in a hairdressing salon in Hillbrow, Johannesburg . . . Catharsis seems to be the presiding principle: all the coarse old prejudices brought into the light of day and washed away in gales of laughter' (23). Akin to 'bourgeois comedy', with its play of reversals and restoration, Melanie's comedy is straightforwardly political, using whatever fragile consensus may exist to affirm a community freed from the past. But its technique is that of farce: part of Melanie's role is to trip over an electric cord and make the lights go out: 'A more Marx Brothers atmosphere', the director urges. Adding to these two types of comedy, we also have Lurie's own biting Byronic wit:

> That sarcastic levity of tongue,
> The stinging of a heart the world hath stung,
> That darts in seeming playfulness around,
> And makes those feel that will not own the wound.[11]

Lurie is himself a quite magnificent comic performer, with a keen satiric eye and a sharp wit. Thinking through his own life as a teacher, he considers the chief irony of his profession to be that 'the one who comes to teach learns the keenest of lessons, while those who come to learn learn nothing'. Then comes the playful dart: 'It is a feature of his profession on which he does not remark to Soraya [a prostitute]. He doubts there is an irony to match it in hers.' (5) Later, reflecting on whether Origen performed the act of castration upon himself, comes a stinging observation:

Severing, tying off: with local anaesthetic and a steady hand and a modicum of phlegm one might even do it oneself, out of a textbook. A man on a chair snipping away at himself: an ugly sight, but no more ugly, from a certain point of view, than the same man exercising himself on the body of a woman.   (9)

It is sharp, expertly timed gallows humour: surely the masterstroke of the first sentence is the immeasurably filthying 'out of a textbook', through which the calm and civility of the classroom and the grotesque spectacle of self-castration glance off each other; in the second sentence the pause over the reflection 'from a certain point of view' times the clinching phrase, 'exercising himself on the body of a woman', to perfection. No need to enumerate the many sharp comic twists with which Lurie's discourse is filled: from fleeting satirical

[11] Lord Byron, 'Lara', ll. 73–6, *Poetical Works* (Oxford, 1970) 304.

reflections ('Country dirt: honourable, he supposes' (61)), to the brilliantly crass ('Do I like animals? I eat them, so I suppose I must like them, some parts of them' (81)), to the downright outrageous ('Sapphic love: an excuse for putting on weight' (86)). Suffice to say that this witty performance contributes a great deal to making Lurie such an engaging, if at times repellent, character to follow.[12]

But if Lurie is said to be 'held' in the comic twang of the banjo, which of these modes—the bourgeois comedy, the farce, the brilliant Byronic wit—is the distinctive comedy of *Disgrace*? The answer (none of the above) comes in a strange place indeed, in the most serious pages of the book—the rape scene. Lucy and David are out walking the dogs, and are passed by three men: they 'reach the plantation boundary' and then turn back for home; back at 'the farm' the men want to be let in, explaining that they need to telephone. Asked where they are from, one says 'From Erasmuskraal': 'Erasmuskraal, inside the forestry concession' (92), a hamlet on the other side of the 'boundary' at which they turned back earlier. Erasmian comedy—a disorienting play with the boundaries of folly and wisdom, the comic and the serious—is of course already familiar to us, both from Coetzee's essay 'Erasmus: Madness and Rivalry', and our reading of the Quixotic endeavours of Elizabeth Curren in *Age of Iron*. But why introduce all this talk of Erasmus (whose emblem, we recall from Chapter 5, was Terminus, the god of boundaries) just before the gang-rape of Lucy—the most deadly serious part of the book?

To answer this we must consider the effect the rape has on the experience of reading *Disgrace*. The rapists emerge from behind one boundary, 'the plantation boundary', and bring nothing but serious-ness in their wake: that is to say, their actions profoundly harden the allegorical boundary-lines of the text. When he was living in Cape Town and teaching at the university, there was an accommodation

---

[12] I have written elsewhere on the unusual sources of Coetzee's interest in Byron: 'Byron, Stavroguine, Lurie: comique et gravité dans *Disgrâce*', in *J. M. Coetzee et la littérature européenne: écrire contre la barbarie*, ed. Jean-Paul Engélibert (Presses Universitaires de Rennes, 2007).

of sorts between Lurie and his opponents: while he was required to teach 'Communications 101' and its equally instrumental compan- ion course, 'Communications 102', his values were not utterly excluded from the academy: he was after all given the opportunity to carry on teaching the humanities, albeit through a rather patron- izing formula ('good for morale' (3)). The divergent political values of the new South Africa lived alongside each other, however uneasy that *modus vivendi* might have been, but his abusive relationship with Melanie swiftly changed everything: the lines hardened, and he was ejected from the university. However, out on the farm with Lucy, away from the *mêlée* of the city and its media circus, the hard and fast boundaries erected by the Inquiry seemed to lapse again. While it was quite apparent that David and Lucy occupied opposite sides of the ideological divide, they had a tolerance of each other, and neither took their differences too seriously. Consider the following exchange, prompted by Lurie's ongoing reflections on the theologi- cal debate over whether animals have souls:

Lucy shrugs. 'I'm not sure that I have a soul. I wouldn't know a soul if I saw one.'

'That's not true. You are a soul. We are all souls. We are souls before we are born.'

She regards him oddly.   (79)

This moment crystallizes the quite absolute difference not only between them, not least by the way it encapsulates the divergent sides of South Africa's pluralism: Lucy's unpretentious materialism is obviously incommensurate with David's concern for the inner human essence. In speaking of 'the soul' David has not suddenly got religion: whether conceived as soul, or spirit, or inner rationality, David means to invoke a sense of the irreducible value of each individual, as well as a sense that all humans are equally valuable.[13]

---

[13] See John Gray, *Enlightenment's Wake* (London, 1995) 144–84, for an analysis of how the type of enlightenment humanism embodied by Lurie in fact emerges from, and depends upon, transcendental ideas relating to human equality that

While they plainly disagree, at this point their disagreement doesn't really matter: Lucy regards David with a certain bemusement, their conversation changes track, and they carry on their lives together.

But the rapists from Erasmuskraal force this relatively peaceful coexistence into the starkest of polarizations. In her decision as to whether or not to report the crime, Lucy is required to make an unforgivingly absolute choice between a sense of the wrong done to her as an individual, and the demands she perceives to be made by the situation she occupies as a white woman—in effect a choice between the politics of equal dignity and the politics of difference. Of course she chooses the latter: rejecting David's insistence upon her abstract equality, she decides on a course of action that seeks to do justice instead to the way in which she is concretely situated 'in this time, and in this place', which eventually leads to her marriage with Petrus. As the allegorical divisions of the text harden, and decisions are forced upon her, Lucy herself becomes an ever more unassailably serious character: the witty playfulness with which she teased her father ('If they prosecuted every case the profession would be decimated' (66)) disappears, and she becomes ever less patient with him: 'Wake up, David. This is the country. This is Africa' (124), she urges; later David complains rather pathetically to Bev that she 'won't listen to me' (139). As the newspaper report of the incident puts it—quite by accident—she becomes 'Ms. Lucy Lourie' (115), louring at David, resolutely ignoring his advice, as she is required to take essentially political decisions about her future in which, as she conceives it, his old-fashioned ideas ('the soul'?) can play no part.

If the Erasmuskraal rapists draw Lucy into the unassailably serious, they have precisely the opposite effect upon David. Whilst he

---

derive from the Judaeo-Christian tradition. In *Disgrace* Lurie's conception of the soul from the very outset (in the classroom, where his concern is with the merely 'soulless image' (22) granted to Wordsworth in his apprehension of Mont Blanc) relates specifically to the distinctively enlightenment ethical stance with which he is preoccupied throughout the novel.

had always been teetering on the edges of the comic, after the rape he is decisively made into a downright fool—someone whose views simply can't be taken seriously. From the very start of the incident, when he sends the 'bulldog' to chase after the third rapist, we are told that 'the dog trots heavily after the boy' (93), and seems unable to do much to stop him: this is because the bulldog is afflicted with constipation, and can't do anything very quickly.[14] From the constipated dog that 'trots heavily', David is himself briefly transformed into a belittling, dog-like state: 'Abandoning them, he rushes back to the kitchen door. The bottom leaf is not bolted: a few heavy kicks and it swings open. On all fours he creeps into the kitchen' (93). Not quite a 'Marx Brothers atmosphere', but David is certainly the fall-guy as he scrambles through the door 'on all fours', only to be pummelled over the head and then summarily thrown into the lavatory. As Lucy is being subjected to the most terrifying assault, whose consequence will be to galvanize her sense of the decidedly serious demands being made by the politics of difference, David— for all his high-flown talk of the soul—has become, to say the least, decidedly non-serious. It is here, locked in the lavatory, that David plunges into the greatest folly he has yet reached in the course of the book, and which will only be matched by his closing revelations of the enduring value of racist discourse:

He speaks Italian, he speaks French, but Italian and French will not save him here in darkest Africa. He is helpless, an Aunt Sally, a figure from a cartoon, a missionary in cassock and topi waiting with clasped hands and upcast eyes while the savages jaw away in their own lingo preparatory to plunging him into their boiling cauldron. Mission work: what has it left behind, that huge enterprise of upliftment? Nothing that he can see. (95)

[14] We were introduced to Katy with the following observation of her constipated state: 'Pinning her ears back, the bitch tries to defecate. Nothing comes....The bitch continues to strain, hanging her tongue out, glancing around shiftily as if ashamed to be watched' (68).

The nonsense starts to pour out from the fool locked in the loo: 'darkest Africa'? 'The savages'? 'Their own lingo'? During and after the rape, the allegorical lines harden, making Lucy the grounds of all seriousness, and David into an irrelevant idiot: 'an Aunt Sally, a figure from a cartoon'. It is at this point that David loses any residual shreds of dignity he may have had: he starts to hear an 'edge of craziness in his voice' (97), and it is no accident that he uses 'baby oil' (98) to soothe his wounds, or that he becomes 'as weak as a baby' (103), either 'a child or an old man' (104), suffering the further 'ignominy of being helped out of the bath' by Bill Shaw.

So with the emergence of the Erasmuskraal rapists, who force David into the realm of Folly, a firmly allegorical reading seems to be granted in which the demands of the politics of difference hold sway in a resolutely absolute fashion. But so far our analysis of *Disgrace*'s Erasmian comic play has been all one way, towards the creation of the fool. As we saw to be the case in *Age of Iron*, Coetzee's text also produces a more complex mixing of the comic and the serious—one that will disturb any attempt to define Lurie as, to recall Beckett, entirely 'beside the point'.

This takes place with the animals David becomes involved with. The presence of animals in Coetzee's writing has been much discussed, but the focus of this discussion has tended either to remain at the level of theme, or to make an overhasty resolution of the problem posed by the text's powerful political allegory.[15] But it is the relation

---

[15] For instance, Laura Wright has recently argued that Coetzee's interest in animals relates both to a concern to de-allegorize their portrayal, and to problematize the boundaries between the human and the non-human (see 'Coetzee's Dogs from Simile to Signified', *Writing 'Out of All the Camps'* 21–51). Jopi Nyman argues that Coetzee redeploys the animal trope, familiar to colonialist narrative, 'to investigate the ways in which the entry of the silenced postcolonial Other into the former centre generates a crisis of modernity relying on Reason and knowledge' (*Postcolonial Animals from Kipling to Coetzee* (New Delhi, 2003) 148). For a more acute suggestion of how animality relates to representation see Jacques Derrida's discussion of the 'animot' in 'The Animal That Therefore I Am (More to Follow)', trans. David Wills, *Critical Inquiry* 28 (Winter, 2002) 369–418.

of animals to aesthetic experience that most concerns David as an artist. At the climax of the composition of *Byron in Italy* David is suddenly taken by another idea that art seems to be teaching him: 'Would he dare to do that: bring a dog into the piece, allow it to loose its own lament to the heavens between the strophes of lovelorn Teresa's?' (215). The lame dog at the end seems to like David's composition, but the opera has always had an animal presence, primarily that of ducks: bewildered by the total loss of his dignity and status after the rape, 'He works in the garden; when he is tired he sits by the dam, observing the ups and downs of the duck family, brooding on the Byron project' (141); back in Cape Town the duck family is one of the things he most misses about life in the country, specifically, it would seem, the clownish, comic character of the ducks: 'Mother Duck tacking about on the surface of the dam, her chest puffed out with pride, while Eenie, Meenie, Minie and Mo paddle busily behind' (178)—two pages later, he is busily at the opera again. These rather silly creatures seem hard to separate from David's own artistic inspiration: our question is therefore, what do animals, as non-rational beings, those creatures least amenable to the serious processes of cultural evaluation undertaken by novels, *do* within *Disgrace*? What does the dog's non-musical howl do to David's opera?

Two 'lessons' from *Elizabeth Costello*, known collectively as 'The Lives of Animals', which were composed alongside *Disgrace*, will help us. Here, Elizabeth's primary dilemma is that the type of discourse demanded of her in the lecture hall 'is the language of Aristotle and Porphyry, of Augustine and Aquinas, of Descartes and Bentham . . . a philosophical language in which we can discuss and debate what kind of souls animals have, whether they reason or on the contrary act as biological automatons, whether they have rights in respect of us or whether we merely have duties in respect of them' (66). This constitutes a dilemma because, Elizabeth argues, the very presumption of such a language immediately places her in a discursive sphere to which animals have no access, and from which they merely look stupid and soulless—'biological automatons', even. Her position is thus equivalent to that of Kafka's Red Peter: 'If I do not subject my discourse to reason, whatever that is, what is left for me but to gibber and emote and knock over my water glass and generally make a monkey of myself?' (68). Clearly, 'The Lives of Animals' invokes a set of important issues worthy of discussion in their own right, and it should not be seen merely as an adjunct to *Disgrace*. But nonetheless, the main formal interest of this text is what happens to Elizabeth when she tries to do justice to animal experience, and this is what concerns us here: as she puts it herself, she becomes more and more remote from seriousness. She attracts a suitably stern judgement from Abraham Stern for her wild comparisons to the Holocaust (94); she is regarded as mad by the rational norms that her daughter-in-law Norma brings to bear upon her. When what John assumes to be a 'kook' or a 'crazie' stands up to ask a question, it becomes apparent that he is not the crazy one: in response to his request for clarity Elizabeth is shaken, explaining that she was 'hoping not to have to enunciate principles' (81–2). Elizabeth finds herself beaten in every argument ('"I don't know what I think," says Elizabeth Costello' (90)), and gives voice to some of the most ridiculous fantasies, including her notion that the insects and the microbia 'may beat us yet' (105) in some kind of war of all the animals. As she becomes increasingly challenged in the debate, her weakness becomes ever more apparent: in trying to credit the autonomy and distinctiveness of animal experience—an experience made 'nothing' by rationalist discourse—she appears more and more absurd, ever more the fool, edging towards a final craziness: 'Am I fantasising it all? I must be mad!' (114).

It is the non-seriousness of animals—the sheer senselessness of the dog's howl and its sheer unamenability to any of the processes of serious representation—that is most important in terms of literary form in *Disgrace*. I will suggest how animals function in the text by first looking at a peculiar little dog-story that is told by David to Lucy before she is raped. In the story we encounter David trying to make a serious articulation of the principles that he considers best defend his relationship with Melanie; drawing upon distinctly (yet absurdly) Kantian political language, he begins by asserting that his case rests on 'the rights of desire,' but swiftly realizes quite how plainly unacceptable such an idea might be to his daughter, and indeed, upon reflection, almost to himself:

He sees himself in the girl's flat, in her bedroom, with the rain pouring down outside and the heater in the corner giving off a smell of paraffin, kneeling over her, peeling off her clothes, while her arms flop like the arms of a dead person. *I was the servant of Eros*: that is what he wants to say, but does he have the effrontery? *It was a god who acted through me.* What vanity! Yet not a lie, not entirely. In the whole wretched business there was something generous that was doing its best to flower. (89)

Realizing that his 'case' simply sounds risible in the words he would wish to use, he 'tries again', with a story about a dog, from the time when they lived in (wait for it) Kenilworth. The dog was an unneutered male, and 'whenever there was a bitch in the vicinity it would get excited and unmanageable, and with Pavlovian regularity the owners would beat it. This went on and on until the poor dog didn't know what to do. At the smell of a bitch it would chase around the garden with its ears flat and its tail between its legs, whining, trying to hide' (90). Lucy doesn't 'see the point' of the story ('And indeed,' David reflects, 'what is the point?'), suggesting it is simply a way for her father to smuggle in the old notion of 'the rights of desire' in a more palatable form: 'So males must be allowed to follow their instincts unchecked? Is that the moral?' But this is not quite 'the moral'. To defend the story David is forced to return to it, and continue to articulate the dog's situation, which ends in a strange moment, half-comic and half-pathetic: '"At the deepest level I think it might have preferred being shot. It might have preferred that to the options it was offered: on the one hand, to deny its nature, on the other, to spend the rest of its days padding about the living-room, sighing and sniffing the cat and getting portly"' (90). The comedy is not now that of the Byronic witty performer, but of an almost clownish bathos—David's story teeters on the brink of self-parody, though without ever quite falling over. The 'point' of the story is not the particular moral meaning that lies within, but that David's serious case about the rights of desire, or in more philosophical terms, the freedom of the individual to pursue happiness without fear of the 'overtones' of so doing, is within the event of telling offset against the bathetic image of the neutered dog. The story leads the reader into an area of doubt: it is unclear how seriously to take it, hovering as it does between David's important ideas and the bathos of the rather louche dog. As an assertion that 'males must be allowed to follow their instincts unchecked', David's case is clearly never going to win the ear of the sceptical Lucy; but within the dog story the value that underlies his liaison with Melanie, so far down it is hardly visible, that value that makes it 'not a lie, not entirely', has a chance of survival. To return to the lesson of the opera: 'He is held in the music itself, in the flat, tinny slap of the banjo strings, the voice that strains to soar away from the ludicrous instrument but is continually reined back, like a fish on a line.' Note that Lucy does not simply dismiss David's idea after the story; instead, her response ('Have you always felt this way, David?') would suggest that she doesn't quite know what to make of it. She cannot translate it back into a straightforwardly serious language of representation, and so it enters her thinking in a way that has a greater 'power to surprise'—potentially, at least.

'So this is art, and this is how it does its work. How strange! How fascinating!' Neither wholly serious, nor wholly parodic (for there remains a certain pathos in the dog that a responsive reading will have to credit), the 'work' performed by David's story is to render a special, and untranslatable, kind of thinking on the status of his ideas.[16]

---

[16] In '"Plink-plunk": Unforgetting the Present in Coetzee's *Disgrace*', Michael Holland argues that *Disgrace* establishes 'the absolute priority of the raw material of language' so as to 'suspen[d] all of the discourses—historical, ethical, political and fictional—by which existence is structured' and instead to put 'the reader of the novel in direct contact with the immediate present of material existence'. My reading clearly differs: while the comic is rooted in an experience of language in its material or semiotic state (language as 'represented'), the particular form of

Within the shifting boundaries of comic experience—neither wholly
serious nor entirely parodic—David finds a chance of survival, a
softening of the hard allegorical boundaries: a refuge, of sorts, in
which he might be 'held'. It is no accident that Bev Shaw's Animal
Welfare Clinic is known as a 'refuge'. 'Bev runs the animal refuge',
Lucy tells him, which sparks a telling moment of introspection: 'His
mind has become a refuge for old thoughts, idle, indigent, with
nowhere else to go. He ought to chase them out, sweep the premises
clean. But he does not care to do so, or does not care enough' (72).
The animals granted refuge in the clinic are as unwanted as the ideas
relating to the soul and to the individual—junkyard legacies of the
enlightenment—that find their 'refuge' in David's 'old-fashioned'
(66) mind. Bev's place is filled with old rubbish, 'galvanised-iron
sheets, wooden pallets, old tyres, where chickens scratch around and
what looks uncommonly like a duiker snoozes in a corner' (73),
things that have been chucked out—rather like David himself, if
the cruelly effective photograph with the rubbish bin poised over his
head be recalled. The refuge is home to all sorts of odd ideas, which at
first only serve as an opportunity for David to sharpen his wit. Not
only does Bev, like Elizabeth Costello, believe there may be, as he puts
it, a 'Great Reckoning' of the animals (82), but she thinks that
animals 'can smell what you are thinking'. ('What nonsense!' (81),
David pronounces.) But nonetheless, he increasingly takes refuge in
this non-serious junkyard milieu from the endless defeats he suffers in
the remorselessly polarized world outside—a world in which he is
merely a fool.

comedy at stake here is brought into being through an oscillation between
representation and parody rather than an outright materialism. David's discourse
is represented, but not wholly parodied: it becomes hard to know *how seriously* to
take it. The dog's howl and the banjo's 'silly plink plonk' are therefore important
in the text not because they enforce 'the absolute priority of the raw material of
language' that 'suspen[ds]' the political discourse in which the text is engaged,
but because they have the power to introduce a complicating and untranslatable
play into the serious problems of that discourse.

The latter half of *Disgrace* works by subjecting David Lurie to an oscillation between the serious world that Lucy is forced to occupy, where he suffers a series of Quixotic defeats, and the 'refuge', where he regains a highly equivocal form of dignity. After the rape of Lucy, the plot in the Eastern Cape around the transfer of lands takes on increased momentum: the harsh workings-out of history, against which David powerlessly rails, begin to aggregate towards what he can only regard as an ever more horrific conclusion. A particularly desolate point comes at the party, where he discovers that Petrus seems to be shielding one of the rapists, and may be more implicated in the rape than had been imagined. The next morning he swallows his pride and helps Petrus lay in the pipes for his new home, also taking the opportunity to urge him to submit himself and his rapist nephew to the judicial procedures of the state. Petrus does not even begin to engage with the terms of debate David puts forward, and their conversation ends with a grim symbolism:

'You know. You know the future. What can I say to that? You have spoken. Do you need me here any longer?'
  'No, now it is easy, now I must just dig the pipe in.'   (139)

A depressing moment indeed: David defends his principles with rising anger, but is straightforwardly dismissed. But then, as an interjection to these 'elegiac' tones ('It is not the erotic that is calling to him after all, nor the elegiac...'), come a few *'plink-plunk-plonk'* plucks on the strings of the banjo: we discover him at the refuge with the dogs. He has now, we discover, embraced one of the odd ideas to which Bev had given refuge: 'If, more often than not, the dog fails to be charmed, it is because of his presence: he gives off the wrong smell (*They can smell your thoughts*), the smell of shame' (142). But what we also find, in this unlikely place, is that some of his own most important ideas—the idea of personal honour, the sanctity of the individual—that had been simply dismissed in the remorseless seriousness of the world outside the refuge, find a rather different status here. This is what we discover:

It would be simple to cart the bags to the incinerator immediately after the session and leave them there for the incinerator crew to dispose of. But that would mean leaving them on the dump with the rest of the weekend's scourings: with waste from the hospital wards, carrion scooped up at the roadside, malodorous refuse from the tannery—a mixture both casual and terrible. He is not prepared to inflict such dishonour upon them. (144)

David's ideas on the value and dignity of the individual are being put forward with the same absolute conviction as ever before. But here in the refuge and at the incinerator they are not wholly caught up in the polarized terms of opposition. They are always at risk of seeming silly, or downright idiotic: as Lurie is forced to observe, 'what do dogs know of honour and dishonour anyway?' (146). Moreover, these are dead dogs, doubly removed from Lurie's claims on their behalf. But Lurie here is not entirely or straightforwardly silly. As we saw in our reading of *Life & Times of Michael K*, Maurice Blanchot spoke of the peculiar anxiety of reading Kafka: 'Whoever reads Kafka is thus forcibly transformed into a liar, but not a complete liar. That is the anxiety peculiar to his art'.[17] The anxiety of reading passages such as these in *Disgrace*, either in the refuge, or by the incinerator, lies in not knowing how seriously to take them. Compare the force this old-fashioned idea of dishonour gathers to itself among the dead dogs, to its weakness and irrelevance a few pages later in David's pathetic letter to Lucy. Here he tells her in no uncertain terms that 'the road you are following is the wrong one. It will strip you of all honour; you will not be able to live with yourself. I plead with you, listen to me' (160). Lucy's response, indeed 'Lucy's last word', is to deny that her father can be 'the guide I need', and (even more hurtfully) to claim he has never even begun to understand her situation. These ideas—including the hints of the 'soul' that will enter the refuge in a more sustained way later in the text (though consider here the description of the incinerator as a divine force: 'On the seventh day it rests' (145))—have no place whatsoever in the

---

[17] *The Work of Fire* (1949) 4.

political choices Lucy makes. But they do have a hold in the text— and a hold upon the reader—through contact with the animals, in all their dumb disruptiveness (for 'that is what he is becoming: stupid, daft, wrongheaded' (146)).

'*O why do you speak like that?* sings Teresa in a long reproachful arc. *Plink-plunk-plonk* go the strings' (185). If David's voice momentarily, among the dogs, here 'strains to soar away' into the most elevated expression of his ideas, the next chapter, the one in which he has sex with Bev Shaw in her clinic, reels him back in, 'like a fish on a line'. If Manfred or Lara could look down and see the type of figure he now cuts, as someone who in Byronic style, 'comes from the big city' with 'scandal attached to his name', making love 'to many women and expects to be made love to by every woman who crosses his path' (149), he would surely elicit their cosmic laughter. Perhaps 'it is not the erotic that is calling to him after all', for when deciding where to have sex, 'the choice is between the operating table and the floor', he reflects grimly: 'Never did he dream he would sleep with a Bev' (149). And yet grim comedy is not the only feature of his sexual encounter with Bev Shaw. There emerges at the end of the chapter, quite unexpectedly, a kind of beauty to their post-coital scene: 'On the horizon lies a last crimson glow; the moon looms overhead; smoke hangs in the air; across a strip of waste land, from the first rows of shacks, comes a hubbub of voices. At the door Bev presses herself against him a last time, rests her head on his chest' (150). Two chapters later David will tell Mr Isaacs that, as a lover, his chief failing is that he 'lack[s] the lyrical' (171). But in these unlikely circumstances, with the glow of the sunset, the rising moon, the suggestions of being among a world thick with populous life ('a hubbub of voices'), and not least Bev's own tenderness, flattering his masculinity by resting 'her head on his chest', the scene finds enough lyricism to modulate away from rock-bottom, away from the utter bathos of the sexual act itself. We gain a first fleeting sense, perhaps, that David is not simply being 'succoured . . . as a man is succoured by a woman', but being loved and valued.

It is a mistake to look to David for any supposedly redeeming change of heart: like Erasmus's Folly, or Cervantes' Quixote, he is not a character who develops, but one who is wrongheadedly entrenched in a certain discursive construction. What changes—and keeps changing, in the most protean and unpredictable fashion—is his status and seriousness in the text. We move from the strained mixture of bathos and resonant twilight lyricism that closes the Bev Shaw chapter, to David back on 'the farm', once again plotting to restore Lucy to the metropolitan existence he cherishes, and wants her to cherish too. It is at this point that David suffers his most crushing defeat, as Lucy now begins to reveal her feelings about the rape in more detail. It becomes ever clearer not only that she does not regard David as a father in the way he wants to be considered, which is to say, as someone acting out of a disinterested bond of human love, but that she regards him in exclusively symbolic identity-based terms:

'Maybe, for men, hating the woman makes sex more exciting. You are a man, you ought to know. When you have sex with someone strange—when you trap her, hold her down, get her under you, put all your weight on her—isn't it a bit like killing? Pushing the knife in; exiting afterwards, leaving the body behind covered in blood—doesn't it feel like murder, like getting away with murder?'

You are a man, you ought to know: does one speak to one's father like that? Are she and he on the same side?   (159)

The polarization of the divergent ideas necessary to South Africa's pluralism has now penetrated into the very heart of his most cherished intimate relationship. David is, in Lucy's eyes, utterly complicit with the rapists because of his gender identity. This is a truly crushing moment, capped off by 'Lucy's last word', already quoted, where she tells her father he is 'not the guide I need'. Yet just as we plunge downwards into the darkest 'elegiac' moments of the text, the '*plink-plunk-plonk*' of the banjo again starts to sound, and Coetzee does indeed 'dare . . . to bring a dog into the piece'. After one line of blank page, the next line of text following 'Lucy's last word' takes us straight to the clinic: 'The business of dog-killing is over for the day, the black bags are piled at the door, each with a body and a soul inside. He and Bev Shaw lie in each other's arms on the floor of the surgery. In half an hour Bev will go back to her Bill and he will begin loading the bags' (161). Here in Bev Shaw's arms the allegorical boundaries of the text again briefly flicker and blur. Swaddled in Bev's love (Bev, whose name reminds David of a cow, and whose appearance reminds him of a 'pointer pigeon'), David and his ideas take on a different resonance—for suddenly, the black bags full of dead dogs seem also to hold the crucial idea of the soul. This idea, as we have seen, is fundamental to David, from the 'soulless image' (22) that afflicts his 'master' Wordsworth, through to his mawkish insistence to Lucy that 'We are all souls. We are souls before we are born' (79), and into the very basis of the distinction he insists on making between the private and the public. We find it again here, but sandwiched between talk of 'the business of dog-killing' and the bathetic spectacle of his affair with Bev Shaw—Bev, who 'will go back to her Bill'. The highly serious and the deeply comic are inextricably mixed: one straining 'to soar away' with high-flown words about the soul; the other, played on a more 'ludicrous instrument', reining it back in. Bev has in fact always believed in David, indeed is the only character in the book who does: 'Bev? You think Bev is part of the repressive apparatus? Bev is in awe of you!' (91). Here she assures him, just as she assures the animals: 'It will be all right,' she whispers. 'You will see' (162).

There is no appreciable change in David's character—no novelistic reintegration of this alienated hero. But there is a continual play with the reader's judgements of him, as the protean text of *Disgrace* shifts between the serious and the non-serious, daring to 'bring a dog in', allowing a 'silly plink-plonk' to open brief spaces of dignity in which David is 'held' and valued amidst the sheer remorselessness of the text's allegorical thrust: the political legacies that David embodies and articulates cannot hold centre-stage, but the novel doesn't let them be 'swept aside', either. For just when we think David is down

for the count—totally 'beside the point', 'less than little', or even
'nothing' at all (220)—the banjo starts up again, the dog starts
howling away, and we cross back to the refuge. We find David at
the end of the novel about to cull one of his dogs—'the one who likes
music', in fact. And here at the end we encounter the text's most
profoundly serious articulation of the idea of the soul—for David,
the common human element, the guarantor of the sanctity of
individual life:

What the dog will not be able to work out (*not in a month of Sundays!* he
thinks), what his nose will not tell him, is how one can enter what seems to
be an ordinary room and never come out again. Something happens in this
room, something unmentionable: here the soul is yanked out of the body;
briefly it hangs about in the air, twisting and contorting; then it is sucked
away and is gone. It will be beyond him, this room that is not a room but a
hole where one leaks out of existence.   (219)

The passage is extraordinary for the way it is so anxiously poised
between high seriousness and low bathos. The idea of the soul being
'yanked out of the body', and 'twisting and contorting' in its sheer
metaphysical splendour, is pushed up close to the image of the dog
simply sniffing around, stupidly not understanding what is going on
(the knowledge of death is something 'his nose will not tell him'),
and an altogether more homely and prosaic register of language ('*not
in a month of Sundays!*'). The departure of the soul in the mystical
chamber is 'held back' by the bathos of 'a hole where one leaks'. But
'held back' certainly doesn't mean 'entirely negated':

A time must come, it cannot be evaded, when he will have to bring him
to Bev Shaw in her operating room (perhaps he will carry him in his
arms, perhaps he will do that for him) and caress him and brush back
the fur so that the needle can find the vein, and whisper to him and
support him in the moment when, bewilderingly, his legs buckle: and
then, when the soul is out, fold him up and pack him away in his bag,
and the next day wheel the bag into the flames and see that it is burnt,
burnt up.   (219–20)

Coetzee spoke of the 'fierce comic anguish' in the prose of Beckett's *The Unnamable*, and that quality is equally evident in his own prose here. It commands a quite awesome rising seriousness, and lays claim to an extraordinary dignity for David and his ideas. Silly, though, to suppose the dog has a soul, or that he even remotely fits into the model of subjectivity Lurie invokes. Funny, too, to find podgy, pigeon-like Bev here, presiding at these mystical rites. For in their straining, soaring intensity, that is what they yearn to be:

He opens the cage door. 'Come,' he says, bends, opens his arms. The dog wags its crippled rear, sniffs his face, licks his cheeks, his lips, his ears. He does nothing to stop it. 'Come.'
    Bearing him in his arms like a lamb, he re-enters the surgery. (220)

David has become so elevated and dignified that he is almost Christ, and the dog is almost the Lamb of God. But did the Lamb of God ever wag its crippled rear, or sniff about like this, licking 'his cheeks, his lips, his ears'?

The ending of *Disgrace* grants an impressive dignity and serious-ness to David as he goes about his ministry among the animals, setting out his faith in the soul. But it simultaneously cancels that seriousness, and presents him as 'little enough, less than little: nothing' (220). As in *The Unnamable*, Coetzee's text tries to find ways of troubling the borderline between nothing and something, such that what counts for nothing might change: 'I have done nothing,' the Unnamable reminds us, 'unless what I am doing now is something, and nothing could give me greater satisfaction' (282). In creating an 'image of our nation', *Disgrace* is committed to 'doing nothing': it is fastidiously reserved towards the claims for representa-tional authority, objectivity, and shared humanity that underpin the classic novel's image-making. It refuses to make a 'nothing' into 'something', as Beckett put it: it won't make any absolute assertion of the political and ethical values Lurie embodies, but stays with the necessarily equivocal process of having 'nothing to recover'. To return to Gerwel: is *Disgrace* therefore 'nonetheless better than Roodt's lightness of spirit'? The originality and value of Coetzee's book does not lie in the strength and seriousness of its claims for the novel's power to bring about a particular form of community. Instead, *Disgrace* finds ways of placing the 'right image of our nation' in continued and productive suspense: through the 'fierce comic anguish' of its prose it tries to open its readers to the complex political demands placed upon the nation's future.

8

Cultural Criticism in the Australian Fiction

Tell us, O Master, we pray, what has gone wrong with our civilization! Why have the wells run dry, why is there a rain of frogs? Look into your mystic ball and enlighten us! Show us the road to the future!

J. M. Coetzee, *Diary of a Bad Year*

In his Australian fiction—*Elizabeth Costello*, *Slow Man*, and *Diary of a Bad Year*—Coetzee has moved away from an overt concern with the politics of difference and the problem of inhabiting a radically intercultural society such as South Africa, to focus on the different, though related, moral debate over what it means to live in a cultural space dominated by the sceptical, rational, and egalitarian side of post-Enlightenment political culture. In *Elizabeth Costello* the different 'lessons' often—though not exclusively—turn on a confrontation with an Enlightenment discourse of some kind: in 'Realism' the feminist literary critic Susan Moebius is set against John Costello's more decidedly transcendent view of his mother's vocation; in 'The Problem of Evil' the coolly rational auditors in the Dutch lecture hall confront Elizabeth's ill-assorted fulminations on evil and the Satanic; in 'The Lives of Animals' rationalist assumptions about the distinction between the human and the animal are pitted against Elizabeth's avowedly supra-rational intuitions of grotesque moral harm. Equally, *Slow Man* turns around a confrontation between a predominantly utilitarian modernity that seems to specialize in an emotionally deadening form of managed happiness, and the sudden demand for spiritual urgency awakened in Paul Rayment following his bicycle accident. Coetzee's interest in developing a general discourse of cultural criticism about the nature and value of modernity is especially evident in *Diary of a Bad Year*, which presents a South African novelist named J.C., resident in Australia, who has been commissioned by a German publishing house to contribute to a book of 'Strong Opinions', in which 'six eminent writers pronounce on what is wrong with today's world' (19). J.C.'s text is an all-purpose Jeremiad on subjects ranging from America and democracy to modern sporting practices and music.

In each text it is obvious that Coetzee chooses to distance himself from the person actually doing the cultural criticism: in *Elizabeth Costello* and *Slow Man* he stages it through the characters of Elizabeth Costello and Paul Rayment; he divides *Diary of a Bad Year* into three sections, structured around a story that emerges 'from below' which often ironizes and implicitly questions the claims being made above, from 'on high'. But it is less obvious why Coetzee goes to all this trouble. To put it simply, why doesn't he just come out and say what he thinks, like other cultural critics past and present?

For some readers there is no particularly good answer to this question. In his review of *Diary of a Bad Year*, James Woods chose to emphasize the 'dazzling' quality of J.C.'s critical essays, believing the distancing and ironizing effects inherent in the structure of the text to be at the very least half-hearted: 'The dynamism of the book is intellectual,' he argued, 'and the real drama is at the top of the page.' While Coetzee makes 'all the right postmodern noises', and plays the standard-issue 'postmodern games', the energy of his writing really lies in a 'besotted relationship to an older, Dostoevskian tradition, in which we feel the desperate impress of the confessing author, however recessed and veiled'.[1] Contrary to Woods, what I am going

---

[1] James Woods, 'Squall Lines', review of *Diary of a Bad Year*, *The New Yorker* (24 Dec. 2007). As the readings I have proposed of *Foe* (Ch. 4) and *The Master of Petersburg* (Ch. 6) must suggest, while Coetzee's sustained engagement with

to argue is that while the so-called 'postmodern noises' made by Coetzee's Australian fiction might at times seem imperfectly achieved, they are nonetheless central to the way these texts engage with cultural criticism. I will show that the best way to understand Coetzee's approach lies in placing him in a much wider tradition of debate on the nature and value of 'high culture'—one that stretches back to German romanticism, and forward to present-day Cultural Studies. I will first—and very briefly—set out a couple of the ways in which *Diary of a Bad Year* signals its relationship to a particular tradition within cultural criticism; then I will outline, in some detail, the contemporary context of the debate on culture into which Coetzee's text intervenes. To do so, I will draw upon Francis Mulhern's useful description of the different forms of 'metacultural discourse' and his exchange with Stefan Collini in the pages of the *New Left Review*. My main claim will be that the dominant rival positions in this debate, which I could equally well represent through other contemporary figures, not least James Woods himself, have reached an impasse, and that this impasse is due to the oversimplification of key terms—particularly the terms 'culture' and 'politics'. By contrast, I will show that Coetzee's writing is designed to refuse this simplification, and to open up a more productive line of cultural criticism—one better fitted to navigating the complex terrain of political modernity. I will concentrate on *Diary of a Bad Year*, which I find to be the most successful of Coetzee's Australian texts, but will end by suggesting some ways of approaching *Elizabeth Costello* and *Slow Man*. In concluding with this chapter on cultural criticism my aim is to place what has been an ongoing argument of mine in a new light. Coetzee's concern with the form of the novel— inseparable, as I have emphasized, from his political concerns—is here connected with another highly related discursive tradition in order to emphasize the wider meaning of what it means to Coetzee to write 'after Beckett'.

Dostoevsky certainly implies an attitude of the very highest regard, this is certainly not a 'besotted relationship', but a complex and critical one.

Early on in *Diary of a Bad Year*, in J.C.'s opening Jeremiad against 'modern political culture', there is a passage in which Nicolo Machiavelli is granted a special, indeed inaugural, place in the hall of blame for the moral chaos in which we are said to live. This is what we are told:

Necessity, *necessità*, is Machiavelli's guiding principle. The old, pre-Machiavellian position was that the moral law was supreme. If it so happened that the moral law was sometimes broken, that was unfortunate, but rulers were merely human, after all. The new, Machiavellian position is that infringing the moral law is justified when it is necessary.

Thus is inaugurated the dualism of modern political culture, which simultaneously upholds absolute and relative standards of value. (17)

In identifying Machiavelli in these terms as the inventor of pernicious modern attitudes towards civil society, J.C. is taking his lead from the cultural critic Julien Benda.[2] In *La Trahison des clercs* (Treason of the Clerks), a text recently repopularized by Edward Said's lectures on the role of the public intellectual, Benda argued that modern 'clerks', a term he deploys to refer to the general intellectual caste of a society, have marked themselves off in history for having betrayed their true role as upholders of higher spiritual values ('non-practical or disinterested values' (103)) against the merely pragmatic and calculative thinking that goes on in civil society.[3] Here Benda enumerates the different teachings on the relation between politics and morality:

---

[2] In fact the most explicit allusion to Benda comes in the passage 'On Al Qaida', where J.C. suggests that 'the *trahison des clercs* of our time' was the Nietzsche-inspired 'academy of the humanities in its postmodernist phase', which taught that 'in criticism suspiciousness is the chief virtue' (33). The suspiciousness inculcated in literature courses led, J.C. argues, in a logical leap that is the argumentative equivalent of high farce, to the paranoid interpretation of innocuous home videos of Muslim families in American courtrooms.

[3] See Edward Said, *Representations of the Intellectual: The 1993 Reith Lectures* (London, 1994). Coetzee makes his own characterizations of intellectuals as a caste in *Giving Offense*, defining their salient features as a 'combination of a close, rational watch over the emotions' and a 'tolerance' of cultural difference. Coetzee notes that

One was Plato's, and it said: 'Morality decides politics'; the other was Machiavelli's, and it said: 'Politics have nothing to do with morality.' Today they receive a third. M. Maurras teaches: 'Politics decide morality.' However, the real departure is not that this doctrine should be put before them, but that they should accept it. Callicles asserted that force is the only morality; but the thinking world despised him. Let me also mention that Machiavelli was covered with insults by most of the moralists of his time, at least in France.[4]

Both J.C. and Benda agree that Machiavelli is a key figure in inaugurating the crisis of modernity, and both describe that crisis as an acceptance that the political organization of civil society be regarded as a space for the enactment of purely instrumental reason. By way of the character of Alan, *Diary of a Bad Year* presents another view of Benda's: namely, that Nietzsche is the philosopher who most clearly embodies the ill effects of political modernity. This is Benda's lament for the influence of what he calls 'Nietzschean pragmatism' on modern clerks:

It is impossible to exaggerate the importance of a movement whereby those who for twenty centuries taught Man that the criterion of the morality of an act is its disinterestedness, that good is a decree of his reason insofar as it is universal, that his will is only moral if it seeks its law outside its objects, should begin to teach him that the moral act is the act whereby he secures his existence against an environment which disputes it, that his will is moral insofar as it is a will 'to power', that the part of his soul which determines what is good is its 'will to live' wherein it is most 'hostile to all reason,' that the morality of an act is measured by its adaptation to its end, and that the only morality is the morality of circumstances. (124)

this tolerance is, 'depending on how you look at it...either deeply civilised or complacent, hypocritical and patronising', adding, on a personal note, that 'I myself am (and am also, I would hope, to a degree not) an intellectual of this kind" (3–5).

[4] Julien Benda, *The Treason of the Intellectuals* (1927), trans. Richard Aldington (1928); reissued with introduction by Roger Kimball (New Brunswick, NJ, 2007) 110. Charles Maurras (1868–1952) was an intellectual leader of *Action Français*, a far-right nationalist movement founded partly in response to the Dreyfus affair in 1898. His concept of 'integral nationalism' anticipated some of the ideas of fascism.

Benda would have had no trouble diagnosing the corrupting impact of these Nietzschean ideas on Alan, an economist and fund-manager, and the novel's main negative embodiment of 'modern political culture'. The market, Alan argues, is necessarily beyond moral evaluation, 'beyond good and evil, like Nietzsche said. Good motives or evil motives,' he explains, 'they are just motives in the end, vectors of the matrix, that get evened out in the long run' (98).

Of course the distinctive literary effect of *Diary of a Bad Year*, an effect that immediately distinguishes it from Benda's text, is that we cannot take these views wholly seriously. Readers of Nietzsche will wonder at Alan's comically crude application of his thinking to justify the supremacy of the free market, for of course Nietzsche never argued for an economism in these or any other terms, nor would he have presented any institution, let alone the market, as a properly 'transcendent' dimension of life—to use Alan's term for the economic sphere (79). Equally, J.C.'s high-minded anti-Machiavellianism is juxtaposed against a storyline at the bottom of the page that ironically emphasizes his own decidedly Machiavellian behaviour: at the very moment of his denunciation he is making a highly duplicitous solicitation of Anya, and is thus by no means living out the moral law in his own public life. Indeed he is, as Alan points out later, not only 'a dreamer', but 'a schemer too' (196). I will return to the particular ways in which Coetzee uses irony in this text, but first I need to delineate the more general context of debate on cultural criticism into which *Diary of a Bad Year* intervenes.

The allusions to Benda signal that J.C. is being staged as a participant in the historically prior of two different forms of 'meta-cultural discourse'.[5] As I have already indicated, Francis Mulhern defines the main characteristic of this type of discourse as the 'mobilis[ation of] "culture" as a principle against the prevailing generality of "politics" in the disputed plane of social authority',

---

[5] This is a term created by Francis Mulhern in *Culture/Metaculture* (London, 2000).

commenting that 'what speaks in metacultural discourse is the
cultural principle itself, as it strives to dissolve the political as a
locus of general arbitration in social relations'.[6] In short, metacultural discourse is an attempt to arbitrate political questions from a
position (often named 'culture') that is assumed to be systematically
beyond, or at least superior to, the terms of political debate. Mulhern
identifies two dominant forms of metacultural discourse, which he
terms *Kulturkritik* and Cultural Studies: these are 'mutually antago-
nistic', and the latter took shape in 'conscious opposition to the
former'.[7] The German term *Kulturkritik* translates literally as 'cultural criticism', but Mulhern uses it to signify a particular variety of
such criticism:

> *Kulturkritik*, in its classic European form, took shape in the later eighteenth
> century as a critical, normally negative discourse on the emerging symbolic
> universe of capitalism, democracy and enlightenment—on the values of a
> condition and process of social life for which a recent French coinage
> furnished the essential term: *civilisation*. Germany was the continental
> heartland of this discourse: it was in the philosophical histories of Johann
> Gottfreid von Herder that *Zivilisation* was first questioned in the name of
> *Kultur*. (p. xv)

Of course a further signal that J.C. is to be read within this tradition
is made by the fact that his Strong Opinions were commissioned by a
German publisher: as Alan remarks (disparagingly), 'in places like
Germany and France people still tend to drop to their knees before
sages with white beards. Tell us, O Master, we pray, what has gone
wrong with our civilization! Why have the wells run dry, why is there
a rain of frogs? Look into your mystic ball and enlighten us! Show us
the road to the future!' (206–7). Mulhern's definition of *Kulturkritik*
takes in a diverse range of European intellectuals—Arnold, Eliot,
and Leavis in Britain; Mannheim, Mann, Ortega, and of course
Benda in continental Europe. What they have in common, he

---

[6] Francis Mulhern, 'Beyond Metaculture', *New Left Review* 16 (2002) 86.
[7] Mulhern, *Culture/Metaculture* p. xv.

claims, is an appeal to a cultural principle, often literalized as high art, but also spiritualized as a state of mind, as that which enables a truer, more distinterested, or more generally harmonious outlook than that available through politics. Its classic Anglophone statement is Matthew Arnold's *Culture and Anarchy* (1867–8), in which culture is represented as that which elevates to a 'best self', a state in which the self can 'see things as they really are': culture is a mix of national institutions, artefacts of high culture, and general spiritual refinement that elevates us from the anarchy into which we descend when we identify with our factional (class and religious) interests merely.[8]

In his analysis of how *Kulturkritik* evolved into Cultural Studies Mulhern stresses the way in which its empowering assumptions failed to survive new arguments made about human identity, and these critiques are replayed forcefully, though crudely, by the figure of Alan in *Diary of a Bad Year*. Foremost is the psychoanalytic critique, which derives most centrally from Freud's *Civilisation and its Discontents* (1930)—in particular his 'monist' interpretation of mental life in which all forms of learned social behaviour, whether designated 'high' or 'low', are equally produced by the logic of repression and sublimation. As Mulhern comments, for Freud culture emerges as 'an activity of restless animals, not a privileged realm apart' (25). In *Diary of a Bad Year* Alan gives voice to a crude and cheapened but nonetheless distinctively post-Freudian account of J.C.'s *Kulturkritik*:

So I ask myself, What is he really up to in this book of his? *Read these pages,* you tell my lady-friend (my lady-friend, not yours), looking soulfully into her eyes, *and tell me what you think of them:* what does that add up to? Shall I tell you what I have decided? I have decided it adds up to you wanting to get your hands on my beauteous lady-friend, but being afraid to make a move in case you get a well-deserved slap across the face. It adds up to

---

[8] As Mulhern comments on Arnold: 'Culture, in this construction, is not merely a repository of value: it is the *principle* of a good society.' *Culture/Metaculture* p. xvi.

courtship of a particularly devious kind. *From the outside I may seem withered and repulsive,* you say to her (no mention of the way you smell), *but inside I still have the feelings of a man.* (201)

Aside from psychoanalysis, the main assault on *Kulturkritik* came from left politics and sociology: primarily from the kind of argument made by Herbert Marcuse in 'The Affirmative Character of Culture' (1937) to the effect that the values to which *Kulturkritik* makes appeal are symbolic merely—illusions that disguise the need for a properly political (in his view, Marxist) transformation of society; one of the most authoritative recent versions of this type of argument was the case made by Pierre Bourdieu in *La Distinction* (1979) that the phenomenon of high culture can be adequately explained in terms of power relations through the concept of cultural capital. *Diary of a Bad Year* lets Alan give voice to his own version of the economistic critique:

You have decided to try your hand at being a guru, Juan. That is what we concluded, Anya and I. You took a look around the job market—this is how we pictured it to ourselves—and saw that it was tight, particularly for the over-seventies... Why don't I give that a shot? you said to yourself. I have not exactly been lionized as a novel-writer—let us see if they will lionize me as a guru. (209)

Alan's view of J.C. is of course extremely simplistic and reductive, but his willingness to reduce even this type of cultural ambition to economic causes evidences a distinctively materialist stance towards culture, just as his crude sexualizing of J.C.'s motives is distinctively post-Freudian.

In polemical opposition to *Kulturkritik*, Cultural Studies emerges out of these new ways of thinking: pioneered in Britain by Raymond Williams and Stuart Hall, it took its lead mainly from twentieth-century Marxism, especially that of Althusser and Gramsci, in the case of Hall. As Mulhern argues, it has a threefold aim: first, to expand critical attention to popular culture; secondly, to revoke the *Kulturkritik* distinction 'between culture in the reserved, positive sense, and the other world of everyday (un)meaning civilisation';

thirdly, to 'demystify the presumptive authority of *Kulturkritik*'
(79). Mulhern's key point, though, is that Cultural Studies' assault
on *Kulturkritik* is radically incomplete. While it has rejected the
distinction between high and low culture, and thus the very basis for
the critical stance taken by Benda and Arnold, it has nonetheless
continued to be 'metacultural' in its discursive structure: that is to
say culture, albeit now popular culture, remains that which replaces
(or 'dissolves') 'political reason itself' (p. xx). Mulhern is particularly
eloquent about the ways in which contemporary Cultural Studies
evidences an 'uncritical populist drift' (139) in its concern to valorize
popular culture: it has become, he argues, a mere inversion of
Kulturkritik, in which 'the popular' is 'promoted as a model of
intellectual practice', not least in the way it pretends to find 'in the
forms and practices of the culture industry the conditions of autonomous popular activity' (139).[9] This countervailing tendency in
cultural criticism towards a 'populist drift' is also represented by
Coetzee in *Diary of a Bad Year.* Under pressure from Anya to
abandon his *Kulturkritik* stance, J.C. begins to renounce his 'strong
opinions', and to look for 'newer, up-to-date ones to replace them'.
This eventuates in the 'Second Diary', and among the general drift of
opinions in this uninspiring (and simply more private and withdrawn) text is to be found just the kind of populism that Mulhern
deplores. In an essay entitled 'The Kiss', J.C. celebrates the oft-
reproduced Robert Doisneau poster of a couple kissing in Paris—
he recalls seeing it in 'a hotel room in the town of Burnie, Tasmania'
(173). J.C.'s analysis of the poster brushes over its commercial
context, and its straightforward participation in mass emotion (indeed he has just questioned whether his own stance of distance from
mass emotion is the right stance to take after all (170)), and culminates in sheer sentimental bathos: 'Who chose this poster and hung
it? *Though a mere hotelkeeper, I too believe in love, can recognize the*

---

[9] This is especially evident, Mulhern points out, in John Fiske's notions of
popular culture as a 'semiotic democracy', and television as a 'liberated cultural
zone'. See John Fiske, *Television Culture* (London, 1987).

god when I see him—is that what its presence says?' (174). A clearer example could not be adduced of an intellectual pretending to find 'in the forms and practices of the culture industry the conditions of autonomous popular activity'. This is a peculiarly depressing passage of the text, for at the bottom of the page we are confronted with the spectacle of a drunken Alan—who, as I have suggested, has been set up as the embodiment of the most deleterious energies of Machiavellian modernity—unashamedly flaunting his plans to rob J.C., and crassly boasting of Anya as 'my adorable lady-friend with the sweet sweet cunt'. The reader feels the absence, when it is most sorely needed, of some more potent critical discourse that might answer back to Alan's outrageous commodification of the most precious of human emotions, and his literally shameless advocacy of the will to power above all moral concerns. But all we get is J.C.'s lame populism—his celebration of a kitsch poster, selling (commodifying) 'love' to help brighten up a cheap hotel room.

So both Mulhern and Coetzee insist on the inadequacy of different types of 'metacultural discourse': the intellectual untenability of *Kulturkritik*, the critical capitulation of Cultural Studies; Mulhern in particular stresses the way both are structured around a denigration of the political. Before focusing on Coetzee's text in more detail, and outlining the type of cultural criticism he develops therein, I first want to stress what I see as the inadequacy of two different attempts to move beyond the terms of metacultural discourse: doing so will set the right context for an appreciation of the ways in which Coetzee's own style of cultural criticism is both distinctive and important.

The first is the position Mulhern himself takes. In place of the merely symbolic resolutions offered by metacultural discourse, Mulhern advocates a practice of 'cultural politics', whose 'field of action is mapped in the discrepancy between its constitutive terms, from which it also absorbs the tension that motivates it' (173). By insisting on a 'discrepancy' or a 'tension' between culture and politics, Mulhern aims above all to restore the authority of what he calls 'political reason', which he conceives in Marxist terms, and requires that it should be that principle 'which is to determine the order of social relations as a whole' (173). By contrast, culture is to be understood as 'a heterogeneous mass of possibilities old and new and never mutually translatable' (174) which 'political reason' must, in order to avoid an empty and impotent abstraction from lived reality, study and mould to its general programme of total social transformation. As he puts it in a *New Left Review* article:

Political practice is *trans*-cultural in its re-working of value as demand, sometimes promoting given identities and preferences, sometimes re-articulating or disturbing or backgrounding them, according to judgements based on a socially determinate programme and strategy ... 'culture', as it enters directly into the space of political practice, negates its ideal self-image, becoming a tactic.[10]

Mulhern's article is part of an exchange with the scholar and cultural critic Stefan Collini, who rightly identifies the central problem with Mulhern's position: that is, his very confidence in 'political reason' as a principle that is able to produce 'judgements' of ultimate direction prior to its encounter with culture, which as such can only ever be a 'tactic'. As Collini points out, it is only by dint of his faith in the ultimate sufficiency of a Marxist conception of political reason that Mulhern is able to make his claim that politics should determine our relationship with culture—but this is a faith that few can share. Although the term 'Marxism' now encompasses a very diverse range of thinking indeed, it is, I think, hard not to agree with Collini's assessment that the central weakness of this tradition

[...] lies in the status of the promised 'resolution' itself, for it is surely now clearer than ever that there is something culpably gestural about Marxism's promise to re-make social relations on some other basis and to abolish those economic and social antagonisms that it identifies as having hitherto been

[10] Mulhern, 'Beyond Metaculture' 103. In this distinction between 'strategy' and 'tactic' Mulhern may be alluding to Michel de Certeau, *L'Invention du quotidian*, i. *Arts de Faire* (1980) (*The Practice of Ordinary Life* (Berkeley, Calif., 1984)): Certeau defines institutions of recognized authority as 'strategies', and everyday, contingent activities as 'tactics'.

the motor of historical change. That claim always rested too heavily on Marx's re-working of Hegel's philosophy of history; and, notoriously, his vision of what kind of society might then succeed capitalism was sketchy in the extreme. In these terms Marxism, too, could be said to offer (no less but also no more than) 'a symbolic metapolitical resolution of the contradictions of capitalist modernity'.[11]

But if Mulhern's attempt to get 'beyond metaculture' is inadequate, rooted as it is in his confidence in the sufficiency of one kind of 'political reason', the alternative offered by Collini himself is no more plausible, and Collini's is the second attempt that I want to consider.

In response to Mulhern, Collini sets out to defend a 'softer', more generally palatable, and more intramundane version of cultural criticism for the post-Freudian, post-Marxist present: one that does not resort to Benda's claim to transcendence, or to Matthew Arnold's highly spiritualized concept of the 'best self', which Collini admits is 'outdated'. To speak from 'a broadly cultural perspective', he argues, need not be to make a 'displacement or supersession of politics', but may instead be a form of address that aims at 'critically supplementing' the political; the cultural perspective is, he suggests, only 'one among the valuable forms of public debate'.[12] But the rhetorical modesty of Collini's stance is unmatched by any substantive rethinking of the position from which culture speaks to politics: 'Culture', he argues, 'still names an ethical move, an allusion to the bearing which that kind of disinterested or autotelic exploration of human possibility, characteristically (but not exclusively) pursued in artistic and intellectual activity, can have upon those processes that are governed by the need to bring about proximate instrumental ends'. (In a more rhetorically-qualified later formulation, he refers to culture as that which 'enable[s] a degree of "standing back" from instrumentality'.)[13] It is evident from these formulations that alongside a sustainedly *Kulturkritik* elevation

[11] Stefan Collini, 'Defending Cultural Criticism', *New Left Review* 18 (2002) 90.
[12] Ibid. 97.
[13] Stefan Collini, 'Culture Talk', *New Left Review* 7 (2001) 51; 'Defending Cultural Criticism' 88.

of the cultural principle goes an equally traditional inability to define 'politics' in any terms other than those that Mulhern rightly calls 'culturalist'. Politics is for Collini exclusively that which is 'governed by the need to bring about proximate instrumental ends'; it is 'instrumental reason' incarnate, which as such is bound to issue in exploitative effects—given the 'narrow pragmatism... of any particular political programme'.[14] Collini makes his case much more tactfully than Benda, speaking of how 'most of everyday activity is necessarily and rightly "instrumental" and "partial"'.[15] But this is only an affable restatement of old ground, and conceals what is in fact a grandiose claim for social authority. For if the 'broadly cultural position'—the position of disinterested judgement, of 'standing back' from instrumentality—were really available in our lives, and were not in fact, as materialists have argued, an illusion rooted in sublimated desire, then it should indeed command general social authority. No matter how much Collini rhetorically tempers his claims, these are still, to borrow J.C.'s term, 'strong opinions'.

There is a shared dynamic underlying both these attempts to move past the merely symbolic resolution offered by metacultural discourse: Collini's reductive view of politics goes along with his hypervaluation of culture, and the same applies in reverse to Mulhern. A different attempt to get 'beyond metaculture' is the argument about the relation of culture to politics that runs through this book, and which as I hope to have shown, is most truly evidenced in the experience of reading Coetzee's fiction. It is not the case that politics is intrinsically inadequate as a general authority in social life, or that there is a cultural perspective that can best order our affairs: to that extent Mulhern's critique of metacultural discourse is right. But what I have argued, and what I think Coetzee's fiction time and again invites us to recognize, is that it is equally the case that no one form of politics can constitute a master-discourse—an adequate foundation

[14] Collini, 'Culture Talk' 48, 51.
[15] Collini, 'Defending Cultural Criticism' 88.

for the truly 'moral community'. It is a mistake to think of politics homogenously either as a degraded form of 'instrumental reason', or as one sufficient and totalizing 'political reason' that can ultimately deliver us from the torsions of power. Both views radically under-describe the valuable, yet incommensurate, ideals of human identity and community that constitute the mixed legacy of our political modernity: most especially, as I have argued, these include the universalist ideals of equal recognition, equality, and autonomy that derive from the Kantian side of the Enlightenment; and the particularist ideals of community and authenticity that emerge from the multifaceted reaction against Kant. If we are de-essentializing politics we must equally de-essentialize culture, and this is what Coetzee's writing tries to do. From his early fiction, especially through his concern to assimilate and adapt Beckett's handling of the form of the novel, Coetzee has tried to find a way out of metacultural discourse that does not at the same time simply collapse fiction into a merely 'supplementary' relation to one particular political ideal. His greatest fiction, I have argued, invites us to regard the ideal of the 'moral community' as a complex demand that requires a continual process of reappraisal, and a sustained hold-ing-open of different moral and political ideas: in its very structure and style it disturbs different types of foundational thinking. Coet-zee's own attempts to theorize his writing have not always articulated this stance successfully—recall, for instance, the irascible commit-ment to 'rivalry' in 'The Novel Today'.[16] But at their best—and the essay that describes Erasmian folly as a response to 'rivalry' is crucial here—Coetzee's theoretical writings are themselves subtle and inno-vative forays into a new critical discourse aimed at pushing beyond the limits of inherited terms.[17]

---

[16] See Ch. 3.

[17] See 'Erasmus: Madness and Rivalry' in *Giving Offense*. As a cultural critic, Coetzee has also written on popular culture—with articles on advertising, rugby, and the comic strip (Captain America). Although Coetzee has suggested that his work in this field 'barely deserves the name of work' (*Doubling the Point* 103) his

For the rest of this chapter, I'm going to suggest what this stance towards culture and politics means for the particular concerns of Coetzee's Australian fiction—and in doing so I will suggest what a cultural criticism that genuinely does move past a 'metacultural' stance towards political modernity involves.

I have argued from the outset of this book that modern concepts of politics are necessarily divided and heterogeneous, and I have focused, because of the particularities of context, on the tension in the modern South African polity between the competing demands of equal dignity and difference. But as I have already suggested, Coetzee's Australian fiction focuses on another type of criticism made of the same political legacy. This is the accusation that a rationalist emphasis on the recognition of human equality and autonomy is not only culturally destructive (that was the argument made by the proponents of the politics of difference), but that it creates a valueless individualist society bereft of any communal norms of moral judgement. *Diary of a Bad Year* does not ultimately confirm the careful reader in this gross oversimplification of the moral achievements of broadly Kantian political ideals, but this type of negative *Kulturkritik* stance towards modern democratic society is indeed the one taken by J.C. As we have seen, J.C. follows Benda in his hostility towards the phenomenon he homogenizes as 'modern political culture', regarding it as essentially Machiavellian in character: in the section on Machiavelli he argues that the 'metaphysical' basis of Machiavelli's separation of public policy and moral ideal must be attacked at the root and shown to be 'fraudulent' (18). The way he in fact tries to close the gap between politics and clerkly morality (the view from

---

1980 essay, 'Triangular Structures of Desire in Advertising', is noteworthy for the way in which it attempts to move beyond 'the humanist critique of advertising' represented by 'the school of F. R. Leavis'. While he acknowledges the 'acumen and moral energy' of this school, he argues that 'the vision of a "time before"' to be found in René Girard's account of desire is 'more historically defensible, less a creation of nostalgia', than the Leavisite approach, which is grounded in a deeply *Kulturkritik* idealization of pre-modern types of community.

'culture') is by trying to resurrect the archaic concepts of honour and shame, and even, at one point, the curse. J.C.'s first reference to honour comes in his admiration for the most notorious opponents of political modernity in today's world—Islamic suicide bombers, who choose 'death over dishonour' (30). Confronted by the robot armies of an imagined American future, 'how can one,' he asks, 'save one's honour except by desperately and extravagantly throwing away one's life?' (30). His invocation of the honour ethic rises to a crescendo in his central Jeremiad against America, 'On National Shame'. Here, having decided that the Machiavellian instrumental stance typifies political modernity, he regards the lamentable conduct of the Bush administration as symptomatic: therefore, the argument runs, the only effective opposition is to strike at the 'fraudulent' Machiavellian root of this society in which 'the old powers of shame have been abolished' (39). J.C. suggests that Americans should learn from the honour code upheld by the suicide bombers: they must ask them-selves 'How do I save my honour?' (39); he speculates that among some good-hearted Americans there may already have been 'honour suicides... that one does not hear of' (40). Towards the end of the essay he looks to the possibility of political action in the form of honour-killings, to avoid the 'shame' that will fall on the community of Americans when they collectively 'appear with soiled hands before the judgment of history' (41).

J.C.'s stance marshals an impressive ('dazzling', according to James Woods) critical force—but what does the concept of 'honour' actually mean, and what does it involve? As Peter Berger has argued, honour is a concept that has 'an unambiguously outdated status in the *Weltanschauung* of modernity': wounded honour is not recog-nized as a motive in American law, and as Berger comments, 'one who claims to have lost it is an object of amusement rather than sympathy'.[18] The reason for this is that one of the central political

---

[18] Peter Berger, 'On the Obsolescence of the Concept of Honour', in Stanley Hauerwas and Alasdair MacIntyre (eds.), *Revisions: Changing Perspectives in Moral Philosophy* (Notre Dame, Ind., 1983) 172.

achievements of the modern period was the replacement of the honour ethic, which had its roots in a pre-democratic politics, with the concept of 'the dignity and the rights of the individual' (173). Both honour and dignity are, as Berger argues, 'concepts that bridge self and society', but they do so in distinctively different ways: honour 'implies that identity is essentially, or at least importantly, linked to institutional roles', and dishonour—a state of being-in-shame that is communally recognized and enforced—comes from a failure to live up to those roles; by contrast, the modern concept of dignity 'implies that identity is essentially independent of institutional roles'. This is Berger's useful distinction:

The true self of the knight is revealed as he rides out to do battle in the full regalia of his role; by comparison, the naked man in bed with a woman represents a lesser reality of the self. In a world of dignity, in the modern sense, the social symbolism governing the interaction of men is a disguise. The escutcheons *hide* the true self. It is precisely the naked man, and even more specifically the naked man expressing his sexuality, who represents himself more truthfully. (177)

Berger assigns no single explanation for the shift from one ethic of human identity, and its related politics, to another, listing the factors generally associated with modernity as each contributing its share of influence: 'technology and industrialization, bureaucracy, urbanization and population growth, the vast increase in communication between every conceivable human group, social mobility, the pluralization of social worlds' (178).

So in attempting to 'speak from culture', as Collini would put it, what J.C. in fact does is make an essentially political assault on the individualist ethic of dignity, in favour of the humiliated pre-modern ethic of honour. It is a powerful and important assault, for it is hard to disagree with J.C. that the good society must include some form of honour-based communal identity—a 'we' that defines the scope of moral accountability for actions taken in 'our' name—and some prevailing norms of moral judgement that go along with that identity, which take emotional hold of us through the feeling of shame. But in setting out J.C.'s thoughts about honour in this way I am already qualifying what he says—perhaps creatively so, but equally, I am detracting from the force of his critique. For Coetzee's text does not exactly qualify or moderate J.C.'s potent revival of the honour ethic, but instead destabilizes it, and does so through the figure of Anya, who is presented to us at the middle and bottom of the page, below the cultural criticism itself. Unlike J.C., Anya does not regard the modern world as 'dark times', but as 'pretty good times' (73), and through her *Diary of a Bad Year* alerts us to the genuine moral achievements of a 'modern political culture' that is based on equal dignity. For instance, when we read J.C. implicitly admiring the honour sacrifice of the Islamist radicals, at the bottom of the page we encounter not, so to speak, the knight in his regalia, riding off to make his own honour-sacrifice, but the 'naked man'—or rather, a J.C. being taunted by Anya for his desire to be a naked man expressing his sexuality with her:

You shouldn't say things like that to a nice girl, Señor, I say. And I turn my back and off I go with a waggle of the bum, his eyes avid upon me. I picked it up from the ducks, I think: a shake of the tail so quick it is almost a shiver. Quick-quack. (30–1)

As crass and stupid as Anya's flirtatious conduct may seem, her very obvious enjoyment of her body, the pleasure she takes in her own sexuality, and not least her power over her own body—these are all political achievements in fact won by 'modern political culture' very recently indeed from the dead hand of the honour ethic. As Anya is quick to point out, the female version of this ethic was the code of chastity, and later on in the text she tries to shake J.C. out of his concern with honour by drawing his attention to the female dimension of the question:

When you tell me you walk around bent under your load of dishonour, I think of those girls from the old days who had the bad luck to get raped and then had to wear black for the rest of their lives—wear black and sit in a corner and never go to parties and never get married. You have got it wrong, Mister C. Old thinking. Wrong analysis, as Alan would say. Abuse, rape, torture, it doesn't matter what: the news is, as long as it is not your fault, as long as you are not responsible, the dishonour doesn't stick to you. So you have been making yourself miserable over nothing. (103–5)

Anya's desire to rebut the claims of dishonour obviously has a very personal resonance, as she was herself raped. If we do regard her breezy rejection of shame and her bottom-wiggling self-confidence as crass, Coetzee's text suggests that may indeed be because we are seeing her through the eyes of *Kulturkritik*: as a sexually violated typist she is after all a literary echo of the typist featured by T. S. Eliot in that central document of modernist *Kulturkritik*, *The Waste Land* (1922). In 'The Fire Sermon' section of Eliot's poem we are presented with the vision of Tiresias, who watches 'the typist home at teatime'—a single, independent young woman in her own apartment—as she receives a 'young man carbuncular', who, like Alan, seems to sum up the malign effects of modern life, and whose sexual advances amount pretty much to rape ('Exploring hands encounter no defence; | His vanity requires no response, | And makes a welcome of indifference').[19] Eliot's text makes a direct appeal to high culture to judge the typist: the lines that follow ('When lovely woman stoops to folly') are adapted from the song of Olivia in Oliver Goldsmith's *The Vicar of Wakefield* (1766), in which, having been seduced and sexually violated, rather than face a life of 'shame' the woman of the song looks ahead to her own death as the only way of redeeming her honour.[20] In Eliot's text, the cultural critic himself is dissolved into a shadowy presence behind an array of acutely judgemental fragments from the past; in Coetzee's, J.C. has to face up to the raped typist, and accept shamefacedly the moral limits on his attempt to revive honour as the basis for social relations. In fact as well as adding a 'gender' complication to J.C.'s powerful Jeremiad,

---

[19] T. S. Eliot, *The Complete Poems and Plays* (London, 1969) 68–9.

[20] 'When lovely woman stoops to folly | And finds too late that men betray | What charm can soothe her melancholy, | What art can wash her guilt away? | The only art her guilt to cover, | To hide her shame from every eye, | To give repentance to her lover | And wring his bosom—is to die.' *The Vicar of Wakefield* ch. 24.

Diary of a Bad Year also uses Anya to add a race complication. One of the most common ways of generating the institutions of community upon which the emotional force of the honour ethic depends has traditionally been, and indeed still is, through ethnicity or religious faith, or (most frequently) some conjunction of the two. Anya, characteristically, has no patience with this communitarianism: in the essay 'On Al Qaida', where J.C. is expanding his thoughts on the Islamic radicals, Anya is at the bottom of the page comically diverting us away from serious identity-thinking: 'Am I not blonde-eyed and blue-haired enough for your tastes?', she jokes; and even her typing errors make a joke of this form of thinking, when she grants J.C. an 'italic identity', making him briefly kindred with Aeneas.

For every attempt made by the voice at the top of the page to homogenize, diagnose, and denounce modernity in general as instrumental, valueless, and Machiavellian, there is a countervoice at the bottom holding it back ('like a fish on a line', to recall *Disgrace*), complicating its diagnosis, diverting its denunciation, and reminding us of the heterogeneity of values within 'the political' that metacultural discourse is inclined to overlook. This process is not—to recall James Woods—an idle 'postmodern game' (whatever that might be), but an important way of tackling one of the most complex of our moral and political dilemmas. After all, as Peter Berger has argued, it makes no sense to denounce the modern destruction of honour without reservation, for this would be to deny the 'vast moral achievements' at stake: 'The same modern men who fail to understand an issue of honor are immediately disposed to concede the demands for dignity and for equal rights by almost every new group that makes them—racial or religious minorities, exploited classes, the poor, the deviant, and so on. Nor would it be just to question the genuineness of this disposition' (173). But equally, Berger counsels, we cannot simply ignore the failures of a purely rationalist and universalist foundation of politics that the destruction of the honour ethic entails:

It seems clear to us that the unrestrained enthusiasm for total liberation of the self from the 'repression' of institutions fails to take account of certain

fundamental requirements of man, notably those of *order*—that institutional order of society without which both collectivities and individuals
must descend into dehumanising chaos. In other words, the demise of
honor has been a very costly price to pay for whatever liberations modern
man may have achieved. (180)

Berger goes on to pose the true moral problem of a modern politics:

It may be allowed . . . to speculate that a rediscovery of honour in the future
development of modern society is both empirically plausible and morally
desirable. Needless to say, this will hardly take the form of a regressive
restoration of traditional codes . . . The ethical question, of course, is what
these institutions will be like. (181)

We must, that is to say, try to find ways of reimagining the place of
'honour' in a modern society: it must play some role, and have some
status in a truly 'moral community', but cannot be allowed to evolve
into the foundation of that community.

   This complex demand on the future is precisely what the form of
Diary of a Bad Year is trying to help its readers to navigate, and the
sustainedly self-qualifying manner in which it delivers cultural criticism is central to the anti-foundational effect it wishes to bring about
in our thinking. The text holds open different forms of politics,
keeping them in a tension that may help bring about—for some
readers—different ways of thinking about the dilemma Berger outlines. For instance, if we return to Anya's feminist assault on the
honour ethic, it is important to acknowledge that this is a finely
poised moment in the text. It is hard not to feel Anya is right to reject
the way J.C.'s thinking makes incursions into the sphere of sexuality,
and right to attack the old spectre of chastity-guilt. But is she equally
right to sweep aside all the critical force that accrues to honour?
'Abuse, rape, torture, it doesn't matter what,' she explains: 'the news
is, as long as it is not your fault, as long as you are not responsible,
the dishonour doesn't stick to you.' Anya thereby refuses the basis of
J.C.'s important critical stance on national corporate responsibility
and, amongst other things, historical guilt in deeply wounded soci-
eties such as South Africa, in a way that at this stage in the text many

readers will find themselves resisting. In fact this moment in *Diary of a Bad Year* opens out onto a particularly effective passage that lasts until the end of J.C.'s strong opinions: in these extremely tense pages the concept of honour becomes subject to a series of especially disorienting revaluations and counter-valuations. In what is typographically marked as the middle section of the text J.C. finds himself humiliated and dismissed by Anya for his idiotic over-extension of the honour ethic. This humiliation, and his desire to win back Anya (the appeal of the 'naked man' identity ethic) leads J.C. to change 'my opinion of my opinions' (136), and to question, though never actually decide, whether 'dishonour is dead'. This passage culminates in the diffuse pages of the second diary, which are generally lacking in a critical standpoint—any feeling for human honour—from which Alan can be criticized. But the two texts revolving around the increasingly dispiriting middle section of the page are more compelling. Below, J.C.'s discourse on honour is actually starting to take hold of Anya, though of course she does not see it this way, insisting to the last that J.C. has not changed her (203), even if he 'opened my eyes somewhat' (204). As she discovers that the truth about Alan's *total* disregard for the ethic of personal honour is a crude will to power, and even a flagrant criminality, she starts to feel her relationship with him is dishonourable. She never puts it in quite these terms, but there is a new flavour in her conversation by the end of the strong opinions: 'Is this your true face, Alan?' she asks; 'Is this the kind of person you really are?' (151). She wants to be able to recognize in Alan a type of knowable sincerity that is at least a version of the honour ethic.[21] In this passage, the text starts to generate some particularly complex moral encounters, and as just one example, consider the first page of 'On Political Life in Australia'. At the top of the page we have a rather arch and even lazy *Kulturkritik* denunciation of the economism and

---

[21] See Lionel Trilling, *Sincerity and Authenticity* (London, 1971) for a suggestive account of this view of identity.

anti-communitarianism of modern political life, made as ever in the name of the values of 'culture'—here the honour ethic to which J.C. is attached. This is then interrupted by Anya's 'pure cold rage' against J.C.'s thoughtless elaboration of the honour ethic into her own life, through his complacent suggestion that 'Dishonour won't be washed away. Won't be wished away. Still has its old power to stick' (108–9). Yet both J.C.'s certainty, and Anya's counter-certainty are then in turn shaken by the emotions welling up from the bottom of the page, where we are starting to learn about Alan's deeply dishonourable economic individualism, the consequences of which make Anya so 'flabbergasted that I cannot speak' (115).

In this passage Coetzee's writing is placing pressure, here in a very compressed way, on the different patterns of thinking differently positioned readers bring to bear on the question of the meaning and value of political modernity. The mode of cultural criticism Coetzee is developing—not always successfully, but sometimes very power-fully indeed—is one that works towards a creative disorientation of the categories and concepts we bring to the text. Avoiding the pitfalls of a merely symbolic 'metacultural' resolution to a properly political issue, *Diary of a Bad Year* makes no strong assertion of the *Kultur-kritik* stance, nor does it accept the countervailing slide into an uncritical populism. Instead it takes what I have been calling a position of creative weakness—a position through which different foundational ways of apprehending the condition of modernity can be put in touch with that which they find 'beside the point'.

'DEPLORING' IN *ELIZABETH COSTELLO*

Although the relation of culture to politics has long been an overt concern in critical essays and in his handling of the novel, Coetzee first began to make the discourse of *Kulturkritik* an explicit theme in his fiction through the character of Elizabeth Costello. Elizabeth first appeared in November 1996, when an earlier version of 'Realism' (the first 'lesson' in *Elizabeth Costello*) was read at Bennington College as the Ben Belitt lecture, and has turned up ever since in public lectures on themes ranging from the humanities to the lives of animals, frequently dramatizing situations familiar to Coetzee, such as receiving a literary prize, or giving a literary interview, or indeed giving a public lecture. These lectures on various themes were then collected into the 'Eight Lessons' of *Elizabeth Costello*, along with two new lessons, 'Eros', and 'At the Gate'. As I have argued, Coetzee's aim is by no means to discountenance the notion of cultural criticism itself, but instead to fashion the *Kulturkritik* stance into something more amenable to his distinctively Beckettian mode of truth-telling. But whereas *Diary of a Bad Year* complicates the discursive status of J.C. through the three-way split in the text, in the figure of Elizabeth Costello Coetzee redeploys the Erasmian fool. As I have already discussed Coetzee's special handling of folly extensively in other texts (especially *Age of Iron* and *Disgrace*) I will focus on one short example of the relation between folly and cultural criticism from *Elizabeth Costello*—the lesson entitled 'The Problem of Evil'.

Like Julien Benda, Elizabeth Costello has come to perceive herself as an upholder of higher values against the incursions of the world outside the realm of culture. In order to do so, she feels, she must renew the old art of 'deploring'—in much the same way that J.C. wanted to restore the emotion of 'shame'. To deplore is to make appeal to a communal consensus that a particular phenomenon is 'beyond the pale' and cannot be countenanced by a good society, and as she strolls along the seafront of the French Riviera with her son John in 'As a Woman Grows Older', she laments the demise of deploring, 'as the English did a hundred years ago with their parasols and their boaters, deploring Mr Hardy's latest effort, deploring the Boers'.[22] It is for her, regrettably, 'An interdicted word, an interdicted activity' (11)—along with so many valuable behaviours that

---

[22] J. M. Coetzee, 'As a Woman Grows Older', *New York Review of Books* (15 Jan. 2004) 11.

have become 'beside the point' in modernity. In 'The Problem of Evil' the deploring in which Elizabeth Costello engages relates to a theme even weightier than Thomas Hardy or the Boers. What she deplores publicly, though in private doubts whether she should in fact deplore, is that the sceptical and rational side of the modern political legacy, especially as evidenced by 'her kind Dutch hosts, her kind, intelligent, sensible auditors in this enlightened, rationally organised, well-run city' (159–60), are incommensurate with the most serious apprehension of human depravity: sheer evil, a transcendentally absolute condition that she is not afraid, in private, to call by the name of 'Satan', and that has the capacity to possess those who come into contact with it.[23] In particular, Elizabeth deplores the way in which the assumptions held by her 'kind Dutch hosts' produce defences of literary freedom that license the portrayal of any horror, however 'evil': an enlightened sensibility will discount the possibility that a novel may not only represent evil, but embody it, and thus be able, in turn, to make evil incarnate in the reader. Her previous feeling that 'the civilisation of the West is based on belief in unlimited and illimitable endeavour' and that 'we must simply hold on tight and go wherever the ride takes us' has been challenged by one of the literary products that the West's commitment to 'illimitable endeavour' has thrown up: a novel by a man himself called West, Paul West, that depicts particularly horrific scenes of torture carried out by the Nazis. Whereas the Western artist, since 'Romantic times', has claimed the 'right to venture into forbidden or tabooed places' (172), Elizabeth 'no longer believes that storytelling is good in itself' (167), or at least that it constitutes a higher good than that of deploring evil.

What is it that makes 'deploring' such a good idea? Should we not leap to Mr West's defence much as we would leap to Mr Hardy's? Elizabeth is quite conscious that her wish to 'deplore' makes her look something of a fool: 'No one with any sense [nowadays] *deplores*,' she

---

[23] This is all 'very Dostoevskian,' as Elizabeth comments in 'As a Woman Grows Older', though she adds, with rather heavy Coetzeean irony, 'I am not sure I have it in my repertoire' (14).

explains frustratedly to John in 'As a Woman Grows Older', 'not unless they want to be a figure of fun.' Or consider the following in 'The Problem of Evil':

A sparrow knocked off a branch by a slingshot, a city annihilated from the air: who dare say which is the worse? Evil, all of it, an evil universe invented by an evil god. Dare she say that to her kind Dutch hosts, her kind, intelligent, sensible auditors in this enlightened, rationally organised, well-run city? Best to keep her peace, best not to cry out too much. She can imagine the next headline in the *Age*: UNIVERSE EVIL, OPINES COSTELLO. (159–60)

A 'figure of fun' to the sensible Australian press, Elizabeth cuts a strangely uncompelling figure, bedraggled and unimpressive, disturbingly vague in her innermost thoughts for someone so strident in public:

From her hotel she wanders out along the canal, an old woman in a raincoat, still slightly light-headed, slightly wobbly on her feet, after the long flight from the Antipodes. Disoriented: is it simply because she has lost her bearings that she is thinking these black thoughts? If so, perhaps she ought to travel less. Or more. (160)

As in Coetzee's South African fiction, there is no attempt here to work towards a compromise: Costello is a fool, absorbed in the most antique discourse (her opponent, West, is a 'dupe of Satan' (164)). Her extreme position is not just at odds with, but utterly irreconcilable to, the situation she confronts. But as we know from having considered Coetzee's earlier fool-heroes, from Elizabeth Curren through to David Lurie, folly, when combined with the protean literary effects of Coetzee's text, is by no means a straightforward condition.

When Elizabeth discovers that not only (to labour the pun) is she speaking in the West, and deploring in general terms one of its most important ideas, but that West himself will be present in the auditorium the next day, she is faced with a dilemma. Should she excise the *ad hominem* attack on West himself from her lecture? Or alternatively, 'what if she tries softening her thesis?' (164). Late at night, she sets to work on the text she has prepared, striking out what she can of the 'bad pages', filling the margins with revisions. But it is a hopeless task: she 'stares in dismay at the mess' she has made, and wonders why, in her foolish panic, she did not make a copy before embarking on the task. So in the early hours of the morning she wanders down to the lobby of the hotel in search of a photocopier:

The young man at the reception desk sits with headphones on, jiggling his shoulders from side to side. When he sees her he springs to attention. 'A photocopier,' she says. 'Is there a photocopier I can use?'

He takes the wad of paper from her, glances at the heading. The hotel caters to many conferences, he must be used to distraught foreigners rewriting their lectures in the middle of the night. The lives of dwarf stars. Crop yields in Bangladesh. The soul and its manifold corruptions. All the same to him.   (164)

Elizabeth's wranglings with sheer evil are brought down with an unforgiving bathos as the gaze of the pleasantly befuddled reception-ist passes over her lecture. It is a gaze exactly consonant with that of 'the *Age*': it takes in only a batty old woman, bumbling about late at night with an obscure and strangely archaic text.

But then, at this very moment, when Elizabeth's authority is lowest, comes a passage in which she recalls an episode in her youth, when she was raped. We suddenly pass from the old woman to her younger self, from the efficient modern hotel to the Melbourne docks, and from the comic to the serious. Her younger self is not sentimentalized: indeed, when the episode begins it seems that the comic mode is going to continue, albeit in a more casually satirical vein. The 19-year-old Elizabeth was 'an art student and a rebel', in whose eyes 'in those days, only the working class and the values of the working class were authentic'. And the opening description of the encounter with 'Tim or Tom' always risks the comic: when she resists him, 'he took it as a game'; then he started hitting her; then he tore up her clothes and set fire to them; when he fell asleep (the rape is only implied), 'Stark naked, she crept out and hid in the bathroom on the landing', as if a character in a bedroom farce; only later, when the coast was clear, could she nip back in to retrieve what she could of the burnt clothes before venturing out to hail a taxi. 'It was her first brush of evil,' Elizabeth states at the opening of the following paragraph. Evil? Are we now inclined to trust the word? Perhaps not entirely, but it now carries more weight than it did three paragraphs ago. Then the seriousness intensifies:

She had realized it was nothing less than that, evil, when the man's affront subsided and a steady glee in hurting her took its place. He liked hurting her, she could see it; probably liked it more than he would have liked sex. Though he might not have known it when he picked her up, he had brought her to his room to hurt her rather than make love to her. By fighting him off she had created an opening for the evil in him to emerge, and it emerged in the form of glee, first at her pain ('You like that, do you?' he whispered as he twisted her nipples. 'You like that?'), then in the childish, malicious destruction of her clothes. (165–6)

It makes for profoundly disorienting reading: the passage doesn't just appear suddenly, it comes, as we have seen, at a moment when Elizabeth is at her most foolish, bumbling around late at night with a photocopying machine and an embarrassed receptionist.

Yet when she tries to bring this experience of her rape to bear upon her present situation, to draw from it a formulable idea about evil that might make the basis for a rethinking of literary freedom, her seriousness dissolves again—not because it would necessarily be impossible to make such a case, but because Coetzee's text disorientingly shifts back into a comic register. Elizabeth starts speaking of 'storytelling' as a 'bottle with a genie in it', and the homely oddity of such a description starts to teeter into bathos as she elaborates: 'When the storyteller opens the bottle, the genie is released into the world, and it costs all hell to get him back in again. Her position, her revised position, her position in the twilight of her life: better, on the whole, that the genie stay in the bottle' (167). Then the archaic language, absent from the narrative seriousness of her encounter with the docker, returns:

A genie or a devil. While she has less and less idea what it could mean to believe in God, about the devil she has no doubt. The devil is everywhere under the skin of things, searching for a way into the light. The devil entered the docker that night on Spencer Street, the devil entered Hitler's hangman. And through the docker, all that time ago, the devil entered

her: she can feel him crouched inside, folded up like a bird, waiting his
chance to fly. (167)

Elizabeth is conscious of how her seriousness seems to dissolve: 'She
is quite aware of how old-fashioned it sounds'; moreover, she is
aware that any verdict will be unanimously in favour of a comic
apprehension of her: '*She has let us down*, they will say. *Elizabeth
Costello has turned into old Mother Grundy*' (168).

The turn back to the non-serious image of a batty old woman
certainly holds back and qualifies Elizabeth's discourse on evil. But
equally important to emphasize is that, paradoxically, foolishness
provided the setting in which her discourse found the status it did: it
was because the shift into the rape episode was so disorienting, and
so baffled our apprehension of the silly and curmudgeonly figure we
thought we knew, that Elizabeth's vision of evil was able to escape the
sensible gaze of the receptionist, or 'the *Age*', so to speak, and find
its own seriousness, however momentary. Consider how flat the rape
episode would read if it was presented in the text not as a fool's fleeting
memory, but as part of an attempt to convince the reader of a case that
was being presented as sensible: it could be unpicked as part of a rhetoric
of persuasion, and rationalized away. As it stands, it haunts our reading
of the text in a way that is hard to decipher—difficult to know how
seriously to take it, or how to rationalize it into the wider debate on
literary freedom; but equally, hard to dismiss it. In renouncing the
authority of *Kulturkritik*, and staging this discourse on evil through
the figure of a fool, Coetzee's text finds that paradoxical kind of strength
in weakness that, as I have argued, is characteristic of his approach.

'TAKING THINGS SIMPLY AS THEY SEEM TO BE': *SLOW MAN*

Slow Man also turns on the question of how to do justice to types of
feeling and thinking that are being made irrelevant—or 'beside the
point'—by the rational and sceptical energies of modernity. The

opening of the text, as Paul Rayment awakens in hospital after his cycling accident, engages the reader in an encounter between Paul's sense of a spiritual crisis, born out of his brush with death, and the ways in which one particular institution of modernity—the hospital—attempts instead to assimilate him to a rationally managed happiness. '*Frivole*', or 'frivolous', is the verdict that seems to be pronounced on his divorced and childless life: 'Something like panic sweeps over him. He writhes; from the cavern within a groan wells up and bursts from his throat' (3). Like Elizabeth Costello in 'The Problem of Evil', Paul perceives in a more sober moment quite how foolishly archaic is this call to spiritual seriousness and the consideration of last things: 'How quaint, how positively antique, to believe one will be advised, when the time comes, to put one's soul in order. What beings could possibly be left, in what corner of the universe, interested in checking all the deathbed accountings that ascend the skies, debits in the one column, credits in the other?' (19). Moreover, his sense of a special calling, encompassing a yearning to do good, and to pass on a worthwhile inheritance, does not find any refuge in the efficient modern hospital, where the nurses engage in a silly sex-talk reminiscent of Aldous Huxley's vision of modern sexuality in *Brave New World* (1932). But 'just when he is about to topple' (27) from this remorseless assault on his sense of his own seriousness, along comes a new nurse called Marijana, and in her he believes he has found someone more amenable to his higher goals: when they talk about his stump Paul feels the conversation is 'devoid of double-entendre' (29); she seems to 'have the ability to annul sex' (30); she also has a son with whom Paul wants to strike up a relationship—a benign relationship, through which he will pass down wisdom from age to youth.

Perhaps the reader is tempted to ask: why all this fuss about an old man's desires? One of the reasons *Slow Man* was felt by many to be a disappointing novel is because of its interest in a subject that, by contrast to what Benda would call the 'political passions' at stake in a novel such as *Disgrace*, seems rather unimportant. But for Coetzee, the yearning for freedom from the taint of desire, and the hope that one might pass on a living inheritance, are realms of experience, and indeed of moral value, for which we should have some concern, and which our modernity is in danger of making entirely 'beside the point'. He expands on this theme in 'Love and Walt Whitman', a *New York Review of Books* essay of September 2005 (the month in which *Slow Man* was published)—an article that is unusual for the extent to which Coetzee sets out what seems to be his own position without using any ironizing and distancing devices. He takes issue with recent literary-biographical assessments of Whitman that treat his love affairs with Peter Doyle and Harry Stafford as being primarily sexually motivated: whereas Whitman's contemporaries seemed to be blind to the homosexual erotic content of the Calamus poems, taking offence instead at the poems about heterosexual love, both David Reynolds and Jerome Loving, in their respective accounts of Whitman, pretend to greater frankness about 'the intimate details' of the poet's homosexuality.[24] However, without denying that Whitman had a concretely sexual relationship with the young men, Coetzee questions the assumptions underlying the well-intentioned (or, at least, liberal-minded) unmasking carried out by the two critics:

Without siding with the censors... might one not argue that, among readers who did not take offense at the Calamus poems, some might have missed the amative content not because they were blinded by preconceptions about what intimacy between men had to consist of but because they did not feel they needed to ask themselves what the amative content of that intimacy might be, that is, because their notion of intimacy did not boil down to what the men in question did with their sexual organs?... In other words, believing that contemporary readers of Whitman's poems of love missed what those poems were really about may reveal more about simpleminded notions of what it means to be 'really about' something than it reveals about Whitman's readers.[25]

---

[24] The works in question are David Reynolds, *Walt Whitman* (Oxford, 2005), and Jerome Loving, *Walt Whitman: The Song of Himself* (Berkeley, 1999).

[25] J. M. Coetzee, 'Love and Walt Whitman', *New York Review of Books* (22 Sept. 2005) 24.

Instead of assuming that 'what the men did with their sexual organs' was the underlying motivation of Whitman's behaviour, an assumption that would draw no complaint from the utilitarian ethic that drives the smutty nurses at Paul's hospital, Coetzee invokes, with apparent seriousness, what might seem a rather chimerical idea: 'There is a certain sophistication, governed by unspoken social consensus, whose nature lies in taking things simply for what they seem to be. It is this sort of social wisdom, whose other name might be tact, that we are in danger of denying to our Victorian forebears' (25). The possible 'social wisdom', or even 'sophistication', of 'taking things simply for what they seem to be' in relation to love—a wisdom akin to the moral norms required by the honour ethic in *Diary of a Bad Year*—is a question with which another of the *Elizabeth Costello* lessons engages. In 'Eros' Elizabeth has been sent a book by 'an American friend' that is 'another telling of the Eros and Psyche story, by one Susan Mitchell' (183). This story seems to Elizabeth to have a quite particular relation to the same problem of modernity she encountered in the previous lesson, 'The Problem of Evil':

Why the interest in Psyche among American poets, she wonders? Do they find something American in her, the girl who, not content with the ecstasies provided night after night by the visitor to her bed, must light a lamp, peel back the darkness, gaze on him naked? In her restlessness, her inability to leave well alone, do they see something of themselves?   (184)

A page later she is meditating on a film of which Mitchell's book has reminded her, one 'that might have been written by Nathanael West' (is she confused with Paul West, or 'the West' again?[26]), 'though in fact it wasn't':

Jessica Lange playing a Hollywood sex goddess who has a breakdown and ends up in the common ward of a madhouse, drugged, lobotomised, strapped to her bed, while orderlies sell tickets for ten minutes a time with her. '*I wanna fuck a*

[26] Elizabeth Costello may have in mind Nathanael West's novel *The Day of the Locust* (1939), set in Hollywood during the Great Depression; it was adapted for the screen in 1974.

movie star!' pants one of their customers, shoving his dollars at them. In his voice the ugly underside of idolatry: malice, murderous resentment. Bring an immortal down to earth, show her what life is really like, bang her till she is raw. *Take that! Take that!* A scene they excised from the televised version, so close to the bone of America does it cut. (185)

It is the particular sensibility of Anchises, 'lover of Aphrodite and father of Aeneas', that interests her. Despite having 'fucked a goddess', as she puts it (185), Anchises did not then seek to uncover the details of his experience: 'he did not think overmuch about it, not as we understand thinking' (186). Elizabeth's concern is that the sort of society whose art is fascinated by the figure of Psyche—a society that cannot take things 'simply as they seem to be'—is one that ultimately makes the experience of love predictable and valueless:

Where in the world today does one find such immortal longings as hers used to be? Not in the personal columns, for sure. 'SWF, 5'8″, thirties, brunette, into astrology, biking, seeks SWM, 35–45 for friendship, fun, adventure.' Nowhere: 'DWF, 5'8″, sixties, runs to death and death meets her as fast, seeks G, immortal, earthly form immaterial, for ends to which no words suffice.' In the editorial office they would frown. Indecent desires, they would say, and toss her in the same basket as the pederasts. (191)

What is at stake in the juxtaposition of the two lonely hearts ads is again the boundary between competing and incommensurable intuitions of value in human identity: between one way of thinking, whether that of Anchises in 'Eros', or the nineteenth-century American readers that Coetzee imagines in 'Love and Walt Whitman', that defers the probing of underlying causes so as to honour the mystery of one of the most important of human intimacies; and another more modern impulse that is devoted to asking questions, liberating us from repressions, probing, examining the doubleness of desire.

As in *Diary of a Bad Year*, *Slow Man* refuses to position itself as a metacultural resolution to (or transcendence of) the problem of inhabiting the competing and incommensurate value-systems that make up our modernity. Paul claims to have been awakened by his accident to a set of rather grandly transcendental accounts of his motivations that cohere around ideals of purity and benign care. But far from 'taking things simply for what they seem to be', Elizabeth Costello's text forces Paul into a number of encounters in which he is required to give a 'deeper' account of his desires—which is to say, one that 'boils down' to, as Coetzee puts it, a concern with what he wants to do with his sexual organs. 'Why?' is the simple question Marijana asks after Paul tells her he will pay Drago's school fees: ' "It is an investment in his future. In the future of all of us." She shakes her head. "Why?" she repeats, "I don't understand" ' (76). The first, and grander, conception of his behaviour is ruled out, and he is forced to couch his hopes instead in the more banal terms of heterosexual desire. Paul is repeatedly confronted with the question 'Why?', and has no particularly effective retort to make, as he discovers when he tries to defend his behaviour to Drago by using an archaic terminology of honour:

> *Nothing dishonourable.* What a funny old form of words! Are they not just a fig-leaf to cover something a great deal coarser, something unsayable: *I haven't been fucking your mother?* If fucking is what it is all about, if fucking is what sends Miroslav Jokić into a jealous rage and brings his son to the edge of tears, why is he making speeches about honour? *I haven't been fucking your mother, I haven't even solicited her: go and tell that to your father.* Yet if he does not plan to solicit Marijana, if he does not aspire to fuck her, what in God's name does he plan or aspire to do, in words that make sense to a youth born in the 1980s?   (133)

Paul cannot defend himself within the discourse of the novel, where he is called upon to speak to others about what motivates him, because he wants to get beyond the desire for 'double-meanings' and narrative complexity in favour of what amounts to a state of grace.[27]

As such the major irony of *Slow Man*—an irony it at times rather labours—is the fact that one of the main barriers to the recovery of

---

[27] As Coetzee defines it in 'Confession and Double Thoughts': 'Grace: a condition in which the truth can be told clearly, without blindness'. *Doubling the Point* 392.

Paul's sense of his own seriousness is the dialogical novel itself. Whereas in 'Eros' and 'The Problem of Evil' Elizabeth Costello was distrustful, to say the least, of the impulse of novelists, poets, and filmmakers (most of whom pass under the name of 'West') towards motivational complexity and the articulation of dialogical countervoices, in *Slow Man* we find her in a different frame of mind. When she enters the text she does so as a writer committed to an art of ambivalence ('She has made a living out of ambivalence. Where would the art of fiction be if there were no double meanings?'), and her chief complaint about Paul is his desire to be a simple soul, unaffected by the dynamic of repression and duplicity. She is of course no mere cipher for the utilitarian institutions whose incursions, by turns rational and infantile, Paul resents and even fears. But nonetheless, she is one of his foes: neither the official institutions nor the literary practices of Australian modernity can find space to credit Paul's idea of himself with the authority he demands. Elizabeth does, at times, try to acknowledge Paul's difference, claiming that he gives her 'faith':

One is embarrassed, that is all, to find oneself in the presence of true, old-fashioned love. I bow before you.

　　She pauses in what she is doing and offers, not without irony, the lightest of inclinations of the head. (94)

But as the 'not without irony' reveals, there are limits to the extent to which she is able to take him seriously. Recall Bakhtin's metaphor of the mirror from our discussion of *The Master of Petersburg*. Dostoevsky was the first to reveal

[...] the complexity of the simple phenomenon of looking at oneself in the mirror: with one's own and with others' eyes simultaneously, a meeting and interaction between the others' and one's own eyes, an intersection of worldviews (one's own and the other's), an intersection of two consciousnesses. (*Problems of Dostoevsky's Poetics* 289)

In Bakhtin's terms, Paul is Dostoevsky's diametric opposite: 'He himself has never been at ease with mirrors. Long ago he draped a cloth over the mirror in the bathroom and taught himself to shave blind. One of the more irritating things the Costello woman did during her stay was to take down the drape. When she left he at once put it back' (163). Paul stubbornly refuses to awaken any counter-voices in himself: if he has a literary genre it is the genre of Friday in *Foe*—the wisdom tale.

I have argued that this type of encounter with the very limits of the expressible—with what his own discourse tends to render 'beside the point'—is crucial to the way Coetzee's fiction responds to the form of the novel itself. As he emphasized in the Tokyo lecture on Beckett, it is a prose style rooted in dissonant tragicomedy that is best fitted to his approach, and it is an aim best figured, as Beckett's own series of paired characters suggests, in the trope of a terminal and non-transcendable companionship of opposites. In a long line of such figures that stretches from Alonso Quixano and Sancho Panza, through to Mercier and Camier and Vladimir and Estragon, stand Elizabeth Curren and Vercueil, Lurie and his dogs, and most recently Anya and J.C. 'Maybe,' Anya speculates, 'in another life, if our ages were more compatible, you and I could set up house together and I could be your inspiration' (204): as J.C.'s critical voice 'strains to soar away', Anya is there to interrupt and provoke, allowing in the process what Coetzee has called 'the play of writing' to take place. Elizabeth Costello's vision of what it means to be an 'Australian novelist' at the end of *Slow Man* is also in this line. She looks to a terminally grouchy life with Paul, within which lies the possibility of becoming 'a well-loved Australian institution' (263): 'What an idea! What a capital idea!' she exclaims, imagining the two of them cycling across 'the whole of this wide brown land, north and south, east and west'. But with a polite kiss, Paul once more refuses to go along with the nove-list's vision of how things should be. In the jocoserious way it com-bines the inspiring reach of Elizabeth's imagination with the stubborn bathos of Paul's refusal, this moment returns us to where we began: to Coetzee's circumspect distinction between being 'a novelist' and being 'a writer working in the medium of the novel'.

Select Bibliography

WORKS BY COETZEE

Coetzee, J. M. 'The English Fiction of Samuel Beckett: An Essay in Stylistic Analysis.' Diss. University of Texas, 1969.

—— *Dusklands*. Johannesburg: Ravan, 1974. London: Random House, 1998.

—— *In the Heart of the Country*. London: Secker & Warburg, 1977. London: Random House, 1999.

—— *Waiting for the Barbarians*. London: Secker & Warburg, 1980. London: Random House, 2000.

—— *Life & Times of Michael K*. London: Secker & Warburg, 1983. London: Random House, 1998.

—— *Foe*. London: Secker & Warburg, 1986. Harmondsworth: Penguin, 1987.

—— 'The Novel Today'. *Upstream* 6/1 (1988) 2–5.

—— *Age of Iron*. London: Secker & Warburg, 1990. Harmondsworth: Penguin, 1998.

—— 'Interview with Paul Bailey'. *Third Ear*. BBC Radio 3, London. 18 December 1990. BBC Sound archive ref. T87063(1).

—— *Doubling the Point*. Ed. David Attwell. Cambridge, Mass.; London: Harvard University Press, 1992.

—— *The Master of Petersburg*. London: Secker & Warburg, 1994. London: Random House, 1999.

—— *Giving Offense*. Chicago: University of Chicago Press, 1996.

—— 'Gordimer and Turgenev'. *Stranger Shores: Essays 1986–1999*. London: Secker & Warburg, 2001, 268–84.

—— 'What is Realism?' *Salmagundi* 114–15 (1997) 60–81.

—— *Boyhood: Scenes from Provincial Life*. London: Secker & Warburg, 1997. London: Random House, 1998.

—— *Disgrace*. London: Secker & Warburg, 1999. London: Random House, 2000.

—— *Stranger Shores: Essays 1986–1999*. London: Secker & Warburg, 2001.

—— *Youth*. London: Secker & Warburg, 2002. London: Random House, 2003.

—— 'He and His Man'. The 2003 Nobel Lecture in Literature, at http://www.nobel.se/literature/laureates/2003/coetzee-lecture-e.html, accessed 19 Dec. 2009.

—— *Elizabeth Costello*. London: Secker & Warburg, 2003.

—— *Slow Man*. London: Secker & Warburg, 2005.

—— 'As a Woman Grows Older'. *New York Review of Books* (15 Jan. 2004) 11–14.

—— 'Love and Walt Whitman'. *New York Review of Books* (22 Sept. 2005) 22–8.

—— Preface. *Samuel Beckett: The Grove Centenary Edition*. New York: Grove, 2006, iv.

—— *Diary of a Bad Year*. London: Harvill Secker, 2007.

—— 'Eight Ways of Looking at Samuel Beckett'. *Borderless Beckett/Beckett sans frontières*, ed. Minako Okamuro, Naoya Mori, Bruno Clément, Sjef Houppermans, Angela Moorjani, and Anthony Uhlmann. Amsterdam: Rodopi, 2008, 19–31.

OTHER WORKS

Adorno, T. W., and Max Horkheimer. *Dialectic of Enlightenment: Philosophical Fragments*. Ed. Gunzelin Schmid Noerr, trans. Edmund Jephcott. Stanford: Stanford University Press, 2002.

Appiah, Kwame Anthony. *The Ethics of Identity*. Princeton, NJ: Princeton University Press, 2005.

Ashcroft, Bill, Gareth Griffiths, and Helen Tiffin (eds.). *The Post-Colonial Studies Reader*. London: Routledge, 1995.

Attridge, Derek. *J. M. Coetzee and the Ethics of Reading: Literature in the Event*. Chicago: University of Chicago Press, 2004.

—— *The Singularity of Literature*. London: Routledge, 2004.

Attwell, David. *J. M. Coetzee: South Africa and the Politics of Writing*. Berkeley: University of California Press, 1993.

—— '"Dialogue" and "Fulfilment" in J. M. Coetzee's *Age of Iron*', in Derek Attridge and Rosemary Jolly (eds.), *Writing South Africa*. Cambridge: Cambridge University Press, 1998, 166–79.

—— 'Race in *Disgrace*'. *Interventions* 4/3 (2002) 331–41.

Attwell, David. 'The Life and Times of Elizabeth Costello: J. M. Coetzee and the Public Sphere', in Jane Poyner (ed.), *J. M. Coetzee and the Idea of the Public Intellectual*. Ohio: Ohio University Press, 2006, 25–42.

—— *Rewriting Modernity: Studies in Black South African Literary History*. Scottsville: University of KwaZulu-Natal Press, 2005.

Auerbach, Erich. *Mimesis: The Representation of Reality in Western Literature*. Trans. Willard R. Trask. Princeton: Princeton University Press, 2003.

Barthes, Roland. *Writing Degree Zero*. Trans. Annette Lavers and Colin Smith. London: Cape, 1967.

—— *The Pleasure of the Text*. Trans. Richard Millar. New York: Hill & Wang, 1975.

Bakhtin, M. M. (Mikhail Mikhailovich). *Problems of Dostoevsky's Poetics*. Trans. Caryl Emerson. Minneapolis: University of Minnesota Press, 1984.

—— *The Dialogic Imagination*. Ed. Michael Holquist, trans. Caryl Emerson and Michael Holquist. Austin: University of Texas Press, 1981.

Beckett, Samuel. *The Beckett Trilogy*. London: John Calder, 1956; Pan Books, 1979.

—— *Disjecta: Miscellaneous Writings and a Dramatic Fragment*. Ed. Ruby Cohn. London: J. Calder, 1983.

—— *The Complete Dramatic Works*. London: Faber & Faber, 1986.

Benda, Julien. *The Treason of the Intellectuals*. Trans. Richard Aldington (1928); reissued with intro. Roger Kimball. New Brunswick, NJ: Transaction, 2007.

Berger, Peter. 'On the Obsolescence of the Concept of Honour', in Stanley Hauerwas and Alasdair MacIntyre (eds.), *Revisions: Changing Perspectives in Moral Philosophy*. Notre Dame, Ind.: University of Notre Dame Press, 1983.

Blanchot, Maurice. *La Folie du jour*. Montpellier: Éditions Fata Mogaria, 1973.

—— *The Work of Fire*. Trans. Charlotte Mandell. Stanford, Calif.: Stanford University Press, 1995.

—— *The Blanchot Reader*. Ed. Michael Holland. Oxford: Blackwell, 1995.

Biko, Steve. *I Write What I Like*. Ed. Aelred Stubbs CR. London: Heinemann, 1978.

Brink, André. *Mapmakers: Writing in a State of Siege*. London: Faber & Faber, 1983.

—— *Reinventing a Continent: Writing and Politics in South Africa 1982–1995.* London: Secker & Warburg, 1996.

Byron, George Gordon. *Poetical Works.* Ed. Frederick Page. Oxford: Oxford University Press, 1970.

Canepari-Labib, Michela. *Old Myths—Modern Empires: Power, Language and Identity in J. M. Coetzee's Work.* Oxford: Peter Lang, 2005.

Chakrabarty, Dipesh. *Provincializing Europe: Postcolonial Thought and Historical Difference.* Princeton, NJ: Princeton University Press, 2000.

Certeau, Michel de. *The Practice of Ordinary Life.* Trans. Stephen Rendall. Berkeley: University of California Press, 1984.

Cervantes, Miguel de. *Don Quixote.* 1605–15. Trans. Charles Jarvis. Oxford: Oxford University Press, 1994.

—— *Exemplary Stories.* 1613. Trans. and ed. Lesley Lipson. Oxford: Oxford University Press, 1998.

Clark, Katerina, and Michael Holquist. *Mikhail Bakhtin.* Cambridge, Mass.: Belknap Press of Harvard University, 1984.

Clingman, Steven. *The Novels of Nadine Gordimer: History From the Inside.* London: Allen & Unwin, 1986.

Collini, Stefan. 'Culture Talk'. *New Left Review* 7 (2001) 43–53.

—— 'Defending Cultural Criticism'. *New Left Review* 18 (2002) 73–97.

Defoe, Daniel. *Roxana.* 1724. Ed. David Blewett. Harmondsworth: Penguin, 1987.

—— *Robinson Crusoe.* 1719. Ed. John Richetti. Harmondsworth: Penguin, 2001.

Derrida, Jacques. *Acts of Literature.* Ed. Derek Attridge. London: Routledge, 1992.

—— *Of Grammatology.* Trans. Gayatri Chakravorty Spivak. Baltimore: Johns Hopkins University Press, 1974, corrected edn. 1997.

—— *Speech and Phenomena.* Trans. David B. Allison. Evanston, Ill.: Northwestern University Press, 1973.

—— 'The Animal That Therefore I Am (More to Follow)'. Trans. David Wills. *Critical Inquiry* 28 (Winter, 2002) 369–418.

Dostoevsky, F. M. *Notes from Underground.* 1864. Trans. Richard Pevear and Larissa Volokhonsky. London: Random House, 1993.

—— *Crime and Punishment.* 1866. Trans. David McDuff. Harmondsworth: Penguin, 1991.

—— *The Idiot.* 1868. Trans. David Magarshack. London: Penguin, 1955.

Dostoevsky, F. M. *Demons.* 1871–2. Trans. Richard Pevear and Larissa Volokhonsky. London: Random House, 1994.

—— *The Karamazov Brothers.* 1879–80. Trans. Ignat Avsey. Oxford: Oxford University Press, 1994.

Eliot, George. *Selected Essays, Poems and Other Writings.* Ed. A. S. Byatt and Nicholas Warren. Harmondsworth: Penguin, 1990.

Eliot, T. S. *The Complete Poems and Plays.* London: Faber & Faber, 1969.

Enns, Diane. *Speaking of Freedom: Philosophy, Politics, and the Struggle for Liberation.* Stanford: Stanford University Press, 2007.

Erasmus, Desiderius. *The Praise of Folly.* 1510. Trans. and ed. Robert M. Adams. New York: W. W. Norton, 1989.

Eysteinsson, Ástrádur. *The Concept of Modernism.* Ithaca: Cornell University Press, 1990.

Fanon, Franz. *Black Skin, White Masks.* Trans. Charles Lam Markmann. New York: Grove, 1967.

—— *The Wretched of the Earth.* Trans. Constance Farrington. Harmondsworth: Penguin, 1967.

Felman, Shoshana. *Writing and Madness.* Trans. Martha Noel Evans, Shoshana Felman, and Brian Massumi. Ithaca: Cornell University Press, 1985.

Fish, Stanley. *Is There a Text in This Class? The Authority of Interpretive Communities.* Cambridge, Mass.: Harvard University Press, 1980.

Fiske, John. *Television Culture.* London: Methuen, 1987.

Frank, Joseph. *Through the Russian Prism.* Princeton: Princeton University Press, 1990.

—— *Dostoevsky: The Miraculous Years, 1865–1871.* London: Robson Books, 1995.

—— *Dostoevsky: The Mantle of the Prophet, 1871–1881.* London: Robson Books, 2002.

Freud, Sigmund. *Group Psychology and the Analysis of the Ego.* Trans. James Strachey. London: Hogarth and the Institute of Psycho-analysis, 1922.

Gaskell, Elizabeth. *North and South.* 1854–5. Ed. Dorothy Collin. London: Penguin Classics, 1986.

Gaylard, Gerald. 'Mastering Arachnophobia: The Limits of Self-Reflexivity in African Fiction'. *Journal of Commonwealth Literature* 37/1 (2002) 85–99.

Gerwel, Jakes. 'Perspektief: Is *dít* die regte beeld van ons nasie?' ('Perspective: Is *this* the right image of our nation?') Trans. Peter McDonald. *Rapport* (13 Feb. 2000) 2.

—— 'Perspektief: Dís tog beter as Roodt se ligsinnigheid' ('Perspective: It is nonetheless better than Roodt's lightness of spirit'). Trans. Charl Engela. *Rapport* (9 Apr. 2000) 6.

Gilman, Stephen. *The Novel According to Cervantes.* Berkeley: University of California Press, 1989.

Girard, René. *Deceit, Desire and the Novel: Self and Other in Literary Structure.* Trans. Yvonne Freccero. Baltimore: Johns Hopkins Press, 1965.

Goodwin, Christopher. 'White Man without the Burden'. *Sunday Times News Review* (16 Jan. 2000).

Gordimer, Nadine. *Burger's Daughter.* London: Cape, 1979.

—— 'The Idea of Gardening'. Rev. of *Life & Times of Michael K,* by J. M. Coetzee. *New York Review of Books* (2 Feb. 1984) 3–6.

—— *The Essential Gesture: Writing, Politics and Places.* Ed. Stephen Clingman. London: Cape, 1988.

Gray, John. *Enlightenment's Wake: Politics and Culture at the Close of the Modern Age.* London: Routledge, 1995.

—— *Two Faces of Liberalism.* Cambridge: Cambridge University Press, 2002.

Guillen, Claudio. *Literature as System: Essays Toward the Theory of Literary History.* Princeton: Princeton University Press, 1977.

Habermas, Jürgen. *The Structural Transformation of the Public Sphere: An Inquiry into a Category of Bourgeois Society.* Trans. Thomas Burger with the assistance of Frederick Lawrence. Cambridge: Polity, 1989.

Head, Dominic. *J. M. Coetzee.* Cambridge: Cambridge University Press, 1997.

Hegel, G. W. F. *Phenomenology of Spirit.* Trans. A. V. Miller. Oxford: Clarendon, 1977.

Heidegger, Martin. *Discourse on Thinking: A Translation of Gelassenheit.* Trans. John M. Anderson and E. Hans Freund. New York: Harper & Row, 1966.

—— *Basic Writings.* Ed. David Farrell Krell. Rev. edn. London: Routledge, 1993.

Hesiod. *Theogony; Works and Days.* Trans. Dorothea Wender. Harmondsworth: Penguin, 1973.

Hillis Miller, J. *The Ethics of Reading: Kant, de Man, Eliot, Trollope, James and Benjamin.* New York: Columbia University Press, 1987.

Hoegberg, David E. '"Where is Hope?" Coetzee's Rewriting of Dante in *Age of Iron*'. *English in Africa* 25/1 (1998) 27–42.

Holland, Michael. '"Plink-plunk": Unforgetting the Present in Coetzee's *Disgrace*'. *Interventions* 4/3 (2002) 395–404.

Holquist, Michael. *Dostoevsky and the Novel.* Princeton: Princeton University Press, 1977.

——*Dialogism: Bakhtin and His World.* London: Routledge, 1990.

Howe, Irving. 'Philip Roth Reconsidered'. *Commentary* 54/6 (Dec. 1972) 69–77. Repr. in Harold Bloom (ed.), *Modern Critical Views: Philip Roth.* New York: Chelsea House, 1986, 71–88.

Huggan, Graham, and Stephen Watson (eds.). *Critical Perspectives on J. M. Coetzee.* London: Macmillan, 1995.

Huizinga, Johann. *Homo Ludens: A Study of the Play-Element in Culture.* Trans. R. F. C. Hull. London: Routledge & Kegan Paul, 1944.

Hutcheon, Linda. *The Politics of Postmodernism.* London: Routledge, 1989.

Jakobson, Roman. *Language in Literature.* Ed. Krystyna Pomorska and Stephen Rudy. Cambridge, Mass.: Belknap Press of Harvard University, 1987.

Jameson, Frederic (ed.). *Aesthetics and Politics.* London: Verso, 1977.

——'Beyond the Cave: Demystifying the Ideology of Modernism', in Paul Hernadi (ed.), *The Horizon of Literature.* Lincoln: University of Nebraska Press, 1982, 157–82.

Jay, Martin, *Downcast Eyes: The Denigration of Vision in Twentieth Century French Thought.* Berkeley: University of California Press, 1993.

Jolly, Rosemary. *Colonisation, Violence and Narration in White South African Writing: André Brink, Breyten Breytenbach, and J. M. Coetzee.* Athens, Ohio: Ohio University Press, 1996.

——'Going to the Dogs: Humanity in J. M. Coetzee's *Disgrace, The Lives of Animals*, and South Africa's Truth and Reconciliation Commission', in Jane Poyner (ed.), *J. M. Coetzee and the Idea of the Public Intellectual.* Athens, Ohio: Ohio University Press, 2006, 148–71.

Joyce, James. *Ulysses.* Ed. Jeri Johnson. Oxford: Oxford University Press, 1993.

Kafka, Franz. *The Complete Short Stories.* Ed. Nahum N. Glatzer. London: Random House, 1999.

—— *The Trial.* Trans. Willa and Edwin Muir. London: Penguin, 1953.

Kaiser, Walter. *Praisers of Folly: Erasmus, Rabelais, Shakespeare.* London: Gollancz, 1964.

Kenner, Hugh. *Flaubert, Joyce and Beckett: The Stoic Comedians.* Boston: Beacon, 1962.

—— *Samuel Beckett. A Critical Study.* London: John Calder, 1962.

Knowlson, James (ed.). *Beckett Remembering, Remembering Beckett: Uncollected Interviews with Samuel Beckett and Memories of Those Who Knew Him.* London: Bloomsbury, 2006.

Kossew, Sue. *Pen and Power: A Post-Colonial Reading of J. M. Coetzee and André Brink.* Amsterdam: Rodopi, 1996.

—— (ed.). *Critical Essays on J. M. Coetzee.* London: Prentice Hall, 1998.

Kristeva, Julia. *The Kristeva Reader.* Ed. Toril Moi. Oxford: Blackwell, 1986.

Kundera, Milan. *The Art of the Novel.* London: Faber & Faber, 1988.

Lawlan, Rachel. '*The Master of Petersburg*: Confession and Double Thoughts in Coetzee and Dostoevsky'. *ARIEL* 29/2 (1998) 131–57.

Lazarus, Neil. 'Modernism and Modernity: T. W. Adorno and Contemporary White South African Literature'. *Cultural Critique* 5 (1986/7) 131–55.

Lukács, Georg. *The Theory of the Novel: A Historico-Philosophical Essay on the Forms of Great Epic Literature.* Trans. Anna Bostock. London: Merlin, 1971.

—— *The Historical Novel.* Trans. Hannah and Stanley Mitchell. Harmondsworth: Penguin, 1962.

McDonald, Peter. 'The Writer, the Critic and the Censor: J. M. Coetzee and the Question of Literature', in Jane Poyner (ed.), *J. M. Coetzee and the Idea of the Public Intellectual.* Athens, Ohio: Ohio University Press, 2006, 42–63.

McKeon, Michael. *The Origins of the English Novel 1600–1740.* Baltimore: Johns Hopkins University Press, 1987.

—— (ed.). *Theory of the Novel: An Historical Approach.* Baltimore: Johns Hopkins University Press, 2000.

—— 'Politics of Discourses and the Rise of the Aesthetic in Seventeenth-Century England', in Kevin Sharpe and Steven N. Zwicker (eds.), *Politics of Discourse: The Literature and History of Seventeenth-Century England.* Berkeley: University of California Press, 1987, 35–51.

Marais, Mike. 'Place of Pigs: The Tension between Implication and Transcendence in J. M. Coetzee's *Age of Iron* and *The Master of Petersburg*'. *Journal of Commonwealth Literature* 31/1 (1996) 83–95.

Mphahlele, Es'kia. *Voices in the Whirlwind, and Other Essays*. London: Macmillan, 1972.

Morris, Pam. *Realism*. London: Routledge, 2003.

Mulhern, Francis. *Culture/Metaculture*. Abingdon: Routledge, 2000.

—— 'Beyond Metaculture'. *New Left Review* 16 (2002).

—— 'What is Cultural Criticism?' *New Left Review* 23 (2003) 35–49.

Nancy, Jean-Luc. *The Inoperative Community*. Trans. Peter Connor, Lisa Garbus, Michael Holland, and Simona Sawhney. Minneapolis: University of Minnesota Press, 1991.

—— *The Experience of Freedom*. Trans. Bridget McDonald. Stanford: Stanford University Press, 1993.

Ndebele, Njabulo. *Fools and Other Stories*. Braamfontein: Ravan, 1983.

Nyman, Jopi. *Postcolonial Animals from Kipling to Coetzee*. New Delhi: Atlantic, 2003.

Parry, Benita. 'Speech and Silence in the Fictions of J. M. Coetzee', in Derek Attridge and Rosemary Jolly (eds.), *Writing South Africa: Literature, Apartheid, and Democracy 1970–1995*. Cambridge: Cambridge University Press, 1998, 149–65.

Pascal, Roy. *Kafka's Narrators: A Study of His Stories and Sketches*. Cambridge: Cambridge University Press, 1982.

Perry, Ruth. *Women, Letters and the Novel*. New York: AMS, 1980.

Phelan, James. 'Present Tense Narration, Mimesis, the Narrative Norm, and the Positioning of the Reader in *Waiting for the Barbarians*', in James Phelan and Peter J. Rabinowitz (eds.), *Understanding Narrative*. Columbus: Ohio State University Press, 1994, 222–46.

Poyner, Jane (ed.). *J. M. Coetzee and the Idea of the Public Intellectual*. Athens, Ohio: Ohio University Press, 2006.

—— 'The Fictions of J. M. Coetzee: Master of His Craft?' Diss. University of Warwick, 2003.

Quasha, George (ed.). *The Station Hill Blanchot Reader: Fiction and Literary Essays*. Trans. Lydia Davis, Paul Auster, and Robert Lamberton. New York: Station Hill, 1999.

Richardson, Samuel. *Pamela*. 1740. Ed. Thomas Keymer and Alice Wakely. Oxford: Oxford University Press, 1999.

Richetti, John. *Defoe's Narratives: Situations and Structures*. Oxford: Oxford University Press, 1975.

Ricœur, Paul. *Freud and Philosophy: An Essay on Interpretation.* Trans. Denis Savage. New Haven: Yale University Press, 1970.

Robbe-Grillet, Alain. *Snapshots and Towards a New Novel.* Trans. Barbara Wright. London: Caldar & Boyars, 1965.

Robbins, Bruce. *The Servant's Hand: English Fiction From Below.* New York: Columbia University Press, 1986.

Roth, Philip. *The Anatomy Lesson.* London: Cape, 1983.

—— *Zuckerman Bound: a Trilogy and an Epilogue.* London: Random House, 1998.

—— *The Facts: A Novelist's Autobiography.* New York: Farrar, Straus & Giroux, 1988.

Said, Edward. *Representations of the Intellectual: The 1993 Reith Lectures.* London: Vintage, 1994.

Sanders, Rebecca. '*Disgrace* in the Time of a Truth Commission'. *Parallax* 11/3 (2005) 99–106.

Sartre, Jean-Paul. *Being and Nothingness.* Trans. Hazel E. Barnes. London: Routledge, 2002.

—— *What is Literature?* Trans. Bernard Frechtman. London: Methuen, 1967.

Scott, Joanna. 'Voice and Trajectory: An Interview with J. M. Coetzee'. *Salmagundi* 114–15 (1997) 81–102.

Spivak, Gayatri Chakravorty. 'Theory in the Margin: Coetzee's *Foe* Reading Defoe's Crusoe/Roxana', in Jonathan Arac and Barbara Johnson (eds.), *Consequences of Theory.* Baltimore: Johns Hopkins University Press, 1991.

Sussman, Henry. 'The All-Embracing Metaphor: Reflections on Kafka's "The Burrow"'. *Glyph* 1 (1977) 100–31.

Stanton, Katherine. *Cosmopolitan Fictions: Ethics, Politics and Global Change in the Works of Kazuo Ishiguro, Michael Ondaatje, Jamaica Kincaid and J. M. Coetzee.* London: Routledge, 2006.

Stone, Lawrence. *The Family, Sex and Marriage in England 1500–1800.* London: Weidenfeld & Nicolson, 1977.

Taylor, Charles. *Multiculturalism: Examining the Politics of Recognition.* Ed. Amy Gutman. Princeton: Princeton University Press, 1994.

—— *Hegel and Modern Society.* Cambridge: Cambridge University Press, 1979.

Tiffin, Helen. 'Post-colonialism, Post-modernism and the Rehabilitation of Post-Colonial History'. *Journal of Commonwealth Literature* 13/1 (1988) 169–81.

——'Post-Colonial Literatures and Counter-Discourse'. *Kunapipi* 9/3 (1987) 17–34.

Tihanov, Galin. *The Master and the Slave: Lukács, Bakhtin, and the Ideas of Their Time*. Oxford: Oxford University Press, 2000.

Turgenev, Ivan Sergeevich. *Fathers and Sons*. Trans. Richard Freeborn. Oxford: Oxford University Press, 1999.

Wachtel, Eleanor. 'The Sympathetic Imagination: A Conversation with J. M. Coetzee'. *Brick* 67 (2001) 37–47.

Watt, Ian. *The Rise of the Novel: Studies in Defoe, Richardson and Fielding*. London: Chatto & Windus, 1957.

Wellek, René, and Austin Warren. *Theory of Literature*. New York: Harcourt Brace & Co., 1942.

Williams, Raymond. *Culture and Society, 1780–1950*. London: Chatto & Windus, 1958.

Woods, James. 'Squall Lines'. Rev. of *Diary of a Bad Year*. *The New Yorker* (24 Dec. 2007).

Wright, Laura. *Writing 'Out of All the Camps': J. M. Coetzee's Narratives of Displacement*. New York: Routledge, 2006.

Young, Robert. *White Mythologies: Writing, History and the West*. London: Routledge, 1990.

Index